# Curse of the Fey

## MORGANA TRILOGY

# ALESSA ELLEFSON

ISBN: 0-9893814-2-0
ISBN 13: 978-0-9893814-2-0

Sequel to: Rise of the Fey.

Jacket design © Sammy Yuen 2019
Background pattern and images © iStock
Author photo by Dhel Reed of deeReed Photography

# Also by Alessa Ellefson

The first two books in the Morgana Trilogy:

*Blood of the Fey*
*Rise of the Fey*

To you, dear reader, who has kept me inspired and stayed with me throughout this long journey.

This wounds me most (what can it less?) that Man,
Man fallen, shall be restored, I never more.

John Milton, *Paradise Regained*

# Chapter 1

I strut up the grassy hill, biting on my lower lip like I can't wait to sink my teeth into a frosted chocolate cake, tall and confident in a way I've never felt, long hair swaying in tandem with my hips. And there Arthur lies, looking beautiful in his sleep, peaceful, his long lashes casting shadows on his stubbly cheeks. Completely unaware of my presence.

Worry flashing in my violet eyes, I look around the moonlit field. But all around is quiet, undisturbed by my sudden presence. I am a shadow within a dream. If only a strange dream.

I kneel beside the sleeping form in a rustle of clothes. My fingers brush against his temple, lightly trace the line of his jaw.

I frown. I wouldn't dare something like that, would I? Even though...

I lean down, brush my mouth against Arthur's, hands slipping in his hair. I smile wickedly as he instinctively turns his head towards me, enjoying the effect I have on him, even in his sleep. I graze his shirt hesitantly, as if afraid to touch him.

2

Or afraid to touch his knight's uniform, a small voice says inside me.

Arthur's eyes fly open, ghostly grey in the moon's silvery light. I pause briefly as his face registers surprise. Then my smile grows warmer, lips parting slightly.

"What—" Arthur starts, but I lean down again, cutting his question off with a second kiss.

His arms are suddenly around my waist, wrapping me into a tight hug.

A wave of cold fear washes through me. This should definitely *not* be happening!

With a satisfied laugh, I press his hands back down, practically pinning him beneath me. I bite playfully on my lower lip, then motion for him to take his shirt off. Arthur tries to kiss me again, but with a predatory grin I push him back down. Even in the moonlight I can tell his cheeks are flushed. My tongue darts over my lips, showing a glimpse of fangs.

"No, Arthur, it's a trap!"

But Arthur can't hear my silent warning. I hear his quick intake of breath, heart beating wildly at the jugular. Despite my fear for him, I can't help but feel absolutely disgusted by him. How could he even think for a moment that I would—

With a low grunt, Arthur kicks his leg out, pulling me down at the same time, then rolls us over until he's the one straddling me, a vicious-looking dagger at my pale neck.

"Who are you?" he growls.

The creature snarls, its jaws unhinged as a pair of saber-toothed incisors push through from behind the first row of teeth. Then, quick as a snake, the Fey wrestles itself free, and strikes.

# Chapter 2

I wake up with a start, my warning cry still echoing in my head. It takes me a moment to realize I'm not on the grassy hill anymore, but inside a dark and narrow cave, the rocky floor hot against my back. My home.

"Sounds like you had an interesting dream," Keva's sardonic voice says across from me.

With a grimace, I push myself into a sitting position, my fraying dress clinging to my sweaty body like seaweed.

"Did you dream of Arthur again?" she asks.

"None of your business," I mutter.

"That means yes."

My gaze slides outside to the wide desert that separates us from an uninterrupted line of rolling hills. All grey. All seemingly empty.

But Keva and I both know better.

"What was it this time that it got you moaning and rolling on the floor like a demented woman?" Keva asks.

"Any signs of the portal being used?" I ask instead, despite knowing the answer already. We wouldn't be talking here right now if there had been.

"I asked you first. What did you dream about? What did Arthur do to you? Or what did you do to him?"

I feel myself blush, and the stones that litter the ground between us burst into thousands of pellets.

"Morgan!" Keva shrieks, diving for cover.

"I'm sorry," I say, mortified. I force my thoughts to calm down, willing the rocks to keep still. "I didn't mean…"

Keva grunts. "You never do, do you?"

"You know I can't control my powers since—"

"Stop using that excuse all the time," Keva says, sitting back up. "It's getting real old."

I wince at the sight of the tiny cuts bleeding down the left side of her face. "Well, it's all I've got," I say. "Besides, this is your fault."

Keva's jaw drops. "My fault?"

"You're the one who keeps…keeps making all these unladylike innuendos."

"Well, it's not like there's anything better to do around here," she says, prodding her face, and turning white as her fingers come back bloody. "You've completely disfigured me!" she shrieks.

I cringe, wishing the cavern's walls could swallow me whole. Keva's here because of me. And if it weren't for her, I'd have languished down here, alone for all eternity, feeling…empty. "I said I was sorry," I say lamely.

Keva breathes forcefully through her nose. "It's OK," she says with great effort. "I'm willing to forgive you this time. *If* you tell me what I want to know."

I repress a defeated sigh. "What does it matter if I dreamed of him or not? It's not like it's going to change anything."

Not after what I've done to him. Not when he could be—

"I knew it!" Keva exclaims, sounding like a fan who's just obtained her idol's favorite boxers. "What did you dream you guys were doing together, then?"

"It wasn't me," I mumble.

"What do you mean it wasn't you?"

"Exactly that," I say. And, because I know she's not going to drop the subject until I've told her everything, I blurt out, "It looked like me, but it wasn't. It moved differently, talked differently, even her kiss was different, and so—"

"Wait, hold on. The one that was you—"

"But *wasn't*," I emphasize, annoyed.

"—was kissing Arthur?" Even in the cave's dimness I can see Keva's eyes sparkle. "But it wasn't like yours, so that means..." She gasps. "You guys have kissed before! When? How? And why did you never tell me?"

I look away, wishing we'd never broached the topic, and grow suddenly still. My eyes narrow on a dark pinprick smudging the dirty-white sky above the distant hills. Surely it can't be a flying demon? In all our time down in Hell, neither Keva nor I have ever seen one. Then again, we haven't dared explore very far, either. Blinking owlishly, I lean slightly forward, but in the span of a breath, whatever it was disappears.

"How could you have done this to me?" Keva continues, her rant building up steam. "You know how I've been rooting for you two from the very start, or at least since I found out you weren't *actually* related. And here you are—"

"Shhh," I tell her, all senses alert. If it was a demon, and it somehow spots us, it'll take it no time to fly over to our lonely mountain spire. And our tiny cave won't give us any protection then.

"Don't you shush me!" Keva explodes, voice bouncing off the stone walls like gunshots.

At this point, there's no reasoning with her anymore.

"I didn't tell you anything because it didn't mean anything," I say in a harsh whisper. "We were out past curfew with a stolen pickup, and there was a cop. We needed a distraction, so he kissed me. That's all there is to it."

And all I want to say, I silently add, rubbing at the tight knot in my chest that appears whenever I think about Arthur.

"That's all there is to it, huh?" Keva repeats, oozing sarcasm. "Funny. It took you over twenty words to explain that to me, which, in your case, means you were rambling. And *that*, Morgan, implies that the kiss *did* mean something. At least to you."

"Drop it!" I say sharply, and immediately regret my tone of voice at the hurt that flashes on Keva's face.

I lean back against the wall, feeling suddenly tired. At this rate, we're going to drive each other completely crazy. We need to do something. *I* need to do something.

I stare at Keva's smudged face, pale beneath the grime. She's sacrificed her life in the human world to save me from myself, and now I need to return the favor. Even if it's not in the way she imagines. Whatever it was that I saw in the sky may have been a false alarm, but it may not always be so.

I take a deep breath, my mind made up. "The Gates haven't opened since you've joined me here—"

"Joined?" Keva snorts. "You mean forced, contrived, threatened, coer—"

"—and whoever carved those journal entries on the steles outside hasn't returned," I continue. "Which leaves us at an impasse."

My fists clench and unclench on my lap as my gaze slides over to the large rock that stands halfway to the edge of the cliff. It is one of ten such carved boulders we've discovered, telling of someone's investigations into the human abductions which I know my brother Mordred is involved with. I had hoped that whoever authored these accounts would know why Carman decided to open the Gates to the underworld. But he or she hasn't shown up since we decided to squat this cozy little piece of Hell.

Keva snaps her fingers together, drawing my attention back to her. "You're scheming on your own again," she says accusingly. "Tell me what kind of insane plan you're hatching, so I can tell you how crazy you are, before you do anything stupid."

I nod slightly. "I was thinking that we can't keep wasting our time waiting here," I say. "Not while Carman's out plotting to do...whatever it is she wants to do.

The witch may have imprisoned me down here, but that doesn't mean I'm totally hopeless.

"So, if our Sherlock, for some reason, doesn't want to come to us," I say, "I'm going to find Sherlock instead."

"The fact that Carman thinks you beaten could play in our favor," Keva says thoughtfully after a long silence. "She won't expect us to be going around, looking for trouble. Especially not trouble for her."

"You mean...you'd come with?" I ask, surprised.

Keva snorts. "Have you not been listening to me all this time? I am bored out of my mind in here. Any excuse so I don't have to stare another second at these walls is good enough for me."

Her eyes go round in shock, and she points outside. Fear coils in my stomach. The flying demon's back! But when I follow her shaking finger, I find myself staring instead at a column of smoke that stretches up into the distant sky like a dark scar.

"Definitely not a good sign," Keva says, betraying a hint of fear and excitement, "but a sign nonetheless. And I bet my panties that it's the one we've been waiting for."

# Chapter 3

Darkness surrounds me, shadows shifting as I move deeper into the woods, heavy footsteps following in my tracks. I duck under an overhanging branch, and a red light flitters around me before settling momentarily on the remains of a rusty car. I watch the pixie as it admires itself in the car's broken sideview mirror before taking off again, straight up into the forest's thick canopy.

The hum of whispered prayers swells around me as I finally emerge into a wide clearing. My footsteps falter at the sight of the crowd gathered under the cloudy night sky, Fey and humans standing uneasily together, heads bowed respectfully. Someone nudges me forward and I start walking again, the throng parting at once to let me through. And as I draw closer to the glade's center, my eyes fall upon a dozen large mounds of stacked wood that have been erected there.

I've seen plenty of these not to know what they are: Funeral pyres. My throat grows suddenly tight with repressed tears. I have witnessed too many of these rites.

A sudden breeze chases the low-hanging clouds across the sky, giving the world below a glimpse of a scattering of stars. The crowd suddenly grows quiet as the stars wink out of sight, only to reappear a second later, closer than before. I watch, entranced, as scores of pixies make their descent in a solemn dance, their warm glow slowly revealing the bodies that lay atop the pyres, before finally alighting upon them like giant, shimmering mantles.

And for a moment, I picture Percy again, the way he looked when I dreamed of his funeral—peaceful despite the dark, gaping wound in his chest.

The pixies' lights suddenly vanish, as if snuffed out, leaving the assembly in total darkness. Then, a couple of heartbeats later, innumerable *pops*, like those of firecrackers, blast through the clearing, and the pyres burst into flames, taking our fallen soldiers with them.

I look away from the blaze, feeling sick, and find myself staring instead at the grieving faces around me.

I easily pick out other Lake High survivors among the gathered Fey, their iron-threaded uniforms reflecting the fires' light. There's fewer of them than the last time.

Lady Ysolt's there, standing in the midst of a flock of scared pages, Laura and Elias the oldest and tallest of them now. The cousins, Gareth and Gauvain, their usual mirth and bantering replaced by a double mask of pain and fury, are a few paces behind, while Hadrian, now sporting a moustache, silently cries beside them.

I tear my gaze away from the group, unable to bear their raw grief etched into every line of their bodies, and find myself staring instead at Lugh's still form. The once impeccable Fey Lord is covered in wounds and bruises, his left eye shut for good. What could have done *that* to him, and made it so bad that not even Blanchefleur could heal him?

Of course, there is but one answer.

Carman.

A voice I know all too well suddenly breaks the silence, spreading goosebumps down my arms.

"We are gathered here to mourn and to give thanks to our lost brothers and sisters who fought bravely at our sides," Arthur intones, his words sadly familiar.

I look frantically about the somber crowd for a glimpse of him, needing to make sure he's alright. But as almost every other time I've dreamed of him, I have to settle for simply listening to his voice.

"I would like instead to speak of their just cause, and of the courage they demonstrated in the face of adversity," Arthur continues. "For no matter how dire and precarious their situations were, never did they falter in the line of duty. Because they knew, as we all do, that we are the only ones standing between Carman and our worlds, the last hope humans and Fey alike have against her unquenchable thirst for destruction.

"It is therefore not only our obligation, but also our honor, to keep the same, unfaltering determination, and to fight until her plans are laid to waste, once and for all. But this cannot happen unless we put aside our differences and work together, Fey and knights, side by side, as our forebears did once before.

"I thus entreat you, with our fallen brothers and sisters as witnesses, to consider each other, from this day on, not as foes, but as friends and allies. Our very survival—"

A long, guttural cry cuts his speech short. "Don't make me laugh, you puny boy!" a bedraggled woman screams, spittle flying from her dry lips as she wrenches herself away from a stunned nurse. The woman points straight at me, her greying hair falling out of a loose ponytail in greasy strands. "My son died to pay for your sins, and now you're asking us to share in his fate? For what else is there for us but death, now that we can only fight with sticks and swords? Though death is all we deserve."

"Lady Elise, please," Lady Ysolt says, her voice strained.

The old woman whirls around. "I won't let you shut me up again, you filthy traitor. You know as well as I do that we're all tainted, yet you continue to parade around as if you're so bloody perfect. But no more. Percy's death should be emulated by all of us here." The woman turns her feverish gaze on the rest of the crowd. "We will cleanse this world of our ilk! Just pray that it will be enough to redeem us all."

And with another cackle, she sweeps her hand towards the fire, before whipping it back around. Bright embers follow her fingers in a sweeping arc, shooting straight into the assembly. Shrieks and startled shouts erupt as people push each other to avoid getting burned, the grass bursting into flames wherever the live coals land.

"Take the children to safety," Lady Ysolt commands as a second figure jumps into the fray—a man, looking as disheveled as the strange woman.

"We will burn away the corruption!" he shouts, a demented gleam in his eyes that reminds me of Myrdwinn.

"I really don't think a funeral is the right moment for you to make a show of yourself," Lady Ysolt says, flexing her fingers until her ogham-encased rings sparkle in response.

The man laughs. "At least these fools died before they could commit the ultimate crime," he says. "Philandering with the Fey is what got us here to begin with. It's sacrilege!" He turns to look at me, left hand held out as if asking me to join him. "And for that, we must all die," he finishes.

With a wild grin, the man snaps his hand closed, and my vision turns white as all the pyres explode, setting the whole clearing on fire.

# Chapter 4

"You're completely off your rocker," Keva says with a hint of worry, as I scan the long stretch of desert still ahead of us, my vision blurry with unshed tears. Despite my strange waking dream, we've managed to make it about halfway through from our cave.

"You did fall pretty hard back there," she continues, eyeing me distrustfully.

"I didn't see the rock," I say, shifting from one foot to the next to ease the cramps starting up my calf.

"It was Puck-sized! How could you miss it?"

"You're missing the point."

"Which is what? That you're losing your brain to some weird, possibly demonic, virus?"

"The point is," I say, "it makes no sense that I keep dreaming of things I've never even seen before."

Keva lets out a theatrical sigh. "It's because you're grieving for your boyfriend, and—"

"He's *not* my boyfriend, and it doesn't explain anything at all." I try not to limp as we resume our trek. "I didn't even know half those people out there."

"Out *there?*" Keva repeats with a cocked eyebrow.

"Nor did I know those two who were talking about tainted blood and—"

"Shacking up with the Fey, I know," Keva says, rolling her eyes. "Between you and me, though, who's never dreamed of doing just that?"

The fleeting memory of the night I met Lugh flashes before my eyes—the music, the dancing, the ambrosia. Back then, he had seemed like a god, charismatic yet untouchable. So unlike my latest vision of him...

Maybe Keva's right and my mental state is rapidly declining.

"But if you're right," Keva continues, fanning herself against the crushing heat with her hand, "and that's a big *if*. But if you are, then it could mean this one, and all your other dreams, are real. Including that nice one where you saw yourself and Arthur getting busy before you went all demon on him. Which would be even more exciting!"

I frown as a small piece of paper drifts towards us, bright red against the dreary landscape as it flutters ever closer, carried by a nonexistent breeze.

"Have you ever heard of the Leanan Sidhe?" Keva asks. "They're Fey that take their powers from the energy created during s—" I raise my hand and Keva stops immediately, looking over her shoulder in fear. "What is it?" she whispers.

I snatch the floating bit of paper from the air, then stare at it in shock.

I hear Keva's sharp intake. "A flower petal? Here? But that's impossible!"

"I thought so too," I say. Which means that someone must have dropped it, and I, like a dumb fish, have just taken the bait. I look around with paranoid fervor, expecting demons to pounce on us at any moment, but our surroundings are still blissfully barren. For now.

"Come on," I say, urging Keva faster, "I don't like how exposed we are here."

"Yeah, yeah," Keva says, "easy to spot, easy to kill. I'm tired of this already. We should've stayed in our cave. My feet are killing me, my skin is parched, my eyeballs sunburned, and this whole place is giving me the creeps."

"You're more than welcome to go back," I say.

My words sound tougher than I feel, and I selfishly pray she's not going to take me up on them. I don't want to be left on my own. But, to my relief, Keva grudgingly tags along.

As the hours lurch by, measured by our increasingly shorter breaths, we manage to cross the rest of the wasteland without another hitch, though the heat has turned us into sweltering gasbags with armpit stains down to our hips.

"Finally," Keva says as we reach the first hill, plunking down onto a small, flat rock to pull her boots off and massage her blistered feet.

"Put your shoes back on," I tell her, "we have to keep going."

"Geez, Morgan, I'm not a Fey like you, I need time to—"

She stops, face paling with fear, and I turn around to find an old man leering at us from around the bend, dusty skin stretched tight over his prominent ribs. Definitely not how I'd pictured our first direct demon encounter to be, but I'm scared out of my mind nonetheless.

For a long second, we all three stare at each other, then the skinny man throws his head back and lets out a hair-raising cry.

"Run!" Keva yells, pulling urgently on my arm.

But it's too late. A series of shouts answers the demon, and we watch as a dozen more emaciated men come hurtling towards us, brandishing long white clubs, scraps of clothing scarcely keeping their modesty in check. Not that modesty seems to be foremost on their minds, a part of my brain notes as they quickly surround us, greed filling their otherwise flat stares.

I flex my fingers, unconsciously reaching for my powers, but the usual fizzy response in my stomach isn't there. I let out a soft hiss. Of course, I can make rocks explode in Keva's face, but when I actually need them, my powers are MIA.

I glance at Keva, the smaller girl holding her steel-toed boot like a weapon, as if it's going to make a difference.

I force myself to breathe. I knew something like this would happen at some point. I just didn't realize it would be so soon. I turn to the one I assume is their leader, and square my shoulders.

"Uh, parley?" I tentatively call out.

My request has about as much success as when I used it with Blanchefleur the first time I met her. With a loud bellow, the demon charges, swinging his mace over his head. I take a quick step to the side, forcing Keva behind me, then lift my arms up to receive the blow, meaty parts out like I was taught in class. But before the man can reach me, a shadow darts in front of him, black knife flashing.

I let out a faint squeak as the demon drops silently to the ground, a bloody smile gracing his neck.

"Look," Keva whispers, as the hunched figure moves onto a second target, cowled robe rustling as it ducks beneath the next man's outstretched arm. A bony hand lashes out, slicing his belly open.

"Banshee?" I say.

The shadow pauses midstride. A second's hesitation too long. With cries of outrage, the remaining men converge upon her. I watch helplessly as the banshee blocks the first attack, dodging a blow to the head before plunging her knife into someone's back. But there are too many of them, and no matter how good the banshee is, they manage to swarm her.

I find myself moving forward, holding tightly onto a large stone I don't remember picking up, dropping inside the nearest demon's reach, then swinging my fist around in a sharp arc. There's a loud *thunk* as my rock connects with his temple. The demon's eyes roll back in his head, and I step to the side as he slumps forward, already aiming for the next one. But as I make my next move, a heavy blow lands on my shoulder, and I fall to my knees with a grunt, the stone falling from my numb fingers.

"Missssstressss!" the banshee howls, as a second blow lands on my ribs.

I fall face-first into the dirt, biting my tongue. Blood fills my mouth with its coppery taste. Coughing, I try to push myself onto my feet, but someone slams my head back into the ground. Pain explodes behind my eyes, my nose flattening with a deafening *crunch*.

And there, as I slowly suffocate on mud and my own blood, something finally stirs in the pit of my stomach, dark and demanding. It spreads, quick as wildfire, up my spine then down my arms, before bursting free. There's a surprised shout, then the weight that was pressing me down suddenly lifts.

Gasping for breath, I roll onto my back, then recoil in horror at the dark mass spewing from the ground a couple of feet away, a geyser of black, viscous liquid that seems to have a will of its own. Even with my broken nose, its stench makes me want to puke. I watch, unable to tear my gaze away, as the thick jet crests languorously over my attacker, before finally tipping sideways and spilling over him, abruptly cutting off his screams.

For a long minute after, I stare at the shapeless lumps floating in the center of the pool of black tar, bubbles popping thickly around it. All that is left of the half-naked demon. Because of me. Bile rises to my throat and I heave, cold shivers running down my back.

"Morgan!" Keva shouts, scrambling over to my side.

I shake my head to dispel the spots dancing in my vision, fighting not to get sick, then look around for the banshee. I let out a relieved sigh as I find her near the base of the closest hill, limping, but still alive.

"Come on," Keva says urgently, helping me up.

The remaining men have turned on me now, their rotten teeth poking from distended mouths as they hiss and snarl.

"Now would be the time to pull that magic trick again," Keva tells me, her back to mine.

"It would, wouldn't it?" I say.

But whatever just happened, whatever it is I did to take that one demon out, has left me completely drained, and I find myself struggling to stay on my feet.

"Watch it," Keva says, yanking me back as a man lands in front of me.

I barely have the strength to duck as he swings for my face, the bone-white club whistling inches from my ear. The demon continues his spin, swiping my legs out from under me with a low kick, and I fall backward, taking Keva down with me. I catch sight of the heavy club as the demon whips it around again, and close my eyes, waiting for the fatal blow.

"What's happening?" Keva asks, voice muffled. "Morgan?"

I crack my eyes open, surprised that my brains haven't been bashed out yet, and find the demon frozen above me, eyes round with shock, the tip of a blade disappearing from his chest in a spray of blood.

"Though I walk through the valley of the shadow of death, I will fear no evil."

The voice is soft and sweet, and makes my skin crawl.

"Morgan, get off me!" Keva says, her sharp elbow digging into my ribs. But when I finally move off her, she presses herself close to me. "What. Is. *That*?" she asks.

We watch mutely as the latest demon goes through the remaining men like a scythe through a field of wheat in a blur of movements. I swallow hard.

"Is it…helping us?" Keva asks.

"I certainly hope so," I say, the words coming out slurred. Or we're totally done for. Especially if I feel the slightest movement's going to make me pass out.

"All right, then, let's go before…" Keva lets her voice trail off.

All at once, the chaos has ended. Slowly, we turn to look back at the newcomer, and I feel Keva go still against me. Standing quietly amidst a pile of dead bodies is another girl, her long, jet black hair hiding most of her pale face.

"Is she praying?" I ask, wiping my clammy hands on my dress.

"More importantly, is that our uniform?" Keva asks instead.

"Saint George's balls, I think you're right."

Keva tilts her head. "You know what? I think I know who that is."

"What?"

"Remember that KORT knight who went missing after her squire was found poisoned?"

"Rei," I say, locking onto the memory of the first black-vein murder at Lake High. One for which I'd originally been accused.

"Well that's her missing knight, Kaede," Keva says.

At the sound of her name, the girl raises her head, and a pair of dark, almond-shaped eyes seeks mine out. There goes our chance to escape. Without once looking away, the Asian girl sheathes her twin swords behind her back, and starts prowling towards us.

"You sure it's her?" I ask, the need to throw up growing stronger with every step the girl takes.

"Well it looks like her…"

With a warning growl, the banshee bounds in front of us, and at last the girl stops in her tracks. Although they're of a same height, this Kaede girl manages to make the banshee look frail in comparison. I flick my eyes to the bodies littering the ground, and have no doubt it would take the knight seconds to take us down too, if she wanted. My gaze slides back to the girl, and my heartrate spikes at the sight of her slowly reaching for her swords again.

"Are you Kaede?" I call out before she can stab the banshee.

The KORT knight's footsteps come to a stop, and I try not to cower as she stares impassively at me over the banshee's hunched figure. "Are you a Collector?" she asks at last.

"A what?"

"Col-lec-tor," the girl repeats, enunciating every syllable like she's talking to a daft child.

My nostrils flare, surprise turning to annoyance. The banshee growls again, as if in tune with my feelings. "Why don't you answer my question first?" I snap.

"Play nice, Morgan," Keva whispers urgently. "We're not the ones with the sharp swords here."

"Maybe she should explain what she means instead of talking down to me," I mutter, feeling that sickening power stir in the pit of my stomach again.

Kaede's lids lower in suspicion until her eyes are but tiny crescents in her moon-pale face, sending goosebumps down my arms. Keva's right. This is clearly not someone to mess with—there's a reason she's survived this long in Hell.

The knight's emotionless gaze slides over to Keva. "Are you not her offering for the Teind?" she asks.

"For the what?" I say.

Keva snorts in derision. "Her offering? *Me*? I can't look that stupid, even if I did come down here for her." She waves at me with a loud sigh. "This is Morgan, and I'm Keva, and we're roommates in Lake High. Or were, before the school was taken over by the Dark Sidhe."

"You're a...knight?" Kaede asks with such genuine surprise that I look down as well.

The beautiful gown I'd worn for the ball is but a tattered memory, leaving most of my legs bare, my blood and dust-coated feet in full display. And despite our precarious situation, I find myself hugging Arthur's jacket closer to myself, face heating with embarrassment.

"I know she looks fishy," Keva says, breaking the awkward silence, "but there are attenuating circumstances. She's a squire, you see, to Sir Arthur, actually. You remember him, right? And since he also happens to be her *lover*, he gave her his jacket at the ball in Caamaloth. Hence the confusion, I believe. But she didn't get a chance to change, as that's when our headquarters were invaded, and she actually was kidnapped. Of course, we got her back, but then Dub—"

"You wear no oghams and yet...," Kaede says, cutting Keva's lengthy explanations short, and motioning to the dark pool behind her.

My insides grow cold. I wish I could deny I had anything to do with the tar's appearance, but it's no use lying. Even if I could still physically do so.

"I, uh,...," I start, panic striking me dumb.

How do you explain your abilities to a blood-thirsty knight before she can skewer you?

"She's half-Fey," Keva blurts out. "But she's just recently started to learn how to use her powers, so she can be a little all over the place. Though I admit she's never done anything quite like this before."

"Fey, but not demon?" Kaede asks.

"No, not a demon," Keva says firmly.

With a slow nod, the knight finally rocks back on her heels, and I finally allow myself to unclench my fists. "It is as was foretold, then," she says.

Keva and I exchange concerned glances.

But before we can ask what she means, Kaede motions towards the hills. "Let's leave before they awaken."

"Where are you going?" I ask the knight as she swiftly walks into the hills, back the way she came.

"Come one," Keva tells me, struggling to put her boot back on.

"But this could be a trap," I whisper to Keva, finding it hard to focus on her small face.

"No, dummy," she says, "she's just following the knights' honor code to help those in need."

"Or maybe it's a trap," I insist.

But Keva ignores me entirely and rushes to the knight's side. "I thought they were dead," I hear her say through the buzzing in my ears.

"For now," Kaede replies.

"You mean they come back to life?"

I shake my head sluggishly, trying unsuccessfully to get my hearing back to normal.

"We're in Hell," Kaede says, already moving. "Nobody dies here unless you give them the true death."

"With a stake to the heart?"

"By destroying their oghams."

I blink slowly as Keva waves impatiently for me to follow. Note her concern. See her mouth move soundlessly. Then the ground tilts sideways, and I'm dimly aware of the banshee catching me before I pass out.

# CHAPTER 5

"Go lick your wounds elsewhere."

I startle at the harsh voice, only to find myself standing in the middle of a wide, hilly field of blue flowers nestled between two steep cliffs. A breeze sweeps through the meadow, making the flowers shimmer under the pale sun. The hairs at the back of my neck stand up.

Bluebells.

Bluebells covering every inch of land like a giant blanket. Which can only mean one thing: I'm in unknown Fey territory.

"This isn't good," I hear Gauvain say ominously as his cousin steps around me.

"Surely he wouldn't set a trap for us?" Hadrian says from further down.

"I wouldn't mind a trap if it's like the one Arthur got," Gareth says, flashing a big smile.

"That's because no girl in her right mind would want to go near you," Gauvain retorts.

"You don't know what you're talking about."

Gauvain smirks. "That's funny coming from you."

Gareth points at his cousin with his war hammer arm. "Your sense of humor is absolutely *déplorable*."

"What I'd like to know," Hadrian cuts in before the two can get into another of their infamous fights, "is who the Leanan Sidhe came to you as."

A glint enters Gauvain's dark eyes. "Great question, you still haven't told us who the lucky girl is."

"Please don't tell us it's that Fey-blooded bastard girl," Daniel's nasally voice chimes in, stifling a yawn. "If it were me, I'd have run away before she could stab me again."

Gareth snickers. "Yes, we all know running away is your favorite course of action."

There's a dull metallic *clang* and we whirl around in time to see Hadrian toppling to the ground over Daniel's unconscious body.

RUN!

My cry remains silent, unheeded, and I'm forced to watch helplessly as, one by one, the knights drop into the flowers like flies, Gareth the last of them. The ground suddenly wobbles around me, too. But before I can drop all the way down to the ground, there's a flash of bright purple, and Lugh's suddenly standing before me, a young Fey boy with pointy teeth at his side.

"Enough, Oberon," he calls out, his chocolaty voice sending tingles down my spine. Without even noting my presence, he turns his brooding face towards the setting sun. "You know we have not come here to fight," he continues, a little louder.

At his words, the soft breeze picks up, leaves and flowers clustering in its wake like a giant swarm of bees, heading in our direction. I squint as the air bends and waves, like on a really hot day, before coalescing into the shape of a man the size of a boulder. The Fey lord scowls at Lugh for a long moment, floral cloak flapping angrily around his stout legs.

"I don't like having to repeat myself, Lugh," the Fey says. "Coming here uninvited means you're trespassing. I believe you know our laws on that."

"Such laws are moot in times of war," Lugh replies evenly.

"A war that I didn't start and will make sure not to get involved in."

"You may want to get all of the facts straight before deciding on anything," Lugh says, looking down his nose at the shorter Fey lord. "Especially when both our worlds are at stake."

"Do not presume to know what I want," Oberon retorts, "except to have you out of my Demesne. So pick up your trash, and leave. Now."

He snaps his fingers together, and the breeze starts anew, this time moving away from him. A minute later, the fallen knights wake up, confused looks turning to angry glares as they realize what's happened.

Only then do I notice the tiny little creatures darting in and out of the knights' reach, tiny wings beating furiously at the air, as if to shoo them all away.

"Dwarf pixies," Gareth says with disgust, spitting on the ground.

At that, a scintillating cloud of blue lifts from the flowerbed to buzz angrily about his head in an offended series of screeches.

"Get those fleas away from me!" a tinny voice shouts, coming from the winged gerbil on Gareth's shoulder, and I recognize the Fey creature I'd seen through Mordred's scrying, the one that turned Gareth's arm into a war hammer with an ill-fated wish.

"What happened to your usual guard?" Oberon asks Lugh, eyeing the weary knights with evident distaste. "Were you forced to adopt these pests because all of your people have deserted you?"

"Unlike others, I do not need a guard," Lugh says, voice dropping dangerously low at the implied insult.

Oberon's gaze lifts to Lugh's eyepatch, and he smirks. "It's not what it looks like to me. Think your daddy would approve of your new look?"

"We came together because we have forged an alliance," Hadrian says quickly before Lugh can react to this new insult.

"I would much have preferred it had you sent Sameerah as your ambassador," Oberon says, ignoring Hadrian completely. He smiles toothily. "She's a damn sight finer to look at than your sorry arse. Not that she would have changed my decision in the least."

"None of us relish imposing our presence upon you, least of all her," Lugh says, a muscle twitching in his cheek with barely repressed impatience, "but the bones have spoken, so here we are."

"You mean *she* has spoken," Oberon says derisively.

"Indeed."

"Then I've certainly got nothing to do with you."

Lugh's eye flashes in anger. "And why, pray, is that?"

Oberon's own glower darkens, the air around him crackling with electricity. "Because I told myself I'd never work with that harlot after she abandoned us in this shithole."

"Perhaps if some of us had not been so pretentious back in the day, we would never have ended down here at all," Lugh retorts. "Besides, you did not seem to mind playing godling in this shithole, as you say, until Myrdwinn taught knights how to fight back."

"There's another traitor whose neck I'd like to wring," Oberon growls.

"There's nothing we can do to change the past," a tired voice says, as if from beyond the grave, "but we can work for a better future. Together."

I feel my heartbeat spike at the sound of Arthur's voice.

Where are you? I want to shout, but I know it's pointless. I can never interfere with my visions, no matter how hard I try. All I can do is watch and listen.

"An alliance with *your* people is like drinking hemlock[1], a derisive idea if I ever heard one," Oberon says with a scoff.

But I've lost all interest in the Fey lord's posturing, my focus lasering instead on the edge of the flower field, where the shadows from the setting sun are deepest. And then I see it again, quick as lightning, the flash of a predatory smile in a tattooed face.

---

[1] A poisonous plant.

# Chapter 6

I must be dying. There's no other explanation for why I keep dreaming of Arthur when there are evidently more pressing matters to attend to, like my own survival. It would also explain why my powers have gone completely wrong, and why I feel so wrung out.

The acrid smell of smoke tickles my nostrils, bringing me fully awake, and I find myself staring into Keva's annoyed face.

"Could you *please* stop passing out?" she says, waving the banshee away. "It's unnerving, and a total waste of time."

"It's not like I choose to do so," I croak out.

I rub my eyes to dispel the black still crowding my vision, though the knot in my chest remains. I know something bad's about to happen to Arthur. And there's nothing I can do about it.

"Listen, I've been talking to K," Keva says, glancing over at Kaede seated a few feet away from us, "and she's willing to help us out. For now."

I follow her gaze across the rocky path. The knight seems completely oblivious to what we're doing, intent upon sharpening her swords instead.

Keva leans in, dropping her voice conspiratorially low. "Of course, I didn't tell her we have absolutely no idea what we're doing, but I figure the longer we stick with her, the longer we stay alive. Which, in my book, is a good thing."

The banshee growls softly and Keva grimaces. "Yeah, yeah, we're glad you're here too. No one else would have bothered to carry Morgan around." Keva crosses her arms. "But admit it, if it weren't for Lady Kaede, we'd all be dead. You too, don't deny it."

The banshee lets out a noncommittal grunt, waving her bony hands around, and muttering something about arriving first. I tune their arguing out as I crane my neck around. Gone are the salt flats that surrounded our mountain spire. Instead, we're now ringed by tall, pebbly hills. And, behind one of them, is the thick column of smoke Keva and I had decided to investigate, its dark fumes spiraling into the grey skies above. I have to admit that now we're so close to it, Keva's right—I have no idea what we're supposed to do when we find its source.

"So, you're saying Kaede's agreed to take us to the fire?" I say, hearing the suspicion in my own voice.

"Right," Keva answers after sticking her tongue out at the banshee in a very unladylike manner.

I look back at Kaede. The girl's finished polishing her sword, and is tipping the blade around so she can inspect her face in its reflection. There's definitely something odd about her, I tell myself as the knight pulls and prods her face like she can't believe she's real.

"Barring your unhealthy obsession for KORT knights, how much do you think we can trust her?" I ask Keva.

"First, who are you to talk about unhealthy obsessions?" Keva replies, cocking her eyebrow in disapproval. "Second, *yeah*! We wouldn't have made it this far without Kaede, especially with you snoring happily away."

"Yes, but this is Hell," I say. "It changes people. For all we know, she could've turned into a—"

"Demon?" Keva says with a scoff. "She's saved our lives, Morgan. Besides, she's not the one who's prone to letting her powers run amok and try to kill everyone around."

I clap my mouth shut, stung.

"Let's go," Kaede says, done admiring herself in the blade of her swords.

"Coming!" Keva replies, jumping immediately to her feet without her usual string of complaints.

"Why did she agree to take us there?" I ask Keva before she can scurry off, and hating myself for the jealous pang I feel at how readily Keva seems to have taken the other girl's side. "She must know what we're up to is dangerous, even if you didn't tell her."

"Can you stop with your whining? I've said she saved our lives, many times over. I don't care what you think, I'm going with her."

And with a final sniff, Keva turns around to rush after the knight.

"I still think there's something off with that girl," I mutter. And, despite feeling lightheaded, I let the banshee hurry me along, scared of leaving Keva out of my sight.

By the time we've gone around our ninth hill, I find myself wishing I were still sick and unconscious. We may no longer be in our cave, but everything here is just as grey and dreary, with the added benefit that I keep jumping at the slightest noise. And when I'm not freaking out, I find my thoughts inexorably drawn to Arthur's plight, wondering how real my dreams are, and if he's all right, or…

"So here's the plan," I tell the banshee to keep myself distracted. "One, we spy on Carman and figure out what she's up to. Two, we head back up our mountain spire, and wait for Mordred to open the Gates."

The banshee grunts, and I wave her doubts away.

"He'll have to at some point or another, if only to let Carman back out," I say. "Then, step three, we get back to Avalon, and warn the others so they can stop her. Easy peasy. Brilliant, right?"

My words are met with stony silence.

"You don't like it?"

"Ssoundssss dangerousssss," the banshee says hesitantly.

"Yeah, well let me know if you come up with something better," I retort, hating her lack of enthusiasm at my scheme.

Trying not to show how stung I feel, I squint up ahead at the other two girls. Kaede's still in the lead, marching like she's been a guide in Hell all her life. A guide who doesn't seem to care much who's following her or not, I note with guilty satisfaction, as the gap between her and Keva grows longer. I still can't shake the feeling that there's something fishy about Kaede rescuing us in the nick of time, only to unquestioningly put her life at risk again to take us deep inside demon territory. Even more shady, is how easily she gobbled up Keva's flimsy explanations. Unless this is a trap, like I fear...

"Keep an eye on Keva for me, will ya?" I tell the banshee, suddenly speeding up.

I quickly catch up with Keva, garnering a dejected look from her. This forced march is certainly taking its toll, turning her slight hobble into a full-on limp.

"Need a hand?" I ask.

"Mind your own business," Keva mutters with a grimace of pain.

I stifle a sigh. In no mood to bear the brunt of another of her bad moods, I hasten ahead of her, and soon leave her far behind.

"Showing off, are you?" I hear Keva shout.

"I'm sure the banshee won't mind carrying you this time around," I say over my shoulder, eyes never leaving the KORT knight's back.

Kaede's finally stopped at the top of the next hill, but she seems confused, looking around uncertainly.

"Are we lost?" I call out, slightly out of breath as I finally catch up with her. "The fire's that way, in case you were wondering," I add, pointing over her right shoulder. "And it seems it's not much further away."

Blatantly ignoring me, Kaede turns to her left instead, and I have to swallow back a curse as I follow her down the other side of the hill.

"Look, I know we got off on the wrong foot," I try again, "so why don't we start all over? Hi, I'm Morgan. I'm a squire and landed here because of the big bad witch herself. What about you? How did you end up in Hell?"

"Collectors," Kaede says, her hooded gaze searching the next hilltops.

"Right, you already mentioned those," I say, as she suddenly backtracks, bowling Keva over into the banshee's bracing arms. "I suppose Keva's already told you about Rei," I say to Kaede's back as the knight starts climbing the hill we've just descended.

"Who?" Kaede asks distractedly.

"Rei, your squire," I say, as she stops dead in her tracks, ears perked. "I wanted to, uh, give you my condolences," I finish lamely. At her silence, I clear out my throat, and add, "I've been thinking, and this plan may need to have a few kinks smoothed out, but—"

"Down!" Kaede cries out, throwing herself to the side just as a black-quilled arrow *thunks* into the ground, inches from where she stood, and barely a foot away from me.

I stand frozen for a second, mind blanked out, when I hear Keva's sempiternal grumbling. Neither she nor the banshee have realized yet what is happening.

"Stay back!" I shout at them.

I drop into a crouch as a second arrow whistles past my face.

"Seriously?" I hear Keva say, sounding way too close for comfort. "Arrows are *so* seventh century!"

"I said get back!" I shout again, scanning our surroundings for the archers.

My breath catches. There! I stare at the spot where I thought I saw a stick poke out. Or the tip of a bow being drawn.

"Kaede, go around while I distract him. I think that...Kaede?" I look back at where the knight dove for cover, but she's gone.

I swear viciously. Another arrow whistles past, and I hear Keva's cry of pain. My stomach plummets.

"Keva!" I shout, scrambling over the rocky ground as fast as I can to get to her.

I find her hunched on her side, the arrow sticking from her shoulder, the banshee trying to keep her from rolling down the hill.

I drop to my knees beside them. "Shitshitshitshitshit!"

My first instinct is to try to heal her like I did so many others back in Lake High. But at the sight of my own blackened hands, I freeze. What if I poison her instead?

The banshee notes my hesitation, and pulls her obsidian knife out instead.

"I'm OK," Keva breathes, before growling in pain as the banshee gingerly twists the arrow's shaft, testing how deep it went.

"Can we pull it out?" I ask the cowled figure.

"Are you insane?" Keva shoots back, eyes glossy with pain.

The banshee shakes her head. "Mussst open moooore," she says.

"Shit."

Keva's hand finds mine, and squeezes tight.

"You'll be fine," I tell her, feeling rather queasy myself.

With precise moves, the banshee snaps the arrow's shaft in two, ripping a scream from Keva. Cold sweat beads on my forehead. I wish I could take her pain away. My free hand clenches and unclenches uselessly at my side. Another arrow flies high overhead, and we both flinch. Only the banshee seems unfazed as she prods Keva's wound.

"W-Where's K-Kaede?" Keva asks, lips trembling.

"She's ditched us," I say, turning a furious eye in the archer's direction. "But I know where our attacker is."

Keva grunts, slumping forward under the banshee's careful instruction. Now's the time for the surgical removal of the arrow.

"Go get…the bastard…," Keva says, knowing what I want to do without me saying it, and she releases my hand.

With a tight nod, I dash away, keeping low to the ground. More arrows zing by in quick succession. I twist sideways as another flies past, feel the burn it leaves along my neck. My breath rushes out, and I nearly loose my footing on the uneven ground. Whoever or whatever it is, it's going to pay.

But as I take a sharp bend around the next hill, I catch sight of a figure ahead, and slide to a sudden stop. Adrenaline pumping furiously down my veins, I take in the hairy creature blocking my way. It's not the archer, but it was definitely waiting for me, and I've fallen right into its trap.

For a long second, we both stare at each other. The beast is massive, the size of a well-fed triceratops. A large hump rises over its blade-thin head where a sharp horn can be seen poking from between two, disturbingly human eyes.

With a blood-curdling bellow, the creature charges, pounding hooves eating the ground with the dizzying speed of an oncoming train. Too fast for me to make a run for it.

I bend my knees, eyes never leaving the monster. Then, when I can feel the beast's stinky breath warm on my face, I kick the ground hard and propel myself into the air, using my powers to push myself higher. I tuck my legs in, curling into a tight ball, feel the tip of the creature's horn graze my arm as I flip over the demon.

And then it all goes wrong.

The world distorts around me, as if yanked sideways by an invisible hand. My stomach heaves, bright sparks blooming in my vision. Then my body hits the beast's back, bouncing off its thick hide to land hard on the stones. Blood fills my mouth as I bite on my tongue, and I gasp wetly, stunned.

Somewhere behind me, I hear the monster turn around, feel the ground shake under the beast's hooves as it charges again. A part of my brain knows I need to move, but my body won't listen.

"Down boy!"

The sudden shout echoes around the hills like a gunshot. There's a deafening *thud* as something falls heavily to the ground, then the world goes still. I let out a shuddering breath, regaining the use of my lungs at last. But each gulp of air brings with it ripples of pain, and the overpowering need to throw up.

I barely have the time to roll onto my stomach before I start heaving. Bile as black as my hands spews forth, wave after nauseating wave, until I'm left empty and shaking.

"The purging's never fun, is it? But the bad's got to come out one way or another." The voice sounds like it belongs to a boy.

I flinch as a cool hand settles on my back.

"Don't worry," the demon boy continues. "The Aether here is impure, makes it hard for newcomers to adjust. Most demons learn not to rely on it directly, but you should be better soon enough."

With a final shudder, I wipe my mouth on my sleeve, and lift my head, blinking blearily at the wiry boy. He can't possibly be more than fourteen, with black hair that falls over a pair of sea-green eyes. My gaze slides over to the beast's carcass lying in a pool of its own blood a few feet away, and my skin prickles uneasily. There's no way someone as young as him could have taken out a beast like that in the span of a couple of seconds. Not unless he's very, very powerful.

The boy catches my look and nods. "Good thinking," he says, snapping his fingers together.

I jump as blue flames burst over the demon's body, quickly consuming its remains.

"I don't like robbing anyone down here of their chances to atone," the boy says, as if any of this is supposed to make sense to me, "but at this point, it would be too dangerous to have it come back only to hunt us down out of revenge."

Revenge. That last word jolts my brain to catch up with what's happened, despite the headache pressing dully at my temples.

"Th-the archer?" I ask feebly.

"Gone too, I'm afraid," the boy says, looking genuinely sad at the news. "In any case, there's no time to tarry. Even with the bodies gone, we're too close to the city. More demons are bound to come by."

"City?" I whisper, headache growing into a sharp pounding.

The boy nods and holds out his calloused hand to help me up, a gesture that seems strangely familiar, and has me instinctively reach out. But as my fingers graze his, I realize what I'm about to do and jerk my hand back.

"Wait, who are you?" I ask.

I expect him to say he's someone from my fevered imagination, another demon who wants to torture me, an envoy from Carman. But, instead, the boy drops into a crouch, his sea-green eyes too knowing for one so young. "You've been searching for me all this time yet you don't even know who I am?"

"I-I have?"

Carefully, the boy leans in and reaches into my pocket. And when he pulls back, a red flower petal is held pressed between his thin fingers. His lips quirk. "You wouldn't have found this if it weren't the case," he says, "and Lady Kaede wouldn't have led you to me."

"You two work together?" I ask dumbly.

Only then do I notice he is wearing Lake High's uniform as well. And on the lapel of his threadbare jacket, the faded embroidery of a Celtic cross over shield and sword can still be seen.

"You're a KORT knight," I say, finally letting him pull me up to me feet. "Or were..." The other shoe drops. "Are you the one who wrote on those boulders?"

"Gale, at your service," the boy says, with a slight bow. "And now that introductions are out of the way, let's go."

He pulls on my hand, getting me to move.

"Wait, my friends...," I start.

"Kaede will take care of them," Gale replies without stopping.

Every muscle aching, I stumble after him, finding it difficult to concentrate on anything but putting one foot in front of the other. Still, my mind keeps spinning back to the boy's name. Gale. Why does it sound so familiar? And then it hits me. You're Lance's brother, aren't you?"

The boy's face breaks into a dazzling smile as he looks over his shoulder at me. "You know him, then? I had hoped… Is he doing well?"

The memory of Lance kneeling at Mordred's mercy flashes before my eyes. I clear my throat uncomfortably. "He, uh, was still alive last I saw," I hazard.

The gleam in Gale's eyes dims. "Things must be quite a mess up there, too," he says somberly. "And they're about to get much worse."

My heart stutters. "Worse? How? What have you found out?"

"It's best if I show you," Gale says.

He steers me up a steep cliffside. The air here is hazy, the thick smell of smoke tickling the back of my throat. I'm about to tell him I need a break, when Gale motions us down.

"Careful, now," he whispers, dropping onto his stomach to crawl the rest of the way up.

With a resigned sigh, I follow suit, struggling to keep my head clear long enough to ask him what this is all about. But when I finally reach his side, my question turns into a shocked gasp.

The demon city's walls rise in the distance, a long, uninterrupted line of black. And darkening the wide valley between us, are battalions' worth of soldiers—men, women, and even children, all standing shoulder to shoulder in concentric circles around the largest bonfire I've ever seen.

"Is that a cauldron?" I ask, unable to tear my stinging eyes away from the cottage-sized pot sitting on the fire, bright flames licking its blackened underside. Dark fumes belch out of its depths, the source of the column of smoke Keva and I had spotted from our cave.

"Unfortunately," Gale replies.

"I don't get it. Are they all waiting to get fed, or something?"

"Or something."

Gale points with his chin, and my eyes bug out as pale arms reach over the cauldron's lip, people slowly pulling themselves out of its steaming insides before toppling awkwardly over onto a raised platform. A dozen of them, all pale and strangely impassive despite having been obviously boiled alive.

My heart lurches. I know what those are.

"Draugar," Gale whispers beside me.

A whole army of them.

"How can there be so many?" I ask, trying not to think about what thousands of draugar could do if unleashed upon the human world. I still vividly remember the two dead children who attacked Inspector Bossart and me back at Caamaloth, and how close we came to not making it out alive.

"That's the Pair Dadeni," Gale explains slowly, "the cauldron of rebirth. It revives the dead and turns them into—"

"Walking corpses," I say, "I know."

"More like fighting corpses," Gale says. He shakes his head. "That cauldron was supposed to have been destroyed ages ago. Another point our Order's Archives got wrong."

"So this is what Carman opened Hell for?" I say, rubbing at the tightness in my chest. "Of course, if they'd kept to the hole Mordred made to sneak them out, most of them would have ended up cut to pieces before even setting foot in Avalon."

I feel Gale's ancient eyes settle upon me thoughtfully, probably wondering how I know about the draugar's previous escape route, when he suddenly returns his attention to the valley below. I scan the motionless ranks, wondering what's going on, when I spot a red-dressed woman making her way toward the gargantuan cauldron.

Gale's shoulder brushes mine as he flattens himself to the ground.

"What is it?" I whisper.

"Asheel."

"Who?" I ask, tracking the female demon's movements as she struts through the ranks of corpse soldiers, her wavy, light-brown hair bouncing around her ample curves with every step.

"Someone you don't ever want to cross paths with if you can avoid it," Gale says.

The woman stops at last before the new recruits, looking at them like a benevolent fairy godmother. Her teeth glint in a wolf-sharp smile as she sidles up to the last of them, a large, bearded man with bulging muscles. The draugar remains impassive while the she-demon runs her hands over his pectorals, rubbing herself onto his sturdy body like a cat in heat.

I tear my gaze away from the disturbing sight. "Is this what you wrote about in your last journal entry when you said they'd increased their activity?" I ask.

Gale nods grimly. "But I'm afraid it's not the main reason for Carman's presence here."

"What then?"

"I don't know. I can't get close enough to her to find out."

I lick my parched lips, a new crazy idea germinating in my already ailing mind. "Are you saying we need to infiltrate her ranks to find out what other surprise she has in store?"

"That would be ideal, but—"

"Something worse than this demonic army?"

"In a nutshell. But we would be too conspicuous, and turning a demon against her, when she has the ability to promise them freedom, is nigh on impossible."

I flex my fingers thoughtfully, trying to ignore the panic mounting inside me as the solution to the problem solidifies. *This is what I'm here for, the way for me to redeem myself.*

I release a shaky breath. "I can do it," I say. "In case you weren't aware of this already, it's because of Carman that I'm stuck in Hell. She's the one who pushed me down through the Gates."

"Yet she didn't kill you," Gale adds, easily guessing where I'm going with this. "And you'd willingly offer yourself as her prisoner?"

I swallow audibly. "I'm already her prisoner. Might as well make it look official."

"She'll wonder why you've decided to show up all of a sudden," Gale says.

"There's nothing else to do around here."

"Have you considered that she's left you alive because she might need you for something?"

Of course, I've asked myself that. I've asked it a million times over since she first pushed me down here. "That'll only make my job easier," I force myself to say.

"Carman isn't stupid," Gale says. But I can tell he's wavering. "There must be a catch somewhere."

"Yeah, but you'll be—"

A sharp shout makes us both look back down, and my blood runs cold. I watch with growing anger as an old woman dressed in too-tight leather clothes struts towards the edge of the draugar army, dragging a bound Keva across the valley floor.

"Don't move," Gale says urgently, putting a restraining hand on my arm before I can bolt to Keva's rescue. "We'll find a way to free her, but not now. Not while we're at such a disadvantage."

"She was supposed to be safely away," I hiss at Gale, watching the hag's colossal horned dog circle them both, jaws snapping excitedly. "You said she was safe. So why does Gwyllion have my friend prisoner? And where is the banshee?"

Far below, Gwyllion stops at last. "Why don't you take a look at the vermin I've found crawling over the territory you're supposed to guard, Asheel!" the old hag calls out.

The she-demon slowly rises in the air to see what Gwyllion's up to, all interest in the bulky draugar lost. Keva lets out another sharp cry as Gwyllion releases her, ripping the whip's bladed lashes out from around her legs.

Fear unfurls in my belly, my tainted power bubbling up sickeningly in response, urging me to fight. But Gale's fingers tighten around my arm.

"Stay down," he whispers harshly, "or you'll be dead before you take three steps."

"Ain't that the truth."

We both jump at the deep voice behind us.

Ever so slowly, we turn around to face a tall, statuesque man sneering down at us. Then a heavy kick to the ribs sends me rolling across the ground.

# CHAPTER 7

Before I can manage a breath, a heavy foot lands on my spine, hard enough to dislodge my vertebrae.

"I believeth she has gotten your point now, Gad," a voice with a terrible lisp says, barely making it through the ringing in my ears.

I force my eyes open, blink the congealing blood away. I immediately catch sight of Gale. The knight is sitting with his hands behind his back, his baby face a mask of cuts and bruises. I wince in guilt at what they've done to him. The boy who managed to evade all these demons for years has gotten caught like a rat, all for reaching out to me.

Another name to add to the long list of people I've sent to their doom.

"Seems a little daft, if you ask me," a cruel voice replies, sending shivers down my spine.

With a grunt, I struggle to sit up so I can glare at our two captors.

One of them reminds me a little of Lugh, tall and strong, with perfectly-proportioned features and the haughty look of a Greek god. But where Lugh's hair is brown, this one's a blond so pale it looks white, making his blue gaze only icier. The demon standing next to him, on the other hand, is so massively muscled that he makes Gareth look like a cute puppy.

"What do you want?" I croak out.

The pretty one laughs. "What do we want?" he repeats. "That is a very good question, don't you think, Az?" The demon starts pacing, as if I've asked him a deep, existential question. "Well, I suppose we could start with the fact that I'd like to get out of this stinking hole. But considering that's not presently possible, I'd settle with killing our time by slowly dismembering the both of you, and cloaking myself with your skin. How's that for a start?"

I repress a shudder, garnering a sadistic grin from the beautiful demon.

"Let us cutteth to the chase," the one called Az says, still sounding like a bad actor in a Shakespearean play. "What are you doing here?"

"Admiring the view," I retort.

A fist as hard as a rock punches me, nearly ripping my head off my neck, and tearing a startled gasp from my cut lips. I blink hard to dispel the stars scattered across my vision as the shock of the blow slowly recedes, leaving behind an intense throbbing that makes it hard for me to think.

"You need to show respect to your betters," the beautiful demon says. His perfect lips split into another cruel smile. "Although, frankly, it doesn't matter what you would have answered. We're going to expunge[2] the both of you anyway."

"It dost appear that these gents art the companions of the lass the lady Gwyllion captured," the beefy demon says, looking down at the plains below.

"More fodder for the Pair Dadeni," Gad says, cracking his knuckles.

[2] To completely erase or wipe out.

My power stirs in outrage, and before I can channel it out properly, the ground splinters around me, deep cracks spreading outward like thunderbolts. I barely have the time to see Az's surprised look before Gad backhands me.

"Cut the crap, or you'll stop breathing earlier than planned."

"I don't think Carman will be happy if you dispatch me without her say-so," I say, cheek burning.

Both of them pretend not to care a word of what I said, but I know I've got them. It's in the bare twinge of a jaw muscle, the stillness of the eyes. And just like that, I've sealed my fate to the will of the very Fey who wishes to destroy all that I care for.

"Thee doth know each other then," Az finally booms out. "Handeth it ov'r, Gadreel."

The beautiful demon gives me another malevolent scowl before reaching into a pocket and flipping a polished stone in his partner's direction.

"Now, prithee, tell us," Az says, addressing me as he pockets his winnings, "why do you think Carman will want you?"

"Why don't you ask her that yourself?" I retort.

I flinch automatically, expecting Gad to smack me again. But instead, I feel his cold fingers slither around my neck, forcing me to look up into his eyes.

"One more impertinent word from you, and I'll make your cute friend there pay," he breathes.

"I'm down here because of her," I answer back, leaving out the juicy bits about us being sworn enemies and all. "In fact, she's probably expecting me."

The last one is conjecture, but they don't know that, and I'm hoping it'll incentivize them to leave us alone quicker.

"She is, is she?" Gadreel squeezes my throat, until I'm scrabbling at his hands for air.

"Just take us over to Carman," I rasp, feeling myself turn purple, "like a good...lackey."

This time the blow does land, a solid *crack* against my cheek that makes me go blind for a second, flooding my mouth with blood.

"It seemeth the lass spake the truth," Az grumbles, sounding displeased.

"However that may be," Gad says, releasing me at last, "I don't think her partner has the same hallowed status she professes for herself."

Cradling my already swelling cheek, I steal another glance at Gale. But the boy hasn't moved an inch, as if turned to stone, and seems completely unaware of the threat looming over him.

"I don't see what business it is for a couple of body snatchers like you to think at all," I say before I can think better of it.

The kick happens so quickly I don't even feel the pain until I'm lying flat on the ground, holding onto my stomach, unwanted tears streaming down my face.

Gad lets out a low laugh. "So much bark for an edentate[3] creature such as yourself. Maybe I should make sure you look the part."

"Gadreel...," the demon named Az says. But the warning comes out more as a plea, and I know that this time, nothing's going to stay Gad's hand as he bashes my teeth in.

Then, from nowhere, a loud, keening wail rends the air, drawing closer.

"What the——" Gad starts.

Banshee?

As if in answer to my silent call, the banshee bursts into view at the bottom of the hill, her grey cloak barely noticeable against

[3] Toothless.

the equally grey landscape. I feel a rush of gratitude towards this ever-faithful Fey, who always throws herself in harm's way to protect me.

But the banshee doesn't stop to face my captors, and I watch her, stunned, as she bullets away again.

A few seconds later, I understand why, as screaming, half-naked men tear across the landscape in hot pursuit, bone maces held high, vengeance burning in their crazed eyes. My mouth drops open as I recognize them for the group of demons who attacked us when we first reached the hills. All bar the one I accidentally drowned in tar. Kaede mentioned people could be reborn here, and even Gale alluded to it, but the reality of it didn't hit me until now.

I mentally shake myself. I needed a distraction, I've got one. It's time to act.

Before Gad or Az can see me, I grab a fist-sized stone and hurl it at the quickly retreating men, willing the projectile to reach at least one of them. Something inside me lets loose, turning my vision momentarily ashen. Then the rock strikes the last man's head, hurtling him straight into the guy in front.

Bingo.

As one, the group of demons swings around to face the new threat. It doesn't take them long to spot us, and, with renewed shouts of anger, they rush up the hillside to fall upon Az and Gadreel in a frenzied swarm.

Now.

I lurch to my feet, meaning to grab Gale and run away, but my legs give out before I can take two steps. Using my power to draw the demons over has wiped me out.

"Careful," Gale whispers, catching me before I hit the ground.

"Gale?" I slur. "You OK?"

"Lean into me," the boy says.

I let Gale half-drag, half-carry me down the rocky slope, trying to move as fast as I can. But I'm too dizzy still, and when I glance back at Gad and Az, I find the two of them finishing off the last of the demented men with practiced ease, looking almost bored.

My stomach heaves, and I trip Gale up in my attempt to avoid my own vomit, sending us both sprawling.

"Sorry," I hiccup.

"Come on," Gale says, urging me back to my feet.

I reach for his extended hand, when the hairs at the back of my neck suddenly stand up. Everything's gone quiet. Then I catch sight of Gad, striding over at a leisurely pace.

"Go," I tell Gale urgently.

"Not without—"

Gad's footsteps speed up.

"GO!" I shout, shoving Gale back.

Gale hesitates for another split second, then nods. "I'll come back for you," he says.

Then, sparing me a final glance, he runs away.

"I can do this," I whisper, willing myself to stay strong.

But hope is a very expensive commodity down here, and I'm quickly running out of it. Especially when I've got two insanely strong demons on my back. Literally.

"Someone's coming," Az says, shifting on top of me so that my lungs are further compressed.

I breathe in shakily, expecting to see Carman's feathery dress swirl up the hill, her hard-set eyes boring into me with all the hatred a demon can harbor. A shadow detaches itself against the nearest hill, long and threatening, before shrinking back down again. Then the edge of a red hat tipped low over a half-melted face comes into view, barely reaching Gad's waist.

"Nibs?" I squeak out, twisting around to get a better look.

The clurichaun shoots me a glare that tells me all about how pleased he is to meet me again, then looks at my captors.

"How much?" he growls.

Gad holds up his left hand, fingers splayed.

Nibs shakes his head. "Too much."

Wrong answer. Gad's beautiful face splits into another one of his cruel smiles and he holds up two more fingers with his right.

"Take it or leave it, swine," Gad says, "or I'll make sure you never see this one again."

My jaw unhinges itself as I finally get what they're doing. "Are you bartering for me?" I ask.

"Shut up, dunghill," Nibs spits at me. He flicks the edge of his hat up, putting his disfigured side in full display. "I told ya five was too much, what makes ya think I'll give ya more?"

A thin laugh escapes Gad's lips. He leans dangerously close to the clurichaun. "We know what she is," he says coldly. "And we know you can't afford to lose her."

"If ya really wanna get yer ticket out of here, ya'd give her over quick, and for free," Nibs drawls out. "Now, I was originally willing to give ya three bags' worth, but since ya're making me waste my time—and ya *know* how much I hate that—I'll bring it down to two. One for each of ya."

Nibs's distended smile makes me cringe, but it seems to do the job, for I feel Az's crushing weight finally lift.

"Here thee are, sweetheart," Az says, grabbing me around my already creaking ribs and gingerly setting me back up on my feet. "And please do excuse my impropriety, but circumstances being what they are…"

"Sure," I wheeze out, as Nibs pulls out two pouches of tinkling coins and hands them over to Gad. "It's been real lovely."

I grimace as my stomach twists viciously on itself at the small lie, garnering a sad smile from the large demon.

"I can tell thy words aren't felt, but I appreciate thy attempt at alleviating my sin," he says. "Mayhap, under other circumstances, our meeting would have been friendlier."

"OK, enough," Nibs says, thankfully batting Az away from me, "we ain't got no time for any of yer awkward wooing, bozo. And you"—he flicks his head at me—"follow me."

Without a hesitation, I limp after the clurichaun, Gad's cold laugh pursuing me like an awful nightmare. Nibs may be half my size, but I struggle to keep up with him.

"Thanks for that," I say, wheezing. "Don't know what would've happened if you hadn't come over to help me."

Nibs suddenly stops.

"What is it?" I ask, the smoke from the draugar-making cauldron so thick around us that it makes everything hazy.

"What were you even thinking?" Nibs barks, jabbing me in the stomach with his tiny finger.

"I'm sorry," I say, stung, "but did I miss something? Aren't you the one taking me to Carman? If I recall correctly, last I saw her, she was intent upon killing me."

The clurichaun snorts. "If she'd wanted you dead, ya pea-brained fatwit, ya'd *be* dead."

"Why does she want me alive then?" I ask, fear and excitement making my skin tingle. If I can get him to spill the beans now, I could move onto the next part of my plan without having to even deal with the witch. Besides, Nibs isn't a bad sort, or Arthur would never have worked with him. Surely there's a part of him that wants to stop Carman too. "She's got what she wanted," I insist, "Hell open, demons everywhere…"

But Nibs clams up immediately. "Nothin' fun, I can promise ya that," he mutters, forcing me to get moving again. Straight, I realize with some alarm, for the army of draugar.

"Still better than that Gad guy, right?" I say, unwilling to let go of the thought that Nibs might still help me.

"That Gad guy?" Nibs repeats with barely contained anger. "Do ya know what Gadreel is known for? War! And ya go an' get yerself captured by him! Do ya even realize what he could've done to ya?"

"I thought it was Lucifer who started the whole war thingy," I say, peeved at his sudden outburst.

Nibs lets out a humorless chuckle. "Fool," he says, pulling out a dented flask from his jacket. "Ya should've stayed away, instead of putting yer nose where it doesn't belong, as usual. Better yet, ya should've taken that silly friend of yers and found another way to get outta here."

I suddenly feel very tired, a weariness that's due to more than the draining experienced after using my powers. My plan to infiltrate Carman's ranks seems so foolish now that the adrenaline has left my body. "Can't you just...let us go?" I ask.

His only response is to grab my arm and resume our march.

Gradually, we wend our way through the ranks of stock-still draugar, the stink of their putrefying flesh mixing with that of the cauldron's acrid fumes. Even a couple hundred feet away from it, I can feel the waves of heat radiating from the bonfire, the Pair Dadeni probably brewing more undead soldiers for Carman's army.

There's a loud rumbling, as of a gathering storm, and Nibs suddenly drops to a knee. I jump as a dark figure lands in our midst, kicking up a cloud of dust and ash. Heart hammering, I find myself unable to look away as a chiseled face framed by lustrous black hair emerges, inky eyes meeting my own.

"It took you long enough to find me, dear," Carman says unctuously. Then her face breaks into a tight smile, and I feel myself go weak with fear. "Welcome to my Demesne."

# Chapter 8

My stomach feels like it wants to crawl out of my throat, along with my drumming heart. Too soon. I'm not ready to face her yet. All my beautiful plans seem so stupid now.

"I can smell her on you," Carman says, taking a long whiff of my hair. "Even all the way down here."

"W-who?" I stutter.

"Your mother." Carman prods my chin up, forcing me to look at her. "Do you think she'll come here to save you?"

"W-why would she?" I ask, hating how much my voice is shaking. "She's n-not even m-my real m-mother."

Carman bares her teeth at me. "I'm not speaking of that low-life human, but of your begetter, she who has already interfered so many times before to shield you."

I exhale sharply, shock momentarily making me forget everything else. "What?"

I catch the hateful gleam in Carman's eyes, before she turns it into a terrifyingly kind look. "I, too, know what it is to be rejected by my own progenitors," she says. Her fingers gently comb my hair back. "The hurt, the confusion, the loss...the anger."

She says this last word so softly, I can barely hear her. I remain as still as possible, afraid the smallest movement is going to trigger her, and she'll rip my throat out.

"And when you confront them with the facts," Carman continues, her face closing up again at some distant, hateful memory, "they pretend they always cared. That it was all for our sake." Her cheeks dimple with another smile that makes me shiver despite the heat. "But we know better—and we're not afraid to show them the error of their ways."

She tenderly pats my cheek, and I catch Nibs's shudder behind her.

"Come," Carman says. "Let us prove to your mother she's no longer needed."

I glance at Nibs, sure that my panic is showing through, but there's nothing I can do except to follow as Carman carves a way through the draugar army, straight for the far demon city walls. My thoughts are a jumbled mess I can't seem to untangle—I have what I wanted, I've managed to attach myself to Carman, but what now?

I barely notice our slowing down, and it's not until Carman finally stops and places her hand on my shoulder that I realize we've crossed the entire plain.

I crane my neck up, blinking blurrily at the megalithic wall towering hundreds of feet over us, its top lost in wreaths of mist. Snaking its way up its side is a narrow, rail-less staircase, guarded by a dozen demons. The men watch us come with slitted eyes, dark scales rippling with unease.

"Now pay very close attention to what I'm about to say," Carman says as we climb the first step. "I want you to know what you're going to help us achieve."

Her hand cleaves the air sideways, and the nearest guard tips forward, holding his neck. We all watch as the demon gurgles his last breath at our feet, dark ichor[4] pooling around his thrashing body. Then, all at once, the other sentries throw themselves at their fallen comrade.

I jump back as one of the demons snarls, fangs glistening with yellowing saliva, before snapping his jaws shut over another guard's arm and ripping it off. The other guard howls in pain, then pulls himself away, holding onto his severed stump, jealously eyeing the frenzy.

"Look at them, fighting each other for a piece of scrap," Carman says contemptuously. "And to think they once fought side by side, fearful warriors in the greatest War of all."

There's a loud *crack* and another demon limps away, giving up. I swallow hard, feeling queasy as the fight redoubles in fury. Finally, one of the last demons standing lets out a loud yelp, and all but one of the guards pull away from the dead sentry's remains.

"This is what this place has reduced them to," Carman continues, as the winner crouches over the lifeless body.

The demon hooks his claws beneath the corpse's chin and yanks the severed head back to expose his torn throat. Then, with a victorious gloat, he reaches inside the dead guard's trachea to pull out a long, oval stone.

An ogham, I realize with a jolt.

Nauseated, I look away, but Carman grabs the back of my neck, and forces my head around.

"Watch," she says, as the champion lets out a victorious bellow. "Do you think it fair that they be forced to spill this precious blood when all they ever dreamed of was their own freedom?"

---

[4] Blood of any Fey, including that of Dark Sidhe and demons. Can have a different consistency or color from that of humans.

The winner's already eyeing the other two injured guards with cupidity, gauging their strength.

"They made their choice," I say feebly. Besides, I want to add, you're the one who started this fight.

Carman chuckles softly. "They never wanted to leave their home," she says, "just to make a few alterations to the rules. Make them more...fair."

"And killing thousands of innocents to get that back is fair?" I ask.

"There is no such thing as innocence. Not when, from the very moment we are conceived, we are prey to desires—free will or no. I know you believe my quest to be vile, an attack on humans who have not done a thing against us. But their ancestors did, and the sins of the parents now reside with their children.

"Besides, I have observed these humans you so cherish, and have found them to be but parasites who abuse their current status of superiority to destroy the very world they inhabit. I'm simply hurrying the process along."

"How can you say that?" I ask. "Not everyone's like that! There are plenty of people fighting to preserve—"

"Too little, too late," Carman says. "They were given the keys to a beautiful, bountiful world, and they raped it in the name of progress, and cupidity. They failed in their guardianship.

"At least, when we Fey ruled the earth, we made sure balance was present, encouraging procreation or culling populations as needed. No exceptions."

"Who are you to judge who deserves to live or die?" I ask. "What right did you have to decide of such matters, what justice?"

"Justice is a matter of point of view," Carman says. "Unadulterated obedience from one's slaves is 'just' in the eyes of the master, not so in that of the serf who's been sent to jail at the former's orders. Wouldn't you agree?"

I'm about to contradict her, but snap my mouth shut instead. She's no longer talking about these demons' rebellion against Heaven, but of my imprisonment by Irene and the Order for fear of what my powers could do.

"A coup is far from the 'little change' you mention," I force myself to say. "All you're doing is imposing your vision of things upon others."

"Such is the way the world works," Carman says, forcing me to resume our climb up the demon city wall. "The strongest always rule, no matter the form. Even your famous democracy is but an illusion.

"It is always those with the most money—your current weapon of choice—who control the outcome of any vote to their liking, whether through purchasing voices, having them removed, or swaying the public opinion through lies and propaganda. Propaganda such that all Fey creatures are to be exterminated, for instance."

"But getting rid of all humans isn't the way to go," I say.

Carman's laugh makes my hairs stand on end. "Indeed? Perhaps, then, it is in your interest to rise to the top, so that you can make sure your vision can come to fruition instead."

"You're saying I should take power away from you?"

"Take, no, but there's always room for negotiation when a relationship is mutually beneficial."

"There is?"

Carman smiles ever so prettily. "Come, and we can discuss the terms."

Discuss the terms. I can't believe I'm discussing anything with a known-psycho witch who, until recently, wanted me dead. Worse, I'm finding it increasingly hard to come up with valid counter-arguments. What Carman's saying has logic. Worser, as

Gareth would say, they hold truth. But that doesn't make her right. Does it?

"Our people," Carman says as we reach the top of the wall, and extending both arms over the battlements.

Fear prickles down my spine at the sight. The demon city is like an ocean of grey pustules, stretching upon the land from horizon to boundless horizon. What ravages the army of draugar can cause is laughable in comparison to what even a tenth of this city's population could wreak.

"Together, we will lead them and take back what is rightfully ours," Carman declares.

"How?" I ask.

"You should be happy to learn that those knights of yours will be the first to fall," Carman says, her dark eyes sparkling with loathing, "for they are the worst of sinners. Done are the days when they usurped our powers for their own gains."

I bite down on my lip, hating how my own thoughts and feelings sound when coming out of her. If the knights hadn't broken their pact with the Fey, if they hadn't decided to hunt them down, Carman would never have been freed, and I wouldn't be in Hell with her, planning for mass destruction.

"So how do I fit in?" I ask.

Carman's smile turns feral. "That depends, dearest."

"On what?"

"What you can do for me."

Saint George's balls, she really does expect me to join her! She must really be insane if she thinks I'll so much as lift a finger to help her.

With a knowing smirk, Carman looks past me, and a jet of dark sparks curls up from her outstretched hand in some kind of signal.

My blood runs cold as a terrible shriek resounds across the valley.

"Keva!" I breathe, lunging across the walkway, all thoughts of the demon city forgotten.

I scan the wide valley below, and my eyes fall on Gwyllion's distant shape as she swings her arm around, bladed whip slashing Keva's bound figure, tearing another heart-wrenching cry from her.

"Stop it!" I scream.

Blazing pain shoots down my arm as Carman yanks me away from the crenellations.

"There, there," she says soothingly, "we wouldn't want you to fall over the wall now, would we?"

"Please," I beg, cringing as Keva's body jerks under a third strike.

"There can be no pity for such a mortal," Carman replies coldly, "not after all her kind's done to us. Unless...you can convince me otherwise."

My knuckles go white over the stone parapet. I taste the sharp tang of blood, before I realize I've bitten my lip open. But the clean pain of it momentarily clears my mind, enough to feel my power rising to my need.

"When Gwyllion finishes her work, your little friend will be just another draugar," Carman continues, hissing in pleasure.

"No."

The word escapes my lips, barely a whisper, but I let my power rip free along with it. It bursts out of my fingertips, long bolts of blue flames arcing through the air and across the valley with blinding speed.

Gwyllion barely has the chance to turn around before the lightning strikes her, over and over again, until the ground is seared black, all trace of the old hag obliterated.

A loud, plaintive whine rises in the silence that follows. Barguest, crying for its mistress, horned head hanging low in distress.

I gasp as Carman yanks me back by the hair, pain slicing through my head at her touch.

"Not exactly what I was expecting," Carman says, with barely-veiled jubilation, "but I believe I can finally see what Dain saw in you. And, my dear, that means it's time for us to negotiate."

# Chapter 9

Every knight's face looks tense in the moon's pale light, eyes drawn outward to the encircling line of trees, as if awaiting an attack. But when I look down, I see that the battle's already taken place.

The ground is gouged, the grass and flowers burned off in large patches, and everywhere my eyes settle are bodies. Those of the tapir-like creatures Mordred likes to use in his army, and those of a few knights I don't recognize, but mostly of pixies. Lots and lots of pixies.

My throat grows tight with sudden tears.

"How many?"

The voice sounds strangled, but I recognize it at once, and the vice that was around my heart loosens.

Arthur.

I know I won't see him, I almost never do in these visions, but at least I know he's still alive.

"Two of ours," Hadrian answers, his face covered in grime and blood, "Bastien and Penelope. Of theirs..." He doesn't finish his sentence. He doesn't have to.

Gauvain tenses next to me, all senses alert.

"Someone's coming!" a girl shouts from the edge of the torn field as a pale figure detaches itself from the forest's deep shadows, carefully picking its way through the rubble and the dead.

All at once I'm moving, heading down to meet the newcomer, the knights parting before me. The pale figure stops at my sight, bows, then straightens up again, and I recognize the plain features of the albino man who used to live in Lake High's asylum before it burned down.

"Sir Rip," Arthur says tightly, "what news do you bring?"

"Nothing that will alleviate your present sadness, I'm afraid," Rip van Winkle answers with a small gesture towards the ground.

"She refused to join us?" Lugh asks, his sudden appearance startling me.

Despite the battle, he looks like he always has: An alabaster statue walking amongst mortals. Only the patch that now covers his missing eye denotes he ever got close to anything life-threatening.

"More like she was prevented from doing so," Rip answers somberly, and my heart skips a beat at the horrifying implication.

"Is it still worth it to offer Lady Maeve our help?" Arthur asks.

Rip shakes his head 'no' as Arthur's pixie settles on his shoulder, casting a red sheen over his pale features.

"How could it be?" Arthur asks. "Her Demesne is further away, surely Mordred's troops couldn't have gotten to her so quickly."

"I would have thought he would go after Aengus next instead," Lugh adds.

"Unless Aengus has joined the Dark Sidhe's forces already," Oberon says, stepping out of what appears to be a tunnel leading inside the hill, its entrance torn open. "Maybe that's what I should've done. Maybe there's still time for me and my people—"

He stops, shoulders hunching as he gazes at what's left of his Demesne. All these pixies were his to protect, and he's failed them. We all have.

"You know the outcome would have been the same had you chosen their side," Lugh says. "Worse, you would then be at Carman's mercy, and you know how little goodwill she bears you. But if you choose to join our side, you can help put an end to all this senseless killing."

"*You* are the one who forced that choice upon me!" Oberon barks, spinning around to face us. "How many times have I pleaded for you to stay away? But each time you came back. And look what it got me!

"Do you know what it feels like to have the deaths of thousands of innocents upon your conscience?" Oberon lets out a grating laugh. "Of course you don't. You *have* no conscience. Let me give you some advice, then, free of charge: Learn to mind your own business. From what I hear, Avalon's falling apart at the seams already. So if you care an ounce for your people, you'd better go back there and defend them."

A muscle twitches in Lugh's cheek, but before he can reply, a dark snake slithers its way out of the tunnel and into the bloody grass, followed closely by a lithe Fey.

"My Lord," Sameerah says, bowing respectfully in front of Oberon. "Please accept my sincerest apologies for failing you tonight. It is as you say: Had we not sought you out today, this terrible calamity would not have happened. At least not tonight. But you know, as well as I, that they would have eventually struck at you, whether we'd come to you or not."

"They might not have known where to find me," Oberon says, voice glacial. "Now get off my land, all of you!"

He turns sharply away, his cape swirling around his shoulders, but not before I see the angry tears glistening on his round cheeks.

"Lord Oberon, your losses are ours to bear," Arthur says. "Believe us when we say we understand the weight you carry, and I do wish we could abide by your wishes, but we cannot afford to wait any longer. Our forces, like yours, are much diminished, while Carman's are growing every day. But if we stand united, we still have a chance to stop her."

Her forces are growing every minute, actually, I silently say, what with that draugar-making pot of hers.

The draugar!

With a jolt, I realize I need to let them know about the impending danger. But no matter how much I try to speak, I cannot utter a single sound, not even the shadow of a whisper.

The world suddenly wobbles around me, and Rip hurries to help me stay up.

"Are you alright?" he asks softly.

As the tremors slowly subside, Arthur's all-too-familiar voice whispers back, "I just didn't expect...I thought I heard...I'm OK, thank you. Just tired, I guess..."

Arthur lets his voice trail off, caught in his own thoughts. Rip looks up then, straight into my eyes, and a light smile touches his lips. I let out a muted gasp. Did he just see me? Does he know I'm watching them?

"If it's any consolation, I did find out more about the Siege Perilous," Rip says. "Before she passed away, the Lady Maeve revealed that it can be destroyed, and, thankfully, the one weapon that can do so is in our possession."

There's a collective intake of breath.

"Excalibur?" Lord Oberon asks, incredulous.

"All's not lost, then," Sameerah breathes, reaching down for the snake slowly twisting its way up her leg.

"I propose we move along with the plan then," Lugh says.

"Plan?" Oberon asks, sounding slightly intrigued despite himself. "To destroy the Siege Perilous?"

"Correct," Lugh says. "But before we do, we need to give others a chance to join us as well."

"There's no time to waste," Arthur says. "We need to get to the other Demesnes before Mordred has a chance to find them."

Shivers run down my spine, for that's the trouble, isn't it? Mordred always seems to be a step ahead of us.

# Chapter 10

"I take it resisting didn't do much good, huh?"

I cough up some more blood, letting it trickle down my chin, too exhausted to spit it out, then nod. I wince as the movement pulls at my bound wrists.

Keva lets out a heartfelt sigh. "Bloody hell."

"Literally," I rasp, my voice grating from too much screaming.

I sag against the whipping post to ease my shoulders, eyes automatically gliding over to the thick fumes still rising from the Pair Dadeni.

From what I've seen over the past few days, the cauldron's kept fed with a constant string of human victims—thanks in no small part to Mordred and his squad—and is churning ever more draugar to strengthen Carman's army.

The only positive thing about it is that these soulless corpses seem to freak the demons out as much as us, so we're usually left alone down on the plain.

"Were you able to find out anything at all?" Keva asks as always, though the answer never changes.

"Not a thing."

Though at first it seemed like the quick plan Gale and I hatched together was working, Carman put an end to it quickly enough. I should've known her taking me under her wing and talking partnerships was just that—an act. A ploy to get me to show her how to use the Sangraal. And when that didn't work, she was quick to force me to do it for her.

Keva grunts in annoyance. "So which *daeva*[5] did she make you heal this time?"

"The one that guards the draugar," I say.

"The necrophiliac?" Keva exclaims. "She's the worst! Have you seen the way she keeps rubbing herself all over those poor draugar? You know, the *handsome* ones. And they're too dead to push her off."

My laugh surprises us both. "Are you going to start a movement against the harassment of handsome draugar?"

"Maybe I should," Keva replies petulantly. "Think how great it would be if I ended up subverting Carman's army right from under her nose."

"I'd not voice that quite so loudly if I were ya."

We both jump at the nasally voice. But it's only Nibs, and I expel an annoyed breath as the clurichaun threads his way through the last of the draugar to stop in front of us.

"Yer both in surprisingly high spirits, considerin' yer current state," Nibs drawls, pulling out his silver flask and waving it at us. "So, what do a starved human and an infected half-Fey have to laugh about?"

"Nothing, thanks to you," I say glumly.

"Don't blame me for ya not runnin' away when ya had the chance," Nibs retorts. He takes a deep gulp of his whiskey, then sputters as something dark jumps onto his back. "Off!" he exclaims, turning a bright shade of violet.

---

[5] A false god in Zoroastrianism.

The cat jumps back down onto the ashy ground, then pads over to rub itself against me, its fur warm and soft against my bare legs.

"Yeah, yeah, stupid pussy showin' off," Nibs mumbles loudly, wiping the spilled whiskey from his shirt front.

The feline lifts its dark head, leveling its one golden eye at him, the other closed shut by a long scar.

"Morgan," Keva whispers.

"I've noticed," I say, wondering whether we're both having the same hallucination.

"Doesn't it look a lot like—"

"The stupid geezer must always be a pain in the ass, mustn't he?" Nibs says, eyeing the cat with unmistakable distaste.

With a sniff, the cat sits on its haunches, looking reproachful. Nibs makes to add something, but grows suddenly still, all senses alert. Then, in the span of a heartbeat, he picks up the furry creature and flings it far into the ranks of impassive draugar.

"Hey!" Keva exclaims.

But Nibs shushes her, and by now I can hear it too. A familiar *clip-clopping* coming from the hills behind us, getting rapidly closer.

"Fraternizing with the enemy?" a laughing voice asks that makes my skin crawl.

"Fraternizing with AC's sister," Nibs retorts as Urim lands next to him in all of his white splendor. "Besides, we're old acquaintances, she and I, goin' back much longer than AC's known her."

"I wouldn't be too sure about that," Mordred says, jumping off his kelpie before it even comes to a halt.

"What are you doing here?" I growl.

"Aw, can't a guy show some brotherly concern?" Urim asks.

"We've seen the results of your latest activities," Thummim says, strolling up to the nearest draugar. "And I have to say that all those newly-restored demons frolicking with humans again is quite a sight to behold."

"But you do seem a little worse for wear," Urim adds.

I flinch as Mordred crouches in front of me, his eyes traveling up my bound arms, taking in the long cuts Carman's given me, the latest one still fresh and painful.

"Ah, Morgan," he says with a soft sigh, "when will you ever learn?"

I keep very still as he slowly reaches over my head. What kind of game is he playing now?

"Why do you keep fighting us?" Mordred asks. His fingers graze my arm, and I have to bite hard on my lip not to cry out. "Is it because of these knights? Because of that…Arthur? Even after all he's put you through?"

"He didn't put me through…," I start, feeling my stomach twinge at the beginning of the lie. "It wasn't like that! Arthur was just trying to stop me from…from…"

"From being yourself," Mordred says through clenched teeth, surprised at my vehement defense of Arthur. "But what did you get out of all those years spent struggling to be like those petty humans? Or is it that you enjoy playing the sacrificial lamb? Does it make you feel special?"

"As special as it is to be here like this?" I retort, thick chains jangling.

"This isn't permanent," Mordred says with a smile that doesn't reach his eyes. "But you've got to understand Carman's reticence to trust your sudden change of heart."

Urim nods. "You've built yourself quite the reputation."

"Traitor, is what they call you at the school," Thummim says offhandedly.

"Heard it was demon strumpet," Nibs says, hawking up phlegm before spitting loudly in the Dark Sidhe's general direction.

"If they only knew you don't stab people in their backs like they say," Mordred adds, tucking a strand of greasy hair back behind my ear. "No, you like to look into their eyes while you do so, just to savor their feelings of betrayal to the fullest. Just like I do."

"Shut up!" I snarl, hurling myself forward.

But my shackles keep me from head-butting Mordred like he deserves, and I'm forced to blow angrily in his face instead, tears prickling my eyes.

"Don't delude yourself," I say at last, "you and I are nothing alike, and never will be."

Mordred smirks. "No matter your wishes, we'll always be linked. In fact, I'll let you in on a little secret—the Gates would have opened for you too, if you'd chosen to sit on the Siege Perilous instead of me. It is, after all, what we were born to do."

Keva lets out a surprised hiccup.

"Don't be ridiculous," I say, blood draining from my face. "Nobody's born to do anything."

"There's evidently a lot for you to learn still," Mordred says with a small sneer. "But we've got time yet, and once I figure out how to keep those Gates open at all times, I'll be able to come visit you down here more often."

"What a lovely thought, truly," Nibs's sarcastic voice cuts in. "And I'd hate to burst yer bubble—"

"Not really," Thummim chimes in, stopping beside the standing corpse of what must have once been a well-fed banker, judging from the dirty suit and spotty shoes.

"—but have ya seen the state she's in?" Nibs continues. "At this rate, I give her a week, tops."

"I concur," Thummim says, poking his finger into what appears to be a bullet wound in the side of the dead banker's head.

"The girl can't even heal herself proper anymore," Urim says, stifling a yawn.

"The use of the Sangraal is drainin' her, figuratively and literally," Nibs adds.

"How many times has she used you?" Mordred asks, his voice dropping dangerously low.

"Four," Keva says from her whipping post.

"And she already looks like that?" Urim says, his eyes going wide.

"Could almost blend right in with these poor suckers," Thummim adds, sniffing his finger before wiping it down his pant leg.

"Where is she?" Mordred asks.

"Right in front of—oh." Urim stops and exchanges a worried glance with Nibs and Thummim. "That might not be such a good idea."

"Asheel said Carman wasn't too pleased when your sister took down Gwyllion," Thummim says, patting the banker on the shoulder, and accidentally dislocating its arm.

"Don't quite see why, the woman was a real pain," Nibs says.

"But we all know Carman's a prickly nut," Thummim says, attempting, without success, to pop the arm back in before giving up.

"Definitely nuts, and certainly single-minded in her vengeful wrath," Urim says. "So now may not be the best of times to sharpen your kitty claws against her."

Keva and I glance at each other in puzzlement. Against her? As in fighting Carman? I look pointedly at Nibs, but the clurichaun shrugs indifferently.

"Unless you want to kiss the prophecy goodbye," Thummim finishes.

"Untie her," Mordred growls, already vaulting onto his kelpie's back.

"As you wish," Thummim says with a defeated sigh.

After a moment's hesitation, Urim grabs the chains holding my arms up, and snaps the metallic links with frightful ease, catching me into his arms as I list forward.

"Are you guys freeing me?" I ask, stunned.

"Guess idiocy runs in your family's genes," Urim mutters as he carries me over to the kelpie.

"Wait," I start, as I'm plunked in front of Mordred. "What are you—"

But the demon horse is already thundering away.

"Remember," Nibs shouts after us, "if she asks, I was never here!"

Only then do I realize that my brother's taking me back to Carman.

"Please don't do this," I say, backing into the rampart, away from the twisty grey streets waiting ominously before us.

I can already smell the acrid stench of excrement, rotting meat and unwashed bodies that pervades the sprawling city. Yet it isn't what lies in plain sight that scares me, but the halls that have been carved beneath, where Carman now resides. And no matter what strange reason Mordred has for taking me there, I still feel like a sow being taken to the slaughterhouse.

"Come into my parlor, said the spider to the fly," Urim chants, shifting restlessly from one foot to the next.

"Let's go away, huh?" I continue, ignoring the Dark Sidhe. "This"—I wave a shaky hand around—"this isn't you. Carman doesn't care about you or your ideas, all she cares about is getting back at everyone for having been locked up." I take a wobbly step toward him, entreating. "Life could be different for us. Father left us a lot of money, enough that we'll want for nothing."

I don't know what I'm saying anymore. The only thing that matters, is that I don't want to go back to her. And for that, I need to find something that would tempt Mordred more than the appeal of power the witch has been dangling in front of him. Especially if Urim's and Thummim's earlier comments are true about him wanting to break free.

"You could go to school with me," I say, remembering how he once questioned me about Lake High classes, "learn new, amazing things!"

Urim and Thummim both make gagging motions off to the side, but Mordred's eyes are intent upon me. I keep forgetting that he's my twin, a boy who's had to live a rough life from the very beginning, and for whom, I expect, a normal life seems so very extraordinary.

"We could hang out with other people our own age," I add, warming up to these ideas myself, "have some fun, chillax... We'll try all these delicious foods, go to the movies, maybe even a concert!" I stop just within reach of him, take a deep breath. "But to do that, we need to leave this place, before Carman crushes us and..."

The rest of my sentence dies on my tongue as Mordred's face closes up again. I've made a mistake. I shouldn't have said anything about Carman besting him. Why is there no *undo* button in real life?

"I didn't mean it like—"

Mordred grabs the front of my dress in his fist. "Do not presume to know anything about me or my life," he says, "or try to tell me how to live it. As for you, you only have two options: Either you join me and do as I say, or try to survive on your own for the little time you have left to live." He leans in so close I can now distinguish tiny little patterns of flames in his woads[6]. "So, which is it? One or two?"

I find myself unable to answer. More so than his words, it's the dead look in his eyes that makes my heart sink.

"So be it." With a disgusted sneer, Mordred shoves me away, and I stumble into Urim's broad chest.

"Nice try, princess, but do try not to distract AC with puny, impossible dreams," the Dark Sidhe says, using Mordred's old nickname as he steers me forward.

"The poor boy's already confused enough as it is," Thummim adds as we follow Mordred down the narrow alleyways and tortuous passages that snake their way in between the city's endless rows of squat buildings.

"It's not puny," I mumble, trying not think about where our steps are taking us.

"No need to look so down," Urim says, his arm still around my waist, more to prevent me from running away than to help me walk, "this isn't your funeral we're going to."

"Could be," Thummim says.

"In which case your troubles will truly be over!"

We duck under a low portico, and I stop short. Instead of being surrounded by more windowless, grimy walls, I find myself staring at an inner courtyard. Crates and boxes have been piled

---

[6] Blue tattoos that Mordred wears, in reference to the tincture he used to make them.

high in one corner, facing a cordoned off area where someone's hung some dirty laundry.

I jump as the sharp sound of a lash hitting flesh cracks wetly from behind them, spraying the garments with blood. And again. Relentlessly.

"No need to worry 'bout it, princess," Urim says darkly, prodding me to start walking again, "it's just a penitent."

Dry-mouthed, I force myself to get moving again. But as we pass by the screened-off area, I find my eyes irretrievably drawn to the hole left between two torn sheets, and the ugly spectacle unfolding behind them.

The demon is kneeling on the hard-packed earth, head bowed, his back already an open wound. Yet still he keeps swinging that cat o' nine tails around, its thick, knotted lashes cutting an ever-bloodier cross between his shoulders and hips.

There's a low hiss from above, and I look up in time to see a shadow slither its way down from the nearest roof onto the top of the stack of crates. I stiffen.

"Though we aren't its target, nor that of the others," Urim says, sounding rather disappointed, "it's probably best for you if we don't tarry."

A chill creeps down my neck. "You mean we're just going to let them kill him while he's...you know...busy?"

Thummim suddenly yanks on my arm as something brushes past me. I look over my shoulder as three demons rip down the line of dirty clothes and converge upon the penitent, sharp teeth snapping.

But at the very last second, the kneeling demon turns around, giant mouth gaping open hungrily. It latches onto the closest assailant's outstretched arm, ripping it apart with a loud *crunch*. Then, still sucking on the severed limb, it strikes the second demon, clawed hand going all the way through the other creature's sternum.

"You were saying?" Urim asks, voice dripping with sarcasm as he leads me down a side passage.

Someone sniggers from behind a shuttered window up ahead. "Has Lucifer decided to join our ranks once again?" a voice grates out.

"Crawl back into your hole, slug," Urim barks, keeping me tight against him now.

I try to pierce the darkness behind the shutters' slats as we hurry past, and the ghoulish laugh resounds again.

"Not Lucifer, I see," the voice hisses. "But the resemblance is uncanny, wouldn't you say, Thummim?"

"I think you need to have your eyeballs straightened," the Dark Sidhe replies. "I'll be more than glad to help you with that."

His grin flashes lightning bright as he suddenly doubles back and jumps up. Urim's long-fingered hand forces me to duck as Thummim rips the window's wooden planks out in a hail of shards and nails.

"What the hell do you think you're doing?" Mordred asks as Urim shoves me out of the alley and into the street beyond.

"Thummim's restocking," Urim says, shifting from one foot to the next impatiently.

Mordred's scowl deepens. "And I suppose you want to join him?"

"Well, it all depends on how well you think your interview with Carman's going to go."

"One minute," Mordred ludges, managing to both sound resigned and pissed off at the same time.

He doesn't have to repeat himself. Urim's already launched himself back into the dark alley, his excited shouts joining those of the others, leaving Mordred and me alone.

"Please don't take me to her," I beg, turning to my brother, hoping to bring him back to my side of things. "You don't know what she's like."

A muscle twitches in Mordred's cheek. "I know plenty more than you do."

"But she's using me to make her stronger! At this rate,..." I swallow convulsively, fear sapping away the rest of my words. "Please don't do this to me. *Please*."

A loud *boom* saves him from having to answer me, shaking the nearest buildings to their foundations. I cling to Mordred to avoid toppling over, as a large cloud of dust and debris billows out of the narrow alley, turning everything white.

"Stand back," Mordred growls.

He raises his hand, and black sparks tear through the dusty air towards a dark figure barreling our way. The blast hits the fleeing demon square in the chest, and I watch the shadow stagger, as if dazed. Then two more shadows appear behind it.

"Where you going to so soon?" Thummim's voice calls out.

The first shape whirls around to face the two Dark Sidhe.

"Thought we were having fun," Thummim continues.

"Bite me!"

The defiant shout makes me jump, and Thummim's low laugh rises in the dusty air. "How tempting," the Dark Sidhe replies.

Then he leaps forward, toppling the self-flagellating demon to the ground. The creature hits the ground with a surprised snarl, but Thummim pins it down with his own body before it can retaliate.

"Now, where were we?" Thummim asks cordially.

"I hope you choke on it," the self-flagellating demon spits.

Thummim's face breaks into a cruel smile. "Let's see if I will, shall we?"

He slams his hand down onto the creature's face. The demon's head explodes with a dull *pop*, spraying bits of flesh and bone across the street, ichor black against the thick layer of dust.

Then, like a mad doctor, Thummim pries the demon's chest open, the ribs cracking sharply under his bare hands. My stomach heaves. This is exactly like what happened to the guard.

I watch helplessly as Thummim plunges his hand up to his elbow into the demon's chest cavity. This isn't right. Fallen angel or not, nobody deserves this never-ending cycle of painful death and rebirth, of having to eat or be eaten, without the slightest hope for deliverance.

"Why are you letting them do that?" I ask, as Thummim finally pulls away from the demon's remains, a dull brown ogham held between his bloody fingers.

Mordred shrugs. "We've all got to survive, and that means feeding ourselves too."

"Feeding? But you guys aren't stuck here, you can find food up in the normal world."

I watch with growing horror as a hole opens in the side of Thummim's neck so he can push the ogham into it. His eyes flutter closed, an addict who's just gotten his fix.

A chill steals over me as I finally understand what Urim meant by restocking.

"Please don't tell me—"

"Time to move," Mordred growls, his hand like a vice around my arm.

"But—"

"Yes, it's how we get our powers," he says, clearly annoyed. "Not everyone wants to mooch off some Danu or other Fey Lordling to stay alive, cow-towing to their every whim, like a bunch of puppets. That's not what we fought for."

"Oh, because destroying each other to steal one's essence is so much better," I retort.

"Seems to me the lady doth protest too much," Urim says, and I find myself staring at his neck to see if I can still spot the hole through which he must have absorbed other stolen oghams. "Does the fact that we took down a few demons really bother you that much? You know they'd have done the same to you and your friends once through the Gates."

"It's no more than what the bastard did to the others," Thummim says, cracking his neck, his pupils so dilated I can't even see his irises anymore.

Urim nods emphatically. "Everyone down here is getting ready for the great outdoors, building up reserves. Can't you feel the excitement in the air?"

"More like humidity," Thummim says with a light giggle.

I freeze as a fat drop falls on Mordred's cheek, red against his blue woads.

"No," I whisper, as we all look up to stare at Carman's rapidly approaching form.

"Guess you'll be getting your meeting earlier than anticipated," Thummim says.

Urim grimaces. "And it looks like she's pissed off again," he says.

"Thanks to you boys," Mordred grumbles, making Thummim laugh even harder.

My whole body's telling me to flee, but I can't move, can't breathe, can't even think. I feel Mordred draw closer to me, and despite it all, I'm grateful for his presence. Maybe things will be different with him at my side. Maybe Carman will leave me be this time around.

"Please tell me this isn't an act of rebellion on your part, Mordred," Carman says, eyeing the damage the two Dark Sidhes have wrought upon the neighborhood. The line of low buildings we cut through is now but a gaping hole in the middle of the demon city. "I don't think I could bear the disappointment."

My heart stops as she turns her cold gaze to us, her black dress fluttering around her like hundreds of crows' wings.

"We were actually on our way to see you," I say without thinking.

Mordred doesn't bat a lash, but I can feel the shock of my taking his defense go through his body.

Carman narrows her eyes. "Pray tell, then, why my property decided to gambol about instead of staying safely stored away where I put it."

"Considering the rarity of the commodity," Mordred says at last, "I thought it wise not to keep her out in the open for anyone to damage further."

The slap resounds like a gunshot. I gasp at the sight of the deep gouges cutting across Mordred's face, but my brother doesn't budge.

"I am not keeping you around to think, boy," Carman seethes, "and certainly not to question my judgment. Besides"—she lowers her eyelids as her gaze slides over to me—"don't let her looks deceive you. She is strong, and gifted. More so than you."

"But her strength is waning," Mordred says, "and fast. I do not presume to know your thoughts, but should you wish to preserve your property a little longer, there are other ways."

"What ways might those be?"

"Instead of trying to restore the five generals to their full power, setting up a geas, like the one at Lake High, might prove more useful."

"A blood oath?" Carman asks.

Mordred nods. "We have seen Mu upstairs," he says. "But something went awry when he tried to use his powers again."

"Penemue rebelled against me," Carman states.

"Not exactly," Mordred says.

"Rather the opposite, actually," Thummim interjects. "Took your orders to the letter, and it backfired."

"It wasn't pretty," Urim says with a barely-repressed shudder.

"And you're saying the geas is meant to fix that?" Carman asks.

"As well as give you an additional benefit," Mordred says. "This being their blood bonding to yours, their loyalty shall never be questioned."

"Unlike yours, you mean," Carman says cooly.

Mordred pales slightly beneath his tattoos. "And by linking them to you through it, they wouldn't need to have their full strength restored through the use of the Sangraal to leave this place."

"Thereby preserving the life of your dear sister," Carman says slowly. "My, my, you certainly have gone to great lengths to protect her."

"I didn't mean to—"

"Enough. I know exactly what you meant. Now run along, and get back to manning the Gates before they close up on you."

For the briefest moment, it looks like Mordred's going to object, but then he lowers his head in submission. "As you wish."

"Mordred...," I say, voice tight with fear.

But my brother keeps his head resolutely down.

Carman's cheek dimples. "The eagerness you've shown in coming to me this time is certainly appreciated, Morgan. Come, we have much to do still." She grabs my arm, and pulls me to her. "Gadreel will be most pleased."

"One! I choose option one!" I say, looking at Mordred in panic, willing him to interpose himself again.

But whatever spark of independence I saw in him before must have been an illusion. Mordred doesn't move an inch as Carman takes off, carrying me with her.

My stomach lurches as we bank above the endless roofs towards the star-shaped city center. Unlike the squalid streets we've just left behind, the plaza is teeming with demons pressing themselves eagerly around the wide scaffolding that dominates its grounds.

When I was here earlier, they were hanging children, betting on who'd kick the longest before dying at last. This time, the crowd's got its hands on a woman, and have her strung tightly over a large wheel. The horde lets out another wave of excited shouts as the executioner brings its spiked mace down over her left calf, tearing a pitiful cry from its current victim.

I grind my teeth together. This is what Carman wants to turn the world into—an abhorrent place where torturing one another for pleasure is commonplace, where nothing is held sacred anymore, and the best one can hope for is true death.

Another blood-curdling cry cuts through the mob's loud jeers.

I can't let Carman do this. Even if it's the last thing I do, I'm taking her down.

Now.

I twist around in Carman's hold and lash out with all the energy I have left. Fire blooms from my fingertips, the dark blue flames quickly burning through Carman's collar. Her grasp on me momentarily loosens, and my fingers finally close around her neck. I squeeze, as hard as I can, crushing her trachea.

I'm dimly aware of someone's shout of alarm far below as we plummet to the ground.

But before we can crash into the crowd, two dark tentacles punch through both my shoulders. I let out a strangled gasp as my numb fingers are torn away from her, arms falling useless to my sides. And just like that, my one chance to get her is gone.

Carman's hand grazes her long neck, the imprint of my fingers prominent above some strange Celtic symbol that seems to have been branded into her clavicle.

"This is going to cost you," she says.

And, looking into her flinty eyes, I know that my own death isn't going to come soon enough.

# CHAPTER 11

I stopped believing in fairy tales and knights in shining armor long before I ever set foot in Lake High, but I never thought I'd wish for one to actually save me.

After what seems like a lifetime, my feet come to a stop before a set of gigantic black doors, two torches ensconced at their sides the only source of light in the dark tunnel. A flurry of shouts comes from the other side, and I take in a deep, shuddering breath, the freezing air burning down my lungs.

Without a word, Carman flicks her hand and the doors swing silently inward to reveal a wide, cavernous chamber filled to bursting with demons.

The throne room.

A loud wail rends the air before we even step inside, reverberating against the walls, driving the crowd into a frenzy of growls and hisses.

As above, so below. Cruelty knows no bounds. I will myself to remain impassive despite the spectacle, wondering what poor soul's been picked to entertain this hysterical mass.

No one has noticed our arrival, all gazes riveted to the raised dais on the opposite side of the room where a man can be seen strutting back and forth. Then his hand shoots up and the terrible screaming starts again. The beautiful demon smiles, reveling in the crowd's cheers, and my heart lurches as I recognize Gadreel. The very one whose full strength Carman is going to make me restore, as if Gad isn't bad enough already.

I repress a shiver as the temperature drops even further, and have a brief moment to register Carman's irate look before she sweeps inside the throne room. The nearest demons don't even get a chance to move out of her way before she pushes past them, turning their flesh to ice. Then someone shoves me in after her, and slams the doors shut behind me.

All my senses screaming for me to run away, I make myself follow in Carman's wake, bare feet sliding over the icy floor. It's pointless to try to run away. I know, I've tried twice already. And Carman's pissed off enough as it is, without me adding oil to the fire. Not if I want to survive this session.

"Aren't we being assiduous today?" Carman croons.

Gad whirls around, face pale, as an uneasy silence settles over the rest of the crowd. All eyes are upon Carman as she slowly ascends the dais, feathered dress fluttering around her. But as I reach the platform behind her, my eyes fall on the poor creature squirming at the throne's foot.

"Banshee!" I exclaim, momentarily forgetting about everything else.

The grey cloak shifts at the sound of my voice, and I scramble to her side. The banshee tries to lift her head in greeting, wincing at some unseen injury.

"Shhh, it's OK," I tell her. "Don't move."

I let out a string of curses, power crackling over my fists. I don't care what Carman will do to me, but I won't let her use me to help Gad. No. I'm going to make him pay instead. But before I can strike the demon down, a cold wind sweeps across me, freezing my hand midway.

My lips thin out in a low growl as I struggle against Carman's control, but all I can do is watch as the witch slowly lowers herself onto the throne. The intricate chair is an exact replica of the Siege Perilous, except that the angels and demons on this one are still as stone.

"I thought you somewhat more duplicitous in your aim to usurp my throne," Carman continues, long white fingers caressing the carvings on her throne's armrest. "Yet here you are, doling out your own justice on one of my subjects."

Gadreel blanches visibly. "This one here isn't one of your subjects, she's a—"

"Every single soul in Hell belongs to *me!*" Carman says, scathingly. "Yes, even yours. And you've only got your own failures to blame for it."

The mood in the room shifts again, getting restless. They want to see more blood spilled today, want to taste it in the air. Especially if it comes from someone as fearsome as Gad. And Gadreel senses it too, for he drops to a knee before Carman.

"My queen," he forces out. "I pray for thy...mercy."

"Such lovely words when uttered by you." Carman pricks her finger on the sharp point of a carved demon's wing, and a drop of blood beads out of the puncture wound. "I can certainly sense your eagerness, this time around. Though your little display right before belies it."

She closes her hand into a fist and a red wave spills out from between her fingers, streaking towards Gad. The beautiful demon's shoulders bunch up as the ruby tide shifts and twists on itself before him, quickly taking human form. I feel myself grow pale at the scarlet shape—an exact replica of Carman's outline, down to the last feather of her dress.

"A blood shadow," a nasally voice says next to me. Nibs is back from the plains, and is eyeing the scene dispassionately.

"W-What's it f-for?" I ask through chattering teeth.

"Watch."

Carman's blood shadow grasps Gad by the neck and forces his head up.

"Does it please you so much to parade up here?" Carman asks.

Gadreel doesn't respond. The blood shadow squeezes a little harder around his neck, and I don't miss the look of pain that crosses his face.

"It was...an offering," he says at last.

Carman gives a disdainful look at the banshee still lying at her feet. "You cannot offer me what I already own. Besides, what do I care about such a useless bag of bones?"

She flicks her finger and a tentacle of black shoots out from her dress to punch into the banshee, sending her rolling towards the edge of the dais.

"Don't you dare touch her!" I shout, straining against the glacial force keeping me in check. "The banshee's mine!"

Carman cuts me a dark glance. "Yours?"

Her blood shadow tosses Gad aside, and the next thing I know it's standing in front of me, its half-translucent form shifting and flickering like candleflame. A gaping hole appears in what should be the shade's head, and, with a sickening feeling, I realize it's smiling at me.

"That would make it two pets for you, sweets," Carman says, and I detect the threat in her hooded gaze. "Seems you're getting a little greedy."

"She is mine," I repeat stubbornly.

Carman considers me for a very long moment while her blood shadow undulates before me.

"If you wish to keep this other pet of yours," she finally says, her voice unctuous, "then you have to give something else in return. Make it a fair exchange, don't you agree?"

My stomach clenches at the sight of the banshee thrashing on the floor, the rope of darkness tightening around her midsection.

"I agree!" I snarl.

"Then let it be so."

"Misssssssstresss, nooooo."

Carman snaps her fingers and the black tendrils around the banshee dissolve into thin air.

"The deal is sealed, then," Carman says with a beatific smile that looks eerily like that of her blood shadow.

I suddenly regain the use of my limbs, steam rising off my warming limbs.

"Nibs, step forward."

At her words, Gad finally looks at me, eyes gleaming in anticipation, his neck still bearing the blood shadow's mark. The mountain of a demon, Az, pulls away from the shadows to pick me up in his strong arms, making sure I can't run away.

"Brace thyself," he says in my ear. "This should beest the last thee are taxed thus."

I keep my eyes firmly on the banshee while Az carries me across the dais to lower me down at Carman's feet.

"A life for a life," Carman says, cheeks dimpling as I stand shivering before her.

Someone sniggers in the crowd. "Negotiating with her captive?"

The pack of demons crammed in the chamber murmur in assent.

"In Balor's time," another pipes up, "this never would've—"

The rest of his sentence is abruptly cut off, and I finally let myself look away from the banshee to look at what's happening.

The blood shadow's moved to one of the demons halfway across the throne room. Its hand is wrapped around the creature's thick neck, just as it did with Gad, but this time I can clearly see the blood seeping out of the demon's every pore, to be absorbed by Carman's shadow. Then, in the span of a long breath, the blood shadow returns to its former station, leaving behind a dry husk, and an uneasy crowd.

"Remember that your word is binding," Carman says, drawing my attention back to her, as if she hasn't been interrupted.

At a signal from her, Nibs shuffles over with that damned bag of his. The velvet pouch bulges over the Sangraal, yet the clurichaun still finds a way to hold it gingerly, as far away from his precious self as he can. I clench my fists together. Gadreel is now on both knees, his face lifted reverently up to me. It makes me sick that such a monster will be rewarded.

"I won't do it," I say past the lump in my throat. "I won't let you restore him or any other of these demons to full power anymore."

Carman lets out a huff of laughter. "Who said anything about restoring anyone?"

Both Gad and I look at her in shock.

"But my queen," Gadreel starts, imploring.

"Who gave you leave to speak?" Carman snaps, eyes sparkling with ire. "You should be glad I'm letting you live at all, or do you need a reminder of your standing?"

For a moment, it looks like Gad's going to complain, but then he lowers his head again. "No, my queen. I apologize for the interruption."

"But then what...," I start.

The blood shadow is suddenly in front of me, its hands cold and slimy on my shoulders, forcing me down to my knees in front of Nibs. I steal another glance at the banshee, then, shaking, I reach inside the bag. My fingers instinctively grip the stone bowl inside, and the Sangraal grows warm in response as I pull it out of its pouch, runes blazing along its rim.

The silence in the room grows deeper, everyone watching with bated breath as the blood shade punctures my arm, letting my blood drip freely onto the Sangraal. With growing dread, I stare as the bowl slowly fills up with a golden liquid, the very same that healed my wounds and restored my powers. Sweat pours down my forehead and my sides as the bout of nausea that always accompanies this moment hits me.

At last, Carman uncoils herself from her throne and I feel her long fingers tilt my chin back so she can look into my eyes.

"I will now collect the lift I am due," she says, grasping the Sangraal over my shaky hand.

Pain rips through my skull, my vision exploding into a million white lights, before the acid burn continues down into my body, tearing a scream from my parched lips. I'm dimly aware of the Sangraal burning through my palm, heat searing my hand to the dull beating of a heart. I can hear myself begging Carman to put an end to me, to make this agony stop. But she never relents.

It feels like I'm being split open, my innards ripped to shreds. I can't see. Can't breathe.

Then a roar suddenly erupts in the cavernous chamber, making the floor tremble, and Carman finally releases me.

I sink to the ground in a useless heap, unable to even lift a finger. The roaring starts again, louder than before. BOOM! The ceiling splinters as something massive pounds against it. The crowd lets out terrified shrieks. *BOOM!* The whole cavern is shaking now, toppling fleeing demons to the floor.

***BOOM!***

The ceiling explodes outward, and I feel someone move above me to protect me from the rocks pelting down on us. Searing heat washes across the cavern, light blooming against my eyelids as a column of fire erupts in the middle of the ruined throne room.

"Missstresss," the banshee howls over the din.

I crack my eyes open, and feel my blood run cold at the sight of the gigantic creature scrambling its way up through the hole in the ceiling, large leathery wings already spreading out for flight.

# Chapter 12

Luther is glaring at me, his whole body vibrating with barely contained violence.

"Don't be a fool," he says. "Your little crusade is bound to get our best knights killed before you even make it inside the school proper. I will not allow it. And if this is the best you can come up with, I suggest you stay put and let the adults take care of matters."

"Let the adults run things?" Arthur's voice cuts in, and the bitterness in it catches me off guard. "Isn't that what we've been doing all along? Sending Caamaloth warning after warning, trusting you to do the right thing to protect us all. But did you listen? No.

"Two years since Carman's been freed, and still you cower away behind your walls, doing nothing but sending empty promises while those whom we're honor-bound to protect keep perishing. And for what? More money? Isn't that also why you treated Morgan like a leper, and kept running programs to exterminate the Fey? Have you learned nothing?"

"Oh, I know what this is about now," Luther says with a sneer that reminds me of Hector. "But if you think I'm going to ruin myself just so you can impress a filthy Fey, and one who tried to kill you, you're out of your mind."

"You forget I am no longer a child," Arthur says. "And the Council has trusted me enough to give me free reign in matters such as these."

"That *carte blanche* can be just as easily taken away if they suspect you of unsound mind," Luther replies coldly.

"We no longer have time for internal discord, Pendragon," Lugh says, stepping out of the garden's shadows with Sameerah at his side, their footsteps silent on the fresh snow. "Algol's rising, a sure sign Carman is growing ever more powerful."

"And we're entertaining severe doubts as to whether we'll be able to resist at all once it reaches its zenith," Sameerah adds, matching Luther's tone.

The Fey warrior looks fierce as always, her black mamba draped around her neck like a heavy necklace. The four of them are standing in the very same garden where Arthur first showed me how to use oghams. Crazy how back in those days I was despairing of ever being able to do any kind of elemental manipulation. How much simpler things back then seem to me now.

Luther spears the two Fey with a scowl. "I will not take threats from the likes of you, either. Perhaps if your kind had stepped in earlier, we wouldn't be where we are today."

"Our kind?" Sameerah repeats, and her snake opens its blue-black mouth as if to strike. "You mean the kind that keeps having to save your asses because you're too much of a craven to fight yourself?"

"Prudence isn't cowardice," Luther retorts. "Unlike you base creatures, we do not wish to uselessly waste human lives. That is not how wars are won. When the time comes—"

"That time is now, Luther," Arthur says, his voice oddly gentle. "That's what I came here to tell you. The Board's officially removed you from the position of General, now that there is more proof that you..."

Arthur's voice trails off, and Sameerah sniggers.

"I think 'proof that you offed the previous leader' is the subphrase you're looking for," she supplies.

Luther's lips thin out. "Don't be preposterous," he says, "nobody 'offed' anyone."

I peer at the ex-Watcher in confusion, the pale scar above her left eye almost glowing against the rich umber of her skin. She's not in any pain that I can see—in fact, she seems to be having fun—which means she's not lying.

My gaze slides back to Luther's hard features. Surely he can't really have killed Jennifer's dad? I try to recall the one and only time I ever met Sir Leo de Lyonesse. It was at the year-end ball, right before Inspector Bossart and I were attacked by the two kid draugar. Sir Leo had certainly not looked sick back then, quite the contrary.

Sameerah's black snake uncoils itself from around her shoulders, its flickering tongue tasting the air curiously as Arthur's pixie lands on its coffin-shaped head.

"The point is," Arthur continues, "that I didn't come here seeking your approval, but to keep you informed that I've already sent out messages to our retired forces, as well as to the—"

"Didn't I just tell you I wouldn't finance your little venture, boy?" Luther snaps.

"I don't think you heard me right the first time, father," Arthur says calmly. "Considering mother's predicament and your involvement in Sir Leo's death, the jury has allowed for the transfer of the estate's management."

Luther blanches. "You?"

"Sir Pelles appointed me himself," Arthur says. "At least until your trial is over. Until then, you are to remain under house arrest."

"Sister Marie-Clémence would never have allowed such a travesty to pass," Luther says.

"Sister Marie-Clémence had nothing to say," Arthur retorts.

Luther's eyes grow wide as the truth finally sinks in that his own son has turned against him. Frankly, neither can I.

Whatever happened to the goody-two-shoes I knew who always followed every rule by the letter?

"So, to finish what I was saying," Arthur continues, "not only have I asked our retired forces to return, but I've also requested help from the other knight factions."

"As in the Errant Companions?"

"Among others," Arthur says.

Luther casts the two Fey a sardonic look. "Well, perhaps you won't be too badly off, then," he says, knowing as well as I do that the leader of the Errant Companions is a born Fey-hater. "But though you've managed to rob me blind, don't think they'll be fool enough to follow a twenty-year-old kid who diddled with a Fey."

I recoil at the insult, feeling like I've just been slapped.

"You're lucky I don't hit a man who's already down," Arthur says, his voice full of barely-contained wrath. "But say that once again, and I won't stop myself."

"I could do it for you," Sameerah offers, with a corner smile in my direction.

"As for the leadership of our combined forces, you are right," Arthur continues. "Sir Cade was picked to lead. You see, funding our armies and leading them are two very different things, father, as you should know. Although they did pick me to lead the joint taskforce to free my people from Lake High."

"They're no longer your people, Arthur!" Luther shouts, and for the first time since I've known him, I wonder if he's truly worried for his son. "They turned their backs on you the moment you lost your place in KORT, so why are you throwing your life uselessly away like this?"

A large shape suddenly lands in their midst, spraying them with snow, and cutting their argument short.

"Sorry for interrupting," Gauvain says, flashing a wide grin at Sameerah, "but I'm afraid I have bad news."

"Funny way of showing it," the Fey warrior mutters.

"Lord Oberon's replied to our latest missive," Gauvain says, sidling up to the Fey warrior despite her evident disinterest, "and this time he made it very clear that he wouldn't join us unless this Danu of yours showed her ass."

"Watch it," Lugh growls.

"His quote," Gauvain says, his eyes not leaving Sameerah a second. "So, I've been thinking. What if we could entice him, and the other recalcitrant lords and ladies who haven't yet spoken for Carman, with something else?" He pauses for effect, looking rather cocky, then adds, "Fey weapons."

"Don't be absurd," Luther says. "There's a reason your Order decided to lock them away."

"Those weapons could give us the edge we need," Arthur says pensively.

"Out of the question!" Luther explodes. "Think of all the knights we lost over the centuries to secure those weapons. And now you want to hand them back to the very same demons we took them from? The ones who abused of their power to subjugate mankind for centuries? I thought you were smarter than that!"

A bright light blazes next to the toolshed, its beam melting the snow as it cuts a circled trefoil pattern on the ground. An instant later, a short Fey boy appears in its center, looking out of breath.

"My lord," Pigfain says, bowing with some difficulty.

"Did they respond to the message?" Lugh asks.

"Not sure, my lord," Pigfain says, "but the package was sent for delivery."

"Then we can only wait and hope," Arthur says.

"Can't wait much longer, I'm afraid," the Pigfain says, sounding strained.

"Another attack?" Sameerah asks, and Gauvain finally stops fidgeting.

Pigfain's throat convulses. "A monster was signaled leaving Lake High, heading for your Demesne, my lord."

"The children!" Arthur exclaims, and the world blurs, as if I've stood up too quickly.

"Take us there immediately," Lugh says, springing into the still-active portal, the others following close behind.

"Hold your breath," Pigfain says, and there's another bright flash.

Screams of terror greet us before the light subsides again, followed by a thunderous roar. A stab of panic goes through me.

Sameerah steps in front of us, looking up. "Don't tell me it's a—"

"Dragon!" someone shouts, barreling through the clearing.

Then the heat wave hits us, turning the whole forest hazy before the treetops burst into flames.

"I thought they were extinct," Gauvain says, his eyes round with disbelief.

They were, I want to say, until Carman had me bring one back to life.

"Get everyone to safety!" Lugh shouts before shooting into the sky to fend off the beast.

"I'll cover you guys," Arthur says.

"Are you insane?" Sameerah hisses, lowering herself into a fighting position. "If anything happens to you, I'll get my hide skinned by that bitchy girl of yours when she returns."

Another wave of heat blasts through the forest, blurring my vision.

"*Raido!*" Arthur intones.

A green sheen envelops me, and I find myself flying, stopping only when I'm high above the burning forest. Sameerah's at my side, and we all watch as the fire spreads in every direction, advancing in waves that devour everything in their passage. Movement at the edge of my vision catches my attention—a flock of small birds that's taken flight, wings batting frantically at the air to get away from the blaze.

"The extra weight is slowing them down!" Arthur shouts at Sameerah.

I realize then that the birds are actually very frightened pixies, many of them carrying small Fey creatures in their tiny hands who couldn't flee the deadly fires on their own.

And, growing larger behind them, is the sinuous shape of Carman's dragon.

"They're not going to make it," Sameerah says.

A light dives at the flying beast, glancing off the dragon's thick hide. Lugh, I realize, heart beating erratically. But not even the Fey lord seems to have any effect on the beast. The dragon rears its head, black scales turning red as it prepares to blast the hapless pixies with its deadly fire.

NO!

Something inside me breaks loose. I hear a distant shout of surprise as a long thunderbolt flashes through the sky, striking the dragon in its flank. The beast bellows, its attack thwarted, and I watch in relief as the pixies fly away, almost out of the creature's range.

"Not bad, hopper[7], not bad," Sameerah says, and I have the strong suspicion that she's talking to me. "Now try to aim for its wings. I'm afraid you've just tickled it, and dragons don't like to be tickled."

I feel faint, bile rising up my throat, like I do every time I use my powers. Did I really just do that?

"It's gearing up for another attack!" Arthur exclaims, and I find myself pelting across the sky to meet it, Sameerah a half-beat behind.

The dragon's belly has started to shine again, its veins standing out against its glowing hide. A series of frantic chirrups erupts from the flock of pixies, and their tiny wings beat at the air ever more furiously.

---

[7] Medium-sized mouse that's fed to snakes, bigger than the pinky and the fuzzy.

"Hopper?" Sameerah calls out, sounding worried.

But whatever I did, I don't know how to do it again. Sameerah hesitates for a long second, perhaps hoping for another miracle, then lets out a long hiss.

"Carnage on the way!" she yells, hurling herself ahead towards the pixies.

The dragon unleashes its fury, fire spewing forth in a long, smoldering jet. Shrieks of pain and terror rise from the first wave of pixies and their passengers, before the flames hit them.

"Sameerah!" Arthur shouts, his voice strangely muffled as the pixies' burning bodies drop out of the sky, a shower of tiny comets.

I scan the skies for the warrior Fey, finding a small group of Fey to have survived unscathed. But Sameerah's not with them. A hole forms in my chest, dark and cold. This can't be happening. The Fey warrior is fierce and strong, she can't just be...gone.

"Help!" someone shouts from somewhere below, the cry barely discernible over the raging forest fire.

Still stunned, I find myself streaking through the air, right under the dragon's nose as it dives towards something far below.

Knights, I realize, quickly picking out the squad in the middle of the devastation. At least a dozen men and women, clustered tightly around a group of children, shields up in a vain attempt to keep the dragon at bay.

Faster! I chance a glance backward. The dragon's catching up with us, maw open wide, teeth gleaming. The children's cries grow louder. Light blazes from inside the dragon's gullet. I whirl around to face Carman's creature, a cold wave spreading through my limbs, and open my mouth in a silent scream of hate and anger. Then the white-hot flames hit us, and the whole world turns into a blinding furnace.

# CHAPTER 13

"Nobody knooows the trouble I've seeeen," a low, raspy voice intones in a familiar if dissonant melody, "nobody knooows but J—"

An annoyed hiss cuts the voice off, and I realize I'm not the one who was singing.

No. I was the one dreaming of dragons turning the world to ashes. I cough feebly, as if still caught in the middle of the flames, and crack my eyes open. I'm back on the plain outside the demon city walls, the sea of draugar standing obliviously still around their fuming cauldron. As if the world above wasn't coming to an end.

"You know what I hate about this place?" Keva asks hoarsely now that I'm awake.

I turn to her, and note that the banshee's been tied to a third whipping post on Keva's other side. At least Carman's kept her word in keeping her alive. If letting us three rot together here counts as living.

"That it's turning me into a pathetic wreck," Keva continues with a mournful sigh. "I don't want to be like you. I actually have aspirations."

The banshee grunts.

"Fine. *Had* aspirations," Keva says with a deep frown. "None of which were to play martyr at your sides, by the way."

A shiver runs down my tied-up arms. I wish I were still passed out so I could find out what's happened to Arthur and the others, instead of being forced to listen to Keva's complaining.

"And if Arthur, Percy, or Lance had kissed me, I sure as hell would have made sure to repeat the act."

I blink at the sudden change in topic. "Percy's dead, Lance is with Jennifer, and Arthur may be gone as well," I say, my voice breaking at the end.

"I know, such a terrible loss," Keva carries on mournfully, "and if—wait, what? Jennifer and Lance? Since when? Does Arthur even know?"

I shrug in annoyance, the movement reopening the scabbing wound on my arm. What does it matter anymore who did what? My eyes settle upon the lone star twinkling brightly from within the grey sky's vast emptiness. The hollow ache inside me since I stabbed Arthur has grown, turned into a black hole, drawing the last of my hope into its abyss.

I should've died a long time ago, as Irene so fervently wished. Then Carman would still be stuck inside her prison, and she wouldn't have had the chance to destroy so many lives.

"Definitely not a good sign when Algol's getting stronger," a young voice says behind us, startling us.

And as I twist around to get a look at Gale, I find myself blushing in shame at the dark thoughts I was just entertaining. I'm the last person on earth who should be allowed to think like this—I've got too many things to make up for.

"You're too late," I tell him accusingly.

"Am I?"

"Who the hell are you?" Keva asks.

"Gale," Gale tells Keva, his upturned face coming into view before the banshee's hunched figure.

"Is that supposed to mean something?" Keva retorts snidely. "Now, why don't you move along instead of staring at us like you're at a zoo. We're rather crowded over here."

"I've got a better idea," Gale says, and I hear the sound of chains hitting the ground.

Keva lets out a shocked moan as Gale eases her away from her post. I cringe as Keva whimpers again. Even with Gale's gentle touch, she's been tied up too long with her hands above her head for every movement not to hurt. Finally, when he's made sure Keva can handle herself, Gale moves onto the banshee.

"OK, let's rewind," Keva says, as the banshee's chains clatter to the ground. "Who are you again, and who's this Algol you mentioned?"

Algol. The very same word I heard Lugh mention in my vision. I frown. Strange.

"Misstressss," the banshee exclaims in a harsh whisper the moment she's set free.

I grin at her as she hurries over, eager to cut me loose despite her evident limp.

"I'm waiting," Keva says with her usual impatience.

"He's talking about Ra's al-ghul[8], you moron," Nibs cuts in.

The banshee whirls around with a growl, but the clurichaun pushes her aside disdainfully.

"Rosh ha Satan[9], Tseih She[10], the demon star?" Nibs continues, eyeing our blank faces with disgust. With a resigned sigh, he points to the single star I was staring at. "Suffice to say that star's

---

[8] Demon's head in Arabic

[9] Satan's head in Hebrew

[10] The piled-up corpses in Chinese

getting stronger because Carman's almost done synching up this place with earth."

"What's your business, clurichaun?" Gale asks curtly.

I groan as the banshee finally frees me, test my joints, and shudder at the still-suppurating black and blue cut on my arm. Trying not to gag, I jerk my coat sleeve down over the wound, hoping that the blood shadow hasn't infected me somehow.

"Eww!" Keva exclaims with a little squeal. "That is seriously the grossest things I've *ever* seen."

I look up to find that Nibs is now staring cross-eyed at the pointy end of a golden spear.

"Tell me what you're plotting now, clurichaun, or I will end you," Gale says calmly, the lance steady in his hand.

"Here might not be the best place to discuss such matters," Nibs says in a strangled voice. "If Asheel comes back, we're all gonna be turned into draugar."

"I actually want her to come here," Gale says evenly. "Now speak."

Nibs swallows audibly. "Let's just say that in the witch's vision of the future, however lovely it may be, there doesn't seem to be much place left for those of us who want to enjoy life's little pleasures."

"You mean alcohol?" Keva says disdainfully.

"Amongst other things. Oh, I'm sure Carman isn't all that bad"—I let out a loud snort, and Nibs rolls his eyes at me—"but Balor's another thing altogether."

The banshee whimpers softly and even Gale's spear dips in surprise. I frown. Who is this Balor? And why does that name ring a bell?

"And even with that toy of yers, Gibborim," Nibs continues, using that strange word the blind Watcher I'd met at Lake High used with me, "you wouldn't stand a chance against him. Lugh himself barely managed to get him locked up, and he got help from higher powers."

"I know our history, clurichaun," Gale says, his spear now leveled at Nibs's belly. "But is that really the reason you're so intent upon helping us escape?"

"Correction," Nibs says, "that's why I'm helpin' Morgan escape."

"You should've done that before," I snap.

"Spare me yer pity party, princess," Nibs says. "Yer the one who sought Carman out. I don't know which part of your bird brain gave ya the idea she'd treat you like anythin' more than a slave. And then ya seriously expected me to come to yer rescue when ya realized ya'd messed up?"

Nibs spits in my direction, and the banshee growls at him, shackles raised.

"So why now?" Gale asks.

"Because her ladyship believes Morgan's of no use to her no more," Nibs replies.

"Because it's too late," I repeat for the third time, teeth clenched.

Nibs raises his remaining eyebrow quizzically. "Look," he says, "Carman's still very much dependent on her troops, despite yer latest gift to her. But rallyin' all of these demons to her cause is no easy feat. Which should give ya some time to work somethin' out."

"Work what out?" I ask.

Nibs's smile stretches the melted part of his face into a hideous grimace. "There's one thin' the witch is still scared of for now. Or rather, one person."

"Lucifer?" I say, recalling all those endless lectures I received from Sister Marie-Clémence.

"Danu?" Keva asks at the same time.

"Exactly." Nibs points at me with his knobby finger. "And ya may be a key to her power. Hence, why yer still alive."

"What?"

But Nibs's attention is back onto Gale.

"Satisfied?" the clurichaun asks. "Now if ya could stop pointin' that fancy toothpick at me, we could get movin'."

After a moment's consideration, Gale finally lowers his weapon, the golden spear retracting into his arm with a wet, sucking sound.

"Absolutely disgusting," Keva says, dry heaving.

"What are you?" I ask Gale in shock. No human, not even a knight, is capable of making a weapon disappear into his body like that. But if he isn't human, then...

"Are you one of those skin stealers?" I breathe out.

Nibs coughs back a laugh. "He's a knight, bozo. And a dangerous one at that."

"But knights can't..." I wave wildly about, as if it's going to make up for my inability to explain what just happened.

"Can't have things sprouting out of their bodies like a bunch of freaks?" Keva finishes for me, still eyeing Gale suspiciously.

"Lance can't do that," I say.

"It works like an ogham," Gale explains, staring at his forearm. "You simply need to figure out how to absorb the object. Granted, it can't just be any object." He extends his arm, the point of the spear already pushing through his skin without so much as a trace of blood. "Want me to teach you how to do it?"

"No, thank you," Keva says with a shudder.

"But if you can do that, why can't Lance?" I ask insistently. "Why can't any of the other knights?"

Gale shrugs. "Hard to accept your full heritage when you're following the laws and regulations of an Order that's anti-Fey." A sad smile tugs at his lips. "But Lance would take to it easily enough, if given the chance."

"Wait, wait, wait, time out," Keva calls out, standing taller so she can look down her nose at Gale. "Are you saying you and Lance are related?"

"Brothers," I say.

Keva's jaw drops open. "You're *that* Gale?"

"Is anybody even listenin' to me?" Nibs says, stomping his foot on the ground. "This ain't some high school reunion here! People actually do want ya dead, believe it or not."

I eye the long lines of draugar, their backs rod-straight, all staring at the Pair Dadeni, waiting patiently for the day Carman will take them into the outside world. Into my world.

"The Gates are currently closed and heavily guarded on the other side," Gale says. "I take it you have another exit in mind?"

Nibs pulls out a piece of cloth from his pocket and hands it out to him. "Here."

"What is it?" I ask, sidling up to Gale as he unfolds the bloody handkerchief.

"Lucifer's sigil?" Gale says, sounding surprised.

I stare at the all-too familiar symbol: A couple of inscribed upside-down triangles with a connecting V at the bottom.

"That's the same one that was next to that hole Mordred used to get his draugar out," I say, stomach turning.

"The portal was never erased," Nibs says.

"You mean there was a secret passage out all this time and you never told me?" Keva asks, her voice pitching higher with barely repressed anger.

I raise my hand to cut her off before her rant can get more steam. "We can't go out that way," I say firmly. "Sure, some of the draugar managed to get through. But most were cut into thousands of pieces trying. This isn't a viable solution."

Keva's eyes go round with horror. "Kind of an important side note," she says, glaring at Nibs.

"Why don't ya people ever listen?" Nibs says, a little louder. "I said Morgan was the key, didn't I? So there's nothin' to worry about." He pauses, then adds, "Theoretically."

"And why, *theoretically*, would that be?" I ask.

"Because yer related to Mordred," Nibs says. "Do ya seriously need me to spell every single thing out for you?"

Keva snorts derisively. "And if this doesn't pencil out then we're minced meat? No, thank you."

But despite my early protest, Nibs's explanation gives me pause. It brings back Mordred's declaration that I could have opened the Gates of Hell if only I'd sat on the Siege Perilous instead.

"I'll do it," I say, hiding my shaking hands behind my back. Even if the odds are low, this may be my only chance to get out of here alive. "But you've got to promise me you'll keep them safe until I can get them out another way."

"Are you nuts?" Keva exclaims.

I shrug. "I've admired Saint George's balls long enough. I think it's high time I grew a pair myself."

"That's not what I meant." Keva crosses her arms. "How dare you even think about abandoning us like that?"

"But I thought—"

She points an accusing finger at me. "We're either all going out together, or none at all. And since I know how stubborn you are, that means option two's out of the question."

To my surprise, Keva flashes me a real, warm smile, and I feel myself respond in kind, momentarily forgetting all about my worries. If even Keva's on board, then surely we can figure this out.

"Earth to the two dweebs, we need to get goin'!" Nibs shouts at us, his patience at an end.

"Sorry," I mumble automatically.

But before I can start after the clurichaun, Gale grabs my arm to stay me. "Are you sure you can trust him?" he asks in a low voice.

"I dunno," I say after a moment's consideration. "He used to work for Arthur, but then finding him here..." I shake my head. "I don't think we have much of a choice in any case. At least not me. Not in our circumstances."

"We could try to look for another way out," Gale insists.

"If there had been one, you'd have found it by now," I say.

With a nod, Gale finally releases me. "Then go ahead," he says, turning away.

"Wait, you're not coming with?" I ask.

"I've got some business to attend to first," Gale says, his arm opening up again to let his golden spear through.

"Because of Asheel?" I ask, remembering what he told Nibs earlier.

"And because of that," Gale says, pointing at the Pair Dadeni.

My mouth runs dry, conflicting emotions running through me. If he destroys the giant cauldron, then Carman won't be able to produce those soulless monsters anymore. But that thing is huge, the size of a small cottage, and Asheel's newly restored to her full powers. I can personally attest to that.

Gale can't take them both down, not on his own.

"A great way to leave with a bang," I say, heart beating loudly in my ears.

"Which is why I recommend you leave before I start," Gale says.

"Didn't you hear Keva? We stick together."

"Not exactly what I meant...," Keva says.

"I'm not working alone, you know, if that's what you're worried about," Gale says, scanning the horizon line.

"You mean Kaede's here? Where?" I ask, belatedly remembering the two knights had been working together long before Keva and I met them.

The corners of Gale's lips curl up. "Keeping Asheel entertained while I freed you guys."

"And then what?" I ask.

"Then we take care of her," Gale says simply.

"Except you've got that giant cauldron to destroy first," I say. Gale nods silently.

"Guess that means you'll be needing a second diversion," I say, though my legs still feel like jelly.

"I'm not sticking around, if that's what you're implying," Keva says.

"Not at all." I smile at Nibs. "Thought you guys could get a head start while we do a little cleaning here first."

Keva's eyebrows lower dangerously. "Don't be stupid, Morgan," she says, and I wince as she grabs my bad arm. "It's one thing for a knight to want to be all brave and show off. But you?"

"Thanks for the vote of confidence," I say. "But don't worry, although my power's changed, it still works fine."

Keva's fingers dig deeper into my forearm, and I have to bite on my cheek not to cry out. "Carman won't be so lenient if she catches you this time around."

"She won't catch us," Gale says. "It'll be too late by the time she comes back. She's currently busy admiring her dragon's work."

I feel the blood drain from my face. "You know about that?"

Gale's green eyes settle upon me. "Everyone here knows."

Keva sighs in defeat. "Don't forget that you're my ticket out of this," she tells me. "I need you alive."

I smile at her. "Get going, then," I say. "We'll catch up as soon as we finish here."

The cloud of dust is growing larger in the distance. They're almost here.

I take a deep, steadying breath, gauging the distance between the approaching demon and the cauldron. Gale's been at it for a while, working his spear around the Pair Dadeni's thick metallic base, slowly weakening its structure. But he won't get to finish his work unless I draw Asheel's attention elsewhere.

Before I can think better of it, I'm moving to intercept the demon, the banshee shadowing my every move. Now that Asheel's closing in on us, I can see the eerie flashes of lightning bolts slashing at the sky. Guess Asheel isn't too happy with Kaede right now. I come to a sudden halt, looking for a good way to get Asheel's attention long enough for Gale to finish the job.

"Dead," the banshee says.

I nod. "Yeah, they're all dead," I say as we reach the last of the draugar. "Or supposed to be, anyway."

The banshee shakes her head. "Deader," she says, pointing at one of the divisions standing a little off to the side.

And I finally get what she's trying to say. The banshee's pointing at a section of draugar that is composed of all the rejects—bodies found way past their expiration dates, or perhaps the Pair Dadeni's first failed batches, for their state of decomposition is such that they can barely stand.

Carnivores always go for the weakest of the pack, and I plan on doing just the same.

To my surprise, I find myself excited at the prospect of finally getting a little action of my own, a small measure of retribution against these monsters. I can already picture Carman's face when she finds out a squad of her army's been torn down while she was away, and that I was responsible for it.

"Make my arm strong and let me not succumb to fear," I pray under my breath, as I take off again.

Power crackles around me as I plunge into the battalion of rotting corpses. The ground splinters on either side of me, twin waves of black tar rearing up from the crevasses. I swing my arm forward and the black lava follows the movement.

The draugar look on dispassionately as the black tides crash into them, ripping through their ranks. Not a single one of them fights back or tries to flee.

I watch as the smallest of them, a little girl with legs bent all wrong—perhaps from a car crash—gets swallowed up, her skin and flesh melting off her bones, absorbed into this dark sea of my making.

My stomach heaves in revulsion, my prior excitement vanished.

"Tut, tut, tut," a voice says from above.

I crane my neck up to find Asheel staring down at me, her chestnut hair falling around her round shoulders in soft waves. Distraction successful. Now I need to survive.

"Didn't think we'd meet again so soon," Asheel says, dropping lower so I can see her impish, snaggle-toothed grin. "You know, I never got to properly thank you for restoring my powers."

"You're *so* not welcome," I say.

"In exchange, how about I show you what I can now do?"

Asheel drops her smile and snaps her fingers. I yelp in surprise as the ground heaves, throwing me down before the still bubbling pools of tar. I roll to push myself back up before my body can process the pain, then spin around to face the she-demon again. But Asheel's no longer there.

I catch movement from the corner of my eyes, then the she-demon's sharp-nailed fingers pierce my right shoulder, shattering my bone upon impact. I howl in pain, vision clouding over.

"That's for moving from your post," Asheel says.

Her other hand slithers around my throat to cradle my head against her bosom, crushing my trachea beneath her iron-like fingers.

"You shouldn't have touched my flock, sweets," she continues. "I'm going to have to replace these now. So I'll start with turning you into another of my draugar. I'm sure Carman won't mind it if—"

With a startled hiss, Asheel suddenly releases me.

"Missssstressss!"

I struggle to stay on my feet, fighting to remain conscious.

"There's another I could add to the lot," Asheel says, eyes flashing as she pulls an obsidian knife out from between her lower ribs.

Without even looking, she hurls the knife away, and it strikes the banshee with the power of a shotgun, sending her flying into the nearest hillside.

That's when the ear-splitting sound of metal cutting metal echoes across the valley, setting my teeth on edge.

Asheel whirls around, her face pale with shocked horror. "The cauldron!"

And I find myself smiling. Finally.

# Chapter 14

Asheel bullets through the sky, blue light flashing in the midst of the draugar army as she casts thunderbolt after thunderbolt at Gale. The cauldron itself is lying on its side like a cracked egg, its contents spilled over the ground. My gaze drifts down to the remains of the latest humans that have been fed to it, bodies mangled and shredded apart, like in some giant cannibalistic stew.

Blood drains from my face as I pick out a woman's face staring blankly back at me, the rest of her body torn away in the explosion. A woman I last saw smiling brightly at her newborn son. The one person I'd managed to save from Mordred's clutches.

"It can't be…," I whisper through numb lips.

"Missstresss?" the banshee calls out in worry, hobbling her way over to me.

"He promised," I say, throat convulsing.

"And a Fey cannot break its promise."

I start at the gravelly voice, and the banshee whirls around with a vicious growl, only to let out a startled yelp. I stare uncomprehending at the slight boy picking his way through the pools of tar I've called up, and my mouth drops open.

Owen, Bri's brother, the one I couldn't free from the Siege Perilous, is standing before me. The boy still looks a lot like Bri—same birdlike build, same dark hair, and straight nose. But the taint from the Siege Perilous that marks my hands has reached his eyes instead, dyeing them entirely coal-black.

But my anger and hurt at the betrayal burn through the shock of seeing him here.

"Mordred isn't just any kind of Fey, Owen, he's a Dark Sidhe," I say, voice raw. "And this is proof that he can lie. We'd made a deal, that he'd leave the woman alone, yet she still ended up here, and now she's…"

The world around me shrivels down to a pinprick, swallowed by a maelstrom of dark emotions—fear, loathing, despair. I thought I'd put them behind me that day Arthur found me cutting myself in the restrooms. But they were always there, lurking beneath the surface. Now they're back in full force, drowning me, and Arthur's not here to show me the light.

"You saved a life," Owen says, his gravelly voice oddly muted.

"She's dead," I say.

"But her son isn't. And you gave her a chance to see him before death claimed her."

"Death didn't *claim* her," I snarl. "She was happy and healthy until Mordred turned her into that!"

Asheel's sinister laugh reaches us from high up in the turbulent sky, pulling my attention back to the battle. Electric bolts light up the darkening clouds as the she-demon launches another attack at Gale. Lance's brother looks so small, standing on top of the upturned cauldron, spear glinting in his hands. A skiff in the middle of a stormy sea, seconds away from sinking into the abyss.

But at the last second, Gale jams his golden spear up, drawing Asheel's lightning to him.

"They'll be fine," Owen says, making me jump. "But you and your banshee won't if you remain here."

I scowl at Bri's twin. "Is that a threat?"

"A statement of fact," Owen says with a half shrug. "This battle hasn't remained unnoticed, and you are both slowed down by your injuries."

Both? I turn to the banshee, mad at myself for not having noticed sooner.

"Are you all right?" I ask.

"Yessss," the banshee says, her trusty obsidian knife clutched in her hand while she watches Gale and Kaede face the she-demon.

From the slight shiver in her shoulders, I can tell the banshee's excited by the scene. This is what she was bred for, to fight until the last breath for her master, and a part of me wonders if she'd have led a peaceful life if Dean hadn't found her. Or if he only allowed her at his side because war was already in her blood.

If she's injured, I can't tell, and the banshee isn't one to complain, and for some odd reason I trust Owen to have stated the truth. I must get the banshee to safety before the whole demon city goes after us. Yet I can't abandon Gale and Kaede like a coward.

"I'm not leaving without making sure we're all safe first," I say.

"The knights can fend for themselves," Owen insists, as Gale throws himself into the air to meet Asheel.

The demon tries to avoid the spear's charged blade, and veers off course at the last second. But Gale twists around, thrusting his spear straight at her legs. The power of a thousand lightning bolts sizzles through Asheel, lighting her up like a second moon. Then, before she can pull free, Gale uses her momentum to swing her around, and flings Asheel straight into the ground.

The earth explodes in a shower of dirt and rocks, taking with it another section of draugar. I shield my eyes as a warm wind howls through the plain, alarmed shouts arising in response, coming from the demon city.

"Mission accomplished," Gale says, landing beside me.

Already his spear is sinking back into the muscles of his forearm. He grabs my hand, running at full tilt in the direction Nibs and Keva took, letting the banshee follow.

"Wait, Owen…," I say, looking over my shoulder at the boy.

But Owen's already gone, lost in the remaining ranks of draugar. My eyes turn to the city, and I recoil at the sight of the demons swarming over its walls like a great tidal wave. Gale pulls harder on my hand, urging me to speed up. I stumble after him, barely keeping my feet under me, vision sliding in and out of focus.

"What about Kaede?" I ask, already running out of breath.

"Creating a false trail," Gale says.

We abruptly turn right between two hills, and the horde disappears from sight. Gradually, the ground steepens, the rocks on our path growing larger and sharper. I'm finding it harder to keep up. Breath ragged. Footfalls clumsy. Everything blurry around me.

"Sssstop," the banshee calls out, jumping ahead of Gale to bar our way.

She points behind us, and Gale lets out a soft curse.

"You're leaving a trail," he says.

I look back, swaying dangerously as the world around me spins, catching sight of bright flecks of red on the ashy ground. Blood. Mine.

The banshee drops to a knee before me, urging me to climb on her back, and a familiar laugh erupts ahead.

"That's quite a show you guys put up there," Mordred says, perched atop his kelpie.

I stiffen. "How did you——" I start, words coming out slurred.

"Know about your little escapade?" Mordred bares his teeth. "I know all about you, sister dear. I know more about you than anyone else. Probably better than you do yourself."

Gale and the banshee draw up on either side of me as my brother jumps off his steed, holding both hands up to show his lack of weapons. As if he couldn't attack us with just the flick of a finger.

"On a scale of one to ten, how much can your brother be trusted?" Gale asks me.

"Minus two," I reply, trying to focus my blurry vision on the approaching figure.

"Didn't think you had it in you to actually fight in broad daylight," Mordred says to Gale, stopping.

"Your sister helped quite a bit," Gale replies guardedly.

"So it would seem. And now you have half a million demons hunting you down." Mordred cocks a brow at me. "Barely able to stand and yet still fighting to protect those pathetic knights of yours," he drawls. "Then again, I always knew you were a slow learner."

"What do you want, Mordred?" I ask through gritted teeth.

Keeping his movements extra slow, he reaches inside a pouch at his belt, grabs my hand, and slips something cool inside it.

"It's a tonic of sorts," Mordred says, pointing at the arm Carman's blood shadow's punctured. "It'll help you more than these knights or that guardian angel of yours ever did."

"What...," I start, opening my hand. My blood chills. "No!" I shout, throwing the ogham back at his face.

Mordred catches the nut-sized jewel, and lets out a loud sigh, before forcing the ogham back into my hand. "You need to get some strength back," he says. "If not, you'll die."

"What do you care?"

Mordred leans in, a sardonic smile on his tattooed face, and I see the banshee grow tense. "I said we would always be linked, you and I, didn't I? And this bond of ours is not one I can ignore."

"I still won't do it," I say, wishing I could slap the smirk off his face. "I'm not some kind of cannibal."

Mordred's knuckles turn white around my hand until I wince in pain, and the banshee snarls in warning.

"Do you think we enjoy this?" Mordred hisses, moving out of reach of the banshee's obsidian knife. "We do it to survive. And we're not the only ones. Where do you think your precious Lugh and his cohort get their strength from?"

"The elements, of course," I say automatically, recalling my lessons at Lake High.

"That only works for basic sustenance, actually," Gale says, looking back the way we came, where the sounds of the demon horde are growing louder.

My eyes widen. "You mean you know about this...this..." I wave my free hand around, at a loss for words.

Gale shrugs, and Mordred snaps his fingers together, drawing my attention back to him. "Have you not been paying attention all this time?" he asks, voice dangerously low. "A Fey's real source of power comes from the Lord of its Demesne. They're as much leeches as they profess us to be. We just have the decency to be honest about it."

"You're lying!" I shout at him, unwilling to believe a word of his. Mordred's a Dark Sidhe. He's never said a true word to me for as long as I've known him. Even if he is my brother, I can't trust him—I told Gale as much just seconds ago. "You just said Lugh was doing...what it is you're doing," I say, taking measured breaths, "but he's the Lord of his own Demesne, so what you're saying makes no sense!"

"His lordship is a front," Mordred says with a sneer, as if he expected my reaction. "He's no better than a steward. And now that you know the truth, why don't you be a good girl for once and do what I tell you to do?"

"Like when you took me to Carman to be used as a sacrifice?" I spit at him, and have the pleasure of seeing him flinch.

"I did it for your own good," Mordred says. "She would have drained you to get that dragon made, even if you'd been sucked dry from restoring another one of her demons first. Like I said, you and I are two peas of the same pod. I know what's good for us."

"Two peas of the same pod?" I repeat through gritted teeth. "I'm nothing like you. *You* are nothing but the devil's son!"

"Which makes you her progeny as well," Mordred says, amusement couching the iron in his voice. "Very well-reasoned. I can see why Sister Marie-Clémence wanted to set you back a year every time."

"What are you? A stalker?"

But his words have done their work. My stomach coils into a tight knot. As surely as Saint George brought the dragon of Silene down, I am demon-spawn. But that doesn't give me the right to absorb and use some other poor Fey's life energy.

"Not that I don't find this talk of yours edifying, but we're out of time," Gale asks. "So speak your business now, or let us through."

"I came to help," Mordred says stiffly. "Or rather Nessie did."

He points to his kelpie, and the beast looks at us with its fiery-red eyes in suspicion.

"Right," I drawl. "As if you'd do anything that didn't serve—"

"Excellent," Gale says hurriedly.

The knight grabs me by the waist and settles me on the kelpie's broad back, before jumping on it behind me. Nessie lets out an annoyed snort, but doesn't otherwise budge.

"You're insane," I whisper to Gale. "Get us off this beast before it tries to kill us."

But Gale only ignores me. "What about you, Dark Sidhe? Are you coming along?"

Mordred's impish smile reappears. "Me? What a strange question for someone who was never even here."

I have no bloody clue where we're headed. Everything looks the same to me—rocky hills of grey under a leaden sky. The demons' shouts have long subsided to nothing, leaving us only with the sound of Nessie's thunderous gallop.

My whole body's aching from gripping the kelpie's algae-like mane. The rough ride's driving my stomach halfway up my throat, and it's all I can do not to retch from motion sickness. I wish I could still fly properly, or at the very least run as fast as the banshee. But I'm still too weak from taking down those draugar.

Unless I use the ogham Mordred gave me... I can feel it tucked away in my jacket pocket, the large gem bouncing against my hip in counterpoint to Nessie's gallop.

I shake the repulsive idea away, disgusted at myself for even thinking it.

Thankfully, the kelpie finally slows down to a stop, and Gale jumps off its sweat-soaked back.

"We're almost there," Gale says.

"Almost?" I squeak, letting the banshee help me down.

Gale points to the top of the nearest cliff, and I squint as I follow his finger to a barely noticeable spot near the top.

"What do you think I am, a goat?" I ask, cringing as I eye the craggy cliffside leading up to what I assume to be a cave.

With a soft nicker that sounds strangely like a laugh, the kelpie takes off again, back to my brother, leaving us three alone.

"Where are the others?" I ask then, worry rearing its ugly head as I find no trace of Keva, Nibs, or even Kaede. "What if they fell somewhere? Or were kidnapped again?"

"They haven't," Gale says calmly.

"How would you—"

A warning growl makes me spin around, just in time to see a figure jump over me and start its rapid ascent, long black hair fanning out behind.

"Hurry up!" Kaede calls down to us, already halfway up.

"The other two are already waiting for us above," Gale says. "But if we don't hurry, others will soon pick up on our trail too, before we can make our way out."

"Supposing the way out actually works," I mutter as Gale tears his shirt up to make a flimsy cord out of it.

"It won't do much," he says, attaching one end of it to my right wrist—the one left untouched by Carman's blood shadow—before attaching the other end to his, "but it'll let me know if you're in trouble.

I eye the steep hill, blanching at how high it is, how much I still need to walk, to climb.

"Let's hurry," Gale says urgently. "Lady Kaede must've seen something serious if she doesn't want to tarry."

The cloth rope pulls at my arm as Gale gets moving, and the banshee nudges me forward. Reluctantly, I start climbing too, foot by painful foot, until my whole body's aching and I'm sweating like a hog. A shower of loose rocks falls upon my head and I look up in annoyance.

"Watch it," I mutter.

The banshee lets out a low growl and I nearly lose my grip in surprise. I stiffen as a shadow ripples overhead. Letting out a string of curses, Gale rolls onto his back to face the new threat, his spear already halfway out his flexors[11].

"What is that?" I ask.

"Harpy," Gale replies.

Petrified, I watch as a large, half-furry, half-feathery bird descends upon us with a loud shriek, gleaming talons out. The winged demon's claws rake the edge of Gale's weapon, sending sparks flying. It lets out another sharp cry, almost human-sounding, and only as it pulls back up do I finally see its head and torso are those of a hirsute woman, hair dangling around its sagging, pale breasts in unkempt locks.

"Morgan!" Gale shouts, startling me out of my paralysis.

The harpy's shadow has circled back and is heading our way again, followed by a second. With a hiss, the banshee urges me forward, and I scramble up the dangerously narrow path as fast as I can.

"Halfway," Gale says, moving sprightly despite the spear still in his hands.

A sudden, strong breeze buffets my back to the pounding sound of the harpies' wings. The banshee turns around with a bark, her knife out. But it's useless against these flying creatures.

I feel the sharp edge of a claw graze my shoulder. I gasp, losing my balance. The rope at my wrist draws taught, then the cloth rips and I find myself slipping down the steep incline. I scrabble

---

[11] Muscles that bend joints and limbs by contracting, like those on the inside of the forearm

at the hard ground in a desperate attempt to find purchase, rocks shredding my palms and knees.

"Missstressss!" The banshee's bony hand latches around my bad arm and I let out a shout of pain, my vision momentarily clouding over.

A screech resounds, so close it makes the ground shake. Then Gale's at our side, thrusting his lance out at the flying beasts. The nearest harpy shrieks in annoyance, flapping away to avoid the deadly weapon.

"You OK?" Gale asks, sparing me a quick glance to look at the damage.

"I-I think so," I say.

"Darknesssssss," the banshee says in warning as the bigger of the two harpies swoops in lower.

"What?" I mumble, arms shaking from the strain.

"She means Celaeno," Gale says, the tension in his body belying his hooded, sleepy look. "The oldest of the three."

"Three?" I exclaim, as the winged demon stops just out of reach of Gale's spear, a smug look on her lined face.

She is twice the size of her sister, her long dark hair merging with the night-colored feathers of its wings, and definitely meaner looking.

"Get her up there, quick, while I keep these back," Gale tells the banshee.

The banshee doesn't hesitate. She hauls me after her, her grip like a vice around my injured arm. I glance back down at the sound of ringing metal. Gale is now fending off the second, smaller harpy. The bird woman is tenacious, diving repeatedly at him despite her evident injuries. As if it's trying to keep him busy...

I look up, searching the grey skies for the second harpy, and panic shoots through me as I realize it's making for the cave.

"Keva!" I shout.

I rush up the hillside in a burst of speed, but I'm too slow. The bigger harpy plunges, sharp talons out, cornering the others inside. I hear a scream of terror. I'm not going to make it!

Before I realize what I'm doing, I slam my foot on the ground, willing my body to take to the skies, and I'm suddenly gliding over the cliffside. But as I fly closer to the cave, the air suddenly thickens, bearing down on me as if to crush me back to the ground. I grit my teeth against the pressure, pulling away again, until I'm soaring high above hill.

Then, releasing a long-held breath, I let myself plummet, straight for the birdwoman.

Sensing my approach, the larger harpy swerves out of the way before my feet can make impact, and I overshoot, flying past Gale as he's prying the smaller harpy off his spear.

I throw my arms out, fingers scraping against the hillside to swing myself around, then kick hard at the ground again with a cry of rage. I surge in a great bound, the ground blurring past, and catch the remaining harpy from behind, fists punching into her feathery back. The demon lets out a sharp croak of surprise, before flying up in retreat.

I twist around on myself, tracking the harpy's movements. My breath is coming in short gasps, muscles burning from the effort. Then everything goes out of focus.

"Above!"

It takes me a while to register Keva's scream. I crane my neck up. "Where—"

I feel the harpy behind me before its talons puncture my back, tearing through flesh and bones to pierce my ribcage all the way through to the front. I let out a strangled cry as the harpy tightens her grip on me, already carrying me away.

"Head down!" Gale shouts.

Something bright flashes in front of me, and I barely have the reflex to duck as Gale drives his spear up, barely missing my head.

The harpy's claws jerk, squeezing my insides tighter as the weapon catches it in the neck. Gale yanks his weapon back out, and the harpy gurgles out a screech, dark ichor gushing out of her wound, steaming hot on the back of my head.

For a second it seems we're suspended in the air. Then the harpy's arrhythmic wingbeat swings us around in a dizzying spiral. The wind whistles in my ears as we plunge towards the bottom of the hill, the ground rushing up to meet us.

I catch sight of a figure racing to keep up with us. A face. Gale, looking worried. Shouting…

I grunt as I try to correct our fall, but it's like I've turned into an old, sputtering engine. There's a grey blur as the banshee jumps towards us, ramming into the harpy's ribs, and altering our deadly course.

We hit the side of the hill in a bone-jarring *thud*, bouncing off the ground several times before skidding to a stop, and the harpy's claws finally unclench.

I take in a shuddering breath, tears leaking from my eyes, dust and ash from the collision slowly settling back down.

I close my eyes against the pounding in my head. I can't feel anything from the neck down, can't move a finger. Sleep pulls at my shattered body, dulling my senses. Then someone slaps me hard across the face, ripping a weak cry of pain from my lips.

"Wakey, wakey, yer moronness," Nibs says, and I open my eyes open. A sneer pulls at the melted side of the clurichaun's face. "Excellent! Now if ya don't mind, we need ya to help out as we get these wings off yer back."

The clurichaun twists his finger, and two sets of hands reach under my back to peel me off the harpy's claws. I scream. It feels like they're gutting me, ripping my spine out. Finally, my body comes free and Gale and the banshee gently lay me back down beside the dead harpy.

"She's gonna bleed to death," I hear Keva say, voice thin with fear.

I want to tell her I'm OK. I don't hurt so bad now.

"She's going into epileptic shock!" Keva shouts.

I try to smile. Keva can be so silly sometimes. My hands and feet contract, muscles seizing, then release again.

"Move aside," Kaede says. She's holding out a round stone that flares for a second as she draws near me. A jewel as bright as the summer sky.

It's not the one Mordred gave me, but it's an ogham nonetheless.

"Great idea," Nibs says, grabbing the stone from the knight's fingers.

I shake my head, struggling feebly to keep Nibs away.

"Sorry, sweetcheeks," the clurichaun says, "but ya've got no choice in the matter. Only way to heal ya."

My body bucks and arches as Nibs pushes the ogham into the open wound in my chest. Another scream rips out of me.

"Stop fighting it," Nibs tells me through clenched teeth. He's pressing both hands over the entry point, keeping the ogham inside me so my body's forced to absorb it.

Angry tears blur my vision anew. Stop. Please! A sob escapes my raw throat. Please make him stop...

I let out a shuddering breath as the pressure suddenly recedes.

"It's being pushed back out!" Keva shouts in surprise.

"Let me go, ya dumbass," Nibs snarls. "She'll die if we don't do this, and then where will we be?"

Out of the corner of my eye, I see Gale shake his head as he holds Nibs up by the collar. "Can't you feel it?" he asks, sounding strangely awed.

"These two might be dead, but there's a third one out there, ya glob of snot," Nibs snaps, waving his bloody fists in the air. "We don't have time!"

"No, Sir Gale's right," Kaede says, sharp profile pointing back to the cave. "There's something there."

And then I feel it too. A strange warmth that reaches out to me, soaking me in its soft, comforting embrace. I let my eyelids flutter closed. My breathing eases, all of my pain and fear receding, gently wiped away.

Then, as quickly as it appeared, the energy vanishes, leaving me feeling cold and empty. But the pain is gone as well. I slowly open my eyes, wondering if I'm not in another one of my strange visions.

"It can't be," Nibs whispers, his eyes even larger with shock.

"You bloody well have to believe it!" Keva squeals. She eyes me from head to foot, as if taking stock. Then, with a satisfied nod, she flashes a big grin at me. "So, you're ready to go kill us some monsters and take back our school?"

# CHAPTER 15

"Even her eyes are back to normal," Keva says.

"We noted," Nibs mutters.

"No, you don't understand. Ever since we got here, her eyes have been dark, and now…" Keva sighs mournfully. "Golden eyes would suit me so much better, though. It's not fair."

"Maybe it's because we're so close to the exit," Nibs says, still sounding stunned, "what with the barrier bein' somewhat breached and all."

Still confused myself, I slowly sit up and run my fingers through my bloodied hair, ash and feathers falling from it in dirty clumps. I test my body, stretching it out luxuriously, reveling in its miraculous healing. And all without having to absorb the ogham Kaede gave me!

Laughter bubbles out of me. "Here," I tell the knight, tossing her the large jewel back.

Kaede snatches the stone out of the air, her dark eyes never leaving my face, as if searching for an answer. Then, with a shrug, she pockets the ogham and jumps onto the harpy's remains.

"There's no need to——" Nibs starts.

He gulps as the knight points her sword at him. "You stay out of my business, clurichaun," she growls, "and I'll stay out of yours."

And without waiting for an answer, she cuts the carcass open, carving it like it's some giant turkey, before jumping inside the bird-woman's thoracic cage.

"That's just foul," Keva says, covering her nose at the stench that emanates from the carcass.

My laughter redoubles at the stupid pun, causing the banshee to fuss about me in worry.

"Relax," I say, patting her hunched shoulder, "I'm fine."

"OK, OK," Nibs whines. "We're all glad to be alive, kisses all 'round, brilliant. Now will you please get yer asses movin' before we get attacked again?"

"There's more of them?" Keva asks.

"Of course, darlin'," Nibs says in his nasally voice, "not everyone's a unique little butterfly like ya."

With a satisfied grunt, Kaede pulls herself back out of the harpy's sternum, gore covering her from head to foot, a bloody ogham the size of an apple clutched in her hand. And looking disgustingly pleased with herself.

"We can go now," Kaede says, shaking the worst of the gunk off her like a she-wolf, before climbing the rest of the way up and disappearing inside the cavern.

"I'm so not going behind her," Keva mutters as the rest of us file after her. "I'd faint from the smell."

"You can go in after me," I suggest as Gale disappears inside the low-ceilinged tunnel.

Keva snorts. "And rely on you if I fall? Don't think so." She cuts me off, rushing inside. "Sir Gale, wait for me!"

131

I chuckle, wondering how Keva's managed to remain the same despite everything we've gone through. "Thanks for taking us this far," I say, looking over at Nibs.

But my eyes fall upon some markings carved along the bottom of the cave's entrance, and I pause, dread seeping into me. The etchings are pale, faded with time, but I have no trouble recognizing the symbol.

"Lucifer's sigil," I whisper.

"Good, yer learnin'," Nibs says, spitting a large gob of phlegm on the ground. "Now step on it. Remember that your friends there won't make it unless yer there with them."

"Because of that?"

Nibs nods. "Though Mordred himself's never tried it, it's been speculated that's how Lucifer high-tailed it out of here so easily. Which means her heirs should be able to as well."

My gut clenches at the idea, and I have to force myself to breathe. That would possibly be the only good thing to come of my parentage. If it works. "Are you saying that our freedom hangs on a stupid theory?"

"It's the best I have to offer," Nibs says. "So either ya go along and test it out, or ya can rot away down here. Your choice."

"That's not a choice!" I exclaim, making the banshee jump.

"It's all ya've got, princess." He pulls the bloodied cloth from his pocket, now turned grey. "But if it makes ya feel any better," Nibs continues, handing me the piece of cloth with the sigil drawn on it, "know that it's his hoity-toitiness who came up with the plan."

"His hoit—" I start in confusion.

He can't mean Mordred. My brother wouldn't have bothered with this bloodied handkerchief to convey his message when he could have told me so directly. But then, who?

The image of the black, one-eyed cat flashes in my mind, quickly followed by that of a brooding face, all high cheekbones, aquiline nose, and full lips. "You mean Lugh?"

"Bingo," Nibs says, casting a weary look around.

Keva's shrill voice echoes down from the cavern before I can say a thing. "Morgan! We need you here!"

I swallow hard. The time for doubts is over. "All right, then," I say, exhaling sharply. "Are you sure you can't come with us?" I ask.

"Dead certain."

I look down at Nibs's ravaged face, feeling guilty. "If we make it out," I tell him, "I'll find your ogham and give it back to you."

Nibs hisses in shock. "Be careful when pledgin' an oath. Breakin' one is anathema, and could result in yer very own demise."

"Trust me," I say, smiling as his mouth gapes wide, "just as I'm trusting you with this."

Squaring my shoulders, I finally step inside the cave, pausing only long enough to let my eyes adjust to the darkness.

"Go find Caim in jail!" Nibs shouts as I hurry up to join the others, the banshee a half-step behind. "If anyone knows Carman's weakness, it's him."

Down, down we go, the darkness so deep I can't see the others in front of me nor the banshee behind. We move slowly through the narrow tunnel, our progress punctuated by grunts and heavy breathing, giving me way too much time to spin a thousand death and doom scenarios in my head: The tunnel caving in, my tainted blood not working so we're all shredded to bits when we try to cross into Avalon, Dark Sidhe waiting for our arrival to enslave us again, Carman's dragon burning us down before we can warn anyone of her plans...

Keva lets out a surprised bleat, and I pull away from my dark thoughts as my center of gravity suddenly shifts. I slam my arms out against the tunnel's rough walls before I can fall face first down the hole, feel the banshee do the same behind me.

"You're good," I hear Gale tell Keva, "I've got you."

"W-What happened?" I ask, disoriented.

Up isn't up anymore, but down. Am I supposed to backtrack? Keep climbing down? Or change tracks instead? I wipe the sweat off my forehead on my shoulder, afraid to make the wrong decision.

"Here, mistresssss," the banshee hisses behind me, which is now ahead.

"O-OK," I say.

The jagged edges of the rock walls scraping roughly against my hands and feet, I carefully turn around to follow the banshee back the other way. I take another shuddering breath, then, after making sure everyone else is safe too, we resume our slow progress.

"We're close," Kaede says after a long while, her clipped voice floating up from the tunnel shaft.

I peer around the banshee's cowled figure, and my heart skips a beat at the soft light filtering down to us through a small, circular hole, suffusing our cramped tunnel with an eerie blue glow. I pause, tension working its way to my shoulders and calves, making my muscles bunch in painful cramps. But not as painful as being torn to pieces if Nibs and Lugh are wrong about this.

"Why are we stopping?" Keva asks, sounding exhausted.

"Because it's dangerous," Gale says, sounding as tense as I feel.

"Well, not moving from here isn't going to accomplish much either!" Keva snaps.

"Right," I say, forcing myself to start moving again. "Just...don't follow until I'm out. You never know..."

With the banshee's help, I manage to climb the last few meters separating us from the exit, and pause only when the tunnel's mouth is within reach.

Beyond it, I glimpse the rafters' wooden beams and caved-in ceiling, bright stars twinkling down benevolently at us from above. I prick up my ears apprehensively, but apart from the soughing of the wind, I cannot hear anything ahead. I hope it means Mordred's crumbling fort has truly been abandoned.

"Well, here goes," I murmur, squeezing around the banshee and reaching up.

My scraped fingers find purchase around the hole's edge, and I pause expectantly. Nothing. I expel a relieved breath and start pulling myself out.

There's a sudden flash of red, and I nearly let go. But the banshee's strong hand shoves me the rest of the way up, and then I'm through.

"We're out!" I exclaim, as the banshee rolls in after me with another red flash. All in one piece.

I laugh, feeling winter's cold touch dry my damp face. It's the type of weather to freeze one's balls off, and I love it! I breathe in the crispy air, relishing the way it burns down my lungs.

Freedom has never tasted so wonderful, and I'm going to make damn sure Hell's foulness never tarnishes it.

"Morgan?" Keva calls out, sounding on the verge of panic.

I crawl back to the hole's edge, grinning widely. "Coast is clear!" I shout down.

Keva's face appears next, a worried frown creasing her pale brow. "How sure are you about this?" she asks through cracked lips.

"Not at all," I say, reaching for her, "but the banshee got out just fine."

The old sigil painted on the side of the tunnel's entrance flashes harmlessly as I pull Keva up to safety, and she tumbles into me. For a long moment, we hang onto each other, shaking, unable to fathom the fact that we're both free at last, and in one piece.

Finally, Keva rolls away from me. "The others," she whispers.

With a nod, I return to the tunnel's edge, praying that whatever luck I've had thus far doesn't suddenly run out. But as I reach down, Gale pulls back.

"Stop," he says.

Sweat drips down my nose, sizzling as it hits the net drawn tightly over the exit, the red threads no longer letting anything through.

"No, no, no, no," I say, punching the side of the hole in desperation. This can't be happening. I need to get Gale and Kaede out! I need to—

"It's all right, no need to panic," Gale says soothingly. "Let's think about this for a moment. You got the others out, so you can do it again. The key is figuring out what's changed since then."

"I don't...I don't know," I say, choking back a sob.

Then the banshee's at my side, and her skeletal hand gently grabs mine. Her cowled face turns to me as she places her obsidian knife over the palm of my hand, and though I cannot see her face, I know she's asking for my permission. Releasing a shaky breath, I nod.

The blade slides across my flesh, black against black, and blood pools in my hand, before spilling over. And when it hits the net, the light flickers out, harmless once again.

"Now," Gale says.

Without another hesitation, I pull both knights to safety, arms shaking from the strain, fingers slick with blood.

"Thanks," Gale says, patting my shoulder. "You did well."

Only then do I finally release my breath, and sag against the wall, feeling wrung out.

"I can't believe we're not dead," Keva says in the silence that follows. She's lying on her back in the middle of the room, staring up at the starry sky.

"Neither can I," I say, staring at my hands in wonder, heart still beating frantically against my ribs. The cut is already healing, Hell's corrupting influence on me no longer in effect.

"I can't believe we could've left anytime we wanted," Keva adds, and I hear the anger in her tone.

"Carman wouldn't have let Morgan go," Gale says, "and you know it."

A strange, scurrying sound from the other side of the wall punctuates his words, and Kaede's twin swords come out of their sheaths with a soft hiss.

"Seems we were expected," Gale says.

Despite our exhaustion, we all jump to our feet, senses alert. But as excited grunts erupt from the hallway leading to the front door, I take an unsteady step forward.

"Wait," I tell the others, holding my hand up. "I recognize that sound…"

And a second later, Puck's chubby form appears from around the corner, running as fast as his little hooves can carry him. At my sight, the hobgoblin snorts in joy, and, holding his chubby arms out, throws himself at my legs to hug me with all his might.

"Hello, you silly boy," I say, picking the hobgoblin up before he can slobber all over my bare feet. "How did you get all the way over here?"

"Ugh, keep that thing away from me," Keva says, quickly moving away. "I'm already filthy enough as it is, I don't need to smell like old cheese on top of it."

I let out a delighted laugh as Puck grabs something from my jacket and starts munching on it.

"What have you got there?" I say, trying to pull the piece of paper from his grubby hands without tearing it apart.

But when I see what's on it, I freeze. Smiling shily back at me across the span of half a decade is fifteen-year-old me.

"A picture?" Keva says, curiosity overcoming her disgust for Puck to take a look at what I'm holding. "Were you carrying it on you this whole time? Did you think you'd be signing autographs?"

"It wasn't in my pockets," I say, stunned.

I let Keva pluck the picture from my numb fingers, remembering very well the day I decided to send it, along with a Christmas card, to the one I'd once called mom. Another letter that went unanswered, another tender hope of spending the holidays with my family crushed. Funny how close innocence is to sheer stupidity.

But it still doesn't explain why the picture's here.

"Maybe it was in the lining, then," Keva says, giggling at my school portrait. "Some knights used to keep pics of their girlfriends like that, instead of the traditional Lady's favor." Her smile widens. "And if I recall correctly, that jacket you're wearing is—"

"Mine," a deep voice says.

I nearly drop Puck as a shadow detaches itself from the collapsed wall and slinks into view, moonlight glinting off the iron-threaded uniform.

Although taller and broader in the shoulders, he looks thinner now, his hair no longer well-combed, and his clothes shows the wear and tear of many a battle. But the shy smile and the glint of his hazel eyes as he looks at me haven't changed.

I find myself holding my breath as he prowls forward, the hilt of a massive broadsword sticking up from behind his dirty blond head like a large cross.

I barely feel my lips move as I whisper his name.

"Arthur."

# Chapter 16

My muscles have locked into place. I can't move an inch. I've dreamed of this moment and dreaded it at the same time for so long. A thousand excuses try to push their way past my clenched teeth, but what do you say to the one you tried to kill, or thinks you did?

Then Arthur's arms are around me, gently cradling my head against his shoulder, and it feels like the whole world has stopped spinning.

"You're back," he whispers, his shaky breath tickling my ear. "I thought I'd never see you again."

My throat's too tight. My mind's a mess. He should be screaming at me, fighting me, not...this.

With an annoyed grunt, Puck wriggles out of my arms, forcing Arthur to pull away. I stand motionless as he looks at my face, as if he, too, can't believe any of this is real. This close, I notice more changes on him—a fuzzy beard has started to grow over his once smooth cheeks, barely covering a new series of pink scars. Even his eyes, which I thought had remained their gorgeous hazel selves, seem more luminous, the green-brown of their irises now flecked with ochre.

"How did you find us?" Kaede asks, ignoring Keva's furious elbowing.

Her harsh voice is enough to break the spell. Feeling suddenly shy, I try to step further away from Arthur, but his hold on my arms only tightens.

"We couldn't track you through the geas," he says, never looking away from me, "not since we lost the school. And knowing Carman had pushed you through the Gates..." His voice cracks. He cups my cheek with his calloused hand. "We were able to get a report from Nibs during one of his rare outings. He's the one who told us of this place, and Lugh then sent his cat through the portal to send the message. We didn't know if it would work, but..."

Something inside me shifts, releasing its hold over my chest, and turning my legs to mush.

"Morgan!" Arthur shouts, catching me.

I giggle at his concern. I haven't felt this light in ages, not even when that strange power healed me after the harpies' attack. My heart is soaring, and it feels like I could too, right through the hole in the collapsed ceiling.

"What's the matter?" Arthur asks. "Are you hurt?"

"She's fine," Keva says, "just absolutely disgusting. Any chance we could go home and get a shower?"

I giggle louder. "I want a bath with lots of bubbles!" I say.

"Ease her down," a smooth, chocolaty voice says.

Lugh's found his way inside the fort. Should've figured he'd be here too, this being his plan and all.

"She has been cut off from her power source for too long," Lugh continues, his one golden eye assessing, "and the sudden reconnection must have shocked her system."

"I like your patch," I tell him, cooing. "Makes you look like a cuddly pirate."

"So she's drunk?" Arthur asks.

"In a way, yes," Lugh says.

"I didn't know it would make her glow," Arthur says.

"Just like what happened in Hell," Keva murmurs.

Lazily, I hook my arm around Arthur's neck for support, and his cheeks turn flaming red. I laugh at his reaction. How did I never notice how cute he is? Or was it I never dared admit it to myself?

"Are you sure it isn't because of Arthur that she's lost her mind?" I hear Keva ask derisively.

"Think of it as having had too much ambrosia," Lugh says, a frown now creasing his otherwise perfect brow.

I press my head more firmly into Arthur's shoulder, looking up at him with what I hope to be the biggest puppy-eyed look I can muster despite my incessant laughter.

"I'm hungry," I whisper-shout, letting Arthur pat me awkwardly like I'm a dog waiting for its biscuit.

There's a bright blue flare, and a Fey boy appears in the middle of the room, flashing his pointy-toothed smile. "Welcome back, princess."

"Pigfain!" I exclaim, letting go of Arthur so suddenly I nearly topple over. I let out another whoop of laughter as both Lugh's and Arthur's arms shoot out to steady me.

"I do hope this wears off soon," Keva says with a grimace. "It's getting annoying."

"Didn't I see you recently?" I ask the Fey boy. I snap my fingers together repeatedly, trying to jab my memory. "You know at my, I mean Arthur's parents' place?"

Pigfain's smile turns into a confused look.

"Actually, you were there too," I say, jabbing Lugh in the chest. "And you," I continue, pointing at Arthur next. "It was like a big, boring party. Then again, nothing's ever fun when your dad's around, eh?" I say, with a wink for Arthur.

"Somebody *please* knock her out," Keva says.

"Puck wasn't there though," I say, as an afterthought. "Oh, but that red pixie of yours was! Where is she, anyway?" I look around the ruined fort, feeling dizzy. "And then Gauvain came over, or was it Gareth? And he kept trying to impress Sameer—"

I stop as the rest of those awful dreams swim back to me, sobering me up. A shiver runs down my arms.

"What happened to them?" I ask. "Where are they?"

Lugh's lips flatten out, the light in his eye dimmed.

"So it was real?" I ask. "All of it? And Sameerah's…dead?"

"I am not entirely sure what you are speaking of," Lugh says, "but yes, Sameerah is unfortunately gone."

"I knew it," I say, my insides crawling. "I mean…I was hoping it wouldn't be…but—"

A loud hiss erupts from the furthest corner of the fort, and I turn towards the sound, only to see a black cat burst away from Puck's reach, to jump into Lugh's arms.

"Why are you not at Caamaloth then?" Gale asks Arthur, moving out of Puck's way as the hobgoblin dives at Lugh's feet. "They should have instated martial law."

"They have," Arthur says, frowning as he finally looks at Gale. "But the Order's suffered a coup, and has only just begun to function normally again."

"Yes, of course," Gale says with a dismissive wave. "But why are *you* here? As a representative of Lake High, your knowledge of Fey activity in Avalon is crucial in terms of strategizing."

"Maybe that's 'cause he got kicked out as KORT President."

Keva and I both turn at the same time to find Daniel loitering by the entrance. Even in the dimness of the fort's ruins, I can tell Arthur's gone pale.

"If a bunch of students couldn't trust him anymore, why should the rest of the Board?" Daniel finishes with evident relish.

"Sir Arthur is still a KORT knight, and thus fully deserving of your respect," Gale snaps at the boy. "Another stray word from you, and I'll tan your hide myself."

Keva's jaw drops open, and I find myself staring wide-eyed at the knight. Not once have I heard Gale raise his voice, not even when he faced Asheel. I clear my throat in the uncomfortable silence that follows.

"Forgot to mention Keva and I picked up a couple of hitchhikers along the way, in case you were wondering," I say. "This here is Sir Gale, and—"

"Lance's brother?" Arthur asks.

"In the flesh, so to speak," Gale says, hand to heart as he makes a slight bow.

"And dumb-dumb still curtsies," Daniel whispers loudly.

"Shut it, Daniel," Keva says. "You may have grown taller since I last saw you, but evidently your brain hasn't kept up."

"I thought you looked familiar!" Arthur exclaims, grabbing Gale by the shoulders with a genuine smile. "I'm so glad to see you again, though you seem so short now. I can't believe that after all this time, you're actually back with us!" His face grows somber. "I do wish Lance were here to greet you too."

"Is he...?" Gale asks, sounding uncertain.

Arthur shakes his head. "When our school fell to the Dark Sidhe, half of Lake High got trapped there as well. Lance was one of them. That is why, when Lugh told me of his plan to get Morgan out, I volunteered to do some reconnaissance work in Avalon."

"And?" Keva asks intently.

"We lost all contact after those inside attempted a full jailbreak," Arthur says softly. "Apart from a few escapees like

Daniel, here"—he takes a deep, shuddering breath—"most didn't make it."

"You can thank Father Tristan for that stupid idea," Daniel mutters.

"It got you out, though, didn't it?" Keva says scornfully.

"There are rumors that Father Tristan has managed to keep the church protected against the Dark Sidhe," Arthur continues before the two of them can get into a fight. "Though who knows how long that sanctuary will last, if it's still there at all... It has been over two years."

"Still safer there than out here getting charred by a dragon," Daniel sniffs.

My muscles bunch up, awash with emotions. Fear. Shame. Guilt.

"We'll figure a way to handle the beast," Gale says, "but it's the least of our worries."

"That's right," Keva intervenes, "there's also the draugar army Carman's building, and it's huge!"

"They've had centuries to build it up," Gale says, "and the pace has accelerated in recent years. If they're released from Hell, I can't tell the damage they'll do. The good news is that—"

"Gale destroyed the giant cauldron that was used to make them," Keva says, cutting him off again.

"I had Lady Kaede's help," Gale says, "as well as that of—"

"Lady Kaede?" Arthur asks.

He scans the fort's remains, his gaze catching on the girl's still form as she leans quietly against a pile of crumbled stonework. Then, with a surprised chuckle, he dashes across the room, stopping short when Kaede flinches away from his extended hand.

"Didn't think I'd ever see you again," Arthur says, laughing self-consciously.

The girl doesn't move nor say a word, her almond eyes emotionless as she stares at him. Finally, with a perplexed smile, Arthur drops his hand altogether.

"A moment," Lugh says, slitting his golden eye. "Something here is not quite right."

Kaede and Arthur stiffen, Gale's eyes stray to the cat now rubbing itself all over his boots, while Daniel slowly backs away from us, his eyes wide with fear. Keva and I exchange worried glances.

"Ah, I think I know what this is about," Gale says.

He drops into a crouch to rub Lugh's cat behind the ear, and sticks his other arm out. Even though I've already seen it happen before, I can't help but hold my breath like everyone else as the skin of his forearm splits open to let a long, golden spear push through with soft, sucking sounds.

"Yeah, that's still gross," Keva says with a shudder.

"Isn't that *Gae Assail*?" Pigfain asks Lugh in awe. "The lance you—"

"It is," Lugh says, gaze fevered. If I didn't know him better, I'd think he's just seen his worst nightmare come to life.

Gale holds the spear out to him. "It's yours, I believe?"

Lugh bares his teeth in a silent growl. "Not anymore," he says at last. "You may keep it."

"But that's the spear that defeated Balor!" Pigfain exclaims.

"It accomplished its purpose, I do not need it anymore," Lugh says, turning away from the weapon as if even its sight hurts him.

"Balor?" I repeat.

"Lugh's grandsire," Pigfain explains, throwing his Lord furtive glances.

"Is that why everyone keeps mentioning him?" Keva asks.

"Who's been mentioning him?" Arthur asks.

Keva shrugs. "Just...random demon gossip, I guess."

"They keep mentioning him because that's the reason Carman's down in Hell," I say, my mouth suddenly dry. "She wants to free him."

A strained silence settles over us.

"Are you sure of this?" Arthur asks at last.

"Yes."

"This is worse than we thought!" Pigfain exclaims, sounding on the verge of panic. "We've got to warn the others, reconvene, figure another way to—"

"It doesn't change our plans," Lugh says.

"But—"

"Enough!" Lugh says with finality. "This talk about freeing Balor is but wishful thinking. If they could open all of the Gates of Hell, they would have so already."

"It's what they said about the first Gate," Daniel grumbles, and for once I have to agree with him. Carman has a knack for getting her hands on what she wants.

"So what are these plans of yours, then?" Gale asks.

"We thought we could catch them off guard by attacking their rears," Arthur says, pointing at the gaping hole behind me.

A chill creeps up my spine.

"You mean by traveling through Hell?" Kaede asks, shocked out of her muteness.

"Are you insane?" Keva blurts out. "We barely made it out alive, and you guys want to hop down there? Do you even know what it's like? On top of the draugar, you've also got whole cities' worth of demons prowling down there! No. Nuh, huh. This is a really stupid idea."

"Agreed," Daniel says.

"Shut up, Daniel," Keva retorts automatically.

"You're not the boss of me," the young boy bristles.

"I can't let our people keep getting massacred without trying to do something to stop it," Arthur counters testily, and only then do I realize how exhausted he must be to have even agreed to such an egregious plan.

"You do have the right idea, though the execution of it isn't coherent," Gale says, commanding our undivided attention. "Your idea is to hit them where they're not looking. And I believe the catacombs should be far enough belowground for us to provide such an opportunity."

"How stupid do you think we are?" Daniel says. "We've tried that way, but the tunnels have all been blocked. Why else would we be desperate enough to come here in the first place?"

"But I don't think all of the tunnels are impracticable," Gale says, a slow grin blooming on his face. "And all we need to verify that, is to send Lady Vivian a message."

# Chapter 17

We hear it moments before the world rights itself again and
Pigfain's portal winks out of existence: The long, insistent bellow
of a horn. My heart stammers—another attack!

With a growl, the banshee steps closer to me, her dagger
already out. We all look up, scanning the dark skies for a sign of
the beast, but find only the twinkling lights of a spattering of stars
through a thick canopy of leaves. It takes me a long heartbeat to
realize this was a false alarm, and I expel a breath of relief. After
everything we've already been through, I don't think I'm ready
for another battle yet, not if it means I'll be facing my brother.

And as my eyes adjust to the darkness, I pick out further details
of our surroundings—faint lights flittering in the trees, the dark
glimmer of a distant creek, the furry tail of a goblin fleeing our
presence. We're definitely in Fey territory.

A knight rushes to meet us, sliding to a stop before Arthur and
Lugh.

"You're back," Hadrian says with a half-salute, his voice
deeper than I remember.

"The horn?" Arthur asks.

"From the team we sent to rescue the refugees at Fort Dubhe." Hadrian clears his throat uncomfortably. "Unfortunately, they arrived too late."

"The dragon," I whisper loudly.

Hadrian looks around owlishly, noticing me for the first time. "A lighthouse came crashing down on top of it," he says at last, before turning away again. But not before I see the flash of hate in his eyes.

"A whole lighthouse?" Keva exclaims, drawing a welcoming nod from Hadrian, and I can't help but feel a twinge at the difference in treatment between us. "How is that even possible?"

"The power keeping Avalon whole and separate from the surface world is dying," a thickly accented voice cuts in.

Gauvain and Gareth have arrived, both grinning widely despite the series of new scars adorning their faces.

"What happened to you?" Keva asks, staring at the right side of Gauvain's face. "You look like you've been scalped!"

Gareth barks out a laugh as Gauvain rubs a hand over the patch where his long dreadlocks used to be.

"Keva," Hadrian growls reprovingly, and Keva's cheeks darken in shame at the reproof.

"Sorry," she says. "I didn't mean…"

"It's all right," Gauvain says. "It does make for a rather edgier look."

"Nearly got his whole head barbecued," Gareth adds. "The dragon didn't like us going for his belly."

"And unfortunately, our E.M. doesn't seem to affect it at all," Hadrian says, with another reproachful frown at Keva. "It seems the literatures were right, and that—"

"Enough with the teachings," Gareth says.

"Have pity for our latest guests," Gauvain adds, garnering a scowl from Hadrian.

"I believe you all know each other already," Arthur says.

"I don't...," Hadrian starts, before letting his voice trail off.

"Is that you, Lady Kaede?" Gauvain booms out in surprise.

The knight seems to draw back into herself before giving a curt nod, her long dark hair swinging over her oval face. Gauvain is about to tell her something else, but Gareth elbows him roughly with his war hammer arm, pointing at Gale.

"Am I drunk, or is that a revenant?" Gareth asks, a tremor to his voice.

"*Oh, la vache[12]*!" Gauvain swears, making me nearly choke on my own saliva. "And he doesn't look a day older, either."

"A draugar?" Gareth asks instead.

"Not yet," Gale replies genially. "You two certainly have filled up quite a bit since I last saw you."

The words are barely out of his mouth that the cousins are grabbing Gale in a tight hug.

"We thought you were dead!" Gauvain exclaims, eyes uncommonly wet.

"Wait till we tell Lance," Gareth says before his cousin punches him in the shoulder. "I mean, when we see him again."

Gale pats the big knight above his war hammer. "That might be sooner than you think," he says, and the cousins grow still.

"You have a plan, then?" Hadrian asks, sounding suspicious.

A sharp breeze cuts through the trees, raising a trail of dead leaves in its wake.

"Ugh, not *him*," Gareth says, slouching dejectedly.

Keva slants a questioning look in my direction, but I've had plenty of visions to know who it is before the round Fey Lord materializes at Lugh's elbow.

---

[12] French expression of surprise similar to "holy cow."

"Back so soon?" Oberon calls out. "I take it that silly scheme of yours didn't pan out?"

"We were successful, at least in part," Lugh says without raising to the bait.

Oberon cocks a derisive brow at us, evidently less than impressed.

"Plans change," Gareth grumbles.

"It's a dynamic approach," Gauvain adds, "made to adapt to new data and events, where—"

"Spare me your lessons, you sodden bear cubs," Oberon says dismissively. "All I want to know is how you're going to get me out of this bloody mess you forcefully plunged me into."

Gareth rolls his eyes at the Fey with such a mournful sigh, I chuckle.

"Indeed," Lugh says, golden eye calculating. "I am glad of your enthusiasm, for we will require your heroic abilities once again."

At my sight, the two cousins break into identical smiles, and amble over to fold me into their crushing arms.

"I don't need to display any heroism!" Oberon shouts, and the cousins release me, tension rippling across their muscles. "That has already cost me a great many of my people, as you very well know."

"My sister wouldn't have died if she hadn't tried to save your people," a sharp voice interrupts.

Blanchefleur, looking pale but fierce as ever, lands besides Lugh to glare at Oberon. Wrapped around her shoulders is Sameerah's black mamba, now as white as snow.

"None of it would have happened if your boss hadn't invaded my territory," Oberon says.

"You let us in," Lugh points out.

"Only to tell you to buzz out!" Oberon exclaims, spittle flying. "You'd been pestering me long enough. And now you dare ask me to risk my people again just so you and your puny army can do"—he waves his hand wildly about—"do whatever it is you've planned to do this time?"

"A preemptive strike, actually," Arthur says, voice a bare whisper, "with the goal of destroying the Siege Perilous."

Lord Oberon and I both sputter at the same time. This isn't what was mentioned at the fort ruins.

"We'll have inside help," Arthur carries on, "and with you distracting them from the outside, they won't notice our presence in their midst until it's too late."

"Nobody is as fast as you and your pixies," Lugh adds placatingly.

"Except for that beast and its hellfire!" Oberon spits. "Don't you try to cajole me into doing something that you yourself refuse to do."

"We would be much obliged," Lugh says, after a slight hesitation.

Oberon opens his mouth to refuse once more, but then snaps it shut again, dark eyes glinting with greed. "How much obliged?" he asks.

"One favor," Lugh says, "as long as it does not harm my people nor myself."

Oberon's face remains impassive, waiting expectantly.

"And I will carve out a portion of my Demesne for you to resettle your colonies," Lugh finishes.

"Deal," Oberon says with a predatory smile. "Remember what happens to those who break their oaths, Lugh," he says, spinning around with great flourish. "Call me when the mission starts."

"I don't mean to bust your balls——" Gareth starts.

"——bubble," Gauvain interjects.

"——but those Dark Sidhe have got wards, you know," Gareth continues, "and we haven't been able to break through them."

We're all seated on a grassy knoll, away from all the preparations that Lugh and Hadrian are supervising. And I'm glad of it, if it means I don't have to deal with the suspicious stares and whispered accusations that have followed me everywhere I go these last couple of days. It is the welcome I'd expected to receive as a traitor, but a part of me had still hoped things would be different...better.

Well, at least I'm clean for once, I tell myself to quell the unease growing inside me. And I've got a new uniform to boot.

"And the catacombs are too well protected," Lady Ysolt adds.

I've learned she's the only faculty member who's both made it out of Lake High and can still fight. Like everyone else, the war has changed her. She's gotten leaner, meaner, and her gaunt cheeks only highlight her fevered eyes.

"I'm actually surprised at how quickly those wards got those up," Gauvain says, bouncing his knee up and down nervously.

"The wards that protected our school for so long were only decoys for the ones that are up now," Gale says. "All it took was for their creator to activate them."

"How do you know all that?" Lady Ysolt asks, fingers drumming the pommel of her sword.

A small smile plays at the edges of Gale's mouth. "There's something about being locked up in Hell that somehow sets tongues wagging," he says.

"I'm not so sure this is a good idea," Blanchefleur says, stopping her pacing long enough to stare at Gale with evident distrust. "How many draugar did you say there were?"

"Close to seven thousand," Gale says, "although our latest intervention may have brought that number down a little. We should thank Asheel, too, as a matter of fact."

"Who's Asheel?" Arthur and Lady Ysolt ask in unison.

"A horrible demon in charge of the draugar," Keva says with a shiver. "She became quite powerful after Carman used Morgan to restore her powers."

All eyes turn to me, and I try not to flinch away from them.

"It wasn't Morgan's fault," Keva quickly adds, but the harm's done.

They already think I tried to kill Arthur, now they can add this whole restoration of demons' powers to my growing list of sins. If only that were the whole extent of it.

"Carman tortured Morgan to use the Sangraal," Keva insists, "and she—"

"The Sangraal?" Lady Ysolt asks, her voice cracking like a whip. "Where is it?"

Keva shrugs, looking uncomfortable. "Still with Carman, I suppose."

"Not exactly," I say, keeping my gaze averted from their accusing stares. "I, uh, think it was absorbed by the dragon when she created it."

I hear Lady Ysolt's sharp intake of breath. "No."

"That would explain its powers," Blanchefleur says, resuming her pacing. "As well as its imperviousness to our attacks."

"And you said Carman's now intent upon freeing Balor," Arthur says, trying to shift the conversation away from me.

I nod miserably, rubbing at my temples where I can feel the beginnings of another headache.

Sameerah's old snake, currently coiled around Blanchefleur's arm, lifts its coffin-shaped head with a hiss. "That's why the Fomori have been sacrificing themselves so obediently," the Fey warrior says, "because she's promised to get their master back. Does Lugh know of this?"

"He is aware," Arthur says. "But if I got this right, he already defeated Balor once."

"A feat once performed might not necessarily be repeated," Blanchefleur states, sending another wave of unease through our little group. "Balor is no fool, he'll know what to expect. He'll make sure to destroy everything beforehand, no exceptions. Lugh wouldn't be able to resist him this time, nor, I fear, the great Danu herself."

"Which brings us back to our plan," Arthur says. "To close the Gates of Hell once and for all, *before* such a catastrophe can happen."

"Very well," Lady Ysolt says, sounding resigned. "I shall inform the Board, and let them know that I will accompany you as well."

The statement seems to shock the knights. From what Keva and I have gathered so far, things at Caamaloth are pretty dire, and Arthur's financial support notwithstanding, the Order doesn't seem too keen to be helping out around here.

"Morgan?"

Startled, I look up to find that everyone's gone but for Arthur. Arthur, who's been a constant presence at my side since I got back from Hell, even though I can barely look at him from shame. Arthur, who's made sure I'm always taken care of, even though he's evidently got more pressing matter to attend to.

Arthur, whose hand I never want to let go again.

Heat creeps from my cheeks all the way up to my hairline at that last thought, and I look quickly away. "Sorry," I mumble, pushing to my feet. "Got distracted."

Arthur gently grabs my wrist in his gloved hand, preventing me from running away like my hammering heart is telling me to.

"Morgan, what is it?" he asks.

"N-nothing," I stammer, feeling myself blush ever more furiously.

My eyes remain determinedly upon the shiny buttons of his jacket, but the rest of my body betrays me at the small lie, and Arthur immediately picks up on it. To my surprise, he doesn't insist, and lets my wrist slide free of his fingers. There was a time when he'd have ordered me to speak, forced the truth out of me. And somehow that loosens my throat.

"Why?" I ask, both terrified and eager to hear his answer. He's taller than me now, so I have to tilt my head up to look at him. "You're the one I stabbed, so why aren't you eager to have me hanged like everyone else around here?"

Arthur's hazel eyes bore into mine. "Because I trust you."

I bite back a shocked gasp, eyes going wide. Arthur can read my disbelief, for he attempts a calming smile that only makes me more nervous.

"I'd be lying if I didn't say that I have doubted you," he starts. "I mean, what happened back there..." He rubs at his side, the side where I stabbed him, and I feel the blood drain from my face. "But I know you, Morgan," his words eerily echoing my brother's. "Better than anyone else around here. Perhaps better than you know yourself, sometimes. And I know that no matter how much you posture and mouth off, you always seek to help those in need."

He flashes me his crooked grin and I feel my chest constrict in response.

"Even if you're not very good at it," Arthur continues. He turns my hand over to trace the faint ridges of the scar Dean gave me the night he freed Carman. "I've dreamed of you so many times while you were gone," he says softly, as if to himself.

I start. Surely he couldn't have had the same types of visions I've been having, could he?

His fingers wrap gently over my own. "It was hard to watch you suffer while being unable to help," he says, his voice sounding oddly strangled. "It's why I now understand...what you did."

"That's why you trust me?"

Arthur lets out a long, shaky breath, bringing my fingers up to his heart. "For ever more."

Tears pool in my eyes, spilling over onto my cheeks, warm against my cool skin. "I'm still sorry," I hiccup. "I'm so sorry I hurt you. Sh-She would've killed you if I h-hadn't made her think I'd k-killed you first. But all the same, I hate myself for what I did to you."

Arthur's arms wrap tightly around my shoulders, drawing my head against him, letting my tears soak his shirt.

I never dreamed this would happen, never dared to believe he'd forgive me this easily. I don't deserve it.

"Please don't cry," Arthur says in my hair. "Dr. Cocklebur told me that you have a perfect understanding of anatomy. A girl with that kind of knowledge wouldn't have been so off the mark if she'd truly aimed for my heart. However clumsy she may be."

I snort out a laugh against him, still unable to stop myself from crying, when a light cough makes us both jump apart guiltily.

"I don't mean to interrupt," Gale says as I wipe my runny nose on my sleeve, "but Puck's arrived."

"Right," Arthur says, looking momentarily dazed. "Right," he repeats. "I'll, uh, gather the troops, then."

Arthur hurries away, leaving me alone for the first time since my return. I can feel Gale's green eyes upon me, unnerving.

"How far are you willing to go?" he asks.

"What?" I squeak out, my face burning up with highly inappropriate images.

"To close up the Gates of Hell," Gale says, and I can't have imagined the wry amusement that flashed on his face. "How far are you willing to go?"

"Oh," I breathe, trying to gather my thoughts. "All the way, I guess," I answer. "Isn't it the case for all of us here?"

"It's your choice that matters most, though," he says. With an enigmatic smile, Gale holds his hand out to show me a poppy cradled in his callused palm, the flower already missing one of its four delicate petals. "For you, when you need a little luck."

# Chapter 18

"Remember that this isn't a suicide mission," Arthur says, pacing in front of our group. The rest of the troops are already spread out across the fields behind us, hiding in ditches and behind trees, waiting for the signal. It didn't take us long to march here, our camp far closer to the school than I'd have expected.

"Not a hundred percent, anyway," Keva whispers to me.

"The key is to draw the Sidhe out of the school," Arthur continues, "which shouldn't be too hard considering their nature, and how long they've been cooped up in Lake High."

The cousins nod their understanding. "Who could resist a good hunt?" Gauvain says.

No one laughs at his attempt at humor. The cousins are to lead the assault on the school with Oberon, while the rest of us make our way into Lake High.

My gaze flits across everyone's face, as if to memorize each and every detail—Keva biting her nails, Daniel brooding silently beside her; the banshee's hooded cloak turned to the sun, as if to soak in its warmth; Kaede staring at her fists; Hadrian tapping his pocket watch nervously; and Arthur, jaw clenching in worry. Only Lady Ysolt and Gale remain impassive as we wait for Blanchefleur and Lugh to return.

I wish I could say something to ease the tension, provide some kind of comfort, but as always, the proper words fail me.

Instead, I finish the last of the cookies Keva obligingly provided me, turning my gaze to the east. Although I cannot see it, I know that one of the school's warding stones stands not too far. And, beyond it, the landing docks, and, within the school itself, Mordred.

My hand tightens around the large ogham in my pocket, the one and only present he's ever given me. Even if I don't ever intend on using it, I simply couldn't find it in me to leave it behind with my old clothes. It is proof that, despite it all, there's some good in him. That Carman hasn't managed to pervert him entirely. But if I end up facing him now, will I be able to take him down if I have to?

"Earth to Morgan!"

I start at Keva's sharp whisper and find that everyone's setting off. I let the banshee help me to my feet, then hurry after the others. We follow Lugh in total silence, down and around a patch of burned-down trees, the remains of their charred trunks sticking out from the ashy ground like the leftover stakes of a pyre, then stop at the bottom of a large hill.

The ruins of another fort crown its top, its demise the same as that of the scorched copse of trees. But what catches my attention is Lugh's cat mewling at some uncommonly thick roots writhing at the knoll's base, like a giant squid's tentacles.

"Watch where you are standing," Lugh says, and I have to hold onto the banshee to keep from falling as the ground starts to buck and cave, until a gaping hole the size of a man is staring at us in the hill's sided.

"Our involuntary host seems to have put up more of a fight than I'd expected," Gale says, greeting Puck as the hobgoblin emerges from the newly-made tunnel with a bottle of milk.

"It does not bode well," Lugh concedes, "but we will have to make do."

"Is this linked to the courtyard?" Lady Ysolt asks, sniffing in suspicion.

"Correct," Gale says. "Now follow me before its owner realizes exactly what's happening."

I don't miss the questioning glance Arthur throws Gale, but Lance's brother just motions us after him. I shake off the feeling of déjà-vu as Blanchefleur summons a couple of floating orbs to light our way and we file in one after the other, remembering quite clearly the time I'd followed Puck down another secret passage to discover the Sangraal.

"You sure this ain't a trap?" Daniel asks, struggling to untangle his sword from a knot of vines protruding from the wall.

"You should know by now there is never any certainty in this world," Gale says. "Less so when dealing with the Fey."

"This is a Fey tunnel?" Daniel gasps, sounding like he wished he'd stayed behind.

"Wow, Daniel, how did you not repeat a year?" Keva asks.

"This is how all Fey Demesnes used to be, when once we lived amongst humans," Lugh says wistfully. "The entry guarded by a tree, the way to the inner sanctum only accessible if it deemed you worthy. Now, only the strongest Lords have the ability to keep such an abode, leaving the weakest of our kind at the mercy of all our enemies."

"What...bloody...tree are we...talking about?" Daniel huffs, nearly taking Keva's head off when he finally manages to pull his weapon free.

"The Apple Tree, stupid, haven't you been paying attention?" Keva says, kicking him in the shin before scurrying further down. "So, is the school, like, Lady Vivian's Demesne then?"

"Not quite," Gale says, straightening up as the tunnel grows larger. "She took over control of it for us. For now, at least. The true master of the place is yet unknown, though I have a hunch."

"I don't understand," I say. "How can a school that trains knights also be presided by a Fey, and one that none of you actually knows?"

Blanchefleur shrugs noncommittally. "There may be a thousand reasons why. But the likeliest is that there's a covenant at play, which means Lady Vivian cannot tell us a thing about it."

"But you've been here before," I say to Lugh's back, still confused, "and you've even been here. So how come you don't know any of this?"

"Because he wasn't there when the school was built," Blanchefleur says curtly.

"But the Watchers—" I keep on insisting.

"—came later," Blanchefleur snaps, as our tunnel forks ahead.

We look down to Puck, who's sucking ravenously on his milk bottle, and the hobgoblin points left, to the narrower of the two passages.

"I read that the school was founded by the first Myrdwinn, and that he was half-Fey himself," Hadrian says after a short while. "It's how he was able to teach knights how to use oghams. And Lady Vivian didn't arrive until perhaps a century later."

"All that is true," Lugh says, ducking under a low-hanging root. "I am at fault for ignoring the happenings at this school for so long. I should have known that, although we wished to live retired from the world and its affairs, the world was far from done with us."

I muffle a curse as I bang my head against the suddenly low ceiling, and the banshee hisses reprovingly at the offending root. By now, the tunnel's grown so narrow we're forced to file one after the other, bent in half.

"What if things don't go according to plan?" Keva whispers, voicing our fears.

"The cousins' diversion should be enough to drive most of the demons out, and Oberon's got the dragon if it shows up at all," Arthur says. "But if any of us gets into any serious trouble, there's only one thing we can do."

"Take cover inside the church," Hadrian says, repeating our prior instructions.

Assuming it's still standing, I mentally add. Daniel said the Sidhe couldn't access it like the rest of the school, but he escaped ages ago. And I doubt Carman would let Father Tristan defy her for so long without taking matters into her own hands. But that's an eventuality none of us dared mention.

"Almost there," Gale whispers.

I find myself holding my breath as we emerge into a concentric room just wide enough to hold us all. It seems to be some kind of extension from the tunnel, its walls and ceiling made entirely of tangled tree roots and smooth heartwood.

"I take it we're inside the tree?" Keva asks in wonder.

"Should we cut our way out?" Arthur asks.

"It won't be necessary," Lugh says.

As if in response, his cat starts rubbing itself against the wooden wall, purring loudly. With a solemn nod, Puck tosses his empty bottle of milk to the floor, sets his small hands upon the spot marked by the cat, and pushes.

A diffuse light blooms under his pudgy fingers, before shooting up in a straight line towards the curved ceiling, splintering at regular intervals in smaller, angled lines like the bones of a fish.

"Better get your weapons ready," Gale says, his spear already poking out of his arm while he presses his other hand against the now door-sized glyph.

The wood parts outward at his touch, like the petals of a flower, and we creep into the fine rain that has started to fall over Lake High's inner courtyard.

"Do you hear that?" Keva whispers.

"It's started," Daniel replies, looking pale.

I repress a shiver at the distant sounds of battle. Gale's plan has worked. Oberon's and the cousins' concerted attack has managed to draw out most of the Dark Sidhe that otherwise haunt the school.

"Come on," Hadrian urges us, and we all find refuge inside Miss Linette's ransacked herbarium.

The spacious classroom is eerily quiet. It smells of mildew and fire, the professor's preciously-tended plants and flowers having been mercilessly put to the flame, every pot and vial destroyed. But despite the carnage, it seems there are enough traces of Fey-repellant plants and concoctions left to have kept the Dark Sidhe at bay.

"Time to split up," Arthur says.

Keva gives me a wobbly smile. "Are you sure you'll be fine without me?" she asks.

This is the first time we'll be separated since getting out of Hell. She's to go with Gale, Hadrian, Daniel and Blanchefleur down to the prison to set whoever's left from our school free.

I let out a raspy laugh. "I've got the banshee with me, don't I?" I say. "Besides, if we succeed, they'll be cut off from their reinforcements."

"Let's hope Carman will get stuck on the other side too," Keva says.

"Let's go, Keva," Hadrian calls out, his eyes flicking over to me, mistrust plain on his face.

"Let's hope," I manage to say, as Keva leaves, flicking her long braid over her shoulder.

Arthur leads us straight into a passage that separates the herbarium from the library, and I gag as I take in a whiff of something that smells suspiciously like a clogged-up toilet. It seems to be coming from a dark archway to our left and, to my greatest disgust, it's where Arthur wants us to go.

Kaede goes in first, followed by Lugh, neither of them making a sound in the dark staircase.

"Watch it," Arthur whispers, motioning to a wet spot on the floor as I finally muster the courage to go up the stairs.

I nod, but no matter how much I wish to avoid it, the thick goo is everywhere, coating every step and the railing itself, as if a giant slug's marked its territory in here. Soon, the sucking sounds of boots treading up the stairs are so loud, I'm afraid we're going to be found out long before we reach the KORT room. Except we're not.

Heart thumping, I finally reach the first floor landing, and wait for Arthur's signal to move into the hallway. I still keep expecting demons to pop out of one of the rooms, or perhaps Mordred, or even Carman herself. But as we pass by shredded tapestries, and door after wrecked door, without meeting another soul, my breathing slowly eases. Gale's plan is working way better than I thought!

At last, we round another corner and the KORT room's carved door comes into view, waiting for us at the other end of the corridor. Our footsteps grow more hurried. Already I can pick out the wooden panel's intricate detail's—the scales on the dragon's body, the raised hackles on the hunting dogs' necks.

"Stand back!" Lugh bellows from behind us.

We skid to a sudden stop as the ebony door swings open, revealing a roomful of demons, and my stomach plummets. Of course, this was too easy. I should've known.

"Miss me much?" a beautiful man says, his eyes the icy blue of winter lakes, blond hair so pale it looks like snow.

"Gadreel," I whisper, stomach sinking.

"It has been a while," Lugh says, edging his way in front of us. "In fact, it should have been a while longer still."

"I thought you'd had your balls cut off, pretty boy," Gad says with a grin that doesn't reach his eyes. "Bet daddy will be happy to do it for you, though."

A muscle twitches in Lugh's cheek. "Balor will remain in the deepest pit of Hell," he says, "and I will make sure you join him back there."

Gad lets out a soft chuckle that makes my hairs stand on end. "I'd love to play with you, but I've got to finish the game I started with your girl first. She's been rather naughty of late."

Lugh lunges forward, energy crackling all around him. Gad doesn't move, doesn't try to dodge the attack. Then a large shadow moves between them, colliding into Lugh with the force of a hurricane. The blast hurls me backward, slamming me against the wall. Light explodes in the hallway as I land flat on the floor, the wind knocked out of me.

I twist around, use the wall to pull myself to my feet, and try to shake the loud buzzing from my ears. Lugh's gone, a large gash cutting across the flagstones the only trace left of his presence.

"Where is he?" I ask, my voice sounding muffled to my own ears.

"Oh, don't expect Lugh to come to your rescue any time soon," Gad says, as more demons crowd in behind him, "Az is keeping him busy."

I swallow hard, telling myself this is good, that we have one less demon to face, that Lugh's strong. But so is Azazel.

"Morgan?" Arthur calls out.

"Fine," I say, catching sight of Kaede at the end of the opposite hallway.

Gad's grin widens. "Ready to play?" he asks.

The banshee scuttles to my side, and I play on my injury to lean into her. "You guys get the chair," I whisper to her.

She goes very still, before I push away from her, eyes boring into the statuesque demon.

"Have you come to steal my power?" I ask him, trying to keep Gadreel's focus on me while I inch away from the rest of my party.

"What power?" Gad asks with a smirk. "You can barely stand."

"Funny you should say that," I say, "cause last time I saw you, you were begging for just a taste of it. On your knees."

The moment I see the vein at his temple throb, I know I've got him.

"Isn't that why Az has to protect you from Lugh?" I continue, reaching for my power.

For a moment, I'm afraid I've gotten too cocky. I haven't tried using my abilities since I've gotten back from Hell. What if they don't work?

But then I feel it respond deep in the pit of my stomach, rolling over, stretching, as if waking from a long sleep. I open my hand and water erupts from my palm in a thick torrent to go crashing into the KORT room.

"Now!" I shout at the others.

Out of the corner of my eye, I see Arthur and Kaede rush inside, but the banshee remains behind me. And as she growls at Gad, I find myself glad she didn't listen.

Gad's laugh resounds through the hallway, water dripping harmlessly down his soaked hair. "I'd take you a little more seriously if you weren't shaking so much," he says.

I sense his attack before I see it. I throw myself to the side, taking the banshee down with me, just as the floor explodes in a shower of dust and pebbles. With a low hiss, the banshee throws herself in front of me as Gadreel punches the air again.

There's a thunderous *crack* and the banshee flies into the arched windows, her body hitting one of the stone pillars before sliding soundlessly to the floor in a pile of grey rags. My mind goes blank with rage. I kick off hard from the floor, vision narrowed down to one target only: Gadreel.

The demon flashes another smile at my approach. This is a game to him. But at the last second, I veer to the left, kicking sideways as I go. His punch connects with my booted foot in a resounding *clap*, sending me flying through the KORT room.

Without slowing down, I use my momentum to bounce off the back of some creature, bone crunching beneath my boots, then hurtle straight back at Gad. The demon spins around, lifting his left arm to counter me. This time, I don't avoid the contact. I ram into Gad, flattening him against the wall. My fingers close around his neck, and I let all my rage and hatred pour out.

Gad's smirk disappears as my power shoots straight into him, wave after burning wave, his alabaster skin turning black around the collar. The smell of burning meat is thick in my nostrils as he punches me in the sides. I feel my rubs crack, but refuse to let go. All I can think of is to make him pay for what he's done to the banshee, and rid the earth of this scumbag.

Gad's eyes grow wide with fear. "What are you?" he croaks, now desperate to pry my fingers off him.

It is my turn to smile as I bring him down to his knees. "Haven't you heard?" I drawl, my hands never leaving his neck as his body starts twitching beneath me. "I am the devil's daughter."

"Enough, Morgan!"

I snarl at Arthur as he grabs me roughly by the arm to pull me away from Gad. He flinches, hazel eyes wide in shock, and I freeze.

"Misstresss!" the banshee calls out.

I blink at my raised hand, note my curled fingers poised to strike, and slowly drop it again.

"I'm sorry," I mumble, shivers running down my back. "I didn't mean…"

My eyes fall upon Gad's body still spasming on the floor, his torso, throat, and half of his beautiful face now a disturbing tableau of blisters and open wounds, as if he's been cooked from the inside. Then, with a final jerk of his foot, the demon stops moving.

It's over. Bile rises to my throat.

"Come, we need to get out of here," Arthur says harshly.

"What about the Siege—" I start.

"Didn't work," Arthur says through gritted teeth.

"Over here," Kaede says, emerging from the KORT room covered in black ichor. "Quick!"

I glance around at the sound of heavy footsteps coming from the other hallway. The banshee takes down the first intruder with a well-placed stab to the neck, but more are coming.

"Come on, Morgan!" Arthur shouts, moving after Kaede.

"Banshee!" I call out, following the others inside the KORT room.

The place is littered with corpses, the massive round table still intact despite the blood sprayed across its dark wood. And, standing innocuously beside it, is the Siege Perilous, its demon and angel carvings motionless now that Mordred's not sitting on it.

Arthur's waiting for me at the entrance of the once-hidden alcove that hid the scrying mirror, the long velvet drapes that covered it now shredded. The very place where I stabbed him.

"Come on," he urges me.

But I can't make myself move. I look back at the Siege Perilous, hating how much we've sacrificed for this chance to destroy it, only to fail.

"There's gotta be a way," I say.

"It must be activated before you can even think to destroy it."

I jump at the soft voice and Arthur swings Excalibur around to point it at the girl making her slow way out of the alcove's recess.

"Jennifer?" Arthur asks.

Jennifer's rosy cheeks dimple, looking breathtakingly beautiful. I frown. There's something off with her, more so than usual. Arthur and I both step back as she continues to advance.

"Arthur," she says, with a slight dip of her head. "It has been a while since we last saw each other."

"Aren't you...I thought you were being held prisoner," Arthur stammers.

"Things have changed since you left me, Arthur," Jennifer says, stopping only when we bump against the round table.

There's a rush of movement at the door and I swing my attention back to the front of the room in time to see the banshee duck beneath a troll's fist.

I raise my hands, fire springing to life above my blackened fingers. "Perhaps you two should have your little lovers' spat another time," I say. "Down!" I shout to the banshee.

She drops to the floor as I send a blaze of fire sizzling over her cowl, hitting the troll in the chest. Jennifer's laugh is a little more strident this time, unhinged. I cock an inquisitive eyebrow in her direction.

"Why are you being so mean to me, Morgan?" she asks.

Yep. Definitely off. Being held captive here must have made her lose the rest of her marbles, and she didn't have that many to begin with.

"After everything I've done for you?" she continues.

I frown. "You mean after you tried to kill me?"

She waves her hand dismissively, before settling it sweetly on Arthur's arm. "Oh, but I sent you a present so you could forgive me," she says, trailing her finger absently on the lapel of Arthur's jacket. "Did you not receive it?"

"Present?" I echo in confusion.

"Hmmm, I recall you getting attached to this one human up on the surface world," Jennifer says in mock thought. "Did I get it wrong?"

"Jennifer," Arthur says in warning.

"You know," Jennifer continues, cruel eyes not leaving my face, "the one who gave birth right after you rescued her? Did you not see her down there?"

"What?" I say feebly. For a second, I'm back in Hell, staring at the cadavers that have poured out of the overturned cauldron.

"I'm afraid returns aren't possible," Jennifer coos. "But I can always get you another one. I hear her son is now with his grandpa."

"It was you?" I ask.

"It did make it to you then," Jennifer says with a feral smile that reminds me of Carman. "No need to thank me then. It was my pleasure."

"Will you shut up?" Arthur shouts, slapping Jennifer across the face so hard, her lip breaks open.

Anger flashes on her beautiful face, but then her smile comes back in full force. "Oh, Arthur, *darling*," she says, licking the blood from her lips. "I know Morgan's always been your weak point. But it's OK. I forgive you. After all, if it weren't for you abandoning me in my time of direst need, I wouldn't have discovered my inner strength."

She raises her hand, red sparks trailing her delicate fingers in the air.

"You see," she continues, "I've found out I'm also part Gibborim. Let me show you."

"No!" I shout, as if from far away.

Jennifer's hand flies towards Arthur, lightning gathered around it. I watch him lift his sword arm in defense. Too slow.

Then Kaede's suddenly behind, deadly blades singing as she swings them down. But, to my surprise, Jennifer evades the attack gracefully, slashing her arm instead in Kaede's direction. The knight ducks under the lightning bolt, spinning around, swords extended, forcing Jennifer away from us.

"Lady Kaede, is that really you?" Jennifer asks, evading Kaede's relentless offensives without ever breaking a sweat.

I find myself unable to tear my gaze away from the two girls, their moves so quick I have a hard time seeing them. When did Jennifer get so good at fighting? Then I hear a slight gasp and Jennifer falls down to one knee, her long dress caught under Kaede's boot.

"Jennifer!" Arthur calls out, making Kaede look up.

"Don't," I say, trying to stop him.

"But she's one of us," Arthur says. "She must—"

His next words are swallowed in the explosion that follows as Jennifer blasts Kaede off her, taking part of the wall with it. Arthur's brows furrow in confusion as Jennifer slowly gets back to her feet, dusting her dress off.

I fling my hands out, ready to defend us at the slightest wrong move from her.

"What did they do to you?" Arthur asks.

Jennifer trains her cold blue eyes on him. "They didn't *do* anything to me, Arthur," she says. "Haven't you been listening? I am a daughter of the Nephilim, just like your beloved Morgan."

A deep chill settles in my bones. What is she saying?

My bewilderment must have shown, for Jennifer's cheeks dimple once again.

"Oh, Morgan, you never were too bright, were you?" she says, raising every hair on my body. "Well, let me spell it out for you: I am part Fey too."

# CHAPTER 19

"Still doesn't make you likeable," I say automatically, my brain unable to compute Jennifer's latest inane assertion.

Surely the girl must be kidding, or she must've been brainwashed. There's no way the one who professed her hatred for the Fey on a daily basis, the one who tried to kill me…also has Fey blood in her. But the way she fought Kaede, the explosion she caused, all without a single ogham on her, give credence to her words.

"Misst—"

The banshee's cry of alarm is cut short.

"Banshee!" Arthur and I shout together as she topples over sideways.

"I hope I'm not intruding," Mordred says, kicking the banshee's body aside to step through the doorway.

I balk at his sight, eyes gliding back and forth between him and Jennifer, mind racing. Mordred's hooded eyes scan the KORT room, taking in the damage we've caused. His woad tattoos are stark against his pale skin, that strange horn of his hanging from a long yellow silk belt at his hip. I narrow my eyes, momentarily distracted by the colorful garment.

"When you escaped from Carman's clutches," Mordred says, brows lowered, "I thought you'd have been smart enough to vanish for good. Instead, you make a spectacle of yourself, and get more of your precious knights killed in the process. Not that I mind this in the least."

His words form a tight knot of fear in my chest.

"Smart isn't part of her vocabulary," Jennifer says with a disdainful sneer, gliding over to Mordred, and snaking her arms around his waist possessively.

I look back down at his yellow belt, comprehension dawning, and bark out a shocked laugh. "A Lady's Favour?" I ask, still giggling uncontrollably. "You two are together, really?"

Arthur's concerned look turns into one of horror as he takes in my brother and his ex.

But I remember the night Mordred kidnapped me, when he'd asked me about my life at Lake High, the classes, and the students. The conversation had quickly turned to Jennifer—the most beautiful girl the world had ever seen, as he'd quoted. I'd taken his curiosity to stem from the desire of someone who wanted to know as much about his enemy as possible.

But it was more than that. I guessed as much back in Hell. Mordred's my brother, a boy whose life was stolen from him when he was little.

And now he's stealing it back.

"Do you remember what I told you, Mordred?" I say. "About finding a better way to get what you want?"

Jennifer smirks. "Mordred doesn't listen to anyone, least of all you."

"It's not too late to make this right," I say, ignoring her.

I can't fault him for what he's done. It's not like he ever really had a choice. Until now.

"I'm afraid it is you who has it all wrong," Mordred tells me.

He looks pensively outside, and I twist around to follow his gaze. Despite the pelting rain, the cousins' squads are still fighting hard, bright flares of power indicating their presence, like beacons in the night.

I squint, heart beating wildly. Is it me or are they getting closer? If so, it can only mean one thing...

"You're losing," I say with a tight smile. "Even with the help of your draugar, your army's falling back."

"Am I?" Mordred asks with a chuckle.

I frown. What is he playing at? I cast another quick glance outside, but I wasn't hallucinating. Our forces have successfully managed to push the enemy back, and I can even distinguish Gareth's war hammer flashing with every strike of his.

So why is Mordred still so confident?

Arthur lets out a strangled sound, and I turn in time to see him backing away from the Siege Perilous, Excalibur pointed straight at the carved demons whirring along its back.

"Mordred, what are you doing?" I say in a strangled voice.

Mordred laughs, his face glowing. "Have you ever stopped to consider why the Siege Perilous came to be here?" he asks instead. "It is because our kind was always meant to have a place at KORT. We are the only ones to whom the seat responds. We are the only *worthy* ones."

"Thought it would actually be an excellent reason not to be here," I say through gritted teeth.

Shrugging Jennifer off, Mordred struts across the room, and sinks into the carved seat with a satisfied air. Smoke billows out from the Siege Perilous's base, and Arthur and I watch with dread as it coalesces into a thick, viscous liquid. As if from its own volition, the tar shoots across the floor to curl around and up the table's legs, forming a large viscous sphere around it that smells of sulfur and putrefaction.

"Please, Mordred, don't do this," I say, unable to tear my eyes away from the opening portal. "You have no idea what you're doing!"

Mordred's tattooed face grows hard. "I know exactly what I'm doing," he says flatly. "I'm going to finish our mother's task—no, her *duty*—and set things right for us again. I'm the one who will break our curse and free everyone from their eternal yoke, just as the prophecy foretold."

"What prophecy?" I shout over the growing din of excited shouts and clanking metal coming from the other side of the Gate. "There's no such thing as prophecies!"

I catch movement out of the corner of my eye, then something flashes, blinding me momentarily, and I hear Mordred swear loudly as something clatters to the stone floor.

"You're going to pay for this, mortal!" Mordred seethes, as I swipe the still rolling object up.

I stare uncomprehendingly at the block of dark wood in my hand, each side carved in delicate whirls like stylized clouds, then hiss in a breath. This is one of the Siege Perilous's finials[13]!

I look up, the thrill of realization sending a rush of adrenaline down my veins.

"Not so fast," Jennifer hisses in my ear, grabbing my arm and twisting it viciously around.

With a cry of pain, I drop to the floor, the lopped off finial sliding through my fingers. Jennifer's knee digs into the small of my back, and with her free hand, she yanks on my hair to force my head up.

"Take a good look at Arthur," she says in my ear. "Might be the last time you get to see him."

---

[13] The carved ornament at the beginning or end of a piece of furniture.

178

My stomach churns at Mordred's bark of laughter. Arthur's hanging upside-down in front of him, his body suspended by thick green ropes of sickly power, Excalibur's point scraping against the floor.

"What a pair you two make," Mordred says disdainfully.

"Put him down!" I shout, straining against Jennifer's hold.

Mordred lets out another laugh. "Now, now," he says, "you should be glad that I can finally get rid of him for you, after all his bullying."

"He didn't bully me," I retort.

"That wasn't the tune you were singing at the beginning," Mordred says, shaking his head, "but perhaps I misspoke. He didn't bully you so much as treat you like a prisoner, a slave. Even tried to drown you on your first day here."

"No, he——" I stop myself short, remembering that long-forgotten day when I dove after Arthur into Lake Winnebago, thinking he was the one drowning. That was before I knew anything about Lake High, the Fey, knights, or Carman.

I blink the memory away. How does Mordred even know about that?

"If you're so worried about avenging me," I say, "then you should take a closer look at your girlfriend. She's the one who bullied me the most." Jennifer's grip tightens, and I swallow a gasp of pain back down.

"All done out of ignorance," Mordred says. "Unlike the object of your infatuation. As I promised you once before, it is high time he and the others of his ilk paid for their sins. Which is why I'm glad you so readily accepted my little invitation."

"What invitation?" I ask, seething.

Mordred motions towards the windows and the battlefield beyond. "This time, when the Gates open, there will have been enough Fey blood spilled on these grounds for the school's wards to keep them open at all times." He grins wolfishly. "Even without my being seated on the Siege Perilous."

My stomach plummets, the pieces of the puzzle finally falling together. He's doing what Dean did to free up his mother, but on a much grander scale. And we helped him do it by leading all these unsuspecting knights and Fey straight into his trap, their very sacrifice the key to our undoing.

"But you helped save me," I say, forcing the words through my constricted throat. "You helped me escape!"

"Oh, honey," Jennifer says, "you didn't actually think someone wanted you for the pleasure of your company, did you?"

With a howl of rage, I shove back, power slamming against Jennifer until I feel her hold relent, then spin around, and punch her in the face. My knuckles shatter her cheekbone, and she drops away, looking stunned and afraid, her delicate hand holding onto her face.

But I don't let myself relish the moment, and rush immediately to Arthur's help. He's still hanging in the air, the vines now wrapped tightly around his torso, binding his arms so he can barely move. My fingers wrap around Excalibur's grip, and I pull the sword free.

Excalibur pulses in my hands as it sings through the air before cutting through Arthur's bindings. I can feel the heat coming through the Gates on my back as I whittle down the green ropes in quick cuts.

Arthur's eyes widen. "Behind...," he gasps.

I look over my shoulder, but I'm too slow to react. Small-fingered hands grab my arms, surprisingly strong, before jerking me away from Arthur. I cry out as teeth puncture my flesh, the draugar latching onto my back like a giant leech.

Tears streaming down my face, I reach around with the sword, but this is a dead person I'm dealing with, impervious to pain. I scream as the draugar rips a piece of my neck off. Hot blood gushes out of my wound, pouring down my uniform. Then the terrible grip suddenly releases, and the severed head of a teenaged girl rolls past me.

An oval face swims in front of me. "You good?" Kaede asks, skewering a second draugar before it can cross into our world.

With a weak nod, I stagger back to Arthur.

"Hurry," Arthur urges me.

I nearly lose my balance as I swing Excalibur around, slicing through the last vine holding him up, and Arthur finally drops to the floor with a muted groan.

"Ready?" Kaede asks.

I can feel her moving around us, hear the wet sound of her swords as they cut demons and draugar open, but I can't take my eyes off of Mordred. He's still seated on the Siege Perilous, watching us curiously like we're some kind of freak show, confident in the fact that no matter what we do, we're doomed.

And he's right. Except for the gap above his right ear, where Excalibur clearly lobbed off a piece of the seat.

"Ready?" Kaede asks again, louder.

My hands tighten around Excalibur's hilt. But there too many demons pouring inside the KORT room now, pressing in, crowding the space between me and my brother.

I flinch as something growls to my left, and turn in time to see Arthur kick an ash-covered beast in the muzzle.

"Ready?" Kaede asks louder.

I blink in confusion, only now noticing Kaede ahead. The knight is carving us a path toward the wall, her twin swords flashing golden in the sputtering torchlights as she fells demons and draugar alike without ever pausing for breath.

"Come on," Arthur says, prying Excalibur from my clenched hands, and we take off after Kaede, catching up with her at the alcove.

"Get in there," Kaede says, shoving us inside the narrow passage before turning back to face the room.

"But—"

"Hurry," Arthur says, forcing me deeper inside the dark recess.

I look back through the tattered drapes in time to see Kaede angling back towards the still open Gates, and my footsteps grind to a halt. What is she trying to do?

"What are you doing?" Arthur asks, out of breath.

"We can't leave them here," I say.

"Your friends will be fine."

I whirl around at the gravelly voice, squinting in the darkness. "Owen?"

Owen cocks his head at Arthur, eyes two pools of black. "But you won't be if you don't leave now."

"Is that a threat?" Arthur asks, voice strained.

"A statement of fact," Owen says evenly, and I remember how his cryptic words down in Hell turned out to be true.

I draw near Arthur. "He's cool," I say. "Let's get—"

Arthur slumps against the wall, and I bite hard on my lip not to scream.

"Arthur, what's wrong?" I ask, reaching for him. I let out a low hiss as my fingers brush against his damp skin, heat rising from him in feverish waves.

"He needs a doctor," Owen says. "Leave now, or it'll be too late."

I nod, trying not to let panic overwhelm me, and shoulder Arthur up into a standing position, ready to carry him if I have to. But even then, I hesitate. Neither the banshee, nor Kaede, as I now know, would abandon us like this. But if I go back in there, Arthur won't make it.

"Hurry," Owen says.

Guilt weighing heavily upon me, I grip Arthur tighter to my side, and start after the boy. Owen presses the catch behind the floor-to-ceiling mirror, and it swings open silently, revealing a set of steep stairs that will lead us outside. Yet I still pause.

"Tell them I'll come back for them," I say, looking into Owen's unfathomable eyes.

Then, like the worst of deserters, I abandon my most faithful friends to their fates.

# CHAPTER 24

I squeal in surprise as an orb of crackling fire the size of a basketball hits the wall behind us, missing my face by inches. Cursing, I raise my free hand in defense, eyes darting across our ravaged surroundings for the attacker.

"Stay back," I tell Arthur, as he staggers away from me, face pale in the storm.

I turn slowly, gathering the water to me until two large discs are floating before us like large shields. Then a shadow darts at the edge of my vision.

"Morgan?"

I try to reel in my attack, the first disc of water veering at the last second to crash into the half-finished wall of the asylum across the path. I squint against the rain as the small girl reappears from behind some of the fallen masonry, short hair flattened to her skull.

"Bri?" I call out tentatively.

"What are you doing here?" Bri asks. She's taller than I remember, but just as skinny as before, giving her the gaunt look of a wraith.

"I should be asking you the same thing," I retort.

"It really is you!" Bri exclaims in an excited whisper, rushing to meet us. "I knew it! You and Arthur got this army to take the school back, didn't you?"

"Uh, close," I say, glancing nervously back to see if we've been followed. "But we haven't exactly been successful."

Bri's shoulders sag. "I guess it was too much to hope for," she says, and for once, I have nothing to add. She approaches us cautiously, nose wrinkling at Arthur's injuries. "What are you doing now then?" she asks more guardedly.

"Getting out of here," I say.

"We need to get to the church," Arthur says, struggling to keep upright.

"Can you help?" I ask.

"Of course," Bri says.

She grabs Arthur's other side, and together we help him up the path, boots squelching in the mud. I try not to gag at the stench that emanates from the old asylum as we slowly make our way past it. Arthur slips at the sight of the mounds that peek from behind the asylum's last standing walls. Piles and piles of bodies stacked on top of each other in varying stages of decomposition, many wearing our uniform.

"Let's take a break," he says weakly.

"Here?" Bri asks, sounding petrified.

But I can also hear her gasping for breath.

"Just a couple minutes," I say, already turning towards the mass grave. Maybe that'll be enough for Arthur to recover enough so he can stand on his own two feet for the rest of the way. As long as nobody notices us.

"Get away from her!"

I wheel around at the shout, pulling Arthur closer, and catch sight of a disheveled boy, tall and wiry, glasses askew on his nose.

And, held threateningly in his fists, a large hammer he must have pilfered from the forge.

"Who…," I start.

"Jack," Bri says, shrinking away from the tall boy, and my eyes go round as I finally recognize him.

"Hi Jack," I start slowly, afraid of making any sudden movement that might trigger him. "This isn't what it looks like. I mean, it is, but we're on your side. Or, rather, you're on ours, right?"

But Jack isn't staring at me.

"It's just us," I continue, "on our way out before all Hell breaks loose."

Never thought I'd say that and mean it literally.

"You're not running away this time," Jack says, his hammer tracking Bri's movements as she carefully edges her way around the remains of an old rusted boat that crashed into the middle of the gravelly path.

I eye him wearily, wondering suddenly whether he has been turned like Jennifer.

"It's not what you think, Jack," Bri says.

"It's *exactly* what I think, and you know it, you filthy traitor," Jack growls, and Bri winces guiltily.

My eyes flicker between Bri and Jack, whom I only remember as being friends. What in the world is going on?

"It's OK, Jack," I say, "Bri's with us. She's helping us escape."

Jack's frown deepens. "You wouldn't be saying that if you knew she's the one who destroyed our school's wards," he says.

I try on a laugh that quickly dies down at the sight of Bri's stony face.

"That can't be right," I say, feeling Arthur shiver against me.

"I was there when Lady, no, that knave Jennifer freed her," Jack says as Bri remains tongue-tied. "There was no room for interpretation."

"It wasn't me," Bri says in a tiny voice.

Quick footsteps draw up to us, and we all four freeze as a shape darts around the boat's rusted hull.

"What are you all doing here?" Keva's sharp voice cracks. "You do realize there's a war going on, and that we're right in the middle of it?"

Daniel emerges behind her, a long gash on his forehead. Seems their operation didn't go smoothly either.

"Excellent timing, Daniel," Keva says. "Why don't you help Arthur, so we can—"

"I'm not going anywhere with that backstabber," Jack says loudly.

A booming laugh rings out from above, and fear spreads across Bri's features like flame to paper. I whirl around, towards the asylum. An old man is climbing his way down from the nearest pile of corpses, long beard tucked in his belt. The old school director snickers as Bri backs into Arthur, his moss-green eyes almost glowing in the rain.

"It's him," Bri says, sounding terrified. "He's the one who played me…who's betrayed us all."

"Myrdwinn?" Keva says, looking at Bri in confusion.

Myrdwinn's shoulders shake with laughter. "Didn't I say following my instructions would bring your brother back?" he asks the timbre of his voice strangely off from its usual wobbly notes, yet also somehow…familiar. "And behold, he's right here. Ask your friend, there"—he points at me with a gnarled finger—"she's seen him. Twice."

Arthur's gloved hand reaches for mine, his other reaching over his head for Excalibur. I don't know what's going on, but one thing's for sure: One of us here is definitely batting for the other team.

The question is, who?

"Are you saying you listened to this mental person, and it led to this?" Keva asks Bri.

"It's true I wasn't myself for a while there," Myrdwinn says, using his pinky like a Q-tip to dig out some earwax, "but that little...setback...has been fixed."

He draws himself to his full height then, his spine straightening from its hunched-over posture. I blink confusedly as his hair grows shorter, going from pearly white to russet brown, the lines of his face smoothing out, until I finally recognize the young man that now stands before us.

It's the same guy I caught speaking with Dean when we were first attacked, the very one I also spied having an intimate moment with—

"Lady Vivian," I say, my insides turning to ice.

It can't be. She's the one who helped us get back inside Lake High. She couldn't have known this man wanted to destroy the school.

Myrdwinn's young, angular face is cut by a cruel smile. "As I said, that particular issue's been fixed," he says. "Now as for the others..."

Without a single warning, the world starts to shake.

"Watch it!" Arthur shouts.

I throw myself to the side as a gaping hole opens beneath us, taking the old boat down with it. There's a loud yell, and I see Bri's dark curls vanish into its depths.

"Hold on!" Arthur shouts, diving in after her.

Myrdwinn's laughter redoubles as he aims for Keva next. His fingers twitch, and a thin vine shoots out of the ground to wrap itself around her ankles. Keva hits the muddy ground with a wet *thud* before being dragged towards the crater.

"Keva!" both Daniel and Jack scream at the same time.

"Leave them be!" I shout at Myrdwinn, jumping back to my feet.

And with a growl, I punch the air. A blast of icy wind tears through the grounds, turning everything it touches to frost. But with the barest of movements, Myrdwinn sweeps my attack aside.

"You do not have what it takes to destroy me, girl," Myrdwinn says. "Do not think I'm like my brothers, who were either too soft-hearted or soft-brained."

I barely have the chance to see him move before his strong arms close around me. My back cracks as I try to break free.

"Mine at last," Myrdwinn breathes.

And before anyone else can do a thing, he's carrying me up into the stormy sky. The howling wind buffets us as we climb ever higher, rain like ice picks stabbing at every exposed part of my body.

"Put me down!" I shout.

"Funny how such an iddy biddy thing like you has managed to cause so much trouble," Myrdwinn says. "And I've got to wonder, is it because of your blood, or are you simply too hare-brained to get anything right? My money's on the second option. But let's see, shall we?"

Pain rips through my chest. Heart stuttering. Muscles spasming. We break through the sky-lake's dome, and the murky water fills my cramping lungs, burning as it steals away the last of my oxygen.

All at once, Myrdwinn's gone, leaving me to drown alone in Lake Winnebago's freezing waters. Panic seizes me. I need to get back to the others. But I can't move, can't see a thing. My heartbeat is slowing. My thoughts sluggish.

Then something hits my sternum hard, and I fling my eyes open, water vomiting out of me. I grab at the person holding me, needing to feel their warmth around me.

"Easy there," Lugh says, rubbing little circles on my back to ease the chills. "I have you now."

I choke back a sob at the sound of his warm voice. I'm alive. And so is he. I clasp my arms around him, hugging him close. Only now do I realize how terrified I was of losing him to Az. My dark, brooding Fey lord who's always watched over me.

"You are fine now," Lugh says, gently helping me up.

He's brought me back to the asylum grounds, and I give the others a wobbly smile, glad to see them all safe and sound, even Bri and Arthur.

"She's not fine," Arthur retorts, sounding furious. "She nearly died!"

"But she is here now," Lugh says. "If it weren't for Lady Vivian, Dother would've—"

"Lady Vivian's a t-traitor," I say, teeth still chattering both from my dip in the lake and nerves.

"Watch what you are saying," Lugh says.

"Who's Dother?" Daniel asks at the same time.

"Carman's third son," Bri replies with a shudder. "He's been posing as Myrdwinn this whole time, and..."

Her voice breaks.

Daniel looks scandalized. "Carman's son was at Lake High this whole time and you guys didn't even know it?" He turns to Lugh. "Not even *you?*"

"As I said, boy, Lady Vivian had him under control," Lugh says cuttingly.

"Under control?" I exclaim. "Lugh, she's been working with him from the beginning, she—"

"Do not speak of that which you do not know," Lugh says, pulling menacingly away from our little group, and for a split second, I can see in him the terrifying warrior he must have been when he defeated Balor.

There's a high-pitched cackle overhead, and we all look up. I flinch as I catch sight of Myrdwinn hurling across the sky straight at us.

"Find Lady Vivian or we will never get out of here alive!" Lugh shouts at us, before launching himself at Myrdwinn.

Light blooms from the collision of the two powerful Fey, turning the whole sky white. The detonation follows a split second later, followed by a scorching wind that flattens us to the ground, turning the rain to steam. Keva whimpers as the scalding water burns her face and neck, until Daniel throws his jacket over her head to shield her.

"There!" Jack says, pointing at a spot far above the burned-down docks.

"But that's not possible," Keva says, staring wide-eyed from beneath Daniel's coat, face blotchy from the burns.

We all watch open-mouthed as a young Myrdwinn pummels Lugh, his blows raining down on the Fey lord so fast I can't even see them.

Now that I know he and Dean were related, I can see the resemblance. But where Dean's eyes always held a sad warmth to them, Myrdwinn's have always been cold, if not downright demented. I clench my hands at my sides, seething.

"We need to find Lady Vivian," Arthur says, back in command.

"Where could she be?" Keva asks.

"I haven't seen her at all since the school got taken over," Bri says.

"And why would you?" Jack asks snidely. "It's not like she'd want to hang out with another traitor, would she?"

With a last punch, Myrdwinn breaks through Lugh's defenses, sending him hurtling down on the other side of the school.

"Morgan, no!" Arthur shouts, catching my intent at the last second.

Too late. Snarling, I slam my foot on the ground and shoot after the bastard.

I swear by all that is unholy, today is the day Carman's going to lose her third and last son.

"I highly recommend you don't intervene this time 'round," Urim says, poking his white face out of a dorm window as I fly up the school building.

I crest over the roof, scanning the skies for a trace of Myrdwinn, who's managed to slip away from me before I could reach him. Ahead, the giant Apple Tree's branches keep quivering and shaking in a way that has nothing to do with the rain and wind. Almost as if it's laughing at me.

I slow down, giving the thick branches a wide berth.

"Ya might wanna look down."

I startle at Thummim's voice, berating myself for not hearing either him nor Urim follow me.

"Is this a trap?" I ask the two Dark Sidhe, narrowing my eyes at them.

Stupid question. What are they going to say? Oh, no, Morgan, we're here because we think we should be BFFs?

Urim shrugs. "Don't mind us," he says. "We're simply curious."

Despite my better judgment, I finally look down. The courtyard is still eerily empty, and from above, even with the torrential rain, the destruction of the gardens is a lot more obvious. Nothing's left but for that stupid Apple Tree and the make-out hedge.

"We've got a bet going as to how long your luck's gonna hold," Thummim adds, nodding emphatically. "Lugh managed a full five minutes against Dother."

"To be fair, he'd already faced Azazel," Urim says, sounding like he lost on another bet earlier.

I'm about to ask them to shut up, when my breath catches. Hanging within the hedge's thorns, is a woman in a long dress of white and red. Lady Vivian.

I react without thinking, diving for her, and only stop when I'm inches from the Fey woman. I hover for an excruciatingly long moment in the air, uncertain as to what to do. Is this what Myrdwinn meant when he talked of taking care of a minor setback? But how could he do this to his acolyte, to his…lover? Unless Lugh was right, and Lady Vivian was somehow preventing him from wreaking havoc all along.

"Lady Vivian?" I call out gently, afraid to touch her in case the thorns holding her up tighten. The smallest of them could pierce her jugular.

"Lady Vivian, can you hear me?" I ask, a little louder.

Slowly, Lady Vivian's eyes flutter open, and I bite back a gasp as pain-filled irises stare back at me, red as carnations.

"Guess it's too late to get them to couple therapy, huh?" Thummim says with a soft snicker, as he and Urim drop to my sides.

"What is this?" I lash out at them, stomach churning.

The two Dark Sidhes give me identical shrugs. "What does it look like?" Urim asks.

With a growl of frustration, I return to Lady Vivian, eyeing the thorny hedge wearily. I may have hated her for a second—she knew Myrdwinn's true nature yet never breathed a word of it to anyone—but she's also the one who showed me kindness when I thought the whole world didn't want me.

"Don't worry," I tell her, garnering a scornful chuckle from Urim. "I-I'll get you out."

I reach for the smaller thorns circling her wrists first, carefully snapping them off one by one, until the ground below is red from the sap. But when I move onto the thicker spines embedded in her side, the hedge suddenly contracts around Lady Vivian, digging deeper into her flesh and drawing a sharp gasp from her.

"Sorry," I say, biting hard on my lip.

"It's OK," Lady Vivian whispers back.

Her eyes close again as the vines jerk her head back by the hair, exposing her white neck to let another thick, black thorn pierce her. Blood flows down the new puncture wound to disappear down her décolletage, draining her.

"It's him, isn't it?" I say, crying freely now. "But why?"

"Watch out!"

Something hits me hard, and I crash into the muddy ground. Myrdwinn's hair-raising cackle resonates from within the Apple Tree. I push myself up, and glare up the gargantuan trunk, trying to pierce the thick foliage to find the Fey. My heart skips a beat at the sight of a blazing pentacle carved halfway up the massive trunk—golden against the tree's bark—the very same mark that was used to seal my powers.

A door slams open. Footsteps. Someone else is coming this way. I fling my arms up defensively, accidentally bringing out the poppy flower Gale gave me.

The intruder bursts into view, only to skid to a halt at my sight. We find ourselves staring at each other for a few heartbeats before I recognize the tall boy.

"Morgan?" Lance asks, dropping his sword arm in surprise.

194

He's skinnier than he used to be, and his skin has lost its sun-kissed hale in prison, giving him a tragic beauty like those of ill-fated knights in troubadour[14] songs of yore.

"Careful," I tell him, returning my attention to the Apple Tree where Myrdwinn is hiding. "Think you're all that for having deceived us, huh?" I call out to the old school director.

There. Movement.

"But I'm gonna make you swallow that leer of yours, and you're gonna wish for the days when you were still locked up in the asylum!" I shout.

Another bough lists ever so slightly. I flex my fingers, the air crackling with power, then launch myself up. I duck as a low-hanging branch tries to swipe me away, swerve around a second before it can shatter my legs. I catch the tail of Myrdwinn's coat disappearing on the other side of the tree, and alter my course to follow him.

But as I fly around the massive trunk, a pulsating mass of amber miasma hits me straight on, catching me across the chest. I see the flash of Myrdwinn's moss-green eyes, crinkling at the sides in laughter, then I'm plummeting to the ground like a rock. I land badly, crying out in shocked pain as my ankle twists beneath me.

"Stay back!" Blanchefleur shouts, bounding forward from the opposite direction. The Fey warrior swings her crystal sword at another projectile, slicing it in two before it can hit her, then twists as another volley whistles past. Myrdwinn's sinister laugh booms out again.

"Can you stand?" Lance asks, offering his hand to help me up.

"I'll manage."

---

[14] A traveling minstrel or poet/musician.

"Good, 'cause it's about to get busy," he says, motioning towards the Herbarium.

I glance over as Keva, Daniel, Bri, and Jack storm out of the building, an angry Arthur closing the rear.

"Anything wrong?" Keva asks me, reaching me first.

"Everything's wrong with her," Daniel says, looking as miserable in his drenched uniform as I feel.

"Ah, well, we're all about to get slaughtered anyway," Keva says with a small pat on my arm.

I throw her a questioning look, avoiding Arthur's seething face.

"Seems the Gates are fully open again," she says, "and we sorta, uh, ran into some of those beasts in the hallway."

"Shields up!" Arthur barks at us.

My stomach tightens into a tight knot as demons swarm the gardens. Flashes pop brightly across the courtyard as knights call on their oghams to defend ourselves. Then chaos hits.

Bri cries out as a dog the size of a pony lunges at her.

"*Laguz!*" Arthur shouts, raising his hand.

A pearlescent beam shoots out of his fingers, and a tall barrier of water cleaves the earth, slicing the demon's head off before it can touch Bri. But already more demons are pressing their snarling faces against the watery barrier.

"*Kano!*" someone roars from behind us, and fire blazes a trail across the old vegetable patches, leaving behind agonizing screams. Hadrian's back, along with the last of the survivors he's managed to free, and they fan out behind him, falling on the horde of demons.

"We need to get everyone out!" Hadrian shouts at Arthur and Blanchefleur.

"We need Lady Vivian!" Bri shouts back at him.

I turn away from the battle to face the make-out hedge again.

"What are you doing?" Arthur asks, rushing to my side.

Excalibur sings as he pushes a draugar away.

"Myrdwinn's up that tree," Lance says, guarding my other side.

Arthur throws me a worried look. "Are you insane?" he yells at me. "Even Lugh couldn't take him, what makes you think you can?"

I swallow hard. Because I have to, I silently tell him.

I reach for my powers again, but this time, instead of flying to meet him, I punch straight out. Dark tendrils shoot out of my knuckles upon impact, boring through the tree like pins in a cushion, and I hear an angry hiss from above.

It's now my turn to smile.

"Why did you teach us to harness Fey power?" I shout over the clash and shouts of the fighting knights and demons.

"It was a perfect way to weaken you self-righteous turds," Myrdwinn says at last, peering at me intently from his perch.

"And to weaken the spell keeping Carman imprisoned," Lugh adds, landing in our midst.

My heart stutters at his sight, relieved to find he's still alive. Hearing Urim and Thummim talking about it made me fear the worst for the second time today.

"Mother should never have been put there in the first place," Myrdwinn snarls. "I was only setting things aright."

"By killing innocents?" Lugh asks coldly. "I thought you were better than that. Guess we all are paying for that mistake"—his golden eye flicks for a moment to the briar hedge—"Vivian most of all."

A long root lashes out from the ground, going for Lugh's feet, but he dodges it easily. The vine rears again, ready to strike, when a sudden clamor resounds from the other side of the courtyard.

"Watchers, Lugh?" Myrdwinn asks, no longer laughing. "And to think you professed you'd never renege your vows of holding peace. Then again, I always knew your word wasn't worth the paper I wipe my ass with."

I glance at the white-clad Fey as they corral the demons and draugar toward the center, their lips moving in whispered prayers. Their presence seems to boost our squad's morale, and I hear Sir Boris redouble his cursing as he strikes another demon down.

The tide is turning at last, if only for a moment.

I reach for my powers again, when something rams into the back of my legs. I gasp in pain as my bad ankle rolls, and Arthur catches me before I drop. I glare down at the white creature trying to climb up my legs, ready to kick it off, and freeze.

"Puck?"

The hobgoblin's large eyes are full of fear and concern as he latches onto me, his tiny body shaking uncontrollably.

"What happened to him?" Keva asks, breathing heavily, blood spattered across her uniform.

"Vivian!" Lugh shouts.

All eyes, even those of the Dark Sidhe, turn towards the hedge. To my surprise, I find the blind Watcher's standing before the wall of thorns, head bowed in prayer. A blazing light spreads from his outstretched hands onto Lady Vivian's still form, making her skin shimmer like a lake under the summer sun, and Puck finally grows still in my arms.

Slowly, the thorns holding her up start to retract, shriveling up away from her body. Until, at last, Lady Vivian opens her eyes again.

"I can't believe it," Arthur says, stunned.

Already Lady Vivian's pulling herself free, and turning toward the Apple Tree beseechingly. Her lips are moving, and I find myself leaning forward to catch her words.

"Come back to me."

The cry of a woman to her lost love.

With a howl of rage, Myrdwinn lands behind the blind Watcher, and curls his fingers up, summoning his power.

"No!" Lugh shouts, throwing himself at them.

Too late. Roots shoot up from the ground, piercing the praying Watcher from all sides. The Fey's blind eyes roll up to the skies, mouth open in a silent cry. His light winks out, and the thorny vines close up around Lady Vivian's slender wrists once more.

Myrdwinn laughs softly. "How does it feel to be trapped?" he asks her. "How does it feel to be unable to help those you care for, huh?"

I tighten my arms around Puck, who's started shaking again.

Lugh turns on Myrdwinn, face contorted in rage.

"Shit!" Arthur shouts, throwing himself on top of me as Lugh's fist connects with Myrdwinn's hastily-raised shield.

The blast crushes us all to the ground, burning through my vision. There's a strange clicking sound, and Arthur and I both look up to find a draugar inching for us, undeterred by the fact that its flesh and hair have been burned away in the explosion.

Excalibur still in hand, Arthur rolls off me, cutting the draugar at the knees. I struggle to my feet, Puck still clutched in my arms, and choke back a gasp.

No. How could it be, Lugh's the most powerful Fey I know, the one who defeated this Balor Carman wants to bring back. Myrdwinn shouldn't be able to withstand such power...

And yet there he still stands, unscathed, strutting before his one-time lover.

"Is that all you have to give me?" he asks, laughing.

Puck shifts in my arms, his attention drawn to a silent shadow that's landed behind the dead Watcher.

"Gale," I breathe.

The knight hefts his golden spear above his shoulder, then hurls his weapon at Myrdwinn. The spear whirs through the air, passing inches above Myrdwinn's head, before landing high in the Apple Tree, the blade sinking deep in its trunk.

"How could you miss?" Keva asks, disbelieving. "He was right in front of you!"

"No, look," Lance says, pointing at the spot where the shaft of the spear is still visible.

The exact place where the glowing pentacle has been carved, I realize.

A loud, thunderous *crack* echoes throughout the courtyard, and Myrdwinn lets out a long, agonizing cry.

Understanding dawns on Arthur's face. "That tree must have been his ogham," he says. "How did he know?"

"Who cares?" I say, my eyes riveted to the tree as it splinters apart.

Myrdwinn spins around to face us all. "This isn't going to change a thing!" he spits, his features growing thicker and more tired. He's going back to his old, crazy schoolmaster self. "Carman's well on her way to getting what she wants and what you all deserve. Soon enough, this world that you love so much will perish."

Spittle flies from his toothless mouth. He's about to shout something else, when Lady Vivian reaches out from the hedge, tenderly wrapping her arms around him. I see her whisper something in the old man's ear, and his eyes grow round with shock.

Then, to everyone's surprise, a fat tear seeps out of the corner of his eye. With a muffled sob, Myrdwinn twists around in her arms and hugs her back. Gripping my arms with his tiny hands, Puck lets out a silent howl of distress.

A lump rises in my throat. I pat the hobgoblin gently, feeling useless before the immensity of his grief, and watch his fur change again, from white to red. But when the red bleeds onto my hands, thick and warm, I look up in fear.

Arthur tenses next to me, our fear reflected in everyone else's faces—Carman's here.

# Chapter 21

Everything Carman's done to me, all the cutting and bleeding, comes back in full force, rooting me to my spot like a rabbit in a snare. No wonder my brother didn't bother following us. The rat bastard knew we'd get caught with our pants down anyway.

There's a shout, and one of the newly-released prisoners falls to a tall, eyeless woman with sallow skin, before she too gets cut down by Sir Boris.

"Keva, to me!" Hadrian shouts, hacking through two massive draugar.

She rushes to his side, shield held high, and throws herself forward as one of them sweeps a sword it's found at Hadrian's legs. The blade hits the side of the shield with a bone-jarring *clang*, before bouncing off. I see Keva wince as it slices her bicep, before Hadrian's own broadsword lops off the draugar's head.

And then, as if in a terrible dream, the whole school vibrates with the urgent peal of the tocsin. A collective shudder runs through Carman's army. The bells' sounds evidently grate on their ears. But they don't let that affect them long.

"To the church, hurry!" Arthur shouts, parrying a Fomori's sharp talons.

"How?" I ask through gritted teeth.

I sweep my arm in a tight arc, and rocks shoot up from the ground to pierce the Fomori through like bullets. But everywhere I turn there are more demons and draugar, the path Lugh's Watchers had carved to get to us already closed up.

Arthur's hazel eyes quickly scan his troops, hair flattened to his scalp by sweat and gore. "Everyone, take flight!" he commands. "Grab anyone who can't. Now!"

At once, flashes of green erupt over the courtyard, and knights and Watchers alike leap into the air. The demons hiss and howl, trying to catch the fleeing soldiers before they can get away. It is just as Gale once said—not one of them can fly unless born to it, or have stolen the ability from another. Thankfully, none of them seem to have gotten the opportunity to do so yet.

Holding tightly onto Puck, I spare the make-out hedge a final look—its leaves and thorny vines have turned to stone, locking Myrdwinn and Lady Vivian in an eternal embrace.

"Goodbye," I whisper.

I follow after the others, the rain whipping at my face. Our troops are still fighting in the distance, but Mordred was right; we're not winning. The earlier retreat the demons suffered was a ploy to get more blood spilled over the school's altered wards. A sick feeling spreads throughout my body at the thought of all those lives lost to unwittingly help the enemy's cause.

"Leaving so soon?" Urim calls out behind me.

"None of your business," I say, picking up my pace.

"We'll miss ya," Thummim adds, stopping so abruptly in mid-air I look over my shoulder to see if he's OK.

"Come back whenever you want!" Urim shouts, waving at me.

Shaking my head in confusion, I finally reach the church tower. I slip on the windowsill as I land, boots slick with blood, and Arthur pulls me inside roughly, his face screwed up in anger.

The space in the bell tower is cramped with knights and Watchers waiting to file out into the staircase.

"What the hell did you think you were doing?" Arthur barks at me.

I pull myself free from his painful grip to let Puck down. "I don't know what you mean."

"Why can't you ever listen?" he exclaims, before toning his voice down to a harsh whisper. "You keep putting everyone at risk all the time because you decide to go off on your own! Can't you for once stop being so…so selfish?!"

My cheeks heat with shame. "I didn't ask you to follow me there!" I lash out.

I immediately regret my words. Arthur's gone sheet white, his lips thinned out. I look down at my scuffed boots, at the blood congealing on its edges, growing increasingly uncomfortable as the silence stretches between us. But what did Arthur expect me to say? Sorry for going after the one who's responsible for the invasion of our school?

There's an awkward clearing of throat. "Tell me again why this is the safest place around here?" Keva asks to no one in particular.

"Saint George's statues," Daniel hastens to respond. "If you hadn't noticed, there's a bunch of them, each with runes circling their base."

"Runes meant to keep everyone out?" Keva asks again, throwing me a pointed look and motioning for me to somehow hug Arthur so all can be pardoned. In front of everyone.

As if.

"Anyone who didn't swear the oath on the altar, and—"

"We should not tarry here," Lugh says curtly, striding for the exit behind the last of his Watchers.

I slip to the front to follow him down the spiraling staircase, glad for an escape. But we haven't made it halfway down when Lugh suddenly flattens himself against the wall, a long, iron-tipped staff aimed at his throat.

"Stop right where you are," Father Tristan growls.

"It is only us," Lugh says calmly despite the sharp weapon inches from his face, "claiming sanctuary before the demons get to us."

"Sanctuary?" Father Tristan asks. "Never thought I'd see the day when the Lord of Avalon would beg me for mercy. How does it feel, huh? I don't recall your showing me any such kindness when I begged for yours once."

His fevered gaze travels up to the rest of us, taking in our bloody attire and worn faces. Finally, after another long second, his shoulders slump and he begrudgingly lowers his weapon.

"I take it by your presence here that I will now have the rest of the hordes to fend off," he says tightly, looking through one of the stained-glass windows. "Again."

My fingers clench around the railing as we continue the rest of the way down, silent but for the sound of boots on stone. Though the church has not fallen, signs of the war are evident here too. Years of being besieged will do that to a place, I suppose.

The rose window above the main doors has been shattered to pieces, the hole boarded up with hasty masonry. Pieces of the stone vault have come crashing down, pockmarking the nave's floor with small craters. But more so than the church itself, it's the stench that permeates the building that's hard to bear. Of feces and spoilt food and unwashed bodies.

"We had expected to have to pack up and go some time," Father Tristan says, chuckling to himself. "Didn't expect it to be in so grandiose a fashion."

We keep pace with him, rejoining the Watchers already gathered in the southern aisle. Ahead, grim faces stare at us from the pews—a few dozen children, teachers and farmers. The last of what once was a thriving community.

As I pass by the pulpit, a burly figure suddenly jumps up, teetering for a moment like a drunken sailor.

"Morgan?" Sir Boris asks, his voice gruffer than I remember.

I freeze in my tracks.

"Thought I'd recognized you out there," Sir Boris continues.

The grizzled man has to hold onto the back of the benches for support as he hobbles his way to me, a soiled bandage wrapped above his left knee. Prison hasn't been kind to him, and our skirmish in the courtyard just now hasn't helped. His cheeks have become sallow, his eyes sunken, and his long handlebar moustache has grown thinner.

I give him a shaky smile. "Glad you were able to make it—"

"No thanks to you," Sir Boris says, Russian accent thick with anger. "How dare you show yourself to us?"

Arthur steps protectively in front of me, trying to shield me as I stand there, stunned.

But to everyone's surprise, it's Father Tristan who speaks up, "Don't speak of that which you don't know, old man."

Funny. That's exactly what Lugh told me about Lady Vivian. The irony almost makes me laugh.

Lady Ysolt springs to her feet, red hair wild. "There's no need to be insulting, Tristan," she says.

"I was only making a statement," Father Tristan says, looking like he's struggling not to curse. "If you took it wrongly, that was not my intent."

"But it was your intent to protect this backstabbing *chort*[15]?" Sir Boris asks, his face turning purple.

"Who are you referring to as a demon?" Arthur asks coldly.

"Gah!" Sir Boris shouts, throwing his hands up in disgust, and nearly losing his balance in the process. "*Slepy durak!*[16] We are not in class anymore. This is no place for philosophizing and—"

An explosion rattles the doors, the deafening sounds bouncing off the church walls and columns. Howls of laughter erupt just outside, so loud it seems like the demons are with us.

"Time's up," Father Tristan intones, as if he's preaching mass again. "Once the true traitors to our Order have decided to take this place over once and for all, they will be unimpeded in their desecration of this holy place." He pauses dramatically, making sure every eye is on him. "And then they'll feed us to the wolves."

Panic sets in.

"But we're mincemeat if we so much as set a foot outside!" someone shouts.

"Only if we are to go out the same way we came in," Arthur says, joining Father Tristan by the altar.

"We can't all fly off again," another voice shouts. "Our oghams aren't workin' proper, and there's too many young'uns for the rest of us ter carry."

More distressed cries arise from our refugees. This has been their home for two years. It's allowed them to survive much longer than most. But despite the fear, they've grown complacent about their precarious safety here, forgetting it's but temporary. Forgetting that the clock's ticking.

---

[15] 'Evil demon' in Russian.
[16] 'Blind fool' in Russian.

"I say we tell them to stuff it and die here instead, if all they want to do is complain about everything," Keva whispers loudly to me.

"Keva," Hadrian growls in warning.

"Oh, take a chill pill," Keva tells him. "This is definitely not the time to quibble over something we both know to be true."

Hadrian frowns, evidently surprised at having his own squire talk back at him, but lets her comment slide as Arthur resumes.

"We will use the Watchers' hall," Arthur says, raising his hand before more people can cut him off. "I know the catacombs are infested as well, but most of the Dark Sidhe have been drawn out by our troops, far beyond the docks. As for the other demons who may still be stationed down there"—he draws Excalibur, light flaring from the sword at his touch—"we'll take care of them."

Just like that, the crowd's appeased. The miracle they've all been praying for has arrived at last. I shift from one foot to the next, unnerved by these people's sudden blind confidence.

"To avoid drawing attention, everyone is to split up into groups," Hadrian says, taking over the logistics. "And each group will be accompanied by a contingent of Watchers who will lead you to relative safety."

"Relative?" a woman repeats, voice hiking dangerously high. "And where would that be?"

"My Demesne," Lugh says, Blanchefleur like a silent ghost beside him.

"A *Fey* place?" another woman asks, holding a baby tightly to her chest.

"Lugh's already saved your life once today," Arthur says calmly, though I can see that all of this arguing is taking its toll on him, the bags under his eyes darkening.

"What if it's a trap?" someone else asks.

This time, Keva can't hold herself back. "Listen here," she shouts, drawing herself up. "I'm gonna keep it simple for you. Either you take a chance at making it alive out of here with us, or you guard our rears when those demons out there finally breach the church's defenses. But let me tell you something else"—Keva's grin turns manic—"I've just come back from Hell, and what Carman's got in store for us is not pretty. So, make your own damn choices, and, by Kali's sword, stop wasting our time. We're short on it as it is."

A second explosion blasts against our outside walls, and another section of the already weakened ceiling comes crashing down, taking a part of the gallery with it. A baby starts shrieking, quickly hushed down by its mother. But nobody else complains anymore as Hadrian resumes his instructions.

"Nicely done," Daniel tells Keva.

Keva shrugs. "Brutal honesty's always the best way to go, I say."

"Definitely something you excel at," Daniel says.

"Daniel, I excel at *everything*. You should know that by now." Keva narrows her eyes at him. "How come you're here with us, anyway?" she asks.

Distracted, I watch Hadrian lead the first group down to the statue of the Virgin and Child that stands in the back of the apse[17]. With a precise movement, he slashes his hand with a dagger and places it over her foot.

The statue flares at his touch, before swiveling on itself, revealing a dark passage behind.

"Then how come I saw Brockton strutting about the place with a Dark Sidhe?" Keva's voice is getting louder, drawing curious glances.

[17] Semi-circular recess at the end of a church where the altar stands.

Daniel's jaw clenches. "He's not my slave to control," he mutters.

"Not for lack of trying, though, right?" Keva retorts.

The sound of metal hitting stones makes us duck. I look to the front doors, expecting a breach, but they're still standing. Then Jack's voice resounds sharply from the chancel. "You have no right to flee, you filthy traitor!"

"Ugh, not that again," Keva says, as we all three turn to find Bri kneeling on the floor, Jack's blacksmithing hammer held above her head.

"These are heavy accusations you bear," Father Tristan says, iron in his voice. Jack must have told him the truth then.

"I saw her fighting out there with us," Sir Boris says gruffly, "didn't seem like a traitor to me."

"She conspired against us with the school director," Jack continues. "Heard her dad finally got that spot on the Board he'd been wanting, thanks to all the death she's caused."

Bri's face looks stricken. "That's not fair."

Jack wheels on her, jabbing her in the back with his hammer. "What's not fair is having Nadia, and Dina, and Laura chopped into bits because you sabotaged our only defense system against the Fey!"

Father Tristan lets out a low hiss. "I knew Myrdwinn was evil all along." He turns his cold gaze upon Bri's prostrated figure, and I have no doubt in my mind he will strike her dead if he judges her guilty. "How many times have I preached against the demon, girl? And still you spurned my advice to listen to that despicable fool?"

The acid in his voice makes even Hadrian flinch, and I find myself striding over to help Bri—I don't care what Jack says she's done, I won't let them burn her like some witch at the Salem trials. She's my friend, and the only reason Myrdwinn could have played her like this was because of her grief and misery at the loss of her twin.

But before I can make more than three steps, Arthur cuts in front of me.

"Her name is Brianna," he says, "and though these accusations are true, it is also true that she acted without knowledge of Myrdwinn's true intent. I believe the old Fey fooled a lot of us, Lady Vivian included."

"She knew enough not to temper with the wards," Father Tristan says scathingly.

"Look who's calling the kettle black," Gale says, moving away from a side chapel where he and his brother have been talking until now. "Didn't you improve upon this church to destroy Avalon from the inside, priest? Myrdwinn just happened to be more efficient than you at it."

Father Tristan's nostrils flare, deep lines of disapproval cutting his face. "I don't know who you are, boy, but I don't appreciate your trying to lecture me."

"If all you want is a name, you need only ask," Gale says, with a cheekiness I hadn't expected from him.

"His name's Gale," Lance says, stepping in.

"*Sir* Gale," Keva shouts from beside me, a little too excitedly.

Sir Boris's moustache quivers. "The one who disappeared six years ago?"

"Were you held captive by the Fey?" Father Tristan asks.

"Not exactly," Gale says brightly, as if getting stuck down in Hell was some kind of pleasure trip. "In any case, priest, I think we can all agree on the fact that what's done is done." He helps Bri back to her feet, gently pushing Jack out of the way. "This young squire has made a mistake. A grave one, to be sure. But it also means that she knows more about Myrdwinn's inner workings than anyone."

The look Bri gives Gale as he keeps her close to him is one of mixed shock and adoration—as if, at the bottom of the deepest pit, she's suddenly seen the light and accepted her fate all at once. I feel a pang of envy at that. How easy it is for her to choose the right path now that someone else has smoothed out all the kinks and wrinkles for her. Whereas I can never fully wash away the taint that runs in my blood.

Lips trembling, Bri nods, then swallows hard. "I know what Myrdw—Dother's done to the wards," she says. She takes a deep breath, then juts out her chin. "If you'll allow me, I wish to stay here to reverse what's been done, as atonement for my actions."

Gale nods at her, then turns to Father Tristan. "You heard her, priest. What say you now?"

"She can't stay here, she'll be killed on the spot!" Hadrian exclaims.

"We're all dead anyway if we don't reverse the wards," Bri says.

A shiver runs down my spine, raising the hairs at the back of my neck. I turn away from the scene, eyes trying to pierce the stained glass windows to see what's happening beyond them.

"She's here," I whisper, hugging myself tightly.

Lugh's suddenly at my side. "There's not another second to lose," he says loudly. "Our sanctuary's compromised."

Bright light floods the church from the eastern side, painting the nave and opposite gallery a gory red.

"Dragon!" Daniel shouts, his sword back out in his shaking hands.

"Everyone out, now!" Arthur shouts.

My footsteps falter at the sight of Gale and Lance, standing side by side in one of the side chapels, watching as Father Tristan taps his staff against the reddening wall. I pick up Puck, the hobgoblin having come back to me for shelter, but I still can't make myself move.

"How long before the wards fall, priest?" Gale asks.

"A few minutes, at best," Lugh says, answering for him.

"I'll try to give you a few more," Father Tristan declares.

"I'll remain at your side," Lance adds.

A choking panic grips me. "Can't you come with us?" I ask, barely making a sound over the roaring fires outside.

"Don't be silly," Father Tristan says. "Someone's got to keep these demons off of you."

"I'll stay and help as well," Lady Ysolt says.

A strange look passes between her and Father Tristan, heavy with meaning. I blink back tears. Nobody should have to say goodbye to their friends like this.

"Come on, Morgan, we can't stay here any longer," Arthur says, trying to steer me towards the secret exit.

"We can't leave them here," I say. "Tell Lance, he'll listen to you. You're the KORT President!"

Arthur's face is closed, unreadable. "Enough, you know what's keeping him here," he says.

He means Jennifer. I know too well how deep Lance's feelings run for the girl, despite her evil personality. Nothing and no one's ever going to change his mind about her, not even his duty.

Except perhaps...

"Hold on to him," I say hurriedly, handing Puck over to Arthur before rushing back to Lance.

The beautiful knight looks at me quizzically as I stop before him.

"I know this isn't the place," I start, "and certainly not the time, but even though I know why you want to stay here, you may not know that Jennifer and my brother..." I pause awkwardly, finding it awful hard to meet Lance's steady gaze. I clear my throat. "That they're…"

"Together?" Lance finishes for me with a rueful smile that pulls at my heart. How can someone so good have fallen so hard for such a self-centered bitch? "It doesn't matter," he continues. "I know what you think, and considering how she's treated you, you have every right to feel that way. But I also know that deep down, there's some good in her, and I can't let that good disappear."

"You've seen her then?" I say, shoulders slumping. There goes my one chance to get him to save himself.

Lance nods. "While I was being detained."

With a defeated sigh, I take his cold hand in mine. "I wish you luck, then," I say, with a wobbly smile. I glance at the few who have decided to make a last stand so the rest of us can escape—Father Tristan, Lady Ysolt, Lance, Bri, Jack… "And I hope, for all our sakes, that when we finally come back to reclaim the school, you'll still be here."

A third detonation shakes the whole building, and this time, the church's doors splinter open. A whoop of victory erupts from outside as a lithe figure steps gingerly over the wreckage. The church's wards flare bright before dissipating again, and the boy steps through unharmed.

"I'm afraid you've run out of time," the boy says, his cruel voice only too familiar.

"Agravain!" Arthur says, surprised.

"And standing on two feet," Lance points out, pushing me towards Arthur before unsheathing his sword.

"How did he—" I start, remembering the knight with his prosthetic leg as he taunted me every chance he got. But I know how he got his leg back—he's evidently joined forces with Mordred. Just like Jennifer did.

"Go," Lance says, stalking forward.

Hot tears blur my vision, spilling freely down my cheeks. I let Arthur pull me towards the Virgin and child's statue, Puck back in my arms.

"Running away again, Arthur?" Agravain shouts angrily as I start down the steps into the tunnel.

There's the sudden ring of metal on metal, and I look back. Lance has intercepted Agravain by the baptistery, and the two knights are now circling each other, like they've done so many times before at practice.

I watch, transfixed, as Agravain parries a blow before thrusting his sword straight at Lance's stomach. Lance twists sideways, bringing his blade down to counter Agravain, graceful even when facing death.

"He'll be fine," Arthur says, urging me to keep on moving. "He's the best the school's ever seen."

There's a soft rasping sound as the statues slides back into place, shutting us inside the dark passage. We find Lugh and Gale waiting for us at the bottom, then file after the tall Fey down the dark tunnels. Not a word crosses our lips, our minds still with those we left behind.

Then a deep rumble rises behind us, carried along by a thickening cloud of dust and smoke.

My heart breaks.

The church has fallen, taking our friends with it.

# CHAPTER 22

The weight of defeat makes us all hunch as we plod through the pristine snow towards Lugh's Demesne, the land of eternal summer overtaken by winter. Ahead, the campfires' flickering lights shine like a string of beacons around the giant oak tree, and the thought of seeing the shock and disappointment on everyone's faces when they find out what happened almost makes me wish I were still stuck in Hell.

Worse is thinking about those who haven't made it back.

"Are you sure we aren't on the surface world?" Keva asks, her voice breaking with fatigue.

"Might as well be, considering how thin the veil between both worlds is around here," Blanchefleur says, greeting us from atop a pine tree's low-hanging branch.

She jumps down from her perch, bows deeply to Lugh, then falls into step behind him. I catch her assessing him, aware of his smallest gesture, and I wonder if Az or Myrdwinn didn't hurt Lugh more than he's letting on.

"Did you guys see that dragon?" Gareth's voice booms out as two burly shadows detach themselves from the surrounding trees.

"Gareth," Gauvain says warningly, immediately catching onto our mood.

"I wish we'd had a chance to fight it this time," Gareth continues, completely oblivious. "Everyone knows fighting a dragon is the epic tome of a knight's quest."

"Epitome," Gauvain growls, waving for him to shut up. "I take it you didn't get to destroy the seat?" he asks, more softly, as if afraid anyone else might hear.

"Not for lack of trying," Arthur says.

The wind suddenly shifts, sending flurries of snow in our face.

"Indeed," an angry voice says as the squall coalesces into Lord Oberon's fuming shape. "Would someone care to explain why I keep having to sacrifice my people against a dragon not even your precious Saint George would have managed to scratch, and all for nothing?"

"The mission might not have been a success, but I would not say it was for naught," Lugh says calmly, motioning for Blanchefleur to make sure no one's eavesdropping on us.

"We found out the Siege Perilous cannot be touched when inactive," Arthur hedges, reaching over his head to place his hand over Excalibur's pommel. "Next time—"

"There won't be a next time!" Lord Oberon snaps. "Not unless you want us all dead. Is that what you were planning all along? Another of those disgusting ploys to get rid of our kind in your unholy crusade?"

"My Lords and Ladies?"

We all start at the sudden intrusion. Rip bows low as we whirl on him, his face almost as white as the snowy ground.

I catch Lugh frowning in the direction Blanchefleur took, evidently displeased at her inability to stop Rip from dropping in on us without anyone noticing.

"Pardon me for the intrusion, but there may be an issue," he continues, straightening up. "In particular when it comes to...space."

Lord Oberon snorts. "Are you saying Lugh's quarters are small?" he asks, with a meaningful glance at Lugh's lower body before barking out a laugh.

"The last few days have unfortunately brought us more injured parties and refugees than at first anticipated," Rip says. "I am afraid that, unless we find a way to expand, we may end up having a riot on our hands."

"Are our people refusing to share quarters with the Fey?" Arthur asks, brow furrowed. "Isn't Hadrian back to settle such matters?"

Rip glances at the two Fey lords. "I'm afraid this time the tensions are coming from within your esteemed ranks," he says.

Lord Oberon's chuckling cuts off, and Lugh's mouth flattens into a straight line of disapproval.

"We shall go this instant," Lugh says.

"Lead the way, my good man," Oberon says, evidently holding Rip in high regard.

"You're too kind," Rip says with another low bow, before moving swiftly away, the two Fey lords flanking him.

"He's rather dashing, isn't he?" Keva says.

Daniel snorts. "That old bald geezer? Are you out of your mind?"

"He's royalty," Keva says with a sniff, "and the finest diplomat our Order's ever had. Which is much more than you can say for yourself."

Daniel's face turns bright red. "Still ended up in the loony bin, didn't he?" I hear him mutter. But to my surprise, instead of storming off, he offers Keva his arm. "Enough drooling though, better get you to the infirmary."

"You're injured?" I ask Keva, mentally kicking myself for not having noticed it earlier.

Keva grimaces. "No," she says, before scowling at Daniel. "Don't you know it's highly impolite to draw attention to a lady's...affliction."

"You're no lady," Daniel retorts. "And what's wrong with saying you're on the rag?"

"Daniel!" Keva exclaims, smacking him loudly on the shoulder under the bemused looks of Arthur, Gale and the cousins.

"What, there's nothing wrong with that," Daniel protests, rubbing his sore shoulder. "Now come on, it's an order."

With a mortified look at me, Keva slogs after a smirking Daniel, the KORT knights' presence making it impossible for her to justly ignore a knight's direct order. Even if it is Daniel who made it.

"On that interesting note, I think we're going to take off too," Gauvain says, wrapping his arm around Gale's shoulders to carter him off. "Gotta show this guy the lay of the land."

"Yes," Gareth says, waving his war hammer arm around, "you'll see Lugh's Demesne is quite the suppository of information."

Gale bursts out laughing at that, shocking even Gareth so much that he forgets to correct his cousin, and the three of them depart, leaving me alone with Arthur. Again.

I throw Arthur a furtive glance, gauging his mood, wondering if I should brace myself for another sermon. But he's just staring at his boots, lost in thought. A part of me wants to use the opportunity to sneak away. Yet I can't make myself leave him.

I know he's hurting. Lance was his best friend. The church was the last bastion against the Fey we had inside the school he lost. And that one last desperate plan he hatched backfired mightily.

Three terrible strikes that make my heart ache for him.

I clear my throat self-consciously. "So," I start.

"So," Arthur repeats right away, which tells me he was very aware of my presence.

"Do you think there's enough room for us at Lugh's place, or do we have to find a room on the surface world?" I ask.

Arthur blushes so furiously his ears go pink, and I feel my own cheeks burn as I realize what I've just said.

"I-I meant rent a room," I stutter. "Each. As in, one for you, and one for me."

Saint George's balls, I'm only making things more awkward. Why can't the ground split open at my feet now, when I want it to?

Arthur picks at the dried blood on Puck's matter fur, much to the hobgoblin's annoyance. "I think it's best if we stay away from high-security civilian places for a while," he says.

"Geez, Arthur, it's not like we're going to rob a bank."

His ears go from pink to crimson. "Or any place with cameras," he adds.

I tilt my head at him in confusion. "Why's that?"

Arthur's eyes remain resolutely downcast. "Because we're both wanted for the murder of the Schultzes."

"What?!"

"Remember when we went hunting for Dub?" he asks, finally setting Puck down before the hobgoblin can clock him with his tiny fists.

"You're talking about the farm where we caught up with him and he nearly killed us?" I ask, quickly putting two and two together.

Arthur nods, still avoiding my gaze.

"But we didn't kill them!" I exclaim, outraged at the injustice of it all. As if we didn't have a hard-enough time down here already. "Any cop can tell that whatever happened to them wasn't…natural." Then the second shoe drops, and I round on Arthur, livid. "I knew we shouldn't have taken their stupid truck! But no, you had to insist it would be fine!"

"It would've been fine if Luther had done his job and smoothed things over with the authorities like he was supposed to," Arthur says, sounding uncharacteristically petulant.

"Did you seriously not think your father wouldn't jump at the smallest opportunity to get rid of me?" I snap.

He finally looks up, and I see on his face that the thought had crossed his mind. Yet he still dismissed it, and now the Feds want me in jail, too.

With a disgusted grunt, I turn on my heels and stomp away. The worst of it is that, for once, I'd been right, and he still did not listen to me.

"Where are you going?"

"Away from you."

"Morgan? Morgan, don't got off on your own!"

I ignore him, too mad to listen to more of his excuses. I hear his heavy footfalls, then Arthur yanks me by the arm.

"Don't you dare walk away from me like that!" he shouts

"Or what? You're gonna lock me up again?" I shout back.

Arthur releases me, as if burned. "That's not…," he starts, then blows loudly through his nose. "How long are you going to hold that against me? You know I had to lock you up for your own safety. If I had to do it all over, I'd lock you up again, and for much longer, if it's the only thing that'll keep you out of trouble."

"You're not the boss of me!" I retort, sounding just like Daniel.

"Actually, until you're knighted, I am the boss of you," Arthur says, crossing his arms.

"Yeah, well, you can go stuff your stupid rules where the sun don't shine, for all the good they've done!"

Arthur's jaw drops open, and I use the opportunity to storm off again.

"Fine, be that way then!" he shouts after me.

This time he doesn't follow me, and I soon find myself deep in foreign land, the forest's charred remains extending to the horizon in every direction. All in all, it must've taken me but fifteen minutes to get well and truly lost.

It's all Arthur's fault. If he didn't always antagonize me, I wouldn't have reacted that way. What's so difficult about saying he's sorry for once in his life?

I hear the break of soft footfalls behind me, and whirl around, heart beating wildly.

"Art—"

I stop at the sight of Puck, trying to ignore the heavy feeling of disappointment at his sight.

"What are you doing here?" I ask softly.

The hobgoblin motions excitedly at me, his tiny arms windmilling about until they get caught in a low bush that's survived the dragon's attack. I release a tired sigh, and kneel down to help untangle him, when excited squeaks suddenly ring out around us. I freeze, eyes darting around in confusion.

"It's her, isn't it?" pipes a small voice from the thicket.

A chorus of tiny laughs erupts as Puck gives a sharp nod then lets himself drop onto his rump, his left arm still stuck inside the bush.

"Wh-Who's there?" I ask, wondering if I should get some help.

The laughter starts again, but this time I see the bramble's lower spines shake, and a small brown mouse appears, its ears almost as big as its fluffy brown belly. With the barest of wheezes, the mouse sits on its haunches to stare more easily up at me, displaying a bright jewel at its throat.

"An ogham!" I let out in surprise.

Another burst of giggling gushes out of the bush.

The sitting mouse nods pridefully, its long whiskers quivering. "They were given to us as a reward for helping out our Lady Danu once," he says, "and we wear them with pride."

The mouse shifts slightly, and only then do I notice the pair of translucent wings that adorn his back.

"She is highly magma"—the mouse pauses, nose twitching— "magmamimouse, she is."

The winged mouse nods again to give weight to its declaration, and the laughter starts anew.

"In any case," the mouse says with a pointed look behind him, "I hear you may have questions for us?"

"I-I do?"

"Or should I call it a request instead?" The winged mouse's large eyes sparkle expectantly.

"I'm sorry," I say, finally releasing Puck from the thorny bush, "but I don't even know who you are."

"Of course, how silly of me!"

The mouse jumps up onto its rear paws, then proceeds to give me a sweeping bow that could rival Rip's, large ears brushing against the snow.

"I am Papillon, longtime follower of the ever-brilliant, kindest-hearted, far-sighted, life-giving, gift-bestowing, mightiest of warriors, the Light Bringer herself!" the mouse proclaims in one breath. "At your service."

Puck grins at me beatifically, as if this is the best thing that could have happened to me.

"Uh, pleased to meet you," I mumble, still baffled.

"Now that we have been properly introduced, feel free to ask me anything you'd like to know," the mouse says excitedly. "I promise that you will not owe me a thing for it!"

The bush's lower branches quiver, and a second mouse rolls into view, its emerald wings fluttering until it comes to a stop before Papillon.

With a delighted hop, Puck flattens himself to the ground so he can be eye to eye with the two small Fey creatures, ruffling their fur with every snorting breath of his.

"Don't be all hoity-toity, Pap," the new mouse squeaks, smoothing her russet coat. "The girl has obviously no idea what you're talking about, and the more turns you take around the pot, the likelier it is the Master of this Demesne will feel our presence."

Papillon sniffs disdainfully. "*He* is not the ultimate ruler. *He* cannot order us around, when we serve a mightier liege."

The russet mouse looks down her nose at Papillon. "How quickly your tune changes when *he* is here," she retorts, the small ogham at her neck scintillating brightly against her fur with every syllable.

The giggling from the scrubs resumes, louder.

"You're saying that you're here on behalf of Danu?" I ask tentatively, and both mice nod at once. "And that you're willing to answer any question I may have?"

"Correct."

"And you'll be able to answer?"

"The thing is, miss," the russet mouse says, "our size makes people easily disregard us."

"Not that we ever pry," Papillon chimes in quickly.

"But our ears are also made to catch the smallest sound, and voices—even whispered—tend to carry."

The two of them have just admitted that they're spies. Spies who do not want Lugh to catch them. Which makes them doubly suspicious.

But Fey cannot lie, not outright, I remind myself, and Puck seems to trust them. So their claim to have come from this elusive

Danu must be true. But why would this Fey Lady want to talk to me now? Unless...

Could it be that this powerful Danu might want to help me out? I shake my head. Don't be stupid, Morgan, I tell myself. This Danu could very well have waited until I was vulnerable, away from any protection, to bait me into a trap.

I glance back down at the two flying mice's guileless eyes.

"OK," I say, tapping my chin thoughtfully, "let's start with something easy. How can we defeat Carman's dragon?"

Papillon opens his mouth to answer, then his shoulders slump. "I'm afraid we do not know that," he says.

"Can Lady Vivian be revived?" I ask instead.

"We do not know that either," Papillon replies, looking more dejected.

"Then how about Carman's next move?" I ask. "I know she wants to free Balor, but what does she need to finally free him? More bloodshed?"

Papillon's face looks positively glum. "We do not know."

I grimace in disappointment. "Not much use, are you?"

"Why don't you ask us about things we actually know instead?" the russet mouse retorts. "Like why Arthur had your picture with him all these years, or who wants to kill you in your sleep, or why the One-Eyed one has gone back on his word not to kill just so he can protect you."

One-Eyed one? Are they talking about Lugh again? I eye the two Fey suspiciously.

"Well, it's been very nice meeting you," I say, getting ready to leave, "but you're evidently talking to the wrong girl."

"We do not have the wrong person," Papillon bristles, "you look just like her! There's no chance at all we wouldn't recogmice Her Wisestness's own daughter."

My breath rushes out. "What did you say?" I ask in a choked voice.

"That we cannot be wrong," Papillon starts.

"No, not that, after." I swallow audibly. "About my...mother."

Two pairs of large, liquid eyes blink up at me questioningly.

"You mean you don't know Danu's your mother?" Papillon squeaks in surprise.

The russet mouse pushes him away. "Of course not, cheese brain, or she wouldn't have asked now, would she?" She twitches her dragonfly wings. "Poor thing, to not have known who her mother was all these years. Why, even the idea of Roquefort, Stilton, Taleggio, Brie, and Munster growing up without knowing how much I love them hurts my poor little heart!"

Blood rushes from my face, and I drop back down into the snow. "You mean to say—" I whisper, the wheels in my mind revving up.

"—that her loftiest-minded—" Papillon says.

"—the Fey warrior you mentioned—" I continue.

"—the Light Bringer herself," Papillon adds with another one of his sharp nods.

"—is my mother."

"The mighty Danu herself," the russet mouse finishes.

"But I thought my mother was Lucifer," I say.

"Lucifer is derived from the Latin Luciferus," Papillon recites, his whiskers twitching meaningfully, "which means the morning star, Dawn-Bringer, she who delivers the light."

"And she sent us to you, sweets," the russet mouse says kindly.

This can't be real. I must've been right earlier—this has got to be a trick of some sort.

A soft breeze suddenly picks up, and I find myself basking in a warm glow, the scent of flowers and sun-ripened fields wafting through the air, surrounding me in a familiar, comforting cocoon.

The same force that held me safe when facing Agravain that time he tried to kill me during practice, that shielded me against Carman, that healed me when I tasted death in the harpy's talons.

A chill snakes its way down my spine. I should've known. Deep down, I should've known who she was, even if she did abandon me.

"Will you take me to her?" I ask.

"Take you to whom?"

I jump at Lugh's sudden voice, and look back down, but the two winged mice have disappeared. My throat constricts at the thought of losing what could have been my one chance to meet my birth mother.

"What are you doing?" Lugh asks again.

"Just minding my own business," I say, more sharply than intended.

Lugh's jaw tenses, golden eye straying to the verdant bush next to me. "Arthur thought you might need help finding your way back," he says at last.

I nod silently. Then, bundling Puck into my arms, I stand back up to look at the brooding Fey Lord. A part of me wants to ask him what he knows about Danu, if it's true she's my mother, and why she ever abandoned me and my brother.

But Papillon was right about one thing. Lugh's hiding something from me, and I need to find out what.

# Chapter 23

"I'll have your filthy head for that!"

Oberon's voice booms out across the circular entrance hall of Lugh's Oak Tree, making everyone there cower in fear.

"Ease up, Lord Oberon," I hear Gauvain say, any trace of his usual mirth stamped out. "I am sure she meant no harm."

I hop onto a narrow staircase made of floating wooden disks to get a better view. Oberon's fuming, his booted foot forcing a red-headed girl's face into the floor. The girl lets out a soft whimper, her eyes rolling up beseechingly. I hiss out a breath as I recognize Marianne, the superstitious knight I once helped out at the infirmary.

Across the hall Gareth is swearing viciously, prevented from joining his cousin by a swarm of pixies. Lightning from his war hammer flashes along the high ceiling, singeing the red oak in long, crooked lines.

Worry coils tighter around the gathered crowd. People and Fey alike are getting restless, and if nobody intervenes, it's going to turn out into an all-out brawl.

Brow lowered dangerously, Lugh leaves my side and cuts a path straight to the other Fey Lord. I jump off the floating step to

228

follow along, but a shadow moves in front of me, stopping me in my tracks.

"Let Lugh handle it," Arthur says, grabbing my hand and leading me away.

"But Oberon's going to kill her," I say, trying to pull free.

"No, he's not. Now for once in your life, stay put!"

A part of me wants to punch him. The other, irrational part, is glad Arthur's talking to me at all after what I said to him earlier, even if it's to bark angry orders at me.

There's another thunderous *crack*, followed by frightened screams. My heart goes still, and Arthur reflexively draws me closer to him, his free hand going up to Excalibur's hilt.

"Have you calmed down, now?" Lugh's chocolaty voice speaks up.

My hands unclench from around Arthur's arm as the tension eases slightly around the room. I can almost hear the collective sigh of relief.

"Will you release the girl?" Lugh asks.

I glance over the crowd at Oberon's puckered face. "She offended me and my people, she needs to be punished for it," he says. "I did not join your rebellion just to see these humans subjugate my kind to their whims. We are *not* slaves."

"I thought we had a truce," Gauvain growls menacingly. "The deal was to fight side by side against Carman, and in exchange we promised to stop hunting your people down, just as you promised not to harm any human."

"Any human on our side," someone adds.

"I've just changed the terms of the contract," Oberon says, eyes glinting dangerously.

"You know very well that once a word is given—" Lugh starts.

Oberon holds up a large ruby-encrusted ring. "These oghams do not belong to them!" he bellows.

"How else are we to fight, then?" Gauvain asks, his biceps bulging as he crosses his arms.

Oberon's lips curl up into a smirk. "Why, however your kind managed before."

"He's askin' us to sign our death warrant!' someone shouts.

"We'll never survive without the use of EM!" another adds.

"So it's OK for us to sacrifice ourselves to save your asses, but not the other way around?" Oberon retorts, flaring up again.

From the strained look on his face, I can tell Arthur's itching to intervene, but he doesn't leave my side. I don't know what's happened, if it's because he lost the KORT Presidency, or because of what his father's accused of. But except for our little raiding party, Arthur's pulled himself away from any leadership position. And I can tell it's gnawing at him.

"Considering our foes," Gale says, appearing silently at their sides, "would you agree to our use of oghams when absolutely needed? We do not have the ability to restore all the Fey whose oghams are currently in use. And forcing us to fight the old way on such short notice, without proper training, is signing our own death warrant—no matter how much Nephilim blood flows in our veins."

There goes that strange word again. Nephilim. I'm apparently not the only one who's confused by it, as shocked whispers rise among the crowd.

Gale tilts his head to the side with a slight smile. "Although I'm sure that under your guidance," he adds before Oberon can object, "we would progress towards it much quicker."

"What say you, Lord Oberon?" Lugh asks, cocking an inquisitive look in Gale's direction.

Oberon's mouth snaps shut, as he considers the offer. "We could start with that," he says slowly, "for I'll be damned if I ever face that dragon on my own again."

At long last, he lifts his foot off from Marianne's face, and Gauvain hurries to help her up. The girl's face is purple, blood flowing freely from her broken nose, but she's alive.

"Come," Arthur says quietly, pulling on my hand again.

He steers me to the wall behind the floating stairs, and presses his foot on a low-hanging conk[18]. The heartwood unfolds outward, like the Apple Tree did back at Lake High, revealing another staircase in the soft light that emanates from thousands of glowworms moving inside the walls themselves.

"What are Nephilim?" I ask as the doorway closes behind us.

"The descendants of humans who procreated with the Fallen Ones," Arthur says, not letting go of my hand.

"You…you mean other people like me?" I ask.

Arthur nods. "Because of their Fey blood, these Nephilim inherited their holy parents' powers. But the ability to manipulate the elements got lost over the generations, though the purer bloodlines still exhibit some latent aptitude. A trait some families tried to maintain through inter-marriage."

I stop dead in my tracks, and Arthur stumbles at the sudden resistance.

"You're saying there are more knights out there who are like me?" I ask. "More like…Jennifer?"

"We all are, to some extent," Arthur says carefully.

I shoot him a withering glare. "You're saying that all these knights who mocked me and treated me like shit because of who my mother is, even tried to have me executed for it, are no better than me?" I take a deep, steadying breath. "How long have you known?"

Arthur looks away. "It has been theorized—"

---

[18] A type of fungi that grows on trees and looks like a miniature platform.

"I'm not as stupid as Keva makes me sound!" I shout at him. "Why can't you tell me the truth for once?"

"I *am* telling the truth," Arthur says. He closes his eyes, letting out a tired sigh. "Look, I don't want to fight. Not with you. This theory has been debated for centuries, but fell out of favor during the Renaissance, and it isn't until recently that it was brought forward again. Jennifer only confirmed my own doubts today."

His mention of Jennifer only makes my blood boil all the harder. But before I can protest further, Arthur leans against the wall, eyes closed, the glowworms' diffused light hollowing his cheeks out and deepening the dark smudges beneath his eyes. I find myself unable to look away from him, eyes drinking him in, noting every new bruise, scar and wrinkle on his face, picking out the few white strands catching the light in his brown hair. Harsh imprints left upon him by this war.

And all the anger drains out of me. In the end, what does any of this matter anyway? Arthur's proven his trust in me over and over again, despite all my slipups, my own doubts, against the judgment of his own parents and friends, and even after I almost had him killed.

My heartbeat picks up at the sudden need to touch him, the desire so strong I forget to breathe. All I want is to hug him tight until he feels better and those deep lines of worry are erased from his forehead.

As if it senses my intent, Excalibur flashes once from its scabbard, and I find myself blinking just inches away from Arthur's face. With a muffled gasp, I back up into the opposite wall, biting my lip hard. What is wrong with me?

"Percy must've known," Arthur says in the barest of whispers. "I think his berserker mode was his way to access his...abilities."

Arthur opens his eyes again, and I feel a stab of guilt at the raw emotion spilling from them. If Percy hadn't been trying to help me, Dub would never have gotten his hands on him.

"Yet he never whispered a word of it to me," Arthur continues with a self-deprecating chuckle. "So I can't blame you for feeling the way you do, when I know even my best friend couldn't trust me."

"Was Percy's line, uh, pure then, that he knew how to use his Fey powers?" I ask awkwardly, still unable to coach my heart into a regular beating pattern.

"Not exactly," Arthur says, eyes lost in his memories. "Not many know this, but that way of fighting only developed after his family was attacked at their home by a Fey servant gone rogue.

"It happened long before he was knighted, and although he never talked much about the event, I think it must have shocked his system into using his own powers." Arthur squeezes his hands into tight fists, knuckles going white. "That's what made his parents lose it. They couldn't bear the thought that their only son was one of *them*. And so they abandoned him."

Arthur rakes his hand in his hair, laughing self-deprecatingly.

"And I was never able to do anything to help him," he adds, voice breaking.

This time, I don't stop myself. The pain in his voice is too deep, exposing years of pent-up remorse, and finding an echo inside my own chest.

I close the distance between us, and wrap my arms around Arthur's shoulders. I feel him stiffen in surprise, then his arms snake around my waist to clutch me tightly to him.

And there, in that deserted staircase, Arthur finally allows himself to cry.

We march in awkward silence down the tortuous hallway to Lugh's Council Room. If I'd hoped letting Arthur cry on my shoulder would have made him open up to me more, I was dead wrong.

If anything, he's gotten worse over the past few days, nagging at me for every little thing. I know that the Board's envoy has been a lot to handle, especially since the clumsy man has a tendency to provoke issues instead of assuaging them. And that Carman's incursions—both in the surface world and throughout Avalon—have become harder to contain since our failed attempt to destroy the Siege Perilous.

But if Arthur keeps this attitude up with me for much longer, I may just sock him.

The floor shifts beneath our feet, turning into another twisted staircase that leads up to a curving door.

Arthur pauses before opening it. "Remember to not—"

"Say a word, I know," I say, rolling my eyes at him. "I should be like Ella: Do as I'm told without a word of complaint."

Arthur presses his lips into a thin line at the mention of the Pendragons' former Fey servant, nostrils flaring. We both know Dean killed her, but I still hold it against his family for not doing more to protect the Fey woman.

With a shrug, Arthur manages to school his expression into a bored mask. "As long as you know," he says, setting his hand on the triquetra[19] chiseled into the door.

At his touch, the likenesses of the four elementals carved around the Celtic symbol shiver to life, then quickly scurry to the

---

[19] Celtic symbol of interlaced arcs that look like three connected leaves.

door's corners, pulling the heartwood open behind them like a curtain.

"Good morning," I say loudly, pushing my way in past Arthur. "Hope everyone slept well."

I wave back at the cousins, then cross the room to stand next to Keva by the wall, like a proper squire.

"We were just waiting for you," Sir Dagonet says.

The Board's emissary motions for Arthur to sit on the giant mushroom stool growing out of the floor to accommodate him. Apparently, Arthur caused quite the stir back in Caamaloth while I was away, his quest to forge a new alliance with the Fey and reclaim Lake High ending in a rift between the Board's two main parties—those in favor of working with the Fey, and those who chose to uphold the old ways.

In the end, Keva told me, the latter prevailed, and tried to shame Arthur and his followers. They even petitioned to cross them out of the Order's register, until they realized more than a quarter of their members were willing to lose their knighthood to follow him. At which point they recanted.

Instead, they keep sending Sir Dagonet to keep an impartial eye on things down in Avalon. A constant thorn in Arthur's side to remind him of his place.

"Must you bring that girl to every one of our meetings?" Sir Boris asks Arthur, lounging to the man's left. "For all we know, she's a spy. Let's not forget it's because of that girl this war even started."

"I thought it was the other way around," Gauvain says casually. "Us betraying our accord with the Fey, and her trying desperately to clean up centuries' worth of our mess."

"Just like her father," Gareth says, nodding emphatically.

"And look where that got him," Gauvain states. "It just shows prophets aren't ever taken seriously until it's too late."

"There's no such thing as prophets and prophecies," Arthur says in a cutting tone that makes me wonder if he's thinking of Mordred right now. My brother's been quite adamant about fulfilling some sort of prophecy, as if any divine message could ever condone his vile acts.

"Are you quite sure about that?" Lugh asks, leaning against the knotted mullion[20] of the floor-to-ceiling window that overlooks his territory.

"Let's get on with the meeting now, shall we?" Sir Dagonet says, dismissing Lugh with a wave of his hand. "I have some bad news to share with you."

"You mean other than the worlds falling apart around us?" Oberon asks, with a little growl that makes Sir Dagonet jump.

His notepad clatters to the floor, and he rushes to pick it up, blushing furiously. "The Board's decided to stop funding your activities," he says, looking down at his copious notes to avoid having to look at either of the Fey lords.

"Out of the question," Arthur says. "If we leave now, we risk losing all of Avalon to Carman, and our chance to close the Gates once and for all goes out the window."

"You've tried twice already, and failed both times," Sir Dagonet says. "And the number of injured parties doesn't cease to grow."

"So does the number of rescued," Hadrian counters.

"Not quite to the same degree," Sir Dagonet says testily. "Besides, I heard the blood of our dead has been used to finish Carman's wards around the school, wards meant to keep Hell's Gates permanently opened."

"They haven't succeeded," Gareth says.

---

[20] Vertical piece of wood that divides a window into sections.

"Nonetheless, the Board believes your activities are no longer justified," Sir Dagonet intones. "Particularly when not even Excalibur was able to destroy the Siege Perilous. Which nullifies your latest argument for mounting yet another attack on Lake High, Sir Arthur."

"Actually, Arthur did manage to lop off a piece of it," I say, drawing an irritated look from both Arthur and Sir Boris.

"It did?" Sir Dagonet squeaks out in shock. He clears his throat. "It did?" he repeats, licking the nib of his pen to start writing. "How did that happen, and why was I not informed of this earlier?"

"My broth…, that is, Mordred was sitting in it," I say, "in the process of opening the Gates, when Arthur went for him."

"We all saw the results of that miss," Sir Dagonet's squire says with a smirk.

"I don't recall seeing you there," Keva snaps at the man.

"And that's when he managed to cut off a piece of the chair," I finish.

"Well that's fantastic news," Gareth says.

"It is?" Sir Dagonet asks, looking up in surprise from his notetaking.

"Of course," Oberon says, voice dripping with sarcasm. "Next time, we can just ask Mordred to please sit in the chair while we turn his source of power into matchsticks."

Sir Dagonet nods, already back to his scribbles.

"There is no need to be flippant, Lord Oberon," Lugh says. "We always knew the Siege Perilous could not easily be destroyed, but at least now we know its weakness."

"Who cares about this precious information of yours if we can't act upon it?" Lord Oberon retorts.

"You seem to be forgetting something," Lugh says, pushing away from the window to slowly circle us. "That Mordred is but a half-Fey."

"That doesn't mean he'd be easy to subdue," Oberon says.

"A half-Fey with a sister whom he's helped rescue once before," Lugh continues, as if Oberon never opened his mouth.

Chills run down my arms as he stops behind me. I know where this is going, and though I understand the logic of it, Papillon's words keep bouncing around my head like an incessant warning. What is it Lugh wants from me?

"A half-human with human needs and desires," Oberon says, tapping his chin in thought.

"Like the desire to reconnect with his family," Lugh says.

"No!" Arthur shouts, jumping to his feet.

"What do you mean *no?*" Sir Boris asks. "What better way for her to redeem some of the damage she's inflicted by going back there to be our own spy?"

And to assassinate my own brother in the process, I silently add. Their intent couldn't be more clear.

Arthur turns his cool eyes upon our former teacher. "If she falls into their hands again, she may not survive it this time."

"It's worth the risk," Oberon says, stretching his legs out. "It would pay to have someone else working for us from the inside, other than that filth of a clurichaun."

"That clurichaun has a name, you know," Keva says, surprising us all with her vehemence. "And if it weren't for Nibs, who knows what else Carman would have used Morgan for beside that dragon of hers?"

I groan as the two older knights' eyes go round with shock at the news. Guess that's one piece of information Arthur chose to withhold from them that's now out of the bag.

"That dragon is actually your doing, squire?" Sir Dagonet asks with a hiccup.

"Yes," I whisper, stomach sinking.

"Against her will," Keva adds, trying to repair the harm she's done. "Carman tortured her and used her blood to activate the Sangraal, and—"

"Well that settles it," Sir Dagonet says, clapping his notebook shut. "If that girl's blood is as powerful as you state it is, then she must be incarcerated, and there's only one place secure enough for her. Caamaloth's dungeons."

"You can't be serious," Hadrian says.

"Dead serious," Sir Dagonet says, standing up with a flourish and handing his precious notes over to his squire. "I will let the Board know right away. Now if you'll excuse me."

I frown as I watch the Council Room's door close behind the pompous man and his squire. Talking about our Headquarters' prison stirs my memory, something Nibs said to me before our escape from Hell.

"I'm so sorry, Morgan," Keva says.

It was something about Cain and Abel, I remember.

"I didn't mean to let it slip out like that. Again."

No. Another name. Like Cabe.

"Don't worry, we won't let them take you," Gareth says, swinging his war hammer arm around dangerously.

"Caim?" I whisper.

Oberon freezes at the name, his eyes flattening to slits. "What did you just say?" he asks, and I don't think I'm imagining the tension in his voice.

"Nibs mentioned that name to me," I say. "Said this Caim would be able to help us somehow."

"And you're only mentioning it now?" Sir Boris says, struggling to get back to his feet with all his injuries.

"I forgot," I say lamely.

"We did have quite a bit on our mind at the time," Keva says, jumping to my defense.

"It would make sense to question the one who was once Carman's lover," Oberon says scathingly, "if he were still around to tell the tale."

Lugh's eyes grow distant. "He could, so to speak. Though I believe him to be under lock and key at the present."

"That's what Nibs said, too," I whisper.

Oberon's face turns purple, but before he can throw another of his dark fits, Lugh continues, "Although he went by another name back in the days."

"And what name is that?" Arthur asks.

Lugh's golden eye settles on me. "Sir Joseph."

I let out a strangled cough, almost choking on my own spit. Surely he can't mean my father's squire. I remember when my uncle introduced me to him through his personal scrying mirror. The squire had looked like a sickly old man. Not at all like a Fey.

Yet why else would the Board have detained him inside the most secure prison in the world?

Perhaps, then, Nibs and Lugh are right, and the one who once was my father's squire can give us the key to Carman's undoing. And, hopefully, before the Council tries to lock me up.

# Chapter 24

I shift restlessly on my moss bed—despite my exhaustion, something's dragged me awake. And then I feel it again, that light, rhythmic breeze against the nape of my neck, as of someone breathing.

"Maybe I should bite her?"

I freeze at the squeaky whisper, heart pounding wildly.

"And make her bleed, you stupid furball?"

"Just a tiny pinch!"

I turn around on the bedding so quickly I hear a squeal of surprise, then the strong whirr of a giant insect's wings.

"She's awake!" Papillon exclaims, the jewel at his throat scintillating in the near darkness. "Why didn't you say so?"

"What are you two doing here?" I whisper harshly, afraid anyone else might notice them, might notice their interest in me.

Papillon buzzes closer to my face, his ogham searing my vision. "You need to come with us."

I suddenly sit up. "Are we under attack?" I ask, looking around for signs of fire.

But the adjoining rooms where the others are sleeping are peaceful, the cousins' hefty snores reaching me through the partitions. I go very still, turning my attention back to the two flying mice.

"Do you mean my...mother?" I ask in a strangled voice.

"Hurry up, she hasn't got much time," Papillon says, zooming away.

"Just follow me," the russet mouse says, flying at a statelier pace.

Still a little groggy, I track the whir of the flying mouse's wings, my feet barely making a sound on the wooden floor. I wonder how the others would feel if they found me creeping out like this?

They'd probably get on my case again. And rightfully so—no matter the size of the creature, a Fey's a Fey, and could be dangerous. I dare a glance towards the rounded recess where Arthur's sleeping, and my footsteps falter.

He must've been really exhausted, for he hasn't bothered to pull down the moss-like drape that serves as a door, and his usually pristine room is now in total disarray—clothes, maps and books covering every inch of the floor.

I promised I wouldn't leave him again without his knowing. And here I am, breaking my word at the first occasion.

"Over here, your ladyship," the russet mouse calls out in a reedy whisper.

I lick my dry lips. I know I'm risking a lot on the word of two mice, but I can't let this opportunity slip me by. Not if they're telling the truth, and this could be my only chance to finally meet my mother.

"What are you two dilly-dallying for?" Papillon asks shrilly, making me jump. "You know her holy-light, the mother-of-all, cannot sustain the opening in the barrier for very long!"

"I know," the russet mouse replies, "but the girl chimes to her own clockwork."

"What is that even supposed to mean?" Papillon asks, bristling. "Nobody should make her most-scintillating-lady-of-the-dragons wait! Not even her own daughter."

I wave the mice to shush, afraid that their angry squeaks are going to wake everyone up. "Alright, alright, I'm going," I whisper at them, trying to ignore the sudden guilt swelling in my chest.

But as I reach the door to our burrow-like suite, a soft moan makes me stop again. I cast another worried look at Arthur's sleeping form, his mussed hair highlighted by Excalibur's soft glow. The sound returns, an anguished sob barely muffled by a pillow. Arthur's hurting! The mice completely forgotten, I dash across the living room and to Arthur's side.

He's thrashing and turning on his bed, as if in the throes of a terrible nightmare. I lean over, and hiss out a shocked breath. Five large bruises stain his shoulders, sternum and kidneys, dark lines spreading out from them like wheel spokes, striating the rest of his torso.

I sink to the floor beside him, a feeling of helplessness spreading through my chest.

"Princess, there isn't much time...," the russet mouse says softly.

I ignore her. My hands hover above Arthur's black and white chest without touching him. This can't be right. Arthur can't have been poisoned by Dub. We killed him!

My throat aches with unshed tears. How long has he been suffering like this?

Out of the corner of my eye, I see the twinkling lights of the two flying mice's oghams as they talk to each other. Then Papillon zooms in front of me.

"I am not sure you are entirely aware of the opportunity that has been offered you," he says once he's certain to have my attention. "Her ladyship is, and may the heavens above strike me for saying so, much weakened from both sustaining us throughout these long millennia, as well as fending off those who wish us ill." He pauses, his large eyes peering at me intently. "Are you sure you wish to spurn her in this here moment?"

Papillon's last words dissolve any doubts I may still have had, and I frown at the flying mouse. "*Spurn* her?" I ask, anger flaring. "Last I checked, she's the one who threw Mordred and me out! Now I suggest you both leave before I call for Lugh."

Papillon draws himself up in affront, his wings beating the air furiously. "Know this, then," he says loftily, "the offer will only take place once again, and not more. I hope you'll choose better then."

And with a sniff, the two mice fly away, out through the nearest window.

"Fine by me," I mutter, trying not to feel the pangs of regret suddenly pulling at me.

"Morgan?"

I start at the raspy voice guiltily. "I'm here, Arthur," I say, placing my hand over his. "Everything's fine."

Arthur's breathing calms at my touch. "I thought...I thought you were gone," he says.

My heart constricts knowing how close he is to the truth. His eyes find mine, the hazel of his irises turning gold under Excalibur's soft light, and he attempts a weak smile.

"Was I making that much noise?" he asks, sounding like a little boy caught stealing cookies. "Sorry if I woke you."

I shake my head, unable to speak.

"Glad you're here," Arthur mumbles, shifting his hold on my hand to lace our fingers together.

Such a small switch, yet so much more intimate. My whole body flushes, as if overtaken by a sudden fever, and I find myself unable to move.

I watch Arthur's eyes close again, the worry lines smoothing away from his damp brow. All this time he's been suffering, yet not once has he let it on. I bite hard on my lower lip. I wish I could heal him, as I've healed him before. But I'm scared. Scared I'm going to make things worse. Scared I'm going to fail him yet again.

So when his breathing deepens with the steady rhythm of restful sleep, I carefully untangle our fingers, pull the covers back over him, and steal back to my sleeping cot, feeling like I'm abandoning him.

Seems I take after my mother after all.

"Sir Cade should have been ready by now," Sir Boris harrumphs, checking his pocket watch for the fourteenth time this morning, as if it's going to make it move any faster.

Sir Dagonet was very clear about us not moving from our post until we got the green light from Caamaloth, and we're all feeling the strain of this latest, useless hold-up. We should've seen Sir Joseph already, and managed to get our hands on some of the Fey weapons that the Order's kept under lock and key in the armory.

I glance at Arthur's pale face. Traces of his nightmare are still evident there, at least to me, and I repress the irascible need to hit something. When I sought out Blanchefleur this morning, while everyone else was at breakfast, to ask for her help, I didn't realize she already knew of his condition. Knew, and didn't bother to tell me. So I was forced to listen to her curt dismissal, telling me Arthur's state was beyond her healing ability. And that the only one who could've done something would have been me, before my little trip in Hell perverted my powers.

"It's unlike Sir Cade to be late," Hadrian says, tapping his boot impatiently on the floor.

"Maybe Pendragon's giving him a hard time again," Daniel says, his snickers cut short when Keva pushes him off his fat mushroom stool.

The burnished trefoil set in the middle of the meeting room floor starts to shimmer.

"He's here," Lugh says, before sweeping his hand over the glossy symbol.

We watch as the three leaves expand, pulling out of the floor, before joining again along the blades to form a round bowl that quickly fills up with limpid water.

"*Sgàthan soilleir,*" Lugh intones.

A thick fog lifts from the water's surface, clouding our images as we eagerly lean forward. When the mists dissipate at last, we find our reflections replaced by the image of a single face. One that I can barely recognize, scars and burns now marking what had once been smooth skin. Yet the square jaw and military crew cut have remained the same.

"Good morning, Sir Cade," Sir Boris says thickly.

"Not good," my uncle replies with a stiff nod. His voice echoes slightly through the copper cup he's holding to his mouth, the Hall of Mirror's only way of communicating through the constant scrying his team does.

Sir Cade's reflection ripples, blurring his features, and Hadrian leans further down.

"What's going on?" he asks.

The crystal-clear water stills once again, and we catch the end of his explanations, "—now the armory's under heavy fire."

Gareth jumps off his stool with a repressed shout. My knuckles whiten on my knees as an assistant appears behind my uncle, bleeding hand curled against his chest. Sir Cade turns away from us as the man's mouth moves, delivering his message. His voice is a distorted murmur, but the meaning is clear in my uncle's bunched shoulders, and the scene unfolding behind them.

The Hall of Mirrors is in total chaos, people moving from one mirror to another, shouting orders. I hear someone yell, followed by the loud crash of glass breaking, and I realize that the whole building must be under attack.

Sir Cade's face turns back to us. "She's here," he says.

Three words is all it takes to instill a deep fear in the pit of my stomach. Something lands on the surface of the water, and everyone jumps in surprise, only to realize a bug landed on my uncle's scrying mirror.

"Locusts," Blanchefleur hisses.

"We'll be right there!" Gauvain shouts, pacing around the wooden basin impatiently. If we could travel through it, he'd be the first to jump in the water.

Sir Cade's eyes find mine, and he mouths something to me, but he's lost the mirror's mouthpiece and I can't hear a word. Then the water fogs over again, and we all find ourselves staring instead at our troubled reflections.

"What are they after that they didn't already take last time?" Gareth asks, putting his iron-threaded gloves back on.

"Sir Cade mentioned the armory," Hadrian says, making sure his sword belt is firmly attached around his hips.

Sir Boris's large mushroom seat tilts its wide cap forward to prop him up. "It's not weapons they want," he says, eyeing me disdainfully. "It's that fake squire of Sir Gorlois."

"Caim," Lugh says, his long fingers tapping nervously against the windowsill.

"It can't be," I say, stunned. "He's our only way to defeat Carman."

"It looks like Carman's figured that out too," Keva says with a grimace.

"We need to get going, stat!" Arthur says. He glances at Lugh. "Do you think Pigfain can manage to transport our knights to Caamaloth?"

The Fey Lord nods. "The portal has been created once before, so transporting that many soldiers should be feasible," he says.

Arthur nods tightly. "Then let's get to it."

The room erupts into action, Sir Boris, Blanchefleur, Hadrian and the cousins slipping away first to get ready for battle, Keva and Daniel close on their heels.

Too soon, yet not soon enough, all the able-bodied troops are ready, filing in the burned-down glade towards Pigfain's portal. Ready to face Carman's ire, and save Caamaloth from her fires.

"I really don't think you should go," Arthur says quietly as we wait for our turn.

"Oh, and are you going to tell any of these other people here to stay as well?" I retort.

We take a few steps forward as another group of knights steps inside Pigfain's Fey circle, many barely our age.

"It's not the same thing," Arthur says.

"Are you saying their lives matter less than mine?" I hiss out.

"Don't put words in my mouth," Arthur says. "What I'm saying is that you're way more dangerous than they would be should you fall into Carman's hands again."

"I thought that was exactly where you guys wanted me," I retort scathingly.

The people in line ahead of us throw curious glances over their shoulders at us, before quickly looking away again when they see me. I repress a flinch, hurt at the thought that these knights would rather face Carman than be anywhere near me.

"But in that, you guys are right," I say at last. "No one around here knows how Carman works better than I do, not even Lugh himself."

It's now time for the group in front of us to move into Pigfain's portal, and with a bright flash they all disappear.

"Morgan, please," Arthur says urgently as the Fey circle starts glowing again, "try to understand—"

"No, *you* try to understand!" I fire back at him. "I know what it's like to be at her mercy, and believe me when I say that I'm the last one who's going to want to fall into her clutches again. But she's used my own blood to create that damned dragon of hers! So I must, no, I *need* to find a way to undo it. And believe me when I say that I'm not going to let anything, nor *anyone*, stop me from fighting her, not while there's a breath left in me."

Shocked at my own outburst I push past him, but not before I see the pain and fear in Arthur's eyes. I know he means well, that he cares for me as any knight would his younger, more inexperienced squire. But if I allow him to sway me today, I'll never get the courage to face Carman again.

I nod to Pigfain as I step inside his wide circle, and the Fey boy nods in return, his features strained with evident exhaustion. The rest of our usual group follows suit, pointedly looking everywhere but at me.

At the last second, Arthur jumps inside the circle too, and I barely have the time to let out an annoyed expletive before we're all sucked into the ground.

# CHAPTER 25

"Watch it!"

Arthur's hand shoots out to stop me from dropping to the ground, and I heave right over his shiny boots instead, the whole world still spinning around me.

"Great," he mutters, patting my back soothingly as Pigfain disappears once more to fetch the next batch of soldiers.

"Disgusting," Keva says with a sniff.

"I hate traveling this way," I mutter, wiping my mouth on the back of my coat sleeve.

Pigfain's taken us to the woods on the southeastern part of the Order's expansive property, far enough away from the battle so as not to warn Carman of our presence. But even under these trees, the trampled snow is blood red, and a strange rumbling permeates the freezing air.

Keva and I exchange nervous glances.

"Maybe she's already gone," I hear someone say as Sir Boris shouts for order.

"Shut up," someone else says. "If she's gone then that means our—"

The sound of a distant explosion sends a flock of birds cawing away in alarm, and a heavy silence settles over what remains of our troops.

"Better hurry," Keva says, taking the lead.

But Hadrian calls her immediately back. "When did I say you could go?" he barks at her.

Keva's cheeks flush red. "But I thought——"

"I didn't ask you to think, I asked you to follow my orders!"

Keva's eyes widen in surprise. Never has Hadrian talked to her with that tone before, and the shock of it seems to be difficult for her to swallow.

"You are to remain at my side at all times, unless I order you otherwise, understood?" Hadrian asks.

I look at Arthur, wondering suddenly if he's going to pull the same I'm-your-mighty-knight-so-obey-me kinda crap, especially after my earlier outburst.

The plan was for us two to slip through Carman's forces, unseen, and head straight for the prison, while everyone else helps Caamaloth survive its latest invasion. But maybe he's changed his mind. Maybe he wants to go alone.

But instead, Arthur gives me a resigned sigh.

"Come on," he says, turning to cut across the trees that border Caamaloth's main compound, and, with a silent thank you, I fall into step behind him.

It doesn't take us long to arrive behind the security hall, or what's left of it. Half the building is missing, as if a giant's swiped it clean off the face of the earth. Bodies litter the ground—mostly those of guards and knights. However Carman's army managed to get in this time, it was a massacre.

We angle right to head up the main road, when my footsteps falter. I glance again over my shoulder, and catch sight of a lone figure roaming about the rubble, poking at the debris with a short spear.

"Wait," I whisper, grabbing Arthur's arm before motioning him towards the remains of the last guardhouse.

"We can't afford to stop," he whispers back at me.

"But it's hunting for survivors," I say, peering around the wall. "We can't let it kill defenseless people like that!"

Arthur's lips thin out. "OK," he says at last, "but we can't—"

"Another transgression, unbelievable!"

We both startle at the deep French voice. I tilt my head to the side in confusion as the figure straightens itself, holding onto what I hope isn't a human head, a cigarette burning red at its lips.

"Inspector Bossart?" I call out in my surprise.

The man jumps, dropping whatever he'd caught on his spike, and reaches for his gun.

"Wait, don't shoot!" I shout, pulling away from the cover of the guardhouse, hands held high above my head.

With a frustrated sigh, Arthur follows suit.

"It's only me," I add, carefully edging towards the weaselly man. "Morgan de Cor—Pendragon," I add, remembering belatedly he only knows me under my old family name. The fake one.

"Morgan Pendragon," Inspector Bossart repeats.

My ears might be deceiving me, but it seems he isn't saying my name with as much venom as he once did. Then again, it's been a couple of years since he last saw me, so maybe he doesn't remember who I am.

"Why am I not surprised to find you here?" the inspector continues. "You seem to attract trouble wherever you are."

I grimace, finally dropping my hands to my sides. The man evidently has the memory of an elephant.

"You really shouldn't be here," I say. "It's too dangerous for...for someone like you."

"Are you saying there are more of those aberrations of nature?" the man asks, holstering his firearm, and I know he means the draugar.

"Look," Arthur says, "I have no idea what kind of reports you've received about our center, though I can venture a good guess. But I'll have to second Morgan on this one. This isn't a place for untrained people to be. So I suggest you hurry back out before—"

"I will not let a couple of emo teenagers tell me what to do," Inspector Bossart says, picking his spike back up to point behind him, its end weighed down by a small creature with pink and black fur.

"Isn't that Lady Tanya's pet?" I ask Arthur.

"I'm twenty," Arthur growls, ignoring me.

Inspector Bossart shrugs, lighting up a second cigarette. "Could be my great-aunt, for all I care. Besides, I need to know what to tell that lot over there."

"Tell who?" I ask, finally looking at what Inspector Bossart's pointing at.

I go very still. Pressing angrily against the entrance gates down the driveway, is a crowd of journalists, their cameras aimed straight at us, flashes going off like machine guns.

"What are they doing here?" Arthur asks tensely. "They shouldn't even have made it this far."

"I'm actually surprised they've never made their way down here before," Inspector Bossart counters, waving the tiny Fey's carcass around, "what with all the exceedingly odd things that always happen around here, and how the whole world seems to have gone down the rabbit hole too."

"Our security team's usually pretty good at intercepting them beforehand," Arthur says.

The security team which was taken down in the assault, I silently add, my skin prickling with dread. I look at the storm clouds gathered over the rest of the compound, wishing I could already be at the prison looking for Sir Joseph. But I can't let these innocent humans get into harm's way either.

"Well, they'll certainly have a ball when the militia finally gets here," the inspector says.

"You didn't!" Arthur exclaims, going pale.

"Of course, I did, boy," Inspector Bossart says, stabbing him with his finger. "Whatever your secret sect may say, there are too many things happening in here, in *my* country. Not to mention those monsters you keep harboring. I'll be damned if—"

"If those soldiers get here, *you*'ll be responsible for their deaths," Arthur says, seething. "Call them off. And you"—he points at me—"get those civilians away!"

"What do you expect me to do?" I ask. "Shoo them away?"

"Exactly," Arthur says, a crazed glint in his eyes. "Remember that time you played with the clouds on our way here?"

"Yeah."

"Do it again."

My mouth drops open. "I don't think that's very wise," I say. "What if the thunderstorm falls over us? We're all carrying a lot of iron on ourselves."

"We'll cross that bridge when we get to it," Arthur says grimly. "All I'm asking is for you to move the clouds lower to create a fog. Anything to hide what's happening from their lenses."

"And what, exactly, is happening here?" Inspector Bossart asks, a little subdued. He may be prickly and an annoying stickler for his rules, but he isn't stupid.

The ground shakes as a loud explosion thunders across the Headquarters. The inspector loses his footing, and Arthur rushes up to catch him before the man can tumble all the way down to the bottom of the pile of rubble. The angry skies above the Tactical Operations Center light up as our troops respond to the attack with elemental power.

"What was that? Another gas explosion?" Inspector Bossart asks, looking like he rather wished it were.

"They must have gotten to the prison," Arthur says in alarm.

"There's a prison here?" Inspector Bossart exclaims, dropping his third cigarette.

Arthur turns on him. "If we manage to repel this latest attack, I'll get someone to answer any question you may have, if that's what you want," he says quickly. "If you're still alive, that is. And the longer you stay here, the lower the probability."

I crane my head up to look at the dark clouds rolling over the Jura mountains, trying to recall my animal figure-making when we were landing here on my first visit to Caamaloth.

"Very well," I hear the inspector say. "I'll do my best to detain those journalists while your people handle…whatever that is. But you better wrap things up quick, cause the militia isn't going to listen to me."

Drawing a deep breath, I point to the closest cloud with my index finger, then sweep it down, an artist painting on her canvas. For a moment, nothing happens, then a sharp breeze picks up, funneling the cloud our way.

"It's working!" I exclaim, as Inspector Bossart casts us weary glance before heading down the long driveway to the gates.

"Don't stop now," Arthur says, keeping a worried look at the back of the compound where we can hear our troops fighting.

Dutifully, I turn to the next cloud, doing the same as with the first, until the whole sky seems to have dropped onto our heads, burying us in a cold, vaporous blanket.

I let out a giddy laugh, all my senses tingling. This is what being Fey is supposed to be: Using the elements to help others, not waging war and destroying everything around.

Then the first rumblings of a storm roll in, and I feel my hair rise with static electricity.

"I think I may have overdone it," I say, as the clouds turn a nasty shade of grey, lightning bolts sizzling all around us.

"It's perfect," Arthur shouts in my ear, pulling me after him. "Now come on!"

We bolt across the rough terrain, navigating around bodies and fallen buildings as quickly as we can. Which is still not fast enough.

"We could fly," I suggest, still buzzed from tampering with the weather.

"Not unless you want to draw the lightning straight to you," Arthur retorts, as we pass by the Research Center.

Debris from shattered windows crunch beneath our pounding boots as we near the thick of the battle. Shouts and cries resound across the Headquarters, drowning out the sound of my pounding heart. Metal hisses and clangs as it connects with claws and fangs. Another detonation rips out somewhere close, throwing us into the Research Center wall. Bodies fly to land at odd angles on the trampled grounds.

I shake my head, eardrums ringing. But Arthur's already helping me back up.

"That way," he shouts, pointing at the Armory's burning warehouses.

I can tell it's costing him not to join the fight. But I've made us waste too much time already.

We plunge between the long buildings, eyes stinging, and coughing on the acrid smoke. The walls on both sides of us seem to pulse with life as the heat of the flames makes them expand and contract. My sweat evaporates, leaving me parched. My uniform feels heavy, and growing hotter, almost burning.

We come out the other side, and I gasp in mouthfuls of fresh air, shivering in the sudden cold. But my relief is short-lived.

Straight ahead is the black cube that denotes the prison's entrance, stark and solitary within its separate enclosure. And, rising from it, dark plumes of smoke.

We're too late.

"Morgan!"

I duck instinctively at the sudden shout, and Arthur wheels around, unsheathing Excalibur in one smooth movement. There's a surprised cuss, and Arthur tries to pull his swing back before he can cut the knight in two.

"Sir Cade?" he calls out.

My uncle halts in front of us, two knights flanking him, Emmerich, and some woman I've never seen before. All three of them look like they've been run over by a tank. But they're alive, and the tightness in my chest eases a fraction.

"Where are the others?" Sir Cade asks.

"They should be here already," Arthur says with a frown. "Sir Boris is leading them. Haven't you seen them?"

Sir Cade's face falls. "I was hoping that was just the front line."

"Afraid not," Arthur says through clenched teeth. He points at the prison with his stubbly chin. "Seen anyone come out of there?"

"Too many, but not Carman herself, if that's what you're asking," Emmerich answers.

"So be it," I say.

My uncle's brow creases in a severe frown as his eyes bore into me, his jaw tensing. "You can't be serious."

"I am," I find myself saying. "I have no choice."

"Of course, you do!" Sir Cade exclaims. "You and Arthur should both leave and let us—"

"Handle things here?" I ask with a pointed look at the war raging on around us.

Sir Cade's face closes again.

"Carman's here for Sir Joseph," Arthur butts in. "The two apparently used to be lovers before she got put away. It's what we wanted to discuss with you earlier."

My uncle blanches. "You can't be serious."

All three of them look at the prison, understanding dawning on their faces.

"Hurry," the woman says, already taking off.

We sprint the last few hundred meters that separate us from the prison block, past its torn-up fence. The front of the building looks like it's been melted through with a giant blowtorch, a large hole where the secret entrance had once been. I take a deep breath, the thick smoke tickling the back of my throat. I blink droplets of mist from my eyes. This is it.

"Wait for my signal," Sir Cade says, already motioning the other two knights inside.

I stare intently inside the hole where my uncle and his knights have gone. One breath. Two. Everything inside is silent, save for the whistling of the wind. Three. Four. Five.

Still nothing.

My nerves twitch. Carman's in there, I know it.

Arthur's hand finds mine, and squeezes it briefly. "Wait a little longer," he says, inching towards the gaping hole, Excalibur flashing in his hand.

A bloodcurdling cry arises from the depths of the prison.

"It's him!" I shout in anguish.

Without waiting for Arthur, I dash inside the prison, springing down the staircase as quickly as my legs can take me. The smoke is thick, blinding, burning down my lungs. But I don't slow down.

"*Ansuz!*" I hear Arthur say behind me.

There's a green flash and the air clears up as Arthur's sylph holds us inside its protective bubble.

"There," I say, pointing at a small puddle of black tar on one of the steps leading further down.

We follow Carman's poisonous trace, taking the stairs three at a time, eyes roving for any sign of Sir Cade and his team.

"Which floor is Sir Joseph on?" I ask, jumping over another patch of tar.

"Don't know," Arthur says, his eyes darting down each corridor we cross, each baring signs of forced entry, trying to count the number of Fey Carman may have freed on her way to Caim.

"Here," Arthur says, skidding to a stop on the twelfth floor down.

Breathing hard, I peer into the dark hallway ahead, trying to make out what's happening inside. Another scream resounds, making the hairs at the back of my neck stand up.

I rush blindly ahead, cold sweat drenching my sides. But before I can get very far, something barrels into me, knocking me down. My head hits the floor, and blood floods my mouth as I bite my tongue.

"Morgan!" Arthur cries out.

I feel the creature shift on top of me, then light flares as it blasts Arthur away.

"No!" I shout, fear making me lash out.

A wave of angry energy bursts out of me as I punch my attacker. I feel its weight lift from me, then hear it slam into the ceiling. I roll and push to my feet, disoriented in the semi darkness. Then pain explodes in my chest as the creature crashes into me, pinning me to the floor, before its cold hand slaps over my mouth.

"Shhhhh," the demon whispers in my ear.

Mordred? I whimper against his calloused fingers.

"The witch is almost done," he says in my ear. "Wouldn't want to interrupt her now, would we?"

I try to move, but Mordred's grip only tightens.

"Listen to me, sis," he continues more urgently. "I'm gonna let you go, but only if you promise to get out of here quietly. Got it? She can't find you here."

Smoke swirls around us, allowing the light from a baby salamander trapped inside one of the wall sconces to illuminate Mordred's tattooed face for a brief instant. And in that second, I see the fear in his eyes.

I nod at last.

"You can't go back on your word now," he says, suddenly releasing me. "So take your boyfriend and go."

Arthur. I scramble back the way I came, mind alight with panic, and find him lying motionless on the landing.

"Arthur," I whisper, feeling around his head for injuries.

He grunts as my fingers graze his bleeding wound, but doesn't open his eyes.

"Out. *Now.*" Mordred urges me, looking in alarm down the corridor as the salamander's light winks out again, plunging the hallway back into obscurity.

Carman must be done with Sir Joseph, and I couldn't stop her. Nor could my uncle. I cradle Arthur in my lap. I won't let her take him from me too.

"Help me carry him," I tell my brother, struggling under Arthur's weight as I pick his sword up with my other hand, its responding glow enough to light our immediate surroundings.

Mordred throws me a disgusted look. Then, seeing I'm not going to move otherwise, he shoulders Arthur on his free side.

"Hold on tight," he says.

And Mordred taps his foot on the floor, propelling us over the railing and down the stairwell.

"Shouldn't we be going up?" I squeak out as landing after landing whizzes past.

"Shut up," Mordred snarls.

I click my mouth shut and resolve to trust my brother, despite all my instincts screaming at me not to. At last, Mordred slows down, and our feet hit the bottom of the prison staircase.

"Don't go back up there until we're long gone," Mordred says, dumping Arthur on the floor.

"But—"

"Carman's too powerful for you. Especially when you've chosen to give yourself a human handicap." I feel Mordred's breath brush my forehead as he leans in. "Remember, sis, you now owe me three times over," he adds before launching himself straight back up the stairwell.

I crouch down, my fingers grazing Arthur's back. He lets out a slight moan of protest at the touch, and I jerk my hand back. Try as he might to hide the injuries Dub gave him, there's no doubt he's weaker than he used to be.

"—seems to me you were speaking to someone."

My insides squirm at the sound of Carman's voice.

"Ran into a couple of stragglers," I hear Mordred say, his voice strangely distorted.

Carman's choking him.

A hole opens in my stomach. Sweat coats the palms of my hands. Any resolve I had left to face her evaporates as my body remembers the pain she inflicted upon me.

"You wouldn't be lying to me now, would you my pet?"

My heart feels like it's about to burst out of my chest.

"Did…hear…interesting…," Mordred wheezes out, "…bones…grange."

"And you're only telling me that now?" Carman shouts.

Darkness erupts far above me. I lean over Arthur's body protectively as black feathers plummet to the ground, burning through everything they touch, leaving behind little pools of fuming slime. I bite back a scream. Mordred!

And then she's gone, the pressure I didn't realize was there suddenly lifted.

Arthur shifts against me. "Morgan?" he calls out tentatively.

"I'm OK," I say, helping him sit up. "Just…stay here for a moment."

I throw myself into the air, flying straight up until I reach Sir Joseph's floor, almost hoping to find Mordred there. I tell myself it's a good thing, that he must have left with Carman, for all I find on the landing are two tar-free patches.

I shake my head to clear it of the fumes still suffusing the air, then dive into the hallway where Mordred intercepted me.

"Uncle?" I call out. "Sir Joseph?"

A strangled whimper comes from the other end of the corridor, and I press forward. I find Sir Cade inside a dank cell that smells of mold and decay, a twinkling orb showing him holding an old man in his arms, no sign of Emmerich or the female knight that went in with him.

"You're alive," I say, a knot of worry loosening in my chest.

"He hasn't got much longer," my uncle says, looking up at me, and I'm surprised to find his eyes moist with unshed tears.

"Is that…young…Morgan?" Sir Joseph wheezes.

I drop down next to them and gently take the old man's spotted hand into my own, a hand that once helped my father.

Now, his paper-thin skin shows every one of his veins as Carman's poison travels through his body, snuffing his life out.

"I-I could try to heal you," I stutter.

Sir Joseph's fingers twitch around mine, and his eyes crack open, amber irises reminding me that he is also Caim, the Fey who once was Carman's partner.

"Do not cry...over me," Sir Joseph says. "It was meant...happen." He attempts a small smile. "Did a lot I regret...but s-saving you was not one..."

He coughs violently, his frail body shaking in Sir Cade's arms, and I finally see the hole in his chest where Carman ripped his ogham free. Not something I could heal, even if I still had the ability to.

Sir Joseph's hand contracts around mine, and he pulls me closer to him. "Remember...anger...not the...answer..."

"The answer to what?" I ask hoarsely.

"She doesn't...understand," Sir Joseph wheezes, eyes staring at a spot above me.

"Carman?" I ask. "What doesn't she understand?"

"Feeding hate...hell...," Sir Joseph whispers, the poison now reaching up to his jaw.

I look at my uncle helplessly, but he seems as lost as I am.

"Sir," I say, shaking the dying Fey by his shoulders, "we know Carman wants to free Balor, but—"

A wet laugh escapes Sir Joseph's parched lips. "Blood can't lie..."—his amber eyes alight on my face again—"true...to both...parents...like hers..."

His hand suddenly unclenches from around mine, the last of his strength used up.

"Like hers?" I repeat dumbly.

But the golden glow has faded from his eyes, and only Sir Cade's floating orb is left to light the prison cell. Another death on my hands.

"He's gone," I say, feeling numb.

"But didn't you hear?" my uncle says urgently. "He's given us what we need to stop Carman."

"What is it?" Arthur asks, stumbling inside.

Sir Cade looks up, grinning widely despite the tears now flowing freely down his cheeks. "Carman's half human too."

# Chapter 26

Silence stretches between us as my uncle's words sink in—Caim's final revelation is huge, and I simply can't fathom it.

Carman's a halfie.

Like me.

And that means the odds of beating her have ever so slightly increased.

"It is as I suspected," my uncle says.

"The bones in Newgrange?" Arthur asks.

Sir Cade nods with a slight wince.

"What are you talking about?" I ask. "You guys already knew she wasn't a full Fey?"

"Just Emmerich, since he was manning the Northern European mirrors the night we received the news," my uncle says. "Then there's myself, and a couple of the more trustworthy knights."

Trustworthy knights like Arthur. I throw them both a scathing look. They knew of this, and yet they didn't even mention a thing. Not even to me, after all I've been through to get them crucial information about Carman's activities.

Anger, deep and wild, boils inside me, making my hands shake. The thick iron door that Carman punched in flies across the cell and hits the far wall with a deafening crash.

"There have been some pretty bad information leaks," Arthur explains, eyeing me with barely veiled surprise. "We didn't want this to get into the wrong hands until our suspicions were proven correct."

"And why did that take you so long?" I ask Sir Cade, breathing deeply through my nostrils to calm myself down. "You and Caim were best buddies, weren't you?"

"I didn't know," my uncle says quietly. He folds Caim's arms over his chest to hide the blackened hole left there by Carman. "I think...I think he didn't breathe a word of it before to protect me, knowing I was under constant surveillance. Then after...I've been too busy to keep up with him like I should have..."

I sneer at the two of them in disgust. If it weren't for all these little secrets everyone likes to keep, we'd have had the solution ages ago. Worse, if Mordred hadn't distracted her away from us, no one would've known the truth.

Fear prickles the back of my neck. Newgrange. That's what Mordred was talking about, the piece of news that had Carman bolting.

"She knows you're aware of the truth," I say, springing to my feet. "We've gotta stop her!" Before she can unleash her fury on everyone else.

I go up the prison staircase as fast as I can, ignoring Arthur's shouts, and burst through the melted entryway into the violent storm outside. Sleet pelts down on me as I throw myself into the air, drenching me to the bone before I even make it past the prison's torn gates.

I fly low over the battle, eyes scouring the skies and grounds for a sign of Carman. But all I see are masses of demons and draugar fighting Fey and knights, bodies tangling and untangling in a deathly dance, blood and ichor spilling over the churned earth. I pause at the sound of a distant rattle, wondering if that could be her, when pain rips through my side.

I let out a surprised gasp as a second bullet tears through my thigh, then feel myself drop, gravity taking over, and I'm falling straight into a mass of snarling demons. I try to slow myself down, regain control. But my thoughts are muddled, body going into shock. I barely register the webbed claws of a Fomori reaching for me before something stops my fall with a bone-jarring jolt.

"Couldn't just wait, now, could you," Arthur growls against me, his sylph enveloping us in its protective bubble.

With a shaky laugh, I let my head fall against his metallic jacket.

"I have to stop her," I say into his neck, using the strong wind as an excuse to cling closer to him. The feel of his arms around me is enough to make me feel safe, even in the middle of a battle.

"Don't be a fool," Arthur says. "Do you really think knowing Carman's half-Fey is somehow going to magically make her any easier to take down? On your own?"

He lands us in the middle of the small courtyard wedged between the Ops Center and the dorms where Inspector Bossart and I encountered our first draugar. The enclosure has somehow managed to remain untouched, both from the fighting and from Carman's blood rain, and when Arthur sets me down on the snow-covered bench, even the sounds of battle seem dimmed.

"Let me see," Arthur says, gently forcing me against the bench's backrest.

I grimace as the movement pulls at torn muscles in my side and leg. "I'll be fine," I mutter, teeth chattering. "I'll heal."

"Probably best if there's no bullet in you, though," Arthur says. "Now stop fidgeting."

I wince as he prods my injuries, and to avoid feeling faint at the sight of my own blood seeping through Arthur's fingers, I stare instead at the statue of a stoic *Charlemagne*. The man's alabaster face is stern, devoid of any mirth, and according to our Lore teacher, Sir Lincoln, it was under this Emperor's reign that our Order started to incorporate Elemental Manipulation as a basic requirement for knighthood. It was also, as Keva added, when the Errant Companions formed, breaking away from what they called a heathen practice.

I wonder how the Errant Companions will react when they find out they've all got Fey blood in them.

"Your leg's OK," Arthur says, pulling me away from my thoughts, "but I don't see an exit wound from the bullet in your side."

"Oh, joy," I say.

"Brace yourself," Arthur adds.

I let out a low groan as he deftly cuts my stomach wound further open to pull out the bullet still lodged within my flesh, the pain making me burn up despite the freezing temperatures.

"Almost done," Arthur says through gritted teeth.

"Do you think our Order would have given up the use of oghams if they knew Myrdwinn taught it to us only to weaken Carman's prison wards?" I ask, feeling the slug sliding out of my body under Arthur's coaxing.

"I frankly don't know," he says at last, rocking back on his heels with a sigh. I watch him clean the blood from his hands in the snow. "Power has a tendency to lure even the best of us. You saw how it's affected Jennifer, Agravain, and the others."

He takes another look at my already closing wound, his hand chilly against my skin, then gives me a small smile as he pulls my shirt back down.

"Good as new," he says. "But I, for one, am glad that such a power has allowed you to stay by my side."

Words of thanks die in my throat as Arthur's other hand comes up to brush my hair back, then lingers along my jawline, so soft I can barely feel it. Heat radiates from my face despite the icy storm, and I quickly look away from his hazel eyes to hide my sudden embarrassment.

"Morgan," Arthur starts, sounding uncertain. "I——"

A loud explosion shakes the whole compound, making me slip off the bench. Terrified screams rise on the other side of the Ops Center.

"It's her," I say tightly, jumping to my feet guiltily. How could I have forgotten about Carman, even for just a second?

"Lugh must be fighting her," Arthur states, pulling his gloves back on and motioning for me to stay close.

We rush across the courtyard, vault over its low wall, then pelt down the once-pristine alleys towards the Dining Hall where the sounds of battling are the loudest. Another detonation sweeps across the grounds, taking with it half the Ballroom's domed roof.

We round the dorms, and fall onto a group of young knights huddling among the rubble, eyes wide with fear as they stare high up at the wrathful sky.

"Retreat by the Eastern Woods!" Arthur shouts, waving them back. "It's too danger——"

*BOOM!*

The force of the blast slams into us, sending us sprawling across the path. I hit the frozen ground hard, cracking my head on a rock. White pain explodes behind my eyes. All slows, sounds gone except for my wild-beating heart. Then the ringing in my ears turns into a dull whine, and I can finally make out the frenzied shouts of those still fighting, the soft sobs of the dying.

A demon lands next to me with a hair-raising shriek, long limbs scraping the ground for prey. I struggle up, fight back a bout of nausea. The creature finally sees me, large eyes slitting at the sight of easy prey. Then a stray blast of salamander fire hits the monster in the head, taking it out.

I scramble to my feet, gaze sweeping the ravaged grounds for Arthur. I find the southern edge of the dorms where the knights had taken refuge, but the building's collapsed into an avalanche of white dust, taking everyone around with it.

"Arthur!" I scream.

I lurch forward, forcing my panic back down.

"Art—"

A kick lands on my back, flattening my back down to the hard ground. Air whooshes out of my lungs with a surprised yelp.

"I wouldn't think about interfering," Urim's distinctive drawl says in my ear as I try to roll away from him. "We won't be nice like we were at that silly school of yours."

"Didn't think you...nice," I wheeze out.

Urim laughs. "Here's the deal, sweet cheeks: We're not gonna meddle, if you don't interfere either."

His knee digs deeper into the small of my back, as a figure detaches itself from the horde of demons swirling around the large fountain.

"Get away from my son!" Luther shouts, pointing off to the side.

"Arthur?" I whisper, craning my neck around to look where he's pointing.

I let out a gasp of fear as I finally catch Arthur facing Mordred, the two of them slowly circling each other. Thummim's there too, watching them with bated breath.

"Oh, please don't let them fight," I beg Urim, as Mordred strikes first, forcing Arthur back.

Urim twists my arm so hard my shoulder pops. "No touchy, I said," he whispers in my ear.

I watch helplessly as Luther tries to run to Arthur's help, only to find himself surrounded by Mordred's creatures, with but a handful of knights to defend him.

One of the Dark Sidhe lashes out, raking the knight closest to it down the face. Bellowing in pain, the man swings his sword blindly around, nearly cutting the woman next to him. Then, with a sinister laugh, another demon punches the knight in the back, its long claws piercing through the iron-plated shirt with ease, and the knight stops moving.

"What are you shitheads doing?" Luther shouts angrily. "You're supposed to be protecting me, not dropping like a bunch of flies!"

One of the knights tries to parry a second attack, but his sword misses wildly, and he lets out a cry of pain as another Dark Sidhe strikes him, pinning him down through the leg with a long bony tail.

Luther reacts immediately, blasting the monster in the chest, then hacking the tail off the injured knight. But a fourth demon uses the opportunity to stab Luther beneath the shoulder blade.

"Father!" Arthur shouts in anguish.

With a vicious growl, Luther twists around to hack at his attacker, then moves onto the next two demons, cutting them across the chest and legs, a tempest of blood and death.

Off to the side, Arthur tries a faint, wanting to rush to his help, but Mordred's always there, blocking his way, corralling him away. He's toying with Arthur, enjoying the sight of his growing despair.

And then I feel it, a slight, distant pull that makes the blood in my veins thrum in recognition. Dread sets in as I look up at the sky, squinting against the sleet. We've run out of time. Carman's called her dragon over, and it's heading this way.

"Get off me!" I shout at Urim, trying to wriggle free.

But the Dark Sidhe sends a shock of power through me in warning. "Your boy will be fine if he stays put," Urim says, misunderstanding my sudden alarm.

Off to the side, Thummim's decided to take part in the fun, sliding inside Arthur's reach while Mordred hops backward, and punches Arthur in the chin. Arthur reels back, slips on the ground, and nearly loses Excalibur as he tries to right himself. Then the Dark Sidhe's elbow connects with the back of his temple, and Arthur's eyes roll back in his head.

I reach for my power, letting it rip out of me. Ribbons of flames whip out of my splayed hand, crackling and hissing as they come into contact with the snow. But with a savage growl, Urim twists my arm further up, and I lose all control in the pain that follows, the fire I summoned exploding in a shower of harmless sparks.

"Hush, he's fine now, princess," Urim says, as Thummim gently lays Arthur on the frozen ground. "Now watch as justice finally takes place."

The Dark Sidhe forces my head around, and through the tears and sleet, I see Mordred's tattooed back advance upon a cornered Luther, power radiating from him in waves.

"Do you know who I am?" my brother asks, stopping a couple feet away from the tall knight's sword in challenge.

"Don't give a rat's ass who you are, demon," Luther spits, eyes cold and calculating.

"It's a shame, for I know a lot about you, Luther Pendragon," Mordred says, a raw edge to his voice. "I know you betrayed my father to satisfy your base urges to bed his wife and take his place on this silly little Council of yours. You should have killed me too, when you had the chance."

Luther's lips curl up as he puts two and two together. "Not for lack of trying," he says. "But your parents had already tossed you out like the garbage you are, so I couldn't find you."

He kicks his last knight from behind, sending her crashing into Mordred. The woman lets out a surprised yelp, raising her sword at the last moment. But with a quick turn of his hips, Mordred dodges the weapon, and hits the knight on the forehead with the palm of his hand, before sidestepping her as she drops to her knees, unseeing eyes crying blood.

"At least you're not denying it," Mordred says, inching forward again.

Luther mirrors his movement, taking another step back, and bumps against the courtyard's fountain.

"My question now to you is this," Mordred continues, "Will you have the balls to fight me, or are you going to run for it, old man?"

Sword held defensively in front of him, Luther steps onto the wide basin, and thrusts his gloved fist down. Purple light blooms outward across the basin, the fountain's ice cracking into hundreds of frozen splinters. Then Luther snaps his hand around, and the shards of ice rush straight at Mordred.

My brother laughs excitedly, flicking the icepicks aside to let them fall harmlessly to the ground.

"You're going to have to do better than that, old man, or it's going to be over too quickly," he says.

Without waiting for an answer, Mordred rushes forward, black flames erupting from his extended fingers. I cringe inwardly at the sight. His power's too similar to Carman's and Dub's, tainted. Like mine is.

Luther's sword sings, cutting through the air. But my brother's too quick, a flash of darkness that cannot be stopped. He ducks, slipping past the blade, then strikes. Luther winces as black fire licks his thigh, melding the iron of his *cuisses*[21] to his flesh. He tries to take another step, falters, then slips off the fountain in a crash of metal on stone.

Mordred lets out another chuckle. "Like I said, over too quickly."

Bile rises to my throat. He's like a leopard, toying with its food, taking cruel joy in the bestowing of pain and fear, all the while knowing he can take his victim's life at any moment. Yet despite all the evidence, I still can't accept that this is my brother's true face.

"Mordred, stop it!" I shout.

I gasp in pain as Urim yanks hard on my arm to keep me subdued, but I've managed to make Mordred pause. He looks over his shoulder at me, confusion and anger warring on his tattooed face.

"After everything he's done to our family, to you, you still want him to live?" he asks.

"Killing him is not the way to go," I say feebly.

A sneer pulls at Mordred's lips. "You're only saying that because you've got a crush on his spawn. But that doesn't excuse the sins of the father."

Behind him, Luther tries again to crawl away, eyes wide with fear. And I finally see it, the dark, writhing mass extending from Mordred's feet to the fountain, consuming all in its passage.

"Blood calls to blood, sis," Mordred says, turning away from me.

---

[21] Thigh armor.

He closes his fingers into a tight fist, and the tar sweeps up to take Luther out. There's a startled shout to my left, then Arthur's suddenly in front of his father, Excalibur held before him as the inky wave crashes over them.

Terror twists my insides viciously, and with a howl of rage, I let my power loose. This time, Urim jumps off me with a string of curses, holding his midsection like he's just been stabbed. I haul myself to my feet, and bolt for the fountain.

I find Excalibur lying in a pool of blood, and I grab it without breaking stride, the sword pulsing in my good hand at my touch, as if in acknowledgment. In the span of a breath, I close the distance between me and Mordred, and swing Excalibur down, aiming for his head.

Searing pain lances down my arm, blurring my vision with tears. I clench my teeth, forcing myself to finish the strike, but at the last second, the blade swerves to the side, leaving Mordred unharmed.

"Did you just try to kill me?" Mordred asks, eyes wide in disbelief.

Excalibur falls from my numb fingers, and I stumble back, seething.

"You would choose *him* over your own flesh and blood?" Mordred continues.

"You killed him!" I shout, my voice breaking with a sob.

"He's fine," Mordred snaps.

He steps away, and behind him I can see Arthur helping Luther up, tar surrounding them like a dark moat, faint traces of a sylph's shield still flickering in the cold air.

I look back at Mordred, the full weight of what I just tried to do dawning on me. I'm not sorry, not truly. Not after what he did. Yet the hurt that flashes on his face makes me doubt myself.

I open my mouth to apologize, then clamp it shut again. There's nothing I can say that'll make any of this better.

That's when the screams erupt. We both look up at the cloudy sky as it lights up a bright, fiery red somewhere to the north. And then I hear it, the steady pumping of giant wings beating at the air.

I forget to breathe.

"I had a feeling things might get to this," Mordred says stiffly. "You should've stayed put, like I said."

Behind him, Arthur raises both arms up, as if to wave the dragon over. Then his voice rings out sharply. "*Tháinig anam sa dragan!*"

I have to avert my gaze as light flares out from his raised hands, then a powerful double roar rends in the air.

"That's only going to piss her off more," Mordred states, sounding oddly calm. "You might want to leave now."

But I can't tear my eyes away from the two red dragons speeding through the sky to intercept Carman's beast. They are half the size of the dragon I helped create, but they don't hesitate. The chest of one lights up, ruby red in the waning day, long neck curved gracefully back. And as the black dragon bellows out its torrent of fire, the smaller one spews out its own jet of scorching flames to counter it.

The two streams of fire meet in a powerful explosion that sends burning embers showering down upon the Headquarters, and the second red dragon launches its attack.

"No way," I breathe. "I thought all dragons were extinct!"

"All wild dragons," Mordred says. "Where did you think the Pendragons got their name from?"

One of the smaller dragons shrieks as it dives in an attempt to rip the larger beast's wing with its talons, missing by inches.

Mordred grabs my bad arm, and I suck in a breath as pain stabs at my dislocated shoulder. "You really should leave," he says tightly, as the heat from another charge blazes above head.

I finally look away from the aerial battle. The world is carnage, disintegrating before my very eyes. Men and women trying to hold the assailants back while not tripping over their fallen comrades. Sneering and hissing demons crawling everywhere, eager to bring down everything that comes in their way, even their own.

"I said to get a move on, and—"

A tinkling laugh floats down to us over the wind. Mordred snatches his hand away. Carman's hanging in the air, feet away from her own dragon, like the angel of death itself. And, caught in some invisible bindings beside her, are Lugh and Blanchefleur.

"Take cover and get ready to fire!" someone shouts.

I blink slowly as Inspector Bossart rushes around the crumbling dorms, frantically waving his arms about.

"Fall back, all of you!" the man shouts at a group of men huddling behind the crumbled wall of the dorms' southern wing.

Men dressed in camo and carrying rifles.

The very ones who shot at me before.

Mordred laughs quietly, following my line of sight. "Oh, this is going to be interesting."

The militiamen start firing in rapid bursts, aiming at the flying beasts without distinction between them. Not that it matters; bullets, it appears, can't pierce dragonhide. Still, the guns keep rattling, casings pinging off stone and masonry, smoke rising from the barrels.

Then Carman swipes a bored hand around, and all at once the bullets reverse their course, a metal hail that's going to take everyone with it. Time seems to slow, yet I can't make myself move to stop this nightmare.

My chest hollows out, despair filling it instead. Why am I so powerless? Why can't I undo the wrong I've done?

Warmth suddenly radiates through my body, nerves singing with power, and time seems to stop. I gasp as my feet lift off the ground, the force carrying me high above Caamaloth, until I'm face-to-face with Carman herself.

Her dark stare fixes me like I'm the plague-bringer. A vein throbs at her temple, hair stuck to her face by the storm. Yet, strangely, I feel no fear. She seems so little now, while I feel so big, so full of energy.

I exhale, the smallest of breathes, and the warm power bursts free, spilling out of my outstretched fingers in a kaleidoscope of colors to sweep through the whole compound like a tidal wave.

I watch as the light dissolves Lugh's and Blanchefleur's bindings, draining them of Carman's poison, without the witch being able to do a thing. Below us, cries of awe and wonder arise as knights and Fey alike find themselves healed, pain and injuries erased in a heartbeat.

Then, as quickly as it appeared, the magic dissolves, and I find myself drifting back down, unharmed.

"Traitor," Mordred says, glaring at me.

I look at my hands in confusion. "That wasn't me," I say, though my fingers are still tingling with the last of the energy.

Jealousy flashes in my brother's eyes, quickly replaced by disgust. But before he can retort, loud cheers erupt across the courtyard. We both look up to find that both Carman and her dragon have gone, not a single trace of them left in the clearing skies.

The tide has turned, and the demon ranks are already splintering away, choosing to flee like their leader before we can retaliate.

"Luther, don't!" Arthur shouts.

I barely have the chance to see Arthur's father lunge at Mordred with a long dagger before I fling my hands out. With a thunderous *crack*, the earth splits open between Mordred and Luther, forcing the latter to skid to a stop, before he can fall into the abyss.

"What the hell do you think you're doing?" Luther shouts at me. "You let the witch escape, and now you dare defend that filth who's been murdering our people?"

"I'm not letting him go," I say, although I'm not quite sure what I should be doing instead. All I know is that I don't want Mordred dead.

But isn't that what's going to happen to him if he doesn't get out of here now?

A bitter smile stretches Mordred's lips. "Oh, but you have no choice in the matter, sister dear," he says. "You owe me three favors now, and I'm calling one back."

A strange torpor spreads through my limbs, as if I've suddenly been caught inside a dream. I watch helplessly as Mordred launches himself over the breach to punch Luther, clocking him in the jaw so hard the man drops to the ground without a sound.

"Don't even bother," Mordred tells Arthur as he tries to come to his father's defense.

Then, with casual unconcern, Mordred bites down on his thumb, and starts tracing symbols with his own blood along the edge of the fountain. I watch, as if from very far away, as the whole water basin starts to shimmer, and a portal appears in its place.

"Retreat!" Mordred shouts to the last of his men.

Urim and Thummim are the first to leap into the fountain, quickly followed by the few Dark Sidhe who haven't abandoned Mordred's side yet.

"Remember that we're two sides of the same coin, sis," Mordred says, ignoring the knights slowly circling him. "Take as long as you need for your wee brain to process that. And when you finally see reason, come join me like you were always meant to."

Mordred looks like he's about to add something, but shakes his head instead. Then, with a final wave at me, he disappears through his portal.

# CHAPTER 27

"Unhand her," Arthur growls.

I try not to wince as the two guards tighten their hold on my wrists instead.

"The sentence for treason is death," Luther says. "And don't you dare throw a temper tantrum, Arthur. This isn't Lake High. She let that Dark Sidhe go, even though she had him in the palm of her hand."

"It's not like she chose to," Arthur says, sounding calm despite his clenched jaw. "And if it weren't for Morgan, we'd all be dead. You saw it. Everyone saw it."

The knights holding me look over my head at each other. I can feel their nerves in the slight tremors of their hands.

Luther's mouth curls into a heinous sneer. "I think a night in jail might straighten you out, *son*. Despite the mounting evidence of her evil purpose, you're still acting like a neophyte around her!"

The virulence of his tone startles me. Never in my wildest dreams did I imagine Luther would look at Arthur, his own flesh and blood, like he's the scum of the earth, like he's...me.

Anger boils inside me. I'm ready to gouge Luther's eyes out if he keeps this nasty business up.

"I would hold your tongue if I were you."

Luther flinches as Sir Cade strides over to us, no trace of injury on him either beneath the grime and soot. My uncle looks pointedly at the knights flanking me, and they wither away under his glare, releasing me.

"That Fey bitch is a traitor," Luther spits, "she deserves to burn!"

Arthur blanches, hands balling into tight fists. I wish I could go to him, tell him not to worry, that such insults have no bearing on me. But now is not the time, not in front of all these people. They may think I've saved them today, but I know it's not enough to get rid of all the prejudice and suspicions that have weighed on my shoulders since the day I was born. And I don't want to have these people cast the same looks at Arthur.

"I believe you are getting things mixed up," Sir Cade says. His chin lifts a fraction higher. "The one who should be arrested isn't Morgan. Emmerich."

My uncle's right-hand man steps up, handcuffs in hand. "As you very well know, anything you say can and shall be held against you," the knight tells Luther in a monotone voice, as if arresting a high-ranking officer of the Order is a daily occurrence.

Luther's face turns purple. "Surely you're not going to put me through this circus of yours again, are you? You've tried me before, and I was proven innocent."

"A 'not guilty' verdict doesn't necessarily mean that you're innocent," Sir Cade says. "As we both very well know. But there are new charges that have been brought against you."

"Sir Luther, you are hereby officially charged with failing in your fiduciary duty to your ward by misusing her funds," Emmerich says, handing the handcuffs over to one of the guards, "as well as embezzling the Order's assets for personal use, bribing other officials, intimidating subordinates, destroying of evidence...shall I continue?

"And unfortunately for you," Sir Cade states, "your actions did leave traces this time around."

I snort back a laugh of derision. The Board could look over the murder of Jennifer's dad, but mess with their funds, and now Luther gets to walk the plank. How typical.

Luther watches in stupor as his men turn on him, snapping the handcuffs around his wrists. The once proud knight and contender to the Board Presidency looks at last to his son for support.

"Arthur, tell them they've got it wrong," Luther says, as the guards march him away through the growing throng of onlookers. "Arthur! This is all fabrications, lies!"

But Arthur remains mute, eyes staring sightless at some distant point, lost in thought.

"Everything I've done, I've done for our Order!" Luther protests, his cries carrying over the buzzing of the crowd.

I stare in shock long after he and Sir Cade are gone, my thoughts in total disarray. Why this? Why now, of all times? We have more important things to take care of, like letting everyone know the truth about Carman, and finding ways to stop her. Or did my uncle feel it necessary to protect me?

"Toppling the status quo, as always," a sarcastic voice says. "And you wonder why so many hate you."

I whirl around to face a grinning Keva. I can't help but return her smile, relieved to find her still in one piece.

"Might wanna keep your distance from that devil spawn," Daniel drawls, scowling at me.

Keva pinches him in reprisal. "Lucifer, for your information, means *Bringer of Light*," she states, reminding me of the two flying mice. "And *that* was quite the lightshow you put on," she adds to me. "Way cooler than anything else I've seen any Fey do. I mean, look at my skin. It's positively glowing!"

"I didn't do anything," I mumble, growing increasingly uncomfortable as those still around turn their attention upon me.

"It can't have been her, she's just a child," I hear someone say, somewhere off to my left.

Keva's dimpling cheeks belie the manic gleam in her eyes. "Quite the Saint Thomas, aren't you?" she says at the woman, tossing her braid back. "You saw it all, and yet you still don't believe. I wonder, would it be the same if the truth smacked you right in the face?"

Daniel puts his hand on her shoulder, as worried as I am that Keva may actually carry out her threat.

"How did she do that?" someone else asks.

"Why didn't she save us before?" an older man juts out, elbowing his way to the front of the growing throng. "My son died out there!" He points at me. "She could have saved him!"

"Hey now," Keva says, sounding a little less certain of herself. "Her powers don't come with a set of instructions. Did you know how to use oghams properly from the get-go? I don't think so."

"She's one of *them*," a younger woman spits. "It's in her blood to know these things. She's been holding back!"

I stumble back, afraid of how quickly their looks have turned from hope and gratefulness to bitter resentment and hate.

"Enough," Sir Pelles says. He may be just inches taller than I am, but his presence is enough to appease the choleric knights. "We have much to—"

"Lady Helen has a point," Sister Marie-Clémence says, arriving at the scene with a contingency of guards.

To my surprise, Bri's father's at her side, looking grave despite the sagging belly peeking through the rend in his mailed shirt where a demon must have stabbed him.

"I don't believe I was done speaking," Sir Pelles says with a withering stare for the nun.

A sudden gust of wind whips around the gardens, raising so much dust and snow that everyone's forced to seek cover. I cough, shielding my stinging eyes.

The bale dies away as quickly as it appeared, and we find Lugh and Oberon standing by the fountain, golden eyes glowing in the burgeoning dusk. Their silent presence is enough to quell some of the dissenting voices in the crowd.

"I entreat you all to remain composed," Sir Pelles states. "This war has already taken too many of ours, why then are you antagonizing those who would be our allies? This squire here has done nothing but try to protect us, as is her duty, and you wish to lynch her like a crazed mob?"

Some of the knights look away in shame at the older man's reproach.

"Because she displays powers you do not possess?" Sir Pelles continues. He lifts a hand before Sister Marie-Clémence can interrupt him again. "Do not judge lest ye be judged," he continues, voice growing louder so even those at the back can hear him. "For if her sin is to carry Fey blood in her veins, then we are all sinners."

Shocked gasps rise from those assembled, and Sister Marie-Clémence's scowl deepens.

"Sir Gorlois was right when he claimed our parentage to those we hunted," Sir Pelles forges on. "We can no longer go on, with our heads in the sand, refusing to believe the truth simply because it doesn't suit our fancy. Let us, therefore, take example on our own children, who have more readily embraced their abilities, under the tutelage of these two Fey Lords."

Lugh and Oberon finally move, parting to let us see a red-haired girl standing just behind them. Marianne. The knight Oberon nearly killed in Lugh's Oak Tree. She looks shyly at the rotund Fey who nods at her obligingly.

Taking a shaky breath, she steps forward, and holds her hands out. At first, it doesn't look like she's doing anything, then a boy cries out, pointing at her feet. And there, peeking from between two slabs of stone, is a growing plant stem, the shoot a vibrant green. Shocked gasps race across the gathered throng. For this time, Marianne isn't using a single ogham.

"I know that our relations have not always been the fondest," Lugh says, as Marianne coaxes the plant up, leaves now unfurling in small bouquets, "not even when fighting side by side these last couple of years. But as demonstrated tonight by Morgan, daughter of Sir Gorlois, it is by embracing our differences that we can grow stronger together, and help each other win.

"To that effect, Lord Oberon has reached out to your very own sons and daughters to help them regain abilities that had been lost for generations. Powers that are yours to command should you choose, and you have only to ask."

At a sign of Lugh, Oberon steps forward. "Pages, please advance."

Keva gasps as seven more boys and girls break timidly away from the crowd to join Marianne's side.

"Is that Brown Bag?" Daniel asks, using the nickname he, Ross and Brockton had come up with for Elias, after the latter had had an unfortunate accident during an EM combat class with Lady Ysolt.

Elias is the tallest of the group—the only one in our class who didn't become a squire like the rest of us, or even a knight, like Daniel. He's the second to demonstrate his newfound abilities. Carefully, almost reverently, he extends his hands and coaxes a bright blue flame to life, letting it drip from one hand to the other like a fiery liquid.

"I think you're the one about to shit your pants now," Keva tells Daniel with a smirk.

Encouraged by Elias, the other six pages follow suit, displaying their own innate abilities, laughing at the adults' gawking.

Sir Pelles uses the stunned silence to speak up again. "As Lady Marianne and these pages can attest, although training sessions have barely started, they are already bearing fruit. Many of you have complained of the unreliability of ogham use. Well, this is your chance to take matters into your own hands. Should any of you desire to learn as well, Lord Oberon has kindly offered to assist in this as well. Everyone else is to report for cleanup duty, and—"

I jump as someone's hand lands on my shoulder.

"Saved by the great Pelles himself," Gauvain whispers in my ear, steering me carefully away from the captivated throng, "and a perfect opportunity to escape."

Exchanging curious glances, Daniel and Keva follow close behind as Gareth falls into step with us, the latter having evidently lost his shirt and jacket in the fight.

"First of all, we'd like to thank you for saving our *derrières*[22]," Gauvain says.

"Truly," Gareth says, pectorals gleaming in the light of a passing torch.

"But we must ask for your help, again," Gauvain says.

"OK," I slowly say, wondering what all the fuss is about.

"See, Arty's somehow disappeared," Gauvain says, hefting a loud sigh.

I try to look back over my shoulder. "But isn't he…here?" I ask. "I thought—"

"Alas, no," Gareth says, scratching his belly with his war hammer.

---

[22] *Butts*, in French.

"Rumors say he disappeared yonder," Gauvain says, stopping finally at the edge of the path, and pointing back the way we first arrived, towards the thick forest that borders Caamaloth's northeaster side.

"Looking rather distressed," Gale adds emphatically.

"Arthur's missing and distraught," Keva says, catching on to the cousins' game. "Gee, I wonder who might be able to cheer him up?"

"A good meal with some *eghajira*[23] always works for me," Gauvain says, smiling thankfully at her.

"I think he'd need a more…delicate touch," Keva says, waving at me to go.

"A soothing presence," Gareth says, voice shaking with barely-concealed laughter.

I roll my eyes at their theatrics. "I, uh, guess I'll go and check up on him," I finally say. "As his squire, you know."

"Would you do that for us?" Gauvain asks, hand on heart.

"Might be preferable to have her away," Daniel grumbles. "Safer for us."

Ignoring his comment and the others' embarrassing giggles, I scamper off in search of Arthur. Everyone was laughing, as if it's some kind of joke, but what's happened with his dad is serious. And his inability to help Luther, even when he asked for help, must be weighing on him. I'm only too familiar with the bitter taste of guilt to want Arthur to taste it as well.

I navigate my way through the wreckage and dead bodies as quickly as I can, my eyes darting to the pockets of darkness where he may have found refuge. But it isn't until I pick my way around the Security Hall's debris that something makes me look up, and

---

[23] Tuareg drink made from goat cheese, millet, and dates.

I catch sight of a tall silhouette melting inside the woods, the cruciform pommel of a sword flashing once above his head.

"Arthur!" I call out, taking off at a run.

My boots hit the packed snow at breakneck speed, thoughts racing. Why is he going away in the middle of the forest like that, all alone? Surely, he can't be thinking about—

"Arthur!" I shout again, heart thumping.

This time, Arthur hears me and he stops, though his back is still turned to me.

"I've been looking all over for you," I say, breathing heavily. "What are you doing here?"

My hand brushes lightly against his elbow as I circle around him so I can see his face, and my heart stops. Tears trail down Arthur's cheeks, his teeth digging into his lower lip so as not to make a sound.

I open my mouth, start to say something, then click it shut again. Nothing I say can make him feel better. So I do the only thing I can think of, and wrap Arthur into a gentle hug, patting his shaking shoulders to let him know I'm here for him, just as he has always been there for me.

"I…I'm really sorry about all this," I whisper to him.

At last, Arthur pulls away, wiping his face with the back of his sleeve. "You shouldn't be the one to apologize," he says. "It is I who"—he takes in a shuddering breath—"I should have prevented this."

"What are you talking about? You haven't done anything."

"Exactly," he says hotly, "I did nothing!"

He looks up at the stars peeking through the forest's interlacing branches, eyes sparkling with the last of his tears.

"Arthur, none of this is your fault," I say.

He pulls brusquely away. "But my father—"

"Is his own man," I say. "You're not responsible for his doings."

Just as I'm not responsible for my parents' actions either.

Arthur looks away, shoulders tense, face unreadable. But I know him well enough now to see that no matter what anyone says, he's going to keep blaming himself. Just like I keep blaming myself for what I am and what Carman's been able to do through me.

I reach for him again, my warm fingers closing around his gloved hand. Arthur's frown turns into a look of surprise as I pull him after me, deeper into the woods, away from Caamaloth's smoldering ruins and corpses, from the Board and the Order's constraints and obligations.

We break into a run, bounding through the trees until our breaths are ragged, sweat pouring freely down our backs and foreheads. We run until our sides ache so much that the pain drives all other thought aside, and only stop when we reach the foot of a wide cliff.

Heart thumping loudly in my ears, I return Arthur's dazzling smile. We've landed in a small clearing, the blanket of snow that covers it untouched by man or beast. The last of the clouds have long since disappeared, leaving us alone beneath the twinkling lights of a thousand galaxies. Staring up at them, it's hard to imagine that what's happening here is so important. I feel so small, and insignificant, and...free.

I laugh, twirling around like I've had too much ambrosia, grabbing Arthur's hands so he can join in this crazed dance. Then, without a word, Arthur suddenly grabs my face and plants a kiss on my mouth. A tingling warmth floods my stomach at the touch of his soft lips. I feel myself respond, eyes fluttering closed, drawing closer into his warmth.

And then Arthur vanishes.

# CHAPTER 28

A bird lets out a lone, high-pitched note before settling on the cross guard of a long sword planted blade-first in the grass like a grave marker. A body lies a few feet away, motionless in the sunlight.

"Arthur?" I call out, knowing it's him.

But my cry echoes forlornly against the cliffside, remaining unanswered. I close my eyes, trying to bring the strange vision back for a hint as to Arthur's location. The cold wind picks up, making me shiver. At least Arthur didn't look like he was going to freeze any time soon. Rather, the vision makes me think he's slipped through a portal into another, sunnier universe...

I bare my teeth in a silent growl, slowly scanning the area—the line of trees, black against the starry sky, its edges blending seamlessly with the mountain's rock wall, in a perfect circle. A Fey circle.

Bastards.

I drop to my knees, staring fiercely at the spot where Arthur and I were kissing just a moment ago.

"Arthur!" I yell at the trampled ground, sounding like a crazed woman. "Arthur come back!"

I punch the frozen ground, sending flurries of snow outward, and keep pounding until my knuckles are shredded and bleeding all over the snow.

Arthur sits up with a groan, rubbing his disheveled head. The bright summer sun reflects off his blood-spattered uniform, and he turns his face to the warm light, breathing in deeply, eyes closed. Peaceful.

"Dammit, Arthur, come back here!" I shout again.

I punch the ground once more, sending a burst of angry energy out that makes the earth ripple, and shakes the snow off the nearest treetops.

There's a sharp squeak of surprise, and I whirl towards the forest line. I slit my eyes as a fresh pile of snow starts wriggling, then a long-nosed mouse pokes its way through, coughing.

"There's no need to be rude," Papillon says with another indignant squeak. "All you had to do was *knock* properly."

"Where's Arthur?" I shout, jumping to my feet. "Where did you kidnap him to? Bring him back here!"

Papillon unfurls his dragonfly wings and flutters over to my side like a mutant bumblebee, then hovers just out of reach to brush the snow off his fur, preening. Shaking with rage, I force my hands into my pockets before I can smack the annoying creature away.

"How about we go to him instead?" Papillon says at last, finally catching onto my mood. "Allow me."

Papillon drops to the ground, lifts his hind leg, and raps it on the bloody snow in a rapid rhythmic patter. I frown, waiting expectantly for a moment or two, but nothing happens.

"I don't have time to play stupid games with you. Tell me where he is, now!" I explode.

"Shh," Papillon says, holding a tiny paw up, giant ears perked. "It's coming."

"What's co—"

I start as the blanket of snow turns to water, a giant pool of warm water that soaks through everything. I stare in earnest at Papillon through the heat now fogging the air, wondering what kind of trick he's playing on me. Then the earth starts to glow, refracting through the water in iridescent colors.

"Arthur?" I shout again, forced to close my eyes against the spreading light. "Are you in there?"

Arthur grows still, as if straining to hear something. He turns around, hazel eyes flickering across the landscape, brow furrowed in confusion.

"Morgan?" he calls back, his voice sounding oddly near.

The air pressure shifts making my ears pop, and I suddenly find myself plunging straight into the ground, the soil swallowing me whole like a giant maw. Then, in the span of a breath, the earth spits me back out the other side, and I'm pelting through a clear blue sky, straight down for the skeletal remains of a massive, six-headed monster.

With a strangled gasp, I try to slow myself down, barely avoiding a gargantuan rib, before I hit the ground with a bone-jarring *thud*.

"That looks like it hurt."

I blink dazedly as Arthur's face appears above mine, a disgraceful groan escaping my lips.

"Where?" I manage to wheeze out after a few painful breaths.

Arthur shrugs, before helping me up. "I have no clue, but..."

"But?" I prod him, testing my legs to make sure nothing's broken.

"But it's kinda nice here, isn't it?" he says. "Quiet, peaceful... You could almost forget about everything that's happening out there."

He looks away in shame, shoulders hunching as if expecting me to laugh at him. But I know what it's like to suddenly lose all your bearings at once and become...orphaned.

"Still would be good to know where we've landed," I say, though I have a strong suspicion.

Papillon may have conveniently eclipsed himself, this is definitely the Demesne of a powerful Fey. I take in the giant ribcage stretching over us. Whatever the beast was, it must've been dead for a long while, for moss is eating away at its skeleton in large patches.

"Well, wherever we are, I'm glad to be here with you," Arthur says haltingly.

I feel myself flush to the root of my hair, and find I'm smiling giddily. "Me too," I whisper, voice thick with emotion. I slide my hand into his. "We're gonna find a solution together, to everything. You'll see."

Arthur squeezes my hand in return, and he lets me lead him to the first of the giant ribs. From up close, I can see the fine cracks in the smooth and polished bones, a grey green sheen coating its surface like the nacreous insides of a mollusk.

"I wish I could ask him why he could never be happy with what he had," Arthur says sadly, lost in his own thoughts.

"It's not too late for that," I say.

"But it is for everything else. What's been done can't be undone, and you know how terrible the Order's punishments can be."

"But he made it through the first trial safe, didn't he?" I say. "And that one was for murder."

Arthur winces at that word.

"Sir Cade's only had him arrested for money matters," I quickly add. "Maybe I could convince my uncle to get him to work his debt off."

He forces a chuckle. "Like doing dishes for the rest of his life?"

"Hey, look at me," I say, stepping close to him. "Look at me."

Arthur's gaze flicks up to meet mine for the barest of seconds, but not before I catch the worry etched there.

"It's going to be OK," I say. "We'll find a solution, I promise."

I don't know how, but I'll fix this too. And for that, I need to find that flying rat so we can get back to Caamaloth. I make to move away, but Arthur pulls me back, keeping me close to him.

My heart flutters, stomach tightening in nervous excitement as Arthur's hand cups my cheek, tilting my head towards his. Then his lips are on mine, warm and soft, setting all my nerves ablaze. Arthur's fingers twine in my hair as he deepens the kiss, forcing me to curve into his body.

My thoughts have gone hazy. I know this isn't the right time, and certainly not the right place, but somehow I can't remember why.

Then, too soon, Arthur breaks away, eyes wild. I stare at him in confusion, hating how cold I suddenly feel.

"I-I'm sorry about that," Arthur says with a shaky voice. "That wasn't"—he clears his throat—"this isn't right."

His words act like a slap. My fingers flex with the sudden desire to punch him, but instead I try to coach my features into a mask of indifference.

"Oh?" I manage to say.

Arthur doesn't even have the balls to look at me. Surely he can't be embarrassed, can he? Is it my breath? Or could it be because I'm a terrible kisser? The thought is enough to make me wish the ground would swallow me whole and send me to the other side of the planet.

"I just mean…" Arthur stops, takes a ragged breath as his gaze slides up to my mouth, then looks away again.

Saint George's balls, it really is because I'm a bad kisser!

"You mean what?" I ask, voice gone hard, the knot in my stomach tightening.

"It's just, with everything that's happened," Arthur resumes tentatively, "what with Luther and what he's done to you and the others… I don't know that this is…proper."

Relief floods through me, and I slowly exhale. OK. This isn't about me, really. I can deal with that.

"Listen to me," I say, gripping both his hands in mine. "I said we'd look into a solution for your father together."

"But—"

"But whatever your father's done has nothing to do with you," I say. "Don't get me wrong, I'm not sure I could ever forget what Luther's done to me and my family. But I could, perhaps, learn to forgive him."

I stop, surprised at my own words. And the lack of pain in my stomach only proves that I'm not lying.

Arthur exhales loudly. "You could?"

I nod, keeping my hair from being blown in my face by a cool summer breeze. Arthur smiles at me, and for a moment, everything seems to be all right again.

Then Arthur stiffens.

"Greetings to the both of you," a woman's deep voice says.

I whirl to meet the new threat, and find a woman smiling benevolently at us. She's tall and pale, jet black hair shot with grey that frames an angular face. Her amber eyes glow softly as she motions behind her. Set deep within the giant skeleton's pelvic bone, is the entrance to a cave, one that wasn't there minutes ago.

"Who are you?" Arthur asks gruffly.

The woman's smile widens, and a strange feeling tugs at my mind, as if remembering a long-ago dream.

"I am Danu, Morgana's mother."

My knees buckle, and a pair of sturdy hands catches me.

"Watch it," Lugh says, smooth voice warm in my ear.

I recoil in disgust, jerking away from his touch. Lugh's presence here proves Papillon right. He knew about this place, but chose to withhold the information from me, when I had every damn right to know!

Now that I am finally in front of this supposed mother of mine.

"I do not think it wise to expose yourself thus," Lugh says.

For a moment, I believe he's talking to me, but the Fey woman shakes her head.

"It matters not," she says. "Our time left here is short."

"Things could still be revert—"

The woman, Danu, lets out a low, raspy laugh. "Ah, my dear Lugh, always the idealist. But the wheels have been set in motion, there is no stymying the flow of things. Not this time."

I snort. Funny how she could be saying the exact opposite of what I told Arthur just a few moments ago.

"These bones are turning to dust before our very eyes!" Lugh exclaims, sounding like this isn't the first time he's had this argument with her. "At this rate, Carman will be able to destroy you in a heartbeat."

"Carman wishes to absorb my ogham, which is not exactly the same thing," Danu says, looking at the monster's moss-eaten vertebrae jutting out of the ground in an uneven path before her. "As she did with the Lapis Exillis."

"All to free Balor," Arthur says pointedly, gaze shifting continuously between us three.

"The Siege Perilous is a bit of an added problem," Danu agrees with a slight nod. "But like with everything, the seat has two sides to it." Her gaze shifts over to Lugh. "Are you not looking forward to finally moving on? There was a time when that was all you wanted."

"Not when it means we could risk losing even the little that we have left," Lugh replies.

"But this is what we asked for," Danu says, "the right to choose our own paths. And with free will come risks as well. We must accept our responsibility in handling our own fate. There is not one without the other."

Her words remind me that Danu isn't just any Fey, but the very angel who lead the rebellion against the Heavens. She may talk now about gaining free will, but I know well enough it's but a paltry excuse to let her and the other Fallen Ones have their vilest desires run rampant.

"Come with me, Morgana," Danu says, interrupting my dark thoughts.

I balk, rage and fear roiling in my stomach. "What for?"

But Lugh pushes me forward. "Go on, we do not have much time for you to waste in pointless tantrums," he says.

I mean to snap back at him, but find my feet are moving of their own accord, and before I know it, I'm standing in front of *her*.

I take in Danu's ragged dress and dirty feet, the strands of white in what had once been midnight hair, the lines forming around her wide eyes and along her thinning lips. I had expected my mother to look somewhat like Irene, or perhaps Lugh's sister. But Danu looks...old.

"What is this place anyway?" I ask, trying for nonchalance and failing miserably as my voice ends up on a shrill note.

"The heart of Avalon, my Demesne," Danu replies.

"Wait, are you saying all of Avalon's your Demesne?" I ask, eyes growing wide in confusion.

But Danu simply nods again. "Now come along."

I cast a long hesitating look at Arthur, but Danu's already disappearing inside the cave, taking with her answers a part of me so desperately wants.

"Go," Arthur mouths at me.

I nod, and finally, against my better judgment, I follow Danu into the darkness. It takes a moment for my eyes to adjust to the dim lighting that emanates from the cavern walls. I'm striding down a long interminable passage after Danu's light footfalls. The whole place smells stale, like a cellar that hasn't been aired out in years, and my mind flashes back to the time I escaped from Hell.

"So why did you make a dead animal your home?" I ask to break the uncomfortable silence.

"An ogham can take many forms," Danu says, her voice echoing down the tunnel. "A gem, a cat, a hobgoblin—"

"You mean Puck?" I ask, stunned. There's no way. She must be playing with me.

Danu presses her pale fingers against the wall, and light flares up at her touch, almost blinding me. "Or a dragon," she continues, blatantly ignoring my question.

I repress a shiver. I think I've had about my fill of dragons for now.

Yet I can't help but look curiously around. This place is where my father met her, where they courted each other and fell in love. At least on his end. She was probably just finding a temporary solution to her infinite boredom.

My fingers graze the ridged surface of the tunnel wall as we progress ever downward, leaving a trail of light that slowly fades again. This is where I was born. Where Mordred and I would have grown up if Danu hadn't abandoned us.

Not a very cheery place, I have to admit, but anything would have been better than the lives we've led instead.

I blink as something bright winks ahead of me, only to reappear on the ceiling above, then again, further down the passage. There are other Fey creatures down here with us, I realize, all senses alert, and they're following us like wolves stalking prey, or...

I stop, staring straight ahead at Danu's back.

Or like moths drawn to a flame.

"You're glowing," I whisper.

Danu's footsteps halt at the edge of a wide arch, a half-smile on her resplendent face. Gone is the old hermit with coarse dress, dirty features and unkempt hair. Instead, stands a goddess, her skin moon-touched, hair sparkling like she's plucked stars from the very sky to adorn it. Only her eyes are the same, their unfathomable gold eyeing me questioningly. Lucifer, the angel of the Morning Star. A title that turns out to be quite literal.

"Is something the matter?"

I shake my head, pulling at the collar of my shirt in a vain attempt to breathe normally. Not until now did the fact that my mother is a fallen angel hit me so hard.

With a knowing smile, Danu sweeps gracefully through the arch, and a heartbeat later, I follow suit.

"If you're hoping this little tour of yours is going to make me change my mind about you, then you're sorely mistaken," I say loudly, hoping to distract myself from the heart attack I can feel coming. "A hole in the ground isn't going to impress—"

I stop midstride, mouth gone slack.

Unfolding in front of me is an endless cave, hundreds of carved columns stretching from floor to domed ceiling, jeweled vines creeping up their graceful shafts in dazzling colors. Lights shift lazily about the cavern as salamanders seek new resting places, away from the playful sylphs flitting around in tiny green gusts.

My head slowly swivels around, taking everything in, and I catch sight of a strange white figure poking its head out from between two spindly columns.

"Ghost?" I whisper.

The spectral form tilts its round, noseless head, black eyes unblinking beneath a pair of vicious-looking antlers.

Danu lets out a low laugh. "Ghosts do not exist, Morgana," she says.

"I know that," I mutter, stung. "And my name's *Morgan*. There's no 'a' at the end."

Danu dips her head in acknowledgment before gliding on ahead, forcing me to get moving again or risk losing her. A thick mist appears as we wend our way through the forest of bejeweled pillars, playing first around our ankles, then steadily reaching up to our knees the further we get from the cavern's entrance.

I occasionally glance back, feeling the weight of unknown eyes upon me, and feel my hairs stand on end as I catch more glimpses of the pale creatures. Soon, others like it join it, following us in silence. All white as death. All observing my every move expectantly.

"Stay close," Danu says.

I start at the disembodied voice, and find I've strayed away from her, the mist so thick now I can barely distinguish her silhouette a couple of feet away.

"What now?" I ask, rushing to her side, ashamed to admit I'm feeling a little scared.

"We cross."

Head held high, Danu lifts both hands to eye level, and the mists part in response, revealing a white skiff hovering in the distance. With a flick of her finger, the small vessel bounds forward, flying to meet us like a swift summer cloud across a limpid sky. It isn't until its shallow hull gently bumps against the ground at our feet that I realize the boat isn't suspended in thin air, but floating on such clear water it appears invisible.

Water sloshes inside the skiff as I trail Danu into the vessel, and I plop down heavily onto the single seating board before I can capsize us.

"Steady," Danu says.

A pale green light bursts from her fingertips, and the skiff bullets back the way it came, cutting through the water towards a bulbous island with nary a sound. I look one last time over my shoulder at the line of white creatures crowding along the shore, and release a long-held breath.

"What are they?" I ask.

"Penitents," Danu says.

"Penitence for what?"

"That is their burden to wear."

I refrain from rolling my eyes at her. "Is that why I couldn't grow up here? Because this place is some sort of...purgatory?"

"We're almost there," Danu says instead.

I grunt in annoyance. What's the point of bringing me here if she's going to spend the entire time talking in riddles?

The boat moors itself gently along the island's shore, and Danu steps lithely onto solid ground, motioning for me to do the same. I wrinkle my nose at the familiar scent that seems to permeate the place—it is the smell of summer blooms and freshly mowed grass, of soft breezes and starry nights.

"Welcome home," Danu says softly.

I resist the urge to throw insults at her, focusing instead on not tripping over the island's strange ground that looks to be entirely made up of knotted roots and twisted vines. We make our way from the dock up the steep and winding path. Sometimes, I also have to use my hands to not tumble back down to the lake, and it seems like ages before the ground flattens out. I want to ask Danu where she's taking me, what the point of this little expedition is, but every time I try, she slips out of view.

Finally, after ducking under another gnarly branch, and climbing over a strange boulder of bark, I see it.

The tree is large, larger even than Myrdwinn's Apple Tree, and half as tall, but its leaves glisten as if cut from the purest emeralds, fruit hanging heavily from its overreaching boughs like giant amethysts.

My gaze drops to the trunk's wide base, taking in the thick roots that snake their way out, twisting and twining across the ground to form the entire island, like a giant Celtic knot.

"What are we doing here?" I ask apprehensively as Danu finally stops beneath the tree's thick canopy.

To my surprise, Danu cups my hands in hers. I shiver at the warm touch, unable to pull away as she takes in the inky stains that span from the tip of my fingers to my elbows.

"There is much healing to be done," she says. "The darkness has become a part of you." Her eyes travel up to my face, and if I didn't know any better, I'd think she's actually feeling sorry for me. "Take care, Morgan, that it does not take you over entirely."

"What is that even supposed to mean?" I ask, stung.

I put my hands in my pockets, finding the ogham Mordred gave me tucked inside the right one. My fingers close around the cool gem, and I find myself taking strange comfort from it, as if my brother were lending me his strength. Even here.

The island's scent is stronger here, beneath the branches, headier, reminding me of the Samhain festivities when I attended Lugh's party, and drank some of that—

"Don't tell me these are the fruit used to make ambrosia," I say, under a flash of inspiration.

"Just so," Danu says. "It is sustenance for my people."

My eyes go round at the implication. Sustenance. Mordred talked before of how the Fey, Lugh included, couldn't survive without receiving energy from the Lord or Lady of their Demesne, like a bunch of parasites.

"You're saying you're feeding all of them with juice from your ogham?" I ask, feeling a little sick.

"I led them to this land, it is my duty to see that they are taken care of." Danu's eyes grow distant. "Without it, many would have long perished. Absorbing power through the elements is enough to survive, for a while at least, but not to thrive and prosper."

I snort in disgust. "So you have them partake in cannibalistic rituals, lovely."

"It is," she says, not picking up on my sarcasm. "What is life, but the transference of energy? I simply choose to give mine of my own free will."

I look away, hating how logical she makes it sound. But to admit it means I might end up agreeing to more of her ideas, and next thing I know, we'll be talking like we're really mother and daughter.

And I'm not ready for that. I don't know that I ever will.

I yelp as the ground suddenly shifts beneath me, the massive root lifting me up to one of the tree's low-lying branches.

"Have one," Danu says.

I swallow hard. "I think I'll pass."

"It will assuage your hunger."

"I'm not hungry." I grimace as the lie twists at my grumbling intestines.

"You may be part human, Morgan, but you also need Fey nourishment."

Another of the tree's roots lifts Danu up until her eyes are level with mine, and she plucks a large fig to present it to me. "If you do not replenish yourself, Carman will have no trouble defeating you. And I may not be strong enough to save you again."

I press my lips together, hating her for bringing that up. I knew, the moment I stepped on this island, that it's thanks to Danu that I'm still alive. It's what Nibs hinted at down in Hell. What Papillon implied. And, if I'm perfectly honest with myself, something I had long suspected, though always discarded.

Why, indeed, bother rescuing me at all, when she's the one who abandoned me in the first place?

The question burns at the tip of my tongue, but at the last second, I wimp out, and snatch the fruit from Danu's extended hand instead.

"Is that how you tempted my father to sleep with you, by getting him drunk?" I ask.

Without waiting for an answer, I take a large bite out of the fig, and have to stop my eyes from rolling back in ecstasy. Sweet juice drips profusely down my chin as I tear into the rest of the fruit, my previous qualms about it evaporated.

Before I know it, I'm reaching for another of the tree's scintillating figs, devouring it in seconds. Then another, and a fourth, until my stomach feels blissfully full. I'm already reaching for a fifth one, sticky fingers grazing the fruit's luminescent peel, when the root drops back down to the ground, nearly sending me toppling over.

"Hey, I wazna done!" I exclaim in outrage.

I blink slowly, taken aback by my slurred speech, then shrug. A deep furrow cuts between Danu's eyebrows, but at this moment, I couldn't care a rat's ass what she thinks of me.

"Come here," she says.

A command—not that of a mother to a child, but of a queen to her subject. I jut my chin forward.

"Dunwanna."

Danu's frown deepens. "When was your last meal?"

I try to think back. There was my running with Arthur and his kiss—I giggle to myself at that—and the battle before that, some time at Lugh's place where I ended up watching Arthur sleep like some kind of creepy stalker... I shake my head to dispel the wooziness.

"Izz bin a while," I manage to say, over-pronouncing each syllable to regain some semblance of dignity.

Danu lets out a long sigh. "Then if you could come over, *please*, there is some water here to quench your thirst. And perhaps it will clear your head some as well."

I totter on my spot, considering her request, trying to find the catch. Finally, not finding any, I lurch forward.

"Here," she says, showing me an oval basin of crystalline water carved at the base of the tree's thick trunk.

I lean over drunkenly, until I find myself staring at a pair of familiar eyes, so very like my own but for the blue woads that circle them.

I hiccup in surprise. Mordred?

# CHAPTER 29

"What is he doing down there?" I ask.

"Your brother is ever a part of you, as you are of him," Danu says. She hesitates before adding, "As both of you are a part of me. It is only natural he would be the first one you see."

"Is this why you brought me here? To talk to me about Mordred?"

I speak more harshly than I intended, angered at myself for feeling disappointed. Why did I even think she'd care about me at all after all this time?

"You are both my beloved children," Danu says.

I jerk away from her reaching fingers, no longer feeling the pleasant buzz from the figs I ate. "Giving birth to us doesn't give you the right to call yourself our mother," I say. "You don't deserve it. You don't deserve *us*!"

"Even if I'd wanted to, I couldn't keep you here, Morgana," Danu says with a flicker of annoyance—the first real emotion I've seen from her thus far. "Keeping either of you here would not only have put you in danger, but would have placed the rest of my people in jeopardy as well."

"I was in danger out there!" I retort, wiping angrily at the tears that have sprung unbidden to my eyes. "Be honest. What you really mean is that you care more about all these other Fey and demons, because you feel guilty. And you are. It's your fault they're all stuck down here. All because of your delusions of grandeur. You really shouldn't have had us at all!"

"I can tell you are still but a child or you would not be voicing these half-formed opinions you have based on hearsay and spurious historical accounts," Danu says icily. "But you will not use that tone of voice with me again."

"Then why don't you enlighten me, oh Almighty Lucifer, destroyer of worlds? What is it that I missed?"

Danu makes a slight grimace. "I am not Abaddon[24]," she says.

I wave her words away. "Not much of a difference to me, is there?"

Hurt flashes across her face. "I may have had your father take you away from here, but I never abandoned you."

"Did my father even know who or what you really are?" I ask.

"He did," Danu says after a long pause.

I watch her intently for any sign of deceit, but I've never been good at reading people, and I don't know if Mordred's ability to lie was inherited from her. Yet, even if what she says is true, it doesn't make me feel any better.

"So what do you want from me?" I say at last.

Danu motions back to the water basin. "Drink," she says.

With a tired sigh, I roll up my sleeves and plunge my hands into the spring water, averting my eyes should I still see Mordred's face in there, only to pull them back out immediately.

"It burns!" I exclaim.

"Cleansing is not usually meant to be enjoyed," Danu says. "You've let the poison get far, further than I had thought."

---

[24] One of the greatest of the fallen angels, whose name means the "Destroyer.'

"I didn't let anything do this," I say through gritted teeth. Why does she keep on accusing me like this?

Without another word, Danu grabs my hands and forces them back into the water. Heat blazes up my arms, and I have to grit my teeth not to scream. A shudder runs through me as the water's surface clouds over, turning black. But this time I keep my hands still, watching as the poison slowly drains from me, and I wonder if this means I'll be able to use my powers normally again.

"I think that should do it," Danu says after a long while.

Biting on my lip, I finally sit back on my haunches, and stare. Gone are the inky spots that were coating my forearms like a pair of long gloves. I turn my hands around, marveling at the sight of the thin blue veins peeking from under my lily-white skin, the scar on my palm visible for the first time since Dean gave it to me.

"Is this for real?" I whisper.

Danu's finger traces the old wound's edges. "I am afraid this one shall not disappear so easily. It cut too deep."

*"Go away!"*

I start at Mordred's distorted voice, and look back down into the tree well's now black waters. I can see him standing sideways to me, casting furtive glances to a spot out of the water's vision. I lean closer to the pool, my knuckles going white around the smooth bark.

Mordred catches my movement, and waves me away impatiently.

*"I said to go away, Morgan,"* he growls.

I frown. His voice sounds off through the water, but there's something eerily familiar about it too. Something that brings me back to all those long-gone internal conversations that carried me through years of loneliness and hard times...

"It's you," I breathe in shock. How did I not catch on until now? "You were my guardian angel?"

Mordred cracks a wry smile.

"Why didn't you ever tell me?"

*"I fancied I was a little more memorable than that,"* Mordred says with a deprecating gesture.

He turns the rest of the way and I have to bite back a shout of horror. Half of Mordred's tattooed face is now ravaged, as if a beast has clawed him across the left side, leaving deep, purplish gouges behind.

"How did that happen?" I find myself asking in a shaky voice. "Why?"

*"You know very well why,"* Mordred says.

"But how could..." My throat convulses. "You're supposed to heal," I finally say under my breath.

*"There are some wounds that cannot be easily mended,"* Mordred says, sounding just like Danu.

He suddenly grows tense, shoulders bunching up as he hears something I cannot.

"Come here!" I say urgently, wishing I could seize him through the scrying pool. "Danu will save you, just like—"

Mordred's eyes swivel back to me, cold and distant.

*"Is that where you are?"* A sardonic smile tugs at his full lips. *"Then you can tell the old hag I'm taking care of things. That prophecy of hers? I'm gonna make sure it happens."*

He stops speaking as a large shadow falls upon him. Worry flitters over his face, quickly replaced by his usual arrogant look.

*"Go away. Now!"* he says, turning his back to me, and obstructing my view.

### "I can smell her!"

Fear prickles down my back, and I find myself holding my breath. Carman's there with him. Then Mordred starts screaming.

"Mordred!" I shout.

Angry red welts burst across my arms, as if I've been burned, and Danu's slender fingers quickly disrupt the water's calm surface, dissolving the vision within.

"Bring it back!" I shout at her, eyes darting over the dark pool in a vain attempt to catch another glimpse of my brother. "We have to stop her!"

"I interfered in her designs, and she is not one to forgive others for her failures," Danu says.

"So you're just going to stand here while she's torturing your son?" I snarl at her.

"I unfortunately have no power where they stand," she says, and I know, without her saying so, that they must be back in Hell. "My last such attempt cost me much," she continues, "and I am afraid that the next show of force I pull may very well be my last."

A flicker of unease traverses me. Is she saying that she's...dying? Surely not! She's a Fey, the mightiest of all the fallen angels. And yet... I recall Lugh's reaction at finding us here, the hints Papillon's given me...

Danu points to my arms, returning my attention to the present moment. Already the blisters are vanishing, as if this is all a strange dream I'm having.

"The link between you two is strong," she says, "a fact Carman has used to her advantage. But the sword can cut both ways." She looks at me through thick eyelashes. "For what one has done, the other can undo."

I frown. "What is that supposed to..." My voice trails off, and I straighten my back. "You're talking about the Siege Perilous, aren't you? Could it be"—I swallow hard—"could it be we don't need Mordred to be sitting on it to destroy it?"

"But note that the destruction of such a powerful Fey object would bring about the annihilation of Avalon and everyone within," Danu says, implicitly agreeing with me.

"Everyone?" I make myself ask.

Danu nods, looking suddenly tired.

"But then we're doomed no matter what," I say, panic rearing inside me.

"Do not let fear keep you from what must be done," Danu says, "and do not fear who you are."

"Accept that I'm the devil's bastard, is that it? You've already got Mordred for that, it seems. Yet you're not even willing to lift a finger to help him."

"You cannot deny where you come from, and the responsibilities that come with it."

"You mean the responsibilities you refuse to bear yourself?"

Danu's nostrils flare out. "Perhaps it would help you see more clearly if I told you about your father."

My heart thumps a little faster at his mention, and I find myself leaning into her words.

"You may have heard already," she continues, "but your father was a great knight, one of the best of his time, rivaled only by Sir Tristan, Lady Ysolt, and the Pendragon."

"Arthur's father?" I ask in disbelief. From what I've seen, Luther seemed more into hogging money rather than fighting the Fey himself.

"The very one. It may surprise you, but all four were very close to each other growing up." Danu smiles wanly. "What differentiated Gorlois from the others was his curiosity and willingness to see beyond conventions. Of course, this open-mindedness is something he acquired over time, after having already enslaved hundreds of my people." Her head tilts to one side, eyes lost in some distant past. "But come around he did."

"You mean you're the one who made him see the light, huh?" I ask, unable to miss the irony.

"I did bring him here," Danu says softly.

"Evidently," I say, annoyed.

"I was tired of this crusade of theirs, and knew it would lead to the total genocide of my people. So I faced him myself, stripped him of all his oghams, and showed him his own abilities."

My mouth goes slack. I knew that long before Gale, Jennifer, Agravain, and now the rest of our troops, my father had discovered that knights carry Fey blood in them. I just never imagined that *she* was the one who'd shown him the truth.

"Was he shocked?" I ask.

"Not as much as one might think. I suspect that he may have already entertained the idea. But when he brought the knowledge to the Council upon his return, he was met with savage condemnation instead. Most of all from the Pendragon."

"Guess showing up with me in tow didn't help either," I mutter.

Danu smiles kindly. "You and Mordred were not conceived until his second visit."

"Second visit?"

She nods. "I do not know how much you are aware of what was done to your father when he returned to Caamaloth after his first visit. Not only was he greatly criticized, but he was stripped of his titles and rank, publicly whipped, then put into a closed house."

"The asylum," I whisper.

"It is only after he escaped that he returned to me."

"And that's when we came into the picture," I finish for her.

"You need to understand that not once did your father blame the Order for his mistreatment," Danu says, laying her warm fingers over my clenched fists. "Hate is what had put a wedge between my people and his, a hate that had been stoked over centuries. He knew that the only way to bridge our peoples was through forgiveness instead."

"Forgiveness, huh?" I say bitterly. "Yeah, I don't think that's gonna work with Carman."

"Peace will never be possible whilst the love of power is greater than the act of loving itself," Danu replies carefully.

"Spare me your philosophical BS," I retort. "I need something concrete. Don't know if you noticed, but Carman's setting the whole world ablaze, not in small part thanks to that dragon of hers. A dragon *I* helped create."

Danu lets out a tired sigh. "Carman is seeking to absorb my powers into herself," she says, repeating her earlier words. "And she partially succeeded in doing so when she merged the Sangraal with her ogham to give it shape."

I slowly let my breath out. "That's it, isn't it?" I say, looking at her for confirmation. "She wants to be just like you, which means that dragon is Carman's ogham, isn't it? Destroy the dragon, and Carman becomes fully human."

"That is correct," Danu says, and for a second I think I see sadness in her eyes.

This is far from the tender mother-daughter moment I've imagined all my life, but at this moment I couldn't care less. What's important to me, though, is protecting my friends. And she's just given me the final piece of the puzzle to do so.

"Thanks for the visit, and all," I say, jumping to my feet, eager to relate my discovery to Arthur, "but I've got dragons to slay, thrones to destroy, and Hell to close back up."

# Chapter 30

"You're out of your mind if you think I'm going to let you do anything to Morgan!"

I startle at Arthur's shout.

"Let me?" Lugh lets the question hang in the air, the threat implicit.

I hurry up the last few feet separating me from the outside, and find Arthur and Lugh staring each other down, Excalibur drawn between them. Neither of them notices me as I step quietly their way.

"Admit it, it's because of that stupid inscription that you're helping us out," Arthur continues, his voice shaking with barely suppressed rage. "All this time I thought you actually cared for her, but you just want to use her like everyone else."

"Trust me boy, I would much rather have let things rest as they were," Lugh says, "but your pitiful Order certainly did not help keep Carman locked away as it was meant to, and now it is too late to return things to their previous state. You are as responsible for what is happening to Morgan as much as we are."

"And what is happening to me?" I ask.

Both of them startle at my intrusion and I refrain from smirking at them.

"What is it you've kept from me, Lugh?" I ask, crossing my arms. "Other than the truth about my mother, that is."

"Here," Arthur says, grabbing my hand to pull me after him.

He marches me up the skeleton's central neck, then out its gaping jaw, between child-sized teeth sticking up from the soil, edges still keen despite their age.

"There," Arthur says, pointing at the dead beast's skull.

"What about it?" I ask, eyes dancing up the sharp-toothed maw until they catch sight of the strange markings that seem to have been burned above the eye sockets. "What is it?" I ask.

"A bloody prophecy," Arthur says through gritted teeth. "And the reason for—" He stops, combs his fingers roughly through his hair, too cross to finish.

I squeeze his hand to let him know I understand, then rise to the tip of my toes to get a better view. If I'm not mistaken, this must be the very same prophecy that Mordred keeps referring to. The etchings are black against the green-tinted ivory of the bone, forming strange shapes that I've never seen before.

"How would you even know what it says?" I ask, wrinkling my nose. "I can't even tell what language it is."

"That's exactly what I asked," Arthur says. "Lugh was kind enough to translate for me. And you know what it says? That for *them* to return to full grace, they need the ultimate sacrifice. Or something to that effect."

I look back at him. "I suppose full grace means Paradise? But 'ultimate sacrifice' could mean anything. Why do you think it's got something to do with me?"

"I don't, but they do," Arthur says. "And I'll be damned before I let them do anything to you just so they can get back to the place *they* left willingly."

I laugh, loving how protective Arthur is of me, feeling truly cared for, for the first time in my life.

Arthur's frown deepens. "How can you laugh about it? This is your life we're talking about."

"I don't believe in prophecies," I say, "even if they're written in fancy letters; They're just a way for lazy people to force their desires for change onto some poor schmuck. And that's not me. I'm not here to make amends for the choices of others. I'm here to make up for my mistakes, and…" I stop, taking a step closer to him.

"And?" Arthur breathes, all iron melted from his voice.

I stare into his eyes, noting the golden flecks sprinkled across his green irises. Slowly, I gently trace the tiny white scars that cross his right cheek.

Maybe it's because I'm still a little drunk on the figs, but I finally make myself say it. "And to protect those I love," I whisper.

Arthur's eyes go wide, as if he can't quite believe what he's heard. Then he's leaning into my touch, stubble prickling my palm. With a smile, I close the small gap between us, and brush my lips against his.

"I take it your meeting was all you wished it to be?" Lugh asks archly.

I grin wickedly at Arthur's beet red face, before turning to face Lugh. Yep, I'm definitely still buzzed.

"Not exactly," I say, "but it was fruitful. Somewhat."

I glance at Arthur who still doesn't seem to have recovered from my sudden public display of affection. Now's the time to lay all the cards on the table. I grin, noting how both shift on their feet uncomfortably, probably wondering whether I've gone completely unhinged. But they'll both lose it too when I tell them everything.

"First off," I say, the words spilling out of me as I start pacing, "do you remember how I used to hear voices?" I ask, ignoring their concerned looks. "Well, it turns out I wasn't crazy, and it was my brother's voice."

"Mordred's?" Arthur asks.

"I know!" I say excitedly. "It must be related to the whole twin thing, and the sharing of blood, or some weird thing like that. Not to mention us being part Fey. Anyway, I've been thinking about it the whole way back here, because there's something that doesn't add up. Why is it I stopped hearing Mordred's voice in my head all of a sudden, when all my life I could? So I tried to remember when it stopped." I whirl on Arthur. "And the first thing that came to me was when you threw me in jail."

"I didn't throw——" Arthur starts.

"But that didn't make sense either, because then shouldn't I have been able to communicate with him again when I escaped?" I continue, talking right over him. "And I didn't. Which means that it must've happened before. Frankly, figuring it out was actually difficult, what with everything that happened... Can't say I was paying much attention. But, I do remember the last time I spoke to Mordred telepathically. Distinctly. And that was when Arthur locked me up in his parents' house."

"I didn't lock you——"

"Then Lake High was invaded by those Fomori, and Dean took me to Carman's tomb to free her, and *that*'s when it stopped," I finish, breathing heavily. I hold my left out, palm up so that my scar is evident.

"Your hands!" Arthur exclaims, having just noticed they're no longer stained.

"Dain used your blood to break the wards," Lugh says slowly, thinking aloud. "Which means Mordred's blood must have been necessary as well."

I nod emphatically as Lugh reaches the same conclusion I did.

"The second and last time your father came to visit Danu," Lugh continues, "he had Excalibur with him. And when he left again, the only thing he was carrying...was you." His face clears from its usual frown. "Did you not find the sword lodged within Carman's altar?"

"Right where Dean poured my blood," I say.

"Could someone explain to me what's going on?" Arthur asks, sounding uncharacteristically petulant.

I turn to him. "The reason Mordred and I could talk to each other telepathically was thanks to our oghams!"

"Oghams which left their bodies along with your blood," Lugh says.

Arthur reaches over his head to grab Excalibur's pommel, eyes round with shock. "You mean to say..."

"Our oghams are in that sword," I finish breathlessly.

"But if your oghams are inside Excalibur," Arthur says, "doesn't it mean your link has been altered? Ruptured, even?"

"I don't think so," I say, looking questioningly at Lugh. I'm still too new at this whole Fey thing to understand all its ramifications.

"Have you ever noticed anything strange since Excalibur was pried out of the altar?" Lugh asks me instead.

I stare at Excalibur's hilt, the large golden and silver cross gleaming in the warm sunlight. "I think it's the reason for the visions I've been having," I say.

"What visions?" Arthur asks, sounding tense.

"I told you before that when I was stuck in Hell, I kept seeing things," I say. "Keva thought it was just me losing it, but then when we came back and it turned out everything I'd seen was real..."

Arthur's face pales. "You saw...*everything*?" he asks.

"Well, not everything, but enough to get an idea," I say, wondering if he's thinking about the visit he got from the Fey girl who took my form.

"What I am worried about," Lugh cuts in, "is whether Mordred may have used the same device to spy on us."

I bite on my lower lip. "That's what I'm afraid of too."

"Could it be?" Arthur asks, an expression of horror dawning on his face.

Lugh stares at me for a moment, before nodding. "It seems there is a distinct possibility of it," he says.

Arthur exhales sharply. "It would explain how he always managed to be a step ahead of us. Do you think he can hear us now?"

"No," Lugh says. "The wards here are strong, too strong even for him."

"Which means he's not aware that we know of his link to Excalibur," Arthur says, relieved.

"Good, because I've got something else to tell you," I say, brimming with excitement. "Carman's ogham is her dragon."

Their reaction, or lack thereof, is not at all what I was expecting, and it's leaving me feeling rather...deflated.

"Um, guys, have you just heard what I said? Carman's dragon is her ogham!"

Arthur shakes his head. "That can't be true. You said so yourself: She used you and the Sangraal to bring forth life."

"No," Lugh says slowly, wiping his hand down his face in a very humanlike way. "The Sangraal was the source of power she needed to shape her ogham into another entity, for she was not strong enough herself at the time. I should have guessed."

"But if that's the case, it'll make her that much harder to defeat," Arthur says somberly, "half-human or not."

"Don't worry," I say, lifting my chin in defiance, "I've got a plan for that."

Arthur looks alarmed. "That's exactly what I was afraid of."

"Are you nuts?"

"Perhaps if you stopped struggling, I might not drop you again," I retort.

Nibs freezes in my arms, and I manage to regain our balance at last, my feet grazing the top of the trees below.

"And just *why* did ya invoke me here?" the clurichaun mutters, finally keeping still.

"Frankly, I had no idea it would work," I say, laughing nervously at the recollection of Nibs appearing in thin air at my call. "Didn't think calling out one's name three times summoned all Fey."

Nibs snorts in disgust. "Only if the dumbass willingly gave ya permission to do so. Which most certainly is *not* my case. And to top it off, ya"—Nibs's heel hits my shin and I grunt in pain—"decided to test it out while *flying*?"

"I needed the exercise," I say. Not to mention that I don't want everyone to know the full extent of my plan. Not yet. It's enough that Lugh and Arthur already don't fully approve of it, I don't need to get the rest of the Order on my back too. Especially with how tense things have gotten since the attack and Luther's arrest. "And I had some questions for you. Thought I'd kill two birds with one stone."

"I certainly hope ya don't mean that literally," Nibs mutters.

I suddenly veer off to the side, keeping Lugh's Oak Tree behind me, and am gratified to hear the clurichaun squeal.

"Don't ya dare do that again!" Nibs shouts at me, his small fingers clutching at my forearms.

"Then answer my questions, and answer them truthfully."

"Ya couldn't have asked me over a bottle of vodka?"

"Arthur, Percy and Lance tried that once, and you bailed out on them, remember?" I say. "Now come on, I need you to confirm a couple of things."

"That your breath stinks?"

"First, that Carman's a halfie like me," I start.

Nibs remains silent, until I start shaking him again.

"OK, OK," he gasps. "She is! But I thought ya knew that already. Or are ya just that dense?"

"Just testing," I reply truthfully, glad to see he is being honest after all. I don't know what I'd have done otherwise. I take a deep breath. "Second, that she's trying to copy Danu, even going as far as turning her ogham into a dragon."

Nibs twists around in my arms to glare at me. "Gee, what gave it away? The fact that the beast always responds to her, no matter how far apart they are? Or the fact that you were bloody there when she created the damned thing to begin with?"

"Why didn't you tell me?" I ask, miffed. "How the hell was I supposed to know what it was? I thought you wanted to help me defeat her."

"Have ya ever heard of a little thing called a geas?" Nibs replies with his nasal twang. "If ya break it, ya suffer the most miserable and excruciating of deaths. Which, needless to say, ain't good for my complexion."

"You and Keva sound so much alike," I say with a sigh.

A geas. It seems like the Fey world really likes to have their unbreakable blood oaths to forge alliances.

"If you've been sworn to secrecy, then why can you talk about it now?" I ask.

"Because ya already know the truth," Nibs says. "Will ya *now* put me back down? Heights and I don't quite agree with each other."

"I'm not done yet," I say, glancing over my shoulder to make sure we're still alone. "What's Carman's next step?"

Nibs remains decidedly mute, even after I threaten to let go of him, and I'm forced to conclude that must fall under the oath of secrecy as well. Not that it matters much. It's not like Carman's worked very hard to hide the fact that she wants to free Balor so he can defeat Danu for her.

So I dive in with the real questions. "How well are Mordred and Carman getting along these days?"

I feel Nibs shrug against me. "They never were the best of buddies to begin with," he says.

"But?"

"But it's true things seem a little arctic these days between 'em. Why?"

"Bad enough she'll try to get rid of him?" I ask.

Nibs tenses up. "Why? Ya wanna see him disappear for good?"

"No!" I exclaim.

This seems to mollify Nibs some. "She won't do a thin' to him till Balor's out," he says. He shudders violently in my arms, and I nearly lose my grip on him. "She won't do anythin' *permanent* to him 'til she's got what she wants," he amends.

Unless someone else can take his place, I surmise.

Perfect.

"I'm gonna let you go now," I tell the clurichaun, dipping towards a patch of trees left untouched among the ashes.

"How sweet of ya," Nibs says. "Couldn't be happier."

"On one condition," I add.

Nibs growls in disgust. "You want a boon?" he asks.

"Yes."

"In exchange for what?"

"Once I find your missing ogham, I'll restore it to you," I say.

"Ya've already promised me that once before," Nibs says dismissively, "and a word once given can't be taken back."

"No, I said I'd return it to you," I say. "Now, I'm saying I'll help you absorb it fully."

On our way back from Danu's cave, I was able to pry a lot of information out of Lugh on the Fey and their oghams. And I know that, once the link between an owner and its ogham has been severed, it requires tremendous amounts of power to be able to restore the bond—power that is often beyond the owner's ability to expend. Especially if the owner's been weakened.

"What is it ya want me to do?" Nibs asks cautiously.

"I need you to put in a good word for me with Carman," I say. "Good enough that she doesn't rip my head off the moment I step back inside Lake High."

"Ya're goin' back to her?" Nibs sputters. "On yer own? Are ya insane?"

"Quite possibly," I say. "But it's the only way I can think of."

"For what?"

"To clean up this mess." I stop, hovering a few feet above the ground. "So, are you up for it?"

"Deal," Nibs says at last. "But don't blame me if this time 'round ya don't make it."

"Just don't forget about your end of the bargain," I say, before finally letting him go.

Nibs flips me off before bounding away in Lake High's direction.

This is it. There's no turning back now, unless at the cost of people's lives. And that's definitely not something I want to gamble on.

324

But Nibs wasn't wrong. After my last showdown, I'll be lucky if Carman' doesn't kill me on sight the moment I set foot back in school. And if she doesn't, then Mordred will believe I've betrayed him, and might balk again at joining me against her.

I sigh, the beginnings of a headache pressing behind my eyes. The bleary sun is low on the horizon, couching the treetops with gold. I've been gone too long. At this rate, the others will be able to tell I've been up to something.

Conflicting thoughts still warring in my head, I force myself to return to Lugh's Demesne, avoiding the main entrance and slipping in through the small oval window that leads straight into our sleeping quarters. I barely make it to my own pallet, when I hear Arthur's voice rise on the other side of the suite's door.

"Where is she? I swear, if she isn't sleeping, I'll be throttling you!"

"Your parents' heads aren't worth much these days," Daniel's voice retorts, which means that Arthur's talking to Keva.

I rush to my moss bed and dive under my covers, shutting my eyes tightly. Arthur may have begrudgingly given his assent to the idea of infiltrating Carman's ranks, but at the condition he goes with me. And that's not something I can accept.

"Why do you care so much where she is at this very moment?" I hear Keva ask as the three of them enter our sleeping quarters.

I try to slow my breathing down, fearful Arthur might be able to hear my erratic heartbeats even from across the suite.

"What if she's gone snogging with one of the cousins' squires?" Keva continues loudly, worry about waking me definitely not on her mind. "You've seen the way they look at her."

"Disgusting," Daniel adds, and I can clearly hear the shudder in his voice.

"Shut up," Keva tells him.

"She wouldn't dare," Arthur says, voice strained.

Keva bursts out laughing. "Are we talking about the same girl?"

There's a muffled sound, as of cursing, and I find myself holding my breath as the footsteps stop close by.

"See? She's right there," Keva says, sounding disappointed. "Satisfied? You can bury that jealousy of yours, now. Really doesn't suit you."

"Wake her up," Arthur says, voice dangerously low.

"Ex-*cuse* me, but I'm not your squire," Keva retorts.

Arthur must've done something, because I suddenly feel Keva shaking my shoulder as roughly as she can. "Nap time over, Morgan. Someone wants to speak to you."

"What is it?" I ask, stifling a fake yawn.

"Pack your bags, we're leaving," Arthur says, still scowling.

"Where?" I ask, pretending to sound shocked.

"Caamaloth."

Keva's shoulders bunch up. "Probably not a good idea right now," she says.

"Why not?" I ask meekly.

Keva shrugs. "No offense, *sir*," she says pointedly at Arthur, "but though there's enough evidence against your father to have him hanged and quartered, he still has quite a lot of followers, some that are also powerful. Going back there means you'll be subjecting Morgan to their insults, and Kali[25] knows what else."

"That's exactly why I need to be there," I say, rolling out of bed, and hoping they don't notice I've still got my boots on. "I don't actually want Luther dead."

"Wait, what?" Daniel lets out.

Keva rolls her eyes up in irritation. "Fine, try to play the hero again," she exclaims. "But I wash my hands of you if any more crap happens while you're there."

---

[25] Goddess of death and destruction in Hinduism.

She makes to leave the room, but I hold her back. "Before you go, I need to speak with you," I say. I look pointedly at the guys, and add, "About girl things."

With a gagging noise, Daniel does a one-eighty and heads back outside. Arthur stays a second longer, our gazes crossing knowingly. His lips thin out in suspicion, but I give him a shy smile and he finally leaves as well.

"Please don't tell me you need some kind of sex ed class," Keva says the moment we're alone. "I know you guys have managed to get past your issues, and I'm glad for you. Truly. But do you really need to rub your relationship in my face?"

"Actually, I need you to do something for me," I say.

"Please tell me you need some kind of sex ed class," Keva says.

"I've decided to join hands with Mordred."

Keva's jaw drops open.

"It's the only way," I say hurriedly. "You've seen it for yourself. Even with the Fey's help, we're not strong enough to defeat Carman."

"You did just fine the other day," Keva says.

I grimace. "That was my mother, not me. And she says she's dying, so she can't do that again."

My voice catches, and to my shock, I have to stop talking to keep from tearing up.

"The only way we can stand a chance to do so," I continue, coughing slightly, "is if Mordred and I work together to separate Carman from her dragon. Only then will she become weak enough for us to face her. I've put some thought into it—"

"Surprisingly."

"—and I think the only way we can do that is to have Carman entirely focused on something else for the time needed."

"Focused on you, you mean?"

"Well, on us," I say, with a slight laugh I hope doesn't sound terrified. "And then the knights can take care of the dragon."

Keva eyes me for a long moment, as if deciding whether she should conk me on the head instead of listening to all the crazy talk.

"Arthur doesn't know, does he?" she asks.

"He thinks he's going to come with me," I say, fingers curling and uncurling around the hem of my jacket.

At last, Keva lets out a resigned sigh. "Very well. But promise me one thing."

"What?"

A wolfish smile pulls at her tired face. "That at the end of all this, you'll make the bitch burn."

# CHAPTER 31

I rush after Sir Cade as he storms on ahead, his disgust rolling off him in angry waves. Luther's trial is over, and as I promised Arthur, I've gone against everyone's expectations and actually taken up the man's defense. Maybe being Gorlois's daughter helped, for in the end, the jury voted in favor of stripping Luther of all his ranks, allowing him to keep his life in exchange for becoming a regular soldier in our army.

"Uncle, please," I call out, "let me explain!"

I turn another corner, and finally catch up with him in front of a tarpaulin wall. The blue canvas has been stretched across the hallway to seal off the now-missing eastern section of the Ops Center.

"I know it's hard to understand, uncle, but—"

Sir Cade lifts his hand, and I clamp my mouth shut, only just now noticing he isn't alone.

"Whatever did you do to the mutt, Cade, that she turned against you?" Sister Marie-Clémence asks, her voice quavering with age. "I had warned you not to trust her, but I thank you nonetheless. Having Sir Luther demoted on baseless grounds was mistake enough."

My uncle hefts a tired sigh. "Has anyone ever told you that you suffer from glossolalia[26], Sister?" he asks instead.

Sister Marie-Clémence's eyes narrow to slits. "You might have won a couple of jousts, Cade," she says, "but that doesn't mean your stream of luck won't tarry. Politics is a long game, boy."

"And I'd suggest you keep your patronizing tone for those who care," Sir Cade says coldly. "I, on the other hand, know you're out of touch with reality, or you'd know we've run out of time to play these silly games of yours."

I can't help the surge of satisfaction I feel at the sight of Sister Marie-Clémence sputtering in outrage, and quickly look down before she can see it on my face. My gaze catches instead on the old newspapers that still litter the floor, and feel any fleeting mirth dissolve at the old headlines.

### Dämon Besitz ! [27]

*Les Templiers sont toujours parmi nous ! [28]*
**The end of days is near – the dead walk again!**

My uncle's right. If Sister Marie-Clémence can't tell we've got more urgent business to deal with than who gets to sit on the Board, then maybe she should be forced to retire.

A gloved hand pushes the blue tarpaulin aside, and two knights freeze at our sight, before saluting.

"News?" Sir Cade asks sharply.

"Another report from Newgrange, sir," the first man says, handing over a manila folder.

---

[26] Random speech that makes no sense.

[27] *Demon possession* in German.

[28] *The knights Templar are still amongst us* in French

I watch over my uncle's shoulder as he opens it up, and riffles through the pictures within. My eyebrows hike up as I immediately recognize the patterns on them. They're the same symbols I saw burned into Carman's clavicle the time I tried to kill her.

"These come from engravings found deep under the site," the knight continues, "down the passage sir Lamorak uncovered before he got caught. As you see, the triple moon superimposed by the sign of a troll cross[29] is surmised to represent Carman herself. And, if you look further down, it appears her people tried to burn her at the stake."

"Still not enough to know her weakness," Sir Cade mutters.

My uncle snaps the file shut before Sister Marie-Clémence can have a good look at what the knight's talking about. I can see it infuriates her, but like my uncle said, they don't matter much at this point, except as further proof of Carman's semi-mortality.

"Get Emmerich to join me in the Hall of Mirrors," Sir Cade says, whipping around to march back the way we came from.

I want to call him back, let him see me with pride as he once did. But it's too late. Sister Marie-Clémence has dismissed the two knights and is already hurrying after him, leaving me alone in the drafty corridor.

I try to swallow the lump in my throat at the thought that my only living relative—scratch that—my only living *human* relative doesn't want to have anything to do with me anymore. Not now that I've broken his trust.

I straighten my shoulders, take a deep breath. Perhaps it's for the best. It'll make my next betrayal easier for him to accept.

Shivering against the cold, I push the tarpaulin aside and make my way between the debris of the old east wing. The sky's clear

---

[29] Circle crossed at the base—a symbol used to cast away evil spirits.

of clouds tonight, the tempest I'd brought down over Caamaloth long gone, but people are still working hard to clear out the rubble, searching for those who are still unaccounted for. In a few hours' time, I'll be gone. Would any of these people miss me, and search for me too? Or will they say good riddance? Yet I know I shall miss my friends.

Keva with her knowing airs, the only one who knows exactly what I've already had to go through at Carman's hands, the only one who's always been brutally honest with me. Then there's the cousins' goofiness, and Hadrian's seriousness. Gale, always there when we need him most. I'll even miss Lugh's brooding, despite his lies, as well as Blanchefleur's fighting spirit.

And, finally, there's Arthur.

Arthur who's stood by me through thick and thin, who's believed in me no matter what, and who's defended me against everyone.

Just the thought of leaving him behind again is like a solid punch to the gut. It'll be like stabbing him in the back again, and, this time, I won't be coming back to ask for forgiveness.

It's this last, heavy secret that leads my feet up the stairs to the dorms' second floor, down the dim hallway, to stop before a simple wooden door marked with the number 327.

Heart pounding, I scratch softly on its panel before cracking the door open, and slipping inside.

"Who's there?" Arthur's sleepy voice growls.

"Shh, it's just me."

"Morgan?" Arthur sounds confused, though more awake.

He's kept the drapes to his windows open, letting the moon's silvery light limn the furniture in his room—the desk, where the notes he took in preparation for his father's trial can still be seen, the dresser, where his clothes have been carefully folded, and his bed.

Arthur sits up, the covers folding back, his hair mussed. "Is everything all right?"

Hanging from the bedpost near his head, is Excalibur. The sword's soft glow reflects in Arthur's eyes, eyes so full of care and concern for me I almost want to scratch my whole plan and toss it in the bin.

I bite on my lower lip to keep from spilling the truth. Instead, I slowly cross the room, taking my boots off, then my gloves and coat. But for once, Arthur doesn't complain, keeping his eyes on me the whole time.

I note the hitch in his breath as I lift his cover and slide into the bed next to him.

"Wh-What are you doing?" Arthur asks at last in a strangled voice.

"Finding a little peace in the middle of this war," I say, sounding braver than I feel.

"Did Keva put you up to this?"

I move closer to Arthur, but he shifts away from me with a low hiss, until his back's flat against the wall.

"No," I say, a little annoyed at his reaction. "But if you don't want me to be here, I can always leave."

"Don't!"

Arthur's hand shoots out before I can scoot away, and a dumb smile spreads on my face.

"Don't," he repeats, softer, his fingers doing little circles around my forearm that send tingles all the way down to my toes.

"Good," I whisper, so giddy with relief I want to laugh. "I didn't want to go."

For a long moment we don't say another word, staring at each other until I can barely breathe. I feel suddenly shy, my thoughts all drawing blank.

"I thought you wouldn't want to see me," Arthur says, and my heart squeezes at the hurt in his voice.

"Why would you think that?" I ask.

The bed shifts as he shrugs. "Because of what I asked you to do for me. For Luther."

"You didn't ask me for anything, Arthur," I say, drawing closer to him so he can see I'm not making anything up. "I did it willingly. You know"—I force myself to breathe—"you know I don't want you to get hurt. Ever."

He lets out a relieved chuckle.

"What?" I ask, suddenly self-conscious.

Arthur brushes my hair back, out of my face. "It's amazing how little you've changed," he says.

I pull a little away from him. "Hell stopped my growth spurt, if that's what you're talking about," I mumble, wondering if it's strange for him to be with someone who still looks like a high schooler, when he could be in college. I'd heard of time flowing differently in some Fey Demesnes and the nasty side effect it can have on humans, as Sir Rip van Winkle can attest. I simply never bothered to think it would be the same in Hell.

"No, I mean, there's still so much…innocence in you."

As I feared. He must be seeing me as a child now. "Yeah, that's exactly why I got here," I say, piqued, "because I'm oh-so-innocent."

"You know what I mean", Arthur says. "It's like none of the horrors you've been through have managed to touch you, touch your soul. And I'm grateful for it."

I pause, turning his words over. "Maybe…," I start, turning back to face him. "I guess…it's how I've learned to cope with life. By forgetting everything that can hurt. That way, I leave plenty of room for the good stuff."

334

Ever so carefully, I reach up in the semi-darkness, my hand coming to rest lightly upon his cheek. I trace his recently-shaved jaw down to the tiny cleft in his chin. Arthur sucks in his breath as my fingers graze his mouth. Smiling, I lean into him, until my lips meet his in a soft kiss full of ache and yearning and barely conceived hopes.

I slide my hand to the back of Arthur's neck, fingers playing in the soft curls of his hair. His lips part, tongue darting over mine, as if to taste me. I gasp in surprise, relishing the feel of him. Then Arthur's hands are at my sides, tentative, exploring, lighting tons of tiny fireworks along my skin.

I wish we'd never stop, that Fey and knights alike could leave us alone, and that Carman would stay holed up in whatever part of Hell she favors.

Arthur's lips leave my mouth to trace a burning trail down my throat, and, in that moment, I forget about everything else.

Keva was wrong.

There is something better than kissing.

I wait until I hear Arthur's breathing slow to the steady rhythm of sleep, his chest rising and falling gently beneath my cheek, then carefully slide out of bed. I quickly dress up, careful not to wake him up, then pause one last long second to memorize every plane of his face. The way his lashes fall over his cheeks. The dark curls framing his face on the pillow. The frown that usually creases his brow momentarily erased.

"Please take care," I whisper, throat constricted. I let my hand hover over his without touching, and, before I lose my will, I flee.

My legs feel like lead as I retrace my footsteps down the long hallway, head lost in thought. This is the best I can do, the best chance of success I can offer, however flawed my plan may be. Yet why do I still feel so wretched?

A slight rustle draws my attention to the left. I start to turn towards it, when I register movement on my other side, and a fist connects with my temple. My head snaps sideways, stars bursting in my vision. My legs give out, and someone catches me before I can fall, wrenching my arms behind me at the same time. I choke back a gasp of pain before a thick piece of cloth is forced into my mouth.

Within seconds, it's all over.

I whimper, still dazed, as both captors carry me away. My knee bangs against the banister as they rush down the stairs. When we reach the bottom, they turn into a narrow hallway that leads to a side exit. Sweat beads on my forehead despite the cold night air. The wind nips at my face. My shoulders hurt, arms tingling from being nearly twisted out of their sockets.

The two men haul me across the gravelly path towards the Central Ops building, and I glimpse the warm fires that line the main alley where knights are standing watch. But they're keeping an eye out for invaders, not for a couple of their own soldiers carrying a girl between them, and we slip by unnoticed. Up a flight of stairs, across another hallway, and out again into a small, inner courtyard.

Finally, the men stop. Light spills on the flagstones as they open a door, stabbing at my eyes.

"Here's the demon," the man to my left says, as both toss me down.

I'm still too stunned, my arms numb, to try to soften the fall, and I crack my head on the stone floor. I moan in the gag, roll slowly into a kneeling position, and blink blearily around.

We're inside a small chapel, judging by the large wooden cross that takes up half the far wall. In front of it is a lonely prie-dieu[30], the wood smoothed down where countless people have knelt before to pray.

And standing to the side, is Sister Marie-Clémence, her pale face stern inside her coif[31].

"It is time for you to repent of your sins," she says.

One of the men grabs my hair, and I growl in pain and fear as he drags me across the chapel towards the forbidding woman.

I try to fight back, scratching uselessly at the man's gloved fist. Sparks shoot out from my fingertips, and the knight jerks back in shock. But the second man is on me in a split second, and drags me the rest of the way, chaining me down to the prie-dieu, before finally removing my gag.

"*You*," I spit.

I glare up at Sister Marie-Clémence's lined face, her own flinty eyes boring into me like a scientist before a dissection of a particularly gnarly toad.

"What do you want from me?" I ask, pulling futilely at my chains.

One of the knights hits me hard on the shoulder with his sheathed sword, and I yell sharply, folding over the prie-dieu in pain.

"You will only speak when spoken to," the man says gruffly.

"I know what this is about," I say, breathing hard. "You're afraid of me. Afraid of what I may have planned for Luther. Didn't think I'd talk for him, did you?"

---

[30] Prayer desk and kneeler combined into one, primarily used for private devotionals, or for praying at church.

[31] A tight white cap that covers the head and is worn under a nun's veil.

This time, the knight hits me in the back of the head. Pain explodes behind my eyes. I pull at my chains, but they're made for the toughest Fey and only cut into my wrists.

"*Sir* Luther would have been found innocent even without your intervention, girl," Sister Marie-Clémence says scathingly. "All he's guilty of is defending our Order against a growing cancer before it could wipe us all out. A cancer *you* are working to bring back."

"Peace is a cancer to you?" I say through gritted teeth.

Sister Marie-Clémence motions with her pointy chin at the man behind me, and a pair of gloved hands grabs the back of my shirt, before ripping it in two. Goose pimples spread down my spine.

"What are you doing?" I shout.

"I don't trust you," Sister Marie-Clémence continues. "I know you're planning our downfall. But our Board's been blindsided by your little display of power the other day. They forget that the only good thing about the Fey is their ogham."

"But that wasn't m—"

The first lash hits my back, tearing a cry from my lips. The second lash hits. Burning pain cuts across my skin. I slump forward on the prie-dieu, body jerking as the whip cracks across my back, again and again, until I lose count.

"In my generosity, I am giving you two choices," Sister Marie-Clémence says as the flogging continues. "Either you tell me where you've hidden your ogham, or we carve you up until we find it ourselves."

A bark of laughter escapes me. "Go. To. Hell," I gasp.

The lash bites into my flesh again, spraying blood across the white stone floor. I scream, dark spots swimming in my vision. Tears stream down my face. My whole back is blazing, throbbing in agony.

Indistinctive shouts reach us from outside. And despite the pain, a little part of me perks up—they're here.

"Make sure we're not interrupted," Sister Marie-Clémence says.

The whip strikes again, tearing another cry from my bloody lips. A shudder passes through me as the knight pulls his arm back, readying for another hit.

"She's in there!"

Keva's voice sounds so distant, but I can still hear the panic in it.

It's time. I grip the prie-dieu, knuckles turning white around the wood. Heat blazes from my hands, and Sister Marie-Clémence jumps back in surprise as it bursts into flames. I grit my teeth as I pull at my chains, flesh sizzling against the now hot iron, until the wood finally disintegrates, and I break myself free.

"Don't let her use her powers!" Sister Marie-Clémence shouts, the flames forcing her further back.

The chapel door bursts open, letting through a group of knights.

"Everyone, stop!" a deep voice booms out. Gauvain.

I whirl around, my manacled hands up, blood dripping profusely around my feet, soaking my boots. The man closest to me drops his whip, reaching for his sword instead.

"Drop it!" Gauvain shouts at him.

"How dare you interfere?" Sister Marie-Clémence says. "This is my jurisdiction! Leave!"

"Our Order is no longer yours to control," Hadrian says, slipping inside with a wide-eyed Keva. "You've been deposed"—he checks his pocket watch—"as of two hours ago."

Sister Marie-Clémence's face contorts in rage. "I will have you boys sentenced for this!" She motions for her men to seize me.

"Get that ogham out of her *now*! I don't care if you have to hack her to pieces to retrieve it."

But the game's over. She's played her role, even if a little too well. It's time to put an end to this charade.

"I wouldn't come any closer if I were you," I tell the two knights as they try to corner me against the wall.

Behind them, the fire is growing bigger, fed by my pain and anger, and cutting me off from my would-be rescuers.

"Come along nicely now," the one who whipped me says, while the other unfolds an iron net used to capture Fey.

I smile grimly. Just as I'd planned.

"Morgan!"

I shiver at Arthur's cry, see him try to drive past Hadrian and Gauvain, Excalibur flashing angrily in his fist. I try not to look at the horror on his face as his friends keep him away from the flames. This is why I didn't give him the details, why I wanted him to sleep through the rest of the night.

**"Stop,"** I mentally tell him, willing him to hear me.

I see Arthur hesitate, looking confused.

**"Trust me,"** I continue pleadingly.

Don't make this harder than it already is, I want to add.

I duck as the iron mesh flies at me, missing my head by inches, then blast the two men back with a strong gust of wind, sending them flying across the chapel. Finally, I return my attention to Sister Marie-Clémence.

"I have tried time and again to be understanding," I say, watching the nun blanch as I stalk towards her. "I've worked so hard to get you to accept me despite my tainted blood, as you like to call it. But no matter what I did, you people always found an excuse to turn a blind eye to my efforts and good deeds."

Someone's shouting to put the fire out, and I think I recognize my uncle's voice.

"Yet you do not mind using our powers as long as it raises you from the mud where you belong," I continue, stopping in front of the old woman, smiling at the fear in her usually malevolent eyes. "But I am done with your hypocrisy."

Steam fills the room with a deafening hiss as people pour water on top of the flames to douse it. But it's too late.

"Help!" Sister Marie-Clémence cries out at them.

I grab her arm, digging my fingers in until she flinches with pain.

"Thanks to you," I say, "my eyes have been opened. I will return to my kind. There, at least, I know I'll be judged not by what I am, but by what I do. And I'll let you in on a little secret…" I lean into her so I can whisper in her ear. "The next time you see me will be the last time you do."

"Over here!" Hadrian shouts.

But as my uncle and his men come rushing at me, I throw Sister Marie-Clémence at them, letting her stumble into their surprised arms. I point at the floor with my index finger, and an invisible hand swipes my blood over the floor in long stroke, tracing a double triangle with a large V on top of its curling edges—Lucifer's sigil.

I catch Keva's look and nod my thanks to her. She nods back in acknowledgment. There's no going back now.

"Morgan, please don't go!"

The pain and fear in Arthur's raw voice make me hesitate, but only for a second. I smile sadly at him from across the room.

"Stay safe," I mentally tell him.

Then I close my eyes, concentrating on the picture of Mordred's face. *Brother*, I call out to him, *I am ready. Bring me home!*

# Chapter 32

You need to have lived with the enemy to understand how its mind works. Father Tristan's words are part of the reason I'm back at Lake High, standing smack dab in the middle of a mass of demons without a single weapon on me.

The sound of Arthur's shout still ringing in my ears, I scan the crowd, faces sniffing the air in my direction, drawn by the blood still dripping profusely from my back. Saint George's balls, but there's a lot of them!

"Well, well, well, what kinda dumbass has decided to land here?" I jump at the sudden voice and scowl at a pimply-faced boy as he ambles over from the other side of the burned-down docks, a large spiked mace weighing his shoulder down. "No longer showing off, are we?"

"Brockton, what a pleasure," I say through clenched teeth.

The boy sneers at me. "Did ya get lost or something?" he asks, before noticing the manacles around my wrists. "Could show ya where the prison is, case ya don't remember."

"Very sweet," I say, a fake smile frozen on my face, "but I doubt that was Mordred's intention when he brought me here."

Brockton frowns so severely, it makes him look cross-eyed. "Mordred, huh?"

I scrutinize him from head to toe with derision, although I know that his presence among all these demons is a sign he's more dangerous than he seems. "I don't suppose you're my escort, are you?"

"I've actually got some serious work to do," Brockton says at last, evidently not wanting to trouble himself with me. "Here's to hoping you die on your way in," he adds, flipping me off as he struts off.

Crap.

A part of me was kinda hoping he would take up the suggestion.

I return my attention to the horde of Dark Sidhe and demons I need to go through to reach the school, gauging their mood, and note their interest in me seems to have grown along with their numbers. Time to get moving.

For a second, I entertain the thought of flying over them, but quickly dismiss it. I'm here to make a mark, impress Carman somehow with my abilities, show her I can be useful at her side instead of locked up. And I won't be able to do so if the first thing I do here is cower before the grunts.

With a resigned sigh, I push my way through the thick bodies, trying not to make any eye contact. My show of confidence seems to work, until I reach the landing docks. Something grunts to my right, feet trample the earth. I duck as a large, hairy arm swipes at me, feeling a serrated claw slice up my cheek before it takes out another demon that venture too close. Ichor sprays out in a dark mist.

Chaos breaks out.

Shouts erupt as demons charge, turning on those trying to push through. I lunge clumsily out of a rusty spear's way, but a meaty hand closes over my foot, and I fall heavily to the muddy ground. I kick back violently, feel something crunch beneath my heel, and the hand finally releases me. I roll out of the way of spike. A beast howls overhead.

I need to do something.

Need to show I mean business.

I let my power crackle along my skin, then hurl it deep into the crush of demons, blasting them away from me. I quickly push to my knees in the temporary breach, and slam my hand down. Power rips deep into the soil until it reaches the aquifer, then, at my coaxing, hurls back up. There's a low rumbling, barely noticeable over the frenzy, before the water punches through the knot of snarling beasts with an earth-shattering roar.

The powerful jet spreads sideways like a giant wall, then the wave crests, blotting out the rising sun. I spread my fingers out, release my breath, and the water comes crashing down like a tsunami, washing demons and Dark Sidhe out like a pile of dead leaves. If leaves could scream in terror.

I raise a shaky hand to wipe the sweat from my brow, and freeze.

No.

No, no, no, no.

I stare at my fingers in incomprehension. The dark spots that the Siege Perilous had left on me are back, spreading to the edges of my wrists like a pair of gloves.

"I was hoping ya wouldn't come," Nibs says, eyeing the wreckage from the top of the burned down docks.

"Ah, did that finally draw your attention?" I ask sharply, storming towards him.

If Nibs had come sooner, I wouldn't have had to make this disgusting show of force, and my hands would still be free of taint.

Nibs eyes my approach with a grimace. "I take it ya're still goin' through with yer bullshit mission?"

"I thought my being here made that pretty clear," I say, still irritated. "Lead on."

Nibs shakes his head as if to say I've gone completely mad, but starts walking anyway, picking his way around the corpses I've sown across the fields, his small boots squelching in the mud.

"Have ya considered not killin' off all her soldiers?" Nibs asks as we draw near a long line of spiked heads. "'Specially considering ya want to get on Carman's good side."

There's a strident sniggering and I startle to a stop.

"Everyone's on edge with Algol up and shining so brightly," a disembodied voice says.

I shiver, recognizing the line of spiked heads as Mordred's. The talking heads are now circling the southern tip of the school's main building instead of the old fort he'd used as a base. His perfect, if oh-so-creepy, alarm system.

"Hello ladies and gentlemen," I make myself say with a stiff nod at the heads still putrefying on their stakes.

"It's soon going to reach its peak," another says, still talking about that star, the very same I'd been able to see down in Hell.

"I'd give it a few more days," the long face of a man says.

"And once it does," the first talking head says, that of Martha, their leader, "the link between here and Hell will be at its strongest, and therefore the most opportune time to free——"

"Balor," I finish for her.

A few more days, only. Guess I did get here right on time, then.

Nibs lets out a loud, moist burp. "Gotta give it to ya, kid, ya've got the balls of a bull on steroids comin' like this. But if I were ya, I'd worry more 'bout Carman rippin' them right off, than 'bout some locked up demon."

The heads start cackling again. "Are you so sure?" Martha asks.

"I think the clurichaun's brains must've melted along with its face," a bald man with decomposing jowls says with a guffaw.

"Nobody asked ya for your opinion," Nibs retorts, kicking the closest head's post, "and ain't nobody that's goin' to, neither. Just stick to yer job."

Without caring for a reply, Nibs trots on ahead, as eager as I am to put as much distance between these creepy heads and us, the cackling of the talking heads following us all the way to the school.

Now that I'm not stealing my way in, I have more time to assess the damage the building has sustained over the last couple of years, and am surprised at the pang of sadness I feel.

The wing where the dining hall once stood is now but an empty, burned down carcass; the façade leading towards the arena is pockmarked from the aftermath of blasts and explosions; and, topping it all, are the blackened branches of Myrdwinn's decaying Apple Tree. Lake High's golden days are no more, relegated to tales, and fading memories.

A pearly-white figure pops out from one of the second-floor windows at our approach, and I instinctively flinch.

"There's a couple loose ones!" Urim shouts excitedly, looking up instead of at us.

Thummim's dark shadow zooms out of the window next to him with a loud *whoop*, followed a split-second later by Urim. Both Dark Sidhe heading for the sky-lake, where I can barely spot a pack of demons trying to break free into the surface world.

"Morons," Nibs says, spitting loudly on the ground. "All that power stolen for nothin'. Though I can't blame 'em for gettin' antsy bein' all cooped up down here with so many helpless humans so close at hand."

"But…I thought the goal was to destroy humans," I say tensely, "so why are the, um, loose demons being chased down?"

"And risk havin' yer knights take us down, little by little?" Nibs says. "No, no, Carman ain't stupid. If she wants to win this war, she needs an army. And an army has to stand together. Or somethin' of the sort. Now come on, Mordred wants to see ya before Her Mightiness comes back."

With a nod, I pull the heavy wooden door open to let us in. A blast of cool air greets us, carrying a faint smell of rotten eggs, a stark reminder that the Gates of Hell are more open than closed these days.

We turn left into a narrow stairwell, and start climbing towards the KORT room. Each time we pass before one of the slitted windows, I can't help but look outside at the multitude of demons shifting across Lake High's grounds. There's so many of them, even my earlier display of power has barely left a dent.

Mordred's voice rings out sharply, bouncing off the staircase's walls before we reach the second-floor landing. "There's a zero-tolerance policy for those who do not obey my commands."

"Tweedle-Dee and Tweedle-Dum worked fast this time 'round," Nibs drawls. "Guess they didn't wanna miss yer arrival."

We emerge from the staircase to find a line of six demons kneeling by the wall halfway down the corridor, heads bowed. I ignore the two Dark Sidhe lounging by the windows, my eyes drawn instead to Mordred's pacing figure. The last time I saw him was in Danu's scrying pool, moment before he was about to feel Carman's wrath. I go over every inch of his tattooed body, but whatever Carman's done to him, there's no trace of it left.

"The message was clear from the start," Mordred continues, sounding almost bored. "You do *not* act, or even *think,* without my say-so. Anyone who disobeys this edict forfeits his eternal life."

Spinning gracefully on his heels, Mordred cuts his hand through the air. There's a gurgling gasp from the nearest demon, then the last in the line falls forward, head hitting the floor with a dull *thud.*

I suck in my breath at the sight of the blood gushing out of the other demons' throats, before they, too, crumple into lifeless heaps.

"Good hunting, guys," Mordred tells Urim and Thummim. "Their oghams are yours to do as you like."

The two Dark Sidhe grin broadly as they each pull out long knives, then fall upon their victims to carve them up. Bile rises to my throat at the slick sounds of flesh and bones being pried open, and I squeeze my hands until my nails dig deeply into my palms to keep from getting sick.

"Hello, brother," I call out. "Miss me much?"

Mordred looks over his shoulder at me, his golden eyes cold and distant. Far from the warm welcome I'd hoped, now that I know he's been my guardian angel all along.

"What exactly do you want here?" he asks guardedly.

A beautiful, crystalline laugh resounds behind me and I stiffen.

"I didn't think it would be a good idea for Mordred to get you here," Jennifer says, strutting past me. "But the sight of your bare back is so worth it. Do tell me you were flogged."

Mordred winces slightly at her words, but doesn't push her away when she wraps her arms around his waist in a proprietary way. Guess he's fine with whatever she says or does, as long as she's his.

"So tell me," Jennifer continues with her honeyed tone, "how does it feel to not be wanted wherever you go?"

A shout from outside the building saves me from having to answer.

"Incoming!"

A second later, a massive shadow drops from the sky before crashing just outside our windows in a deafening *BOOM* that makes the whole building rock on its foundations. Jennifer grimaces prettily, leaning slightly over to look out the windows.

"What was it this time?" she asks in annoyance.

"That would appear to be a fishing boat," Thummim says offhandedly, cleaning himself off with a rag. "Again."

"But this one looks like it may have taken the forge down," Urim adds, his usually pristine clothes now covered in gore.

I let out a breath I didn't realize I was holding. Mordred seems to notice, and says, "Avalon's been seriously compromised, and is unraveling at the seams. Here faster than in other places, but I'm sure it'll spread to the rest of the place soon enough."

"You could save this place if you would only stop what you're doing here," I say.

"It is of no concern to me what happens to Avalon," Mordred says with a light shrug. "This is but a temporary residence until we finally take our rightful place on Earth."

"You know, I never saw the appeal of ruling over everyone else," I say, abruptly changing tacks. "You're constantly hounded by people who want something from you, while at the same time you have to worry about those who want to take your place. It all sounds rather fatiguing."

"Little people will never be able to fathom what great minds think," Jennifer says with a smirk, "least of all try to understand them."

"There's no need to put yourself down like that, Jen," I retort.

Anger flashes in her beautiful eyes, but Mordred pulls Jennifer along as he heads back for the KORT room.

"I didn't bring you here so you could have a hissy fit with the object of my wooing," he tells me over his shoulder.

I snort back a laugh, enjoying Jennifer's cringing at the old-fashioned word. But as I follow them down the long hallway, all feelings of mirth leave me, replaced by a sense of doom. I can feel the Siege Perilous's power flowing out of the KORT room, cold and demanding, making my skin prickle with the need to grab for it.

I hug my arms to my chest, willing myself to keep moving, to cross the room's threshold. Gone are the pennants of the old knight families that used to hang proudly on the walls. Gone, too, are the chairs where the KORT members used to sit. And, floating above the spot where the round table once stood, is the portal, the air inside it shimmering as of extreme heat, the Siege Perilous standing innocuously beside it.

"I've got a little surprise for you," Mordred says, his smile chilling me to the bone.

He motions me around the portal. My stomach feels tight. Slowly, I edge around the room, until I can see what he's pointing at, and swallow a curse back down.

"Fancy meeting you here," I manage to say, eyes fixed on the diminutive woman kneeling on the hard floor.

For some reason, Mordred's decided to bring Irene out from whatever cell she's been kept in. Despite her bound hands, the woman I once considered my mother turns to face me. Her hands have been tied behind her back, and her greasy hair, streaked with white, hangs over half of her face in clumpy strands. But it can't hide the black-rimmed eyes staring at me with unabashed hatred.

At least that part of her hasn't changed.

"I thought you might enjoy this present, at least," Mordred says with a wolfish smile.

"Luther was right," Irene says, her voice hoarse. "We should have drowned you as a baby."

"Why didn't you?" Jennifer asks. "I mean, you did marry the one who killed your fiancé, surely one more murder wouldn't have been such a big deal." She catches the confusion that flashes in my eyes, reflected on Irene's grimy face. "Oh, don't act like you're surprised. Did you sincerely believe no one would ever find out?" Jennifer's cheeks dimple in another of her signature cruel smiles. "I must say, though, that the face Artie made when I showed him the evidence was priceless."

Irene blanches. "You ungrateful swine! What kind of filthy lies have you been feeding my s—"

Her eyes bulge out, a choked gurgle escaping her cracked lips. My gaze slides over to Jennifer. The girl's left hand is clenched, a vein throbbing at her temple as she slowly strangles Irene from across the room. I grit my teeth together until my jaw feels like it's going to shatter. No matter what Irene's done, she doesn't deserve this.

Yet I do nothing to save her. Don't even voice an objection as Irene's face turns purple, blood vessels in her eyes bursting.

"Stop."

Mordred's voice is barely a whisper, but it acts like a gunshot on Jennifer, and she releases her hold on Irene. The woman slumps to the floor, wheezing.

I turn questioningly to Mordred, and find that he's watching me. Can he tell I didn't want Irene to die, that my coming over is a sham, a trick?

"Why stop me?" Jennifer asks, seething.

Mordred shrugs. "She's still a valuable prisoner. But if you're so keen to have a little fun, I have other choice prisoners for you. I hear one of them was even a KORT knight, and is parentless. So completely useless to me."

I feel myself turn white, aware of my brother's allusion. Mordred knows about her and Lance, then. And as part of me rejoices in the news that Lance is still alive, another fears how Jennifer's going to react.

"Would you, darling?" she asks prettily, sliding her arm in Mordred's in a simpering way that makes me want to punch her so very bad. After everything Lance has done for her, sacrificed for her, this is her response?

But she doesn't ask for Lance to play with. Instead, she keeps her mouth uncharacteristically shut, her eyes flickering to Mordred, gauging. My weariness increases a notch. For if the supposed love of Mordred's life is jittery around him, then, brother or not, I need to be extra careful.

# Chapter 33

"What are you doing here?"

It's the tenth time Bri's asked me that question since I've run into her, and still I don't know what to say.

When Mordred sent me away, tired of my constant bickering with Jennifer, I found my feet automatically heading for the old storage room down by the kitchens, the very place where Arthur secretly taught me to control my powers. I needed some peace and quiet, so I could figure out a way to corner Mordred away from his sadistic girlfriend and work on having him switch sides.

Instead, I've got to contend with a confused and suspicious friend. But if I tell her the truth, my whole plan might unravel, and would put her at risk too. Wouldn't it be easier to let her assume the worst of me, and continue this whole thing on my own, like I've always done?

"I thought you were going to stay away until I finished working on those wards," Bri continues intently. She's grown as thin as a piece of stick in the last few days. But something sharp has entered her eyes. Self-confidence.

I blow out a sigh. Truth then. "We've found Carman's Achilles' heel, and I'm here to help pry it open," I say."

"You've found her weakness?" she says slowly. "The wards?"

Owen tilts his head at me. He's sitting cross-legged on the floor, gathering books and papers. His presence alone explains how Bri's managed to evade the enemy thus far, even when working in the middle of them.

I shake my head. "No," I say at last.

Bri's lower lip starts to shake, her act of bravado slipping. "So everything I've done is useless?"

"No," Owen and I say together.

"Not at all," I say. "OK. Let me go about it another way. How's your work coming along?"

Bri looks down at her feet, her short dark hair forming little question marks around her head. "Slow," she says at last. "It's turning out to be harder than I thought."

"The alteration will happen if you will it so," Owen says, pushing to his feet, books and papers under an arm.

"You keep saying that, but nothing's happening!" Bri says, her pale brow creasing more severely. "And I keep losing precious time trying to avoid that sneaky pig Brockton."

I grab both her hands. "And that's exactly what I'm talking about," I say. "What if you don't succeed?"

"She will," Owen states calmly.

"Or not in time?" I continue. "Or you do, and Carman still manages to succeed in freeing Balor? We needed a backup plan, one to take care of Carman while you do your work, and Caamaloth gets ready for battle, so…" I shrug.

"So you decided to, like, sacrifice yourself?" Bri says.

I shake my head. "Not sacrifice, spy," I say, trying to sound more confident than I feel. "As I said, we've found the chink in Carman's armor, but we can't take advantage of it from afar."

I open my mouth to finally explain the whole plan, when the door to the storage room slams open, making us both jump.

"Well, well, well," says Agravain, striding inside. "What have we here?"

My stomach does a backflip. The last time I saw him, he was leading the charge against the church, forcing Father Tristan, Lance, Jack, and Lady Ysolt to sacrifice themselves so we could flee. He must've seen me leave the KORT room with Mordred and Jennifer, and decided to follow me down here. And like the big dolt that I am, I didn't notice a thing.

Agravain sniffs the air. "Smells like a couple of conspirators," he says, smirking as I rush to place myself in front of Bri.

"Conspiring to get your ass kicked," I retort with a sneer of my own, motioning for Bri to leave through the back door with her brother. "Again."

Agravain's smile turns into a frown. "Watch it," he growls. "Nobody's gonna save your skin this time around."

Out of the corner of my eye, I see Owen gently pulling Bri away. "I don't need anyone to save my skin wherever you're concerned," I say, to keep Agravain focused on me. "I can take you whenever I want."

"Doubt that," the boy says, turning to track Bri's and Owen's movements.

And what I see in his eyes chills me to the bone. This isn't a boy anymore, but a killer.

Without waiting another second, I charge, power rippling over my blackened fists. But before I can make contact, I slam into an invisible barrier. My power backfires, sizzling through me, and I'm sent flying across the room. Wood explodes into splinters as I crash into the old wardrobe.

Agravain lets out a low laugh. "What is it with you people trying to be all noble all of a sudden?" he asks. "Do you really think I don't know about your little friend? It's only a matter of time till I get my hands on her, too."

I hear him lunge, and roll to the side just as a flaming fist swings down. Agravain's knuckles hit the floor, blasting through the flagstone in a shower of sparks, and leaving behind a small, burned out crater where my head was.

I swallow hard, neurons firing in all directions. I'm not used to fighting in close quarters. My power is too erratic, wild. If I keep this up, I might bring the whole school down. If Agravain doesn't take me out first.

So I do the only thing I can think of.

I turn around and run.

"Wait here, you damned coward!" Agravain shouts, tearing after me.

Heat burns down my back as I burst into the staircase, barely avoiding a second attack. I stumble forward, veering into the staircase so fast my head hits the sharp edge of the railing. Stars dance before me, but I make myself keep moving, taking the steps three at a time.

"When I say stop, you stop!" Agravain bellows, entering the staircase behind me.

The flames dancing above his outstretched hand sear my vision as I turn to face him again.

"When I say roll over, you roll over," he continues, eyes sparkling brightly in the firelight, rabid with bloodlust. "And when I say play dead, you keel over and die."

He punches his fists out and the fire blazes out toward me. I fling my arms up, gathering wind around me. The flames hit my shield, spreading wide instead, before I shift the tide and send them leaping back the way they came.

Agravain drops to the floor, flattening himself to the stairs before he can get roasted. I don't wait for him to recover, and dash the rest of the way up.

"You're gonna pay for that, bitch!" Agravain shouts.

"I'll aim better next time," I tell him as I burst onto the main floor.

A demon grunts in surprise as I barrel into her. I trip over a fallen torch. Scramble to keep my feet under me. The demon shrieks behind me. Bones crunch.

I glance over my shoulder as I pelt down the long hallway. Agravain's there, a long, angry red patch where his hair's been burned. The demon I ran into is lying in a heap at his feet, motionless.

"You should stop following me," I shout at him. "You're only going to make a bigger prat of yourself if you let me beat you again in front of thousands of witnesses."

Agravain storms after me, and I speed up. The exit is just a dozen feet away. Five... I'm already reaching out to push the door open. Then something cold punches into my shoulder with the force of a harpoon, and I spin sideways to crash into the wall.

"Fiiiight!" someone bellows out excitedly at the opposite end of the hallway.

I grunt, hand going automatically to the ice pick sticking out from beneath my clavicle. "OK, now you're really pissing me off," I say.

I let my temperature flare up, melting the icicle in seconds, then bring my arms together, before pushing my hands out. For a long second, nothing happens, then I can feel them. Small tremors in the floor that are growing stronger. Someone screams in the distance. Then a dozen vines puncture the wall around Agravain like deadly tentacles to wrap themselves around his limbs, long thorns lacerating his flesh.

"I did warn you to leave me alone," I say, pushing away from the wall, my shoulder already healed. "But you wouldn't listen to me, would you?"

"No reason to," Agravain replies with a smirk. I frown. Something's off. He shouldn't be that cocky, considering I've got him tied up.

Footsteps echo all around us as more demons hurry to watch the spectacle. I flex my fingers and the vines tighten around Agravain, constricting his airway. All it would take for me to end his miserable life is to have that large thorn by his neck pierce his jugular. Cold sweat breaks out over my back at what I'm contemplating to do.

"What's it to be, Agravain?" I ask, my voice tight. "Truce, or death?"

"You don't even have the balls to end me," he replies.

I clench my teeth together, getting angry with myself. He's right. Despite knowing that if the roles were reversed, he wouldn't have hesitated. Just as I didn't hesitate when I faced those demons and Dark Sidhe. My chest tightens at my hypocrisy. What makes Agravain so different that he deserves to live, when the others couldn't? Wasn't it I who condemned the Order for treating the Fey like soulless tools and weapons? And here I am doing exactly the same.

Agravain smirks as I drop my arm back down. We lock eyes, and his grin falters.

"Remember you chose this," I say.

I jab my index finger inward. The long thorn follows the movement, piercing Agravain's neck. It's just a tip, but it's enough for it to leach him of blood, to show him his life is now in my hands. Perhaps now—

There's a bright flash as Agravain swings his leg up, then the vines are falling off him in pieces, spraying black sap across the floor. Demons grunt and whistle in appreciation as he brings his leg back down with a sharp metallic *click*. I stare at the silvery limb in confusion, pants ripped where the blade cut through.

"You like it?" Agravain asks, pulling the long thorn from his neck and tossing it aside. I frown as the leg shimmers, returning to its normal, human shape. "I actually don't mind so much what you did to me now," he says, admiring his leg. "I find it to be an improvement, actually."

"Too bad you couldn't alter your face," I say, taking an unsteady step back. I knew he wasn't a boy anymore, but this...this makes him so much more dangerous!

With a furious growl, Agravain lunges at me, before stopping dead in his tracks again.

Silence builds around us, spreading across the wide hallway. And in it, I can finally hear the first notes of thunder rolling in. And quickly drawing closer.

Shit.

A gust of wind slams the door open, revealing a dark figure outside.

This was definitely not how I'd planned our reunion, but as the cousins like to say, I need to roll with the punches. Eyes never leaving the pale-faced woman, I bow. "Greetings, Carman. I've been waiting for you."

# Chapter 34

Carman's laughter raises goosebumps down my arms. "Greetings?" she repeats. "You mean goodbyes are due, sweets?"

I clasp my hands behind my back, trying to look non-threatening as I straighten up again to stand in front of her, almost her equal.

"No, no, you heard me right the first time," I say, working hard to keep my smile in place. "I came here offering peace."

"There is no peace to be had between gods and mortals, only serfdom from the latter."

I cock my head. "I didn't mean for all the human race," I say. "Just myself. Considering we're in the same basket, you and I."

Carman lowers her eyelids. I'm really bad at innuendos, but I think she's caught my drift, so I press my advantage.

I lean forward until the slightly putrid stench of her breath tickles my nostrils. "I know what it is that you want," I whisper, "and I can give it to you."

Whatever she needs to keep me at her side.

In a blur of movement, Carman catches my jaw in her hand, and I have to bite hard on the inside of my cheek not to cry out at the pain that tabs all the way down to my chin.

"Will you kill your mother for me, then?" she asks, eyes boring into me.

"No," I say, deliberately slow, as if talking to a dull-witted child. "I would kill her for *me*."

Carman takes my declaration in silence, her flinty eyes never leaving mine, and I know she's waiting for the tell-tale gut-wrenching agony that accompanies each lie I make. But the pain doesn't come.

Danu's already dying, she's said so herself, and mostly because of this war for which I'm partially responsible. In a way, I've already killed her.

I cough back a laugh. "Why do you even think I'd dare lie to your face?" I ask. I shake my head, using the movement to free myself from her painful grasp. "I'm not as stupid as I look."

"I wouldn't be quite so sure," Carman says.

She snaps her fingers together and this time I let out a surprised grunt as the dark vines I'd called upon spring to encircle my own wrists, lifting me up until my feet can no longer touch the ground. But the vines do so gently, their long thorns curving away so as not to scratch my limbs. Slowly, Carman circles me,

"Is this why you decided to trade your allegiance?" she asks, trailing her fingers down my bare back, leaving a burning trail where hours ago Sister Marie-Clémence's henchman whipped me. "It seems so light compared to what I had to put you through. Yet here you are, begging me to take you back. How very intriguing."

I shiver against my restraints. "What you did was nothing compared with a lifetime of poisoned lies," I say, meaning every word. A flesh wound can heal, whereas the deep cuts Irene's willful neglect of me over the years have left numerous scars that will never go away, even if I like to pretend they never were.

"So here you are," Carman says, caressing now the vines holding me up. "And Dother's briar has decided to adopt you, it seems. As if to encourage me to trust you."

"I am your best solution," I say.

"You would like to think so, wouldn't you?" Carman says.

"What Mordred can do for you, I can do better," I say. "Weren't you the one who once said so?"

"Only with regards to the Sangraal, but that's already taken care of. I don't see any further use for you. But let's ask your brother, shall we?"

She turns as Mordred makes his way over, Urim and Thummim trailing in his wake with identical looks of curiosity plastered on their faces.

"Why did you bring her here?" Carman doesn't need to raise her voice to make her disapproval clear.

"I know it was presumptuous of me," Mordred says, bowing low, "but I thought it best to give you a choice before the knights decided to burn her at the stake."

"Choice?"

"Of whether or not you truly want her gone."

The offhanded way Mordred mentions my demise is like a cold vise around my heart. Carman came back too soon, didn't give me the chance to work on him, open his eyes to other possibilities. And now he's offering me up to her, like lamb to slaughter.

"Frankly, I'm not entirely sure she's trustworthy either," Mordred continues, still not looking at me. "Let me suggest, therefore, a more entertaining way for her to demonstrate her commitment to this proposed alliance of hers. One that would benefit you whatever the outcome."

"And what would that be?" she asks.

Mordred's wolfish grin appears. "What better way for her to prove her worth than through a combat to the death?"

"The Ancient Greeks believed war should be waged once every twenty-five years so each new generation would know how bad it is," Mordred recites to me, Urim and Thummim hanging off to the side, having lost all interest in us for now.

If this were another time and place, I'd roll my eyes at him and ignore him too. But instead, I watch with growing horror the masses of demons pressing against each other on the stone benches that rise above the arena in tiers. Their excited cheers and yipping fill the chill air as they soak in the latest bloodbath.

They may have left Hell behind, but it certainly has not left them.

"But they failed to mention that it's a great way to cull the population and do some cleansing," Mordred continues, "for the greater good of the stock."

"Is this why you have these games?" I ask. "To cull the weak from your army?"

"You don't know what it's like to have to manage so many people in one place," Mordred says. "Give them entertainment enough to forget they can't stand each other, until we're ready to get moving."

I let my gaze fall to the poor souls fighting on the arena's floor, wondering when I'll be expected to join them. One of them is Barguest, Gwyllion's old pet. The hairless demon dog is pawing the ground angrily, head lowered in defense as a couple of demons circle him. The taller of the two swirls to his left, curved sword whistling in the air as she slashes her weapon down.

Barguest lets out a pitiful whine as the blade cuts through his back paws' tendons, rear end buckling under him. Yet still he tries to fight for his life, jaws snapping bravely. It's painfully clear, however, that the demon dog isn't going to make it.

With a grunt of disgust, I turn away from the cruel show.

"You need to watch it till the end, sister," Mordred says, putting a restraining hand on my shoulder. "Watch and learn." His voice drops to a whisper. "And remember that you're under observation. If you want to be part of the inner circle, this type of show should leave you cold."

I cast a nervous glance over to the box on the opposite side of the stadium, where Carman sits, watching. Her beast is roaming the school grounds, too big to fit even inside the large arena, but not too far off she can't call it to her at a moment's notice.

"The smallest wrong move on your part," Mordred adds, "and you'll be cut to pieces like that poor bastard down there. But without the chance to defend yourself."

I breathe slowly through my nose, knuckles white as I tighten my hold on the railing. I may not know what game Mordred is playing, whether he's trying to save me or helping me sink further, but it's true I can't afford to blow my cover now.

To ease my worry, I remind myself of my plan. Step one, separate Carman from her dragon.

Down below, the tall demon impales Barguest on her sword, to the crowds exuberant clamor.

Two, encase her ogham in iron.

The demon twists her sword viciously. Barguest's ribcage opens with a *crack*, like the sound of dry wood splintering, and his whimpering suddenly stops. Then, with evident pleasure, the woman plunges her hand inside the dead beast's thoracic cage to pry his ogham out.

Three, kill the bitch.

The demon holds the blood-covered ogham above her head in triumph, and the crowd goes wild, whistling and shouting, demanding for more.

That's when the second demon finally decides to make his move. He's shorter, but lither, flowing across the trampled earth like water, unstoppable. The woman is slowly pivoting on herself, still holding the ogham up like a trophy, drinking in the crowd's approval.

Then she sees him. Dropping Barguest's ogham, she lunges for the curved sword still stuck inside the dead demon's body. But the other demon's already on top of her, and with quick movements, rips her head right off.

The crowd is stunned into silence. They didn't expect the fight to end so quickly. My eyes move to the sole survivor with a shiver. This is what Carman expects me to face. What she expects me to kill, if I want to stand at her side.

I hiss out a breath as the demon finally turns to face my side of the arena.

No. Freaking. Way. What is Gale doing down there? He's supposed to be with Caamaloth's army, getting ready for my signal to take the dragon down.

"Someone you know?"

I cough to hide my surprise. "Just another knight," I say meekly.

Urim leans forward. "Yessss," he hisses excitedly, sounding a lot like the banshee. "Pay up!"

Mordred's brown creases in barely repressed anger.

"Hey, blame it on the freak," Thummim says, as Mordred reaches inside the heavy pouch hanging at his hip.

"Looks like it's your turn," Urim says, sounding annoyingly cheerful as he pockets his winnings.

"Think your mama's gonna come all the way here to save you this time around?" Thummim asks me.

"Certainly would please someone we all know," Urim says, staring across the arena at Carman.

She hasn't moved an inch since the start of the combats. The only movement comes from her dress, as it billows out in front of her in a sudden gust of wind, like a dark, foreboding cloud. I wonder if she'd even bother with this whole charade if she knew Danu doesn't have the strength to help me anymore.

"Enough stalling," Mordred says.

"Please don't," I say, balking at the idea of fighting Gale.

I look in panic at my brother, who grabs my hands and gently pries them off the railing.

"Don't worry," he says, "we've got another opponent for you. And I think you'll like the surprise."

Then, with a shove, he sends me flying over the wall and into the fighting pit.

"Show us what you've got!" I hear Urim shout as I land sprawling in the sand.

Cheers and laughter arise at my sudden entrance. I climb unsteadily back to my feet, whirling on any would-be attacker. But the only other ones down on the floor with me are a couple of silent Fey who are rushing to clear the latest two corpses, while a Dark Sidhe frog marches a chained Gale back out.

I look up as the crowd suddenly goes quiet, waiting with bated breath as Carman finally shifts in her seat to raise her hand, signaling someone by the entrance.

Goosebumps spread up my arms as a cage is slowly wheeled through the gate, creaking under its weight. It is huge, the height of four men, and requires a dozen demons to pull. Old curtains that must have been torn from dorm room windows cover half of it, obstructing whatever's locked inside from view.

The wheels stop with a groan as the demons finally let go of the ropes. I watch with dread the lead demon sprint for the back of the cage before vaulting on top of it. Then, muscles bulging under the strain, it pulls the cage's door open with a loud *clang*, before fleeing the stadium with the other demons.

Time ticks away. Cold sweat beads on my forehead. The wind picks up, howling miserably around the arena. Then, with deliberate slowness, a giant creature emerges, pale as a corpse, six long pairs of arms and legs extending and retracting at odd angles, like a deformed spider. It is a thing made of nightmares; a cruel experiment gone massively wrong.

Hesitantly, the monster swivels its head, and my stomach tightens in revulsion as I recognize Father Tristan's face, empty eye sockets staring straight at me. The creature takes another awkward step, long red hair swinging stiffly about its shoulders, and my knees grow weak at the sight of the second head pushing through where the neck should be—long nose ending prettily above red, red lips stretched in a rictus. Lady Ysolt.

The monster lurches towards the edge of the arena, as if it can't quite figure out how to use its new limbs. There's a strange, mewling sound, and it takes me a moment to realize it's coming from a third face protruding from behind the first set of arms.

I bite back a gasp as the monster twists around to give it a better look.

"Jack," I hiccup, staring at the boy's small face. He looks younger without his glasses.

Jack's mouth opens, pink tongue darting out, and he lets out another of those pitiful cries. I really have to puke.

I turn away, glaring at the ecstatic crowd, hating them all for what they've done to my friends. I wish I could destroy them all at once right here, right now. I catch sight of Mordred, still as stone between Urim and Thummim's shouting figures, and remember his words. Lashing out now is exactly what Carman expects me to do.

I expel a shaky breath. Time to play my part. I turn towards Carman's box, and bow with flourish.

"My lady, it shall be a pleasure to fight for you," I yell so she can hear me above the crowd's cheers.

My shout jolts the chimera[32] to action before Carman can bother to respond, and the crowd's eager shouts redouble as the monster storms at me in a sudden burst of speed. I drop into a low crouch, watching as the creature's long legs close the distance between us, long arms swinging wildly at its sides. Ten feet. Five. Adrenaline pumps through my veins as I wait. Two feet.

The chimera lets out a high-pitched bellow, a long-fingered hand already reaching for me. But at the last second, I dive to the side.

The monster slides to a stop in a cloud of dust, then spins around to face me again. I cringe at the sight of Lady Ysolt's forehead bulging beneath Father Tristan's chin. She opens her mouth wide, and I stare, frozen, as her jaws dislocate completely to let out a terrible shriek.

I cover my ears with a cringe, expecting my eardrums to burst, but not a sound emerges from her distended lips. For a split second, the chimera seems to waver, then the pressure wave hits me with the power of a running train.

Pain rips through my body as I'm hurled through the air, lungs no longer functioning. My right leg hits something solid, and I flip around to slam into the screeching crowd. I can't breathe. Everything hurts. I fear I've shattered my leg. My right arm's

---

[32] Monster made up of dissimilar parts that give it a grotesque and horrifying appearance.

pinned at an odd angle beneath me. And all I can do is stare blearily at the sky-lake.

A high-pitched ringing starts in my ears. I suck in a short, burning breath. A second. The bleachers shake beneath me with the roaring cheer of a thousand demons.

They think I'm done for, vanquished by that horror, fruit of Carman's retribution. I blink slowly once. Even that hurts. Another shuddering breath.

I need to move. Have to. Through the haze and the pain, I finally manage to roll onto my stomach. But before I can summon the strength to push myself onto my feet, a foot stomps on my good arm.

"I'd stay right where you are, girly," a demon says, adding weight to his words by placing a rusty dagger at my throat. "Got good money on this game, and you ain't gonna ruin it for me."

Cold fury wipes all my pain away. With a startled hiss, the man snatches his foot away. Too late. Within seconds, his whole body's writhing next to me, bright flames quickly turning the demon to ashes. I glare at the crowd around me, and this time they pull away from me, no longer heckling.

Rage swelling through me, I get back up, testing my injured limbs, making sure they're setting properly, before returning my attention to the arena floor.

The chimera's waiting, all three heads twisting grossly around, seeking me out. I swallow bile back down. I can't let myself think of it as *them*, as the people I cared for.

Still holding onto the ramp for support, I release all my pent-up anger, fear and frustration, and stamp my foot down repeatedly on the stone step.

*BOOM! BOOM! BOOM! BOOM!*

On the fourth stomp, the floor craters out beneath me, power carving out giant boulders from the stadium in a series of deafening explosions. Demons shriek as they try not to fall into the crevices. The chimera whirls on itself, confused by the sounds. I don't see Lady Ysolt's mouth open again, don't hear her second cry, but the tiered benches on the other side of the arena explode under her blast.

I slide my hand out, and the boulders shoot through the air to circle the monster. The chimera turns on itself again, confused by these different targets.

A shudder goes through its long-limbed body, and I pause, hesitating, wondering why it's shifting its stance. I can feel everyone's eyes boring into me, wondering what I'm doing. Sweat slowly tracks its way down my neck. Come on, you fool, I tell myself, just finish it.

But I can't get images of Jack, Lady Ysolt and Father Tristan out of my head. Can't help but hope there's a way to revert what's been done to them.

The chimera's shoulders slump, all three pairs of hands dropping to its sides as its faces turn to me in anguish.

Saint George's balls, they know!

Shock ripples through me at the realization that my friend and professors have been locked together into this formless creature, all the while being aware of what was done to them. I bite back a sob. It's sick. Morbid. Vicious.

"Morgan? Morgan is that you? What's wrong? Where are you?"

Arthur's sudden voice acts like a cold shower, cleansing my muddled thoughts until only one thing's clear: I'm going to put an end to this horror, and make Carman pay for it. *All* of it.

I'm fine, I mentally tell Arthur, not knowing whether he'll hear me or not, and hoping he can't see what I'm seeing.

Standing a little straighter, I close my hand into a tight fist, and the boulders plummet to the ground, pounding the chimera repeatedly until there's nothing left of the monster, nothing left for Carman to desecrate.

Only then do I plaster a sickening smile to my face and bow before Carman's lodge.

"I hope the spectacle was agreeable to you, my lady," I shout over the incensed crowd's clamor.

Carman's answering laugh makes me want to rip her eyes out. The witch leans forward in her seat, long, dark hair falling over her shoulders in lustrous waves.

"I think I may keep you after all," she says.

And, just like that, my most ardent wish and deepest fear come to be.

# ᚲᚺᚨᛈᛏᛖᚱ 35

"I don't think it's as simple as that," Bri whispers, and I try not to wince at how grating her murmurs sound to my ears.

I stretch my legs out on my pallet, ever so slowly so as not to scream from the pain. Carman may have decided to keep me alive for now, but she still didn't appreciate my destroying her latest creation, and half the stadium with it.

I doubt she'd be so lenient if she found out I've been holding secret meetings in my cell to plot her demise since she locked me up three days ago. I don't know how Gale and Bri have managed to find me, but I have a strong suspicion it has something to do with Owen, who's currently keeping watch just outside the door.

"Of course it is," Gale says, turning the book around so he can show her what he means on the graph. "This symbol here is clearly a Bindrune[33]—"

"I know what Bindrunes are," Bri says, sounding annoyed, "but this clearly...oh."

"It's a simple pattern, really," Gale says, as engrossed in the ward patterns as Bri, "one rune here, and another, followed by a

---

[33] The joining of two or more runes into one.

binary Bindrune, then a triple one, so these here should be five, and seven, to follow the Fibonacci sequence[34]."

I tune out their voices, glad that they, at least, are making some progress.

Unlike me. My efforts to bring Mordred to our side have been fruitless. He barely spared me a minute when I first arrived, and since the fight in the arena, he hasn't bothered to come down to visit me once. Maybe it's just as well. I can't forgive him for what he's done to my friends. Every time I close my eyes, all I can see are their distorted faces, screaming at me to free them.

"Now that's done, let's talk about the next step in our plan," Gale says, drawing me out of my nightmarish memories. "I'm here to take down the dragon——"

"You really think you can do anything while Carman's around?" Bri retorts, still taking notes from her runic book.

"You've got it wrong. I need to find a way to cut the dragon up and encase its ogham in iron. Carman is Morgan's problem."

"Thanks," I retort. "But in case you hadn't noticed, even if you do manage to cut Carman off from her Fey powers, my hands are kinda tied at the moment."

Gale cocks his head at me. "Whatever happened to the strong-willed girl who defied both a knight and a Fey lord to come here?"

"She's wizened up," I mutter.

"Or given up," Bri says. She looks down, as surprised as I am by her outburst. "Sorry," she adds in a small voice.

"No, I'm sorry," I say, the words struggling to get out. "It's just…I thought I knew what I was doing, what I was getting into. I had a plan. But nothing's going the way it was supposed to. And now I'm lost. And I've dragged you guys into it…"

---

[34] Infinite series of numbers where the next one is found by adding the two numbers before it: 0, 1, 1, 2, 3, 5, 8…

"Morgan, don't you know nothing ever goes according to plan?" Gale says. And, as he's done before, he reaches inside the remains of my jacket to pull the poppy he'd given me out of my pocket, the flower bearing but a single red petal now. "That's why we work together, as a team."

"So we can watch each other's back?"

"So we can catch each other's mistakes," Gale says with a nod.

"You mean *you* make mistakes too?" Bri says, sounding like Keva.

"But it doesn't mean we don't believe in you anymore," Gale says. "Besides, you're soon going to get the opportunity to cause all the mischief you're apparently so good at making."

"What is that supposed to mean?" I ask, with a strangled laugh.

Gale's about to reply, when he suddenly goes still. "We better get going," he says, as distant footsteps reach us, getting louder.

But Bri doesn't move, her eyes on me, filled with worry.

"She'll be fine," Gale says, grabbing her arm, "she's a survivor."

There's a little scratch at the door, and Owen pokes his head in, eyes like pools of darkness that reveal nothing. "Time," he says.

And in a flash, all three leave, locking the door behind them. I find myself holding my breath, ears perked for any sound of scuffle. But when I hear the heavy footsteps stop before my cell, I know they've managed to slip away safely.

A key turns inside the lock, and the door creaks open once more. I stare, slack-jawed, as Mordred struts inside, the flickering light of a torch pouring in behind him.

"Aren't you a sight for sore eyes?" Mordred says, eyeing me coldly, like a mortician studying the next body to embalm.

He, on the other hand, looks just peachy.

"Come here to gloat?" I ask, leaning my head against the stone wall, grateful for its coolness against my feverish skin.

"You actually did a nice job on that ghoul," Mordred says, crossing his arms over his pectorals. "Impressed quite a few."

"What does that matter anymore?" I ask angrily.

"It matters if it's the only thing that will keep you alive," Mordred says.

"Oh, and forcing me to fight these horrible monsters is the way to do it?"

"You and I share the same blood, the same abilities. Surely you don't think the ghoul would have posed me any problem, do you?"

I look away from him, unwilling to answer. I wish he'd leave me alone. Instead, however, Mordred drops into a crouch in front of me.

"Morgan, these people don't understand things like pity, or mercy. They are signs of weakness, and weakness among them means death. The only way, therefore, you could have blended in—if you could ever truly blend in anywhere—was if you shared these same instincts as theirs."

"Could have? *Was*?" I ask, finally looking back at him.

Mordred brushes my hair back to look at the side of my face, where Carman scored me from temple to jaw, and lets out a disgusted grunt before tossing something onto my lap. My fingers brush the old iron-threaded jack in dismay. It's the one Arthur had given me eons ago at the ball, the one I wore my whole time down in Hell, and that I tossed out the moment I got back here. And though it's now threadbare, it's better than the ripped-up jacket I'm wearing now.

"Where did you find this?" I ask.

"That's not important," Mordred says. "What's important is for you to finally understand that there's nothing anyone can do against Carman. No one's stronger than she is. Not Lugh, not your boyfriend's paltry army, not Danu, and certainly not you."

I glare at him, bunching up my old vest in my manacled hands, wishing I could slap some sense into him. "You took all this trouble to get down here just to tell me that?" I ask. "To be careful? You shouldn't have bothered."

"Shut up, Morgan. I know exactly what I'm doing, unlike you, who keeps bumbling about all the time, making a mess of things."

"Well if it's Carman's plans I'm making a mess of, then I'm not sorry at all," I retort. "I can't let her free Balor."

Mordred snorts in derision. "You mean *I* need to free Balor. She can't open Hell's seventh gate on her own, not even with the way Dother's changed the wards. Only I can do that." He pauses, golden eyes locking with mine. "Or you."

"You can't be serious," I breathe out. "You'd honestly let Carman use you so she can destroy this whole world?"

Flashes of Mordred's punishment for what happened at Caamaloth come back to me, the vision from Danu's cave still fresh in my mind. Carman's hate for Mordred was evident, and the only reason she kept him alive was because she needed him still. So why is Mordred still OK with playing her lackey?

Mordred's smirk turns into a soft snarl. "I am nobody's servant," he says, leaning so fast I jerk back and hit my head against the wall, "and you'd better remember that."

"That's certainly not what it looks like," I bite back, annoyed.

But I immediately regret the taunt at the flat look he gives me in return. I need to remind myself that Mordred's my brother, that he's like me, trying to find his place in the world, one where we wouldn't constantly have to be afraid for our lives and freedom because of what we are. He's just going about it a different way.

If only I knew how to show him my way's the right one…

Mordred suddenly pulls away from me. "Look, I've come down here to let you know to be good these next few days," he says, pinching the bridge of his nose. "I won't be here to defend you if you don't."

"Why—"

"And that includes your little friends," Mordred continues."

Blood drains my face. "What—"

But Mordred's already out, the door closing behind him

I hunch back down on my pallet in the sudden darkness. Despite my exhaustion, I keep mulling over his last words, turning them over and over in my mind until I think I'm going crazy.

And maybe I am, for I can't help but think that he just admitted to being on our side.

"I smell something frying," someone sniggers as the door to my cell creaks open, making me jump.

It feels like ages since I saw Mordred, though Bri says it's only been two days. And still I don't know what to make of his last visit. Bri says to ignore him, that unlike me, he can lie through his teeth. Which is true. But somehow, I don't think he did this time around.

My gut tightens as Urim's pale face pokes inside my cell. Right on cue, Thummim squeezes behind him, flashing me his commercial-bright smile. "Neurons, I think," he says. "The frying, I mean."

"Can't you guys give me a rest?" I mutter, shifting uncomfortably on my pallet.

"You've had 7,614 minutes of rest already," Thummim says. "Time to get moving."

I snort in derision. Right. "What do you guys actually want?"

"Oh, so many things," Urim says, as if he was waiting for me to ask him just that. "Carrot cake and some absinthe would be good for a start."

"Going to a water park, making dogs out of balloons," Thummim says.

"Fulfilling the prophecy, driving a Formula 1 car, going to a spa, and getting our nails done."

"But we're always so busy," Thummim finishes with a theatrical sigh.

"Wait," I say, looking up at the strange pair. If they're talking about prophecies, then... "Are you guys saying you want to go back to Paradise, too?"

"We've been away from home for a while," Urim says.

"Never really thought I'd miss it," Thummim adds.

"Home," I repeat. "Last I checked, that wasn't in Carman's plans. So why are you working for her."

"Last I checked, we were working with your brother," Thummim says.

"Who's helping Carman, so it's essentially the same thing," I say.

Except it's not, I realize as I look at their mischievous faces. Working *with*, not *for*. Which means they chose to go with Mordred.

Mordred who left me with a warning not to get into trouble.

"Where's Mordred?" I ask.

Thummim shrugs. "Not at Lake High, that's for sure."

"Threw Carman all up in a tizzy," Urim says, sounding rather pleased.

"I think she might be leveling a city or two up in the human world for that," Thummim says thoughtfully. "Something about deadly hail..."

Saint George's balls.

I was right. Mordred and these guys have turned against Carman at long last.

A memory pushes its way to the forefront of my mind. "When I came back here the first time after you guys had taken over the school," I cautiously hedge, "you were waiting outside for someone..."

Both Dark Sidhe stare at me, unblinking.

"You mentioned you were waiting for a different mutt," I forge on. "You meant you were waiting for Carman, didn't you? That means you guys have known all along that she's only half-Fey. Was that your way of giving me a hint?"

"Took you long enough to figure that one out," Thummim says, scratching his jaw. "At the rate you were going, we figured we'd drop a few more hints."

"The geas wouldn't allow us to tell the truth outright," Urim explains with a disappointed sigh. "But I thought we'd nonetheless been quite obvious."

I nod slowly, though this is still too much to take in at the moment. "Thanks for...trying to help me," I say at last.

Urim's smile deepens. "No, no. Thank you for letting us help *you*."

Both Dark Sidhe move at once, and before I can make sense of what's happening, they're upon me, one of them holding me down, the other grabbing my arm and exposing it, flesh part up.

Panic fills me as I struggle to shove them away. They played me, and the eager idiot I was fell right for it!

"Stop struggling, princess," Thummim says, pulling out a sharp knife. "It'll hurt less if you do."

"I thought you wanted to help," I say, angry tears leaking out the corners of my eyes.

"But we are," Urim says, pressing down on me harder. "Didn't you profess to be one of us now?"

"And those of a feather...," Thummim says, pressing the tip of the knife into my forearm.

I whimper as he drags the knife down my arm, my flesh splitting easily beneath the blade.

"...eat together," Urim finishes, as Thummim pulls out a large, yellow gem from his pocket.

"Present from Gadreel," Thummim says before shoving the demon's ogham into my arm. "*Bon appétit.*"

"NO!" I shout, thrashing against their hold.

Urim's other arm snakes around me, until he's practically covering me with his entire body.

"Just hold on," Thummim says through gritted teeth as he keeps both hands pressed firmly around my arm, until the wound closes up again.

My legs kick out, spasms overtaking me. My stomach cramps up as the foreign presence burns through my body, spreading goose bumps across my skin. I buck against their combined weight, lifting Urim up, then slam my head against my pallet so hard, stars burst across my vision. I want to grab Thummim's knife and slice myself open to rip the ogham back out and stop this agony.

"Shhh," Urim says, holding my head to stop me from bashing my brains out. "It's gonna get better."

A scream tears through my throat. My fingers clamp onto Urim's arm, and I feel his bones shatter beneath them.

A maniacal laugh escapes Thummim. "Stop fighting it and enjoy the rush!" he shouts, struggling to loosen my grip on Urim.

I arch on my pallet so violently I feel tendons and muscles tear in my back. It's too much. My body isn't meant to absorb all this foreign power at once. I'm barely conscious of both Dark Sidhe diving before my cell echoes with a resounding *BOOM*!

The walls and ceiling explode, the grey stone pulverized to dust in less than a second. Warm tears flow down my face, and I can't tell if they're of relief or...relish. My whole body's thrumming with the energy I got—no, *stole*—from Gad.

I roll over and heave, chills coursing down my body.

"That wasn't so bad now, was it?" Thummim asks, coughing.

A Fey light pops into existence, a purple glow that casts a devilish sheen over the destruction I've just caused.

"Better than I thought it would be," Urim says.

He picks himself up, eyes traveling first to the door hanging halfway off its hinges, then around the crater that's become my prison cell, and finally up at the cracked ceiling through which the sky-lake is now visible.

"Though perhaps not as discrete as one might have hoped," he finishes.

"Who cares at this point?" Thummim says, wiping the dust from his face.

A silent sob escapes my lips. My arms have turned entirely black, and I can feel the taint spreading slowly to the rest of my body, as if I've gathered all the darkness inside me and it's eating me alive. Yet at the same time, I can feel Gad's energy coursing through me, hot and violent, eager to escape. And it scares me how much I enjoy it.

"Ready?" Thummim asks me after a while.

I take a deep, steadying breath. It's OK, I tell myself, willing the last of my tears back. If this is what it takes to save the others, I'll become a monster too.

# Chapter 36

"What's this, Morgan?" Bri asks, eyeing Urim and Thummim suspiciously.

At my orders, the two Dark Sidhe have gathered my friends in the library's book repair room. It smells like glue and rot, and our only source of light comes from a narrow window set in the far wall, but the two have sworn this is one of the safest places left in the school.

If they are to be trusted, and it's clear neither Gale nor Bri do. I can't fault them for that. Even now, I find it hard myself to believe this isn't a trap.

"Exactly what it looks like," I say, trying not to sound as nervous as I feel. "We're finally getting this show started."

Too soon, a part of me says, while the other itches for some action. Anything to let my stolen powers loose. My hand closes over the ogham in my pocket, the one Mordred once gave me. Would I get the same kind of rush if I were to absorb that one too?

I yank my hand back out, as if burned.

"You never mentioned…them being in on it," Bri says tensely, drawing me away from my disturbing thoughts. "We can't rush things like this, not when so much depends on these plans of yours."

"Plans, schmance," Thummim says. "Learn by doing, that's what I always say."

"And risk getting us all killed for nothing?" a deep voice asks from the entrance, startling us.

"Lance?" Bri asks, eyes going round with shock.

"You're alive?" I ask at the same time.

"Loverboy!" Urim exclaims, mirth dancing in his dark eyes.

With a tight smile, Lance walks over to our corner, and I note with some concern that he's favoring his right leg.

"What's happened to you? Where were you?" I ask, giving him a tight hug.

"Not in any prison cell I know," Bri says, sounding a little curt.

I throw her a puzzled glance, and she has the grace to look ashamed at her tone.

"I'm here, that's all that matters," Lance says.

Up close, he looks even paler than I remember, long scratches marring his once perfect skin. I frown. "Did Jennifer do that to you?"

"We had...an argument," he says.

My stomach drops. "Does she know you're here?" I ask.

"No," Lance says.

His blue gaze slides down to my collar, and his brow furrows. My heart skips a beat, and I refrain from reaching for my neck, knowing that the dark stains must already be showing there. I wonder what will happen when it's spread to my whole body. Will I die? Will I go crazy? Or will I turn out to be just like Carman?

"Morgan?" Bri asks tremulously.

I blink, shaking the disturbing thoughts away, and notice that all the loose papers and books in the room have started to rise in the air, their edges smoking as with the beginning of a fire.

"Sorry," I mutter.

I try to put a leash on my powers again, but this is turning out to be much harder than it used to be. My whole body is humming with energy, and I feel like the slightest wrong manipulation is going to snap me in two. Or make the whole school explode. I grit my teeth together, and at last, the books and papers thud harmlessly to the floor.

"OK," I say, feeling a little nauseated, "let's start over."

"AC's on his way to meeting up with your Arthur," Thummim says.

"Who's AC?" Lance asks.

"He means Mordred," I reply, though I'm as worried as he looks.

What if this whole thing is a ploy to get rid of us once and for all? But then, why bother giving me Gad's ogham when I know how precious they are to them?

"And while they're working to get our troops here, we must lure..."

My voice trails off as a hunched figure slips in between the fallen bookcases.

"Banshee?" I whisper.

"Thought it best to get all available hands on board if we are to take Carman down," Urim says grinning up to his ears.

The cowled figure hovers hesitantly by the wall. "Mmmissssstressss," she says hesitantly, as if unsure what kind of welcome she is to receive. As if getting caught here was her fault!

With a strangled cry of joy, I run for her and throw myself into her arms, hugging her bony frame close.

"I thought I'd lost you!" I say through my sudden tears.

"I'm ssssoorrry," the banshee says, her voice muffled against my jacket.

I pull back, wiping my eyes. "What are you sorry for? I'm the one who should be apologizing!"

"Could we please get started?" a cool voice behind the banshee says. "There's too many lice around for comfort."

"Kaede? You're here too?" I say, grinning like a fool. This is too good to be true.

"Just tell me what we have to do now that we didn't try before," Kaede says.

The knight stiffens as Urim throws his arm around her shoulders. "I know the reports from down under weren't exactly glorifying," he says, "but can't you tell a revolution when it's staring straight at you?"

"Is that what this is?" someone asks from the other side of the fallen bookcases, and we all grow still at the honeyed voice.

"Jen?" Lance says, growing even paler. "What are you—"

I turn on him. "I thought you said she didn't know!" I growl.

Lance winces. "I thought...I didn't mean..."

Bri releases a shocked cry, springing back as the bookcases that were shielding us from view burst into flames. Owen puts his hand on her arm, fathomless eyes calm. Next to them, Urim and Thummim look panicked. And through the acrid smoke, I can see Jennifer turn towards someone else.

"Didn't I say they were acting strange?" she asks, her words tumbling out. "So, will you believe me now about Mordred's little expedition?"

The other person laughs, sending shivers down my back. I was wrong. I should never have doubted Mordred. Jennifer's the one I should've kept an eye on instead.

"I know all about Mordred's whereabouts," Carman says, and Jennifer's boastful smile drops.

Tendrils of dark smoke come out of her dress to smother the fire, and my stomach turns at the stench of sulfur that quickly overpowers the smell of burning books.

"In fact," Carman continues, finally stepping into our line of sight, "I believe he and the Pendragon heir are meeting right about now. Though perhaps not under very amicable terms as some here might think."

The lump in my stomach grows to the size of a fist. How can Carman know what's happening with Mordred and Arthur if none of us do? Unless...

"She's sent her dragon after them," Gale says, voicing my own fears.

Carman's smile deepens across the smoldering remains of the bookcases, dimpling her cheeks. "Did you not think I'd know about your silly plotting?" she asks unctuously. "Well, at least this way I can get rid of all these nuisances at once, and get my hands on your oghams."

My heart's hammering so loud, I can't make out what she says next.

"What did you plan for this predicament?" Urim asks me in a rush.

"I say screw the plans," Thummim says, sounding scared.

Carman sweeps her hand sideways and the remains of the bookcases crumble to the floor, leaving the passage free for her to go through.

No.

I won't let her even so much as lay a finger on any of my friends.

I gather Gadreel's power, feeling it pulse urgently under my skin.

"Run," I tell the others.

The wind shifts behind me as I throw my arms out, energy blazing around our small group in a wide arc, covering my friends' retreat through the single window.

"No, you're mine!" Carman shouts.

I flinch as her power slams into mine, cords of darkness writhing across my shield, looking for a weakness. I risk a look over my shoulder. Thummim is pushing Bri up through the window, Lance and Owen waiting for their turns.

"Missstressss," the banshee says in warning.

My feet slip on the cluttered floor as Carman pushes me back, the veins in her face darkening.

"It's time to stop playing," she says. "Now be a good girl, and come along."

I grit my teeth, straining against her. "Over. My. Dead. Body!"

My power flares at that last word. There's a bright flash, and the dark tendrils disintegrate, forcing a hiss out of Carman's mouth. I stare in shock as she holds onto her arm, smoke drifting up where I burned her.

I feel empty, my newfound energy spent, a migraine pushing behind my eyeballs, but I find myself laughing. I can't believe it! I thought for sure she was going to kill me, but instead I'm the one who hurt her!

"I always said she was unhinged," I hear Jennifer mutter from a corner.

With a snarl, Carman wheels on her, flinging Jennifer into the wall with a sharp *crack*.

Still giddy and somewhat lightheaded, I turn to follow the others out the window, but the air around me suddenly thickens until I can hardly move.

"You little tramp! You dare defy me even now?" Carman seethes, breathing heavily.

Her power's pressing down on me, an unbearable weight that makes my bones groan. She wants me on my knees, begging for my life, for those of my friends, though we both know she'd kill us all the same.

388

Spots dance in my vision as I will myself to stay standing. I blink slowly as one of the spots grows larger, turning into a flying rat. I blink again, and the rat is now bobbing through the air behind Carman, waving its tiny arms about frantically. Papillon?

Then everything goes black.

The whole world explodes before my very eyes, earth heaving and splintering, sending knights, Fey and beasts alike sprawling to the ground. There's another mighty roar, then fire blazes through the forest, one massive gust that burns everything down indiscriminately.

Arthur...

The silent cry echoes through my mind in a wave of panic. My eyes try desperately to adjust to the sudden brightness, but all is purple smoke and orange flames. White light pulsates to life, and I allow myself a breath of relief as Arthur swings Excalibur around.

Another thunderous growl rips through the air, fanning the flames higher. The dragon's right above us.

Arthur.

But Arthur doesn't react to my cry. And while he's tracking the dragon's destructive path, I keep my focus on the man creeping towards us through the smoke, unhindered. Mordred's tattooed face splits into a smile, sending shivers down my back.

*Arthur!*

Fear courses down my veins, sending my thoughts into a frenzy. Mordred's brought the dragon into Lugh's lair, and they're killing everyone I love. I should never have left Arthur's side! I should have never trusted my brother...

The ground splits at Arthur's feet, clearing a path through the flames. Through the shimmering heat, I see Gareth and Gauvain rush over, their dark faces glistening with sweat.

"The tree's done for!" Gauvain shouts, wincing at the sound of distant screams.

"At least Lugh's had time to take everyone to safety, but—"

"We need to keep that beast occupied," Arthur says with a strangled cough.

My heart is beating so wildly I feel like throwing up. How can nobody see him? Mordred's almost upon us.

"Stop!" I shout at him.

Despite the vision, a part of me is still aware of what's happening inside the library, and I see Carman cock her head, squinting at me in confusion.

To my surprise, Mordred pauses. "Convinced now, boys?" he asks aloud.

"Yeah," Gareth replies, face sheening with sweat. "Ready to skin the thing?"

"Ready," both Mordred and Arthur reply at the same time.

My heart skips a beat. My mind stops spinning. Did I hear that right? Then, at last, I feel a smile tug at my lips.

And at last, understanding dawns on Carman's face, while in the vision, her dragon rears in anger, knowing it has been betrayed.

"Mistressssss!"

I blink at the banshee's shout, breathing heavily, before realizing that Carman's left.

"Where is she?" I ask shakily.

The banshee motions wordlessly towards the rest of the library. I shake my head to try to clear it. Why did she leave? I've spent most of Gadreel's powers, she would've won, she—

"Can't believe it, but I believe she got scared."

I jump at Lance's voice. The knight is leaning against an upturned table, holding Jennifer's limp body in his arms.

"Didn't realize you'd come back, and for *her* nonetheless," I say thickly, trying to ignore the tightness in my chest.

Everyone left when I told them to, everyone but the banshee. And he would have gone too if it hadn't been for Jennifer, even if it meant facing Carman's wrath.

Lance's arms tighten around Jennifer, pressing her to his chest. "She's all I have," he says simply.

"She dumped you a long time ago," I say, "traded you in for another the second you were no longer cool or useful. Saint George's balls, she's betrayed us all to Carman! And yet here you are—"

"She's all I have," Lance repeats, a little more fiercely.

I swallow the insult I was about to throw at him.

He's still in love with her. Always has been. Always will be. No matter how vile she is, no matter all the damage she's caused, the blood on her hands. He'll always run back to her.

"You make me sick," I finally say.

Lance blanches, but remains otherwise motionless, and a part of me feels ashamed at having lashed out at him. He can't help how he feels. It's not his fault Jennifer's a soul-sucking troll.

I point a blackened finger at him. "Just...just keep her out of my sight," I growl.

He nods, already moving to take her some place safe.

"Oh, this is not good," a tiny voice says, buzzing around my ear, and I find myself staring at a scared Papillon.

"So it was you," I say, surprised to find the flying mouse here. With Danu's permission, Arthur and I enrolled the small creature to help us coordinate our attacks, without drawing any undue attention. "I thought you were supposed to be with the others at the front?"

"Came to say they're on their way, and that the girl's waiting for your sign so she can finish the ward reversal," Papillon says, wringing his tail in his paws. "But this is bad. This is very bad, indeed, if Carman's escaped."

"She's still here," I say, licking my parched lips.

Carman didn't leave because she's scared. She sensed we made a pact with my brother, and now that he's left the school, she can't afford to kill me. I'm the only one left who can open the seventh Gate.

"This is exactly what we wanted," I continue. "You need to go back to Arthur, and let him know to get here ASAP."

"You mean they've found the d-d-dragon?" Papillon asks, eyes growing larger than his wide ears.

I smile weakly. "No, my friend. The dragon found them. Now they need to bring it here."

And I must make sure Carman stays here, within the school boundary, where she can cause the least trouble.

Adrenaline pumping down my veins, I rush across the library, no longer caring who sees me or not. This is it. Time to put the monsters back in their box.

I burst through the doors into the dark hallways, slipping over a wet patch of tar. I catch myself on the wall, then make for the exit, the banshee on my tail.

"Upssstaiirsss," she says.

Without breaking pace, I turn into the nearest staircase. We've barely made it up a couple of steps when a figure jumps in front of us, metallic leg gleaming despite the darkness.

"You again," I mutter, shoulders bunching in annoyance.

Agravain grins fiercely. "Me. Always me. Until your dying breath."

"You know, if you have a crush on me, you should just say so," I say, sounding strangely like Keva.

Agravain's sunken cheeks twitch, then, in a flash, he pounces forward. I raise a hand to parry his attack, power surging in response. But before either of us can make contact, the banshee slips in between us, and catches Agravain's blow on her obsidian knife.

Agravain lets out an unhinged laugh. "Letting your pet do the dirty work for you?" he asks, following his strike with an elbow to her head.

The banshee dodges, aiming her knife at his legs next, not knowing it is no longer flesh and bone. Stone hits metal, spraying sparks across the stairs.

"Off, you hag!" Agravain mutters, slashing his sword down.

Blood lashes my face, warm and slick, and the banshee falls silently to the floor.

Power flaring in anger, I vault over my friend's body, whipping my arms around. Wind whistles in my ears before punching through the wall behind Agravain in an explosion of stone and plaster.

"That was closer than I thought," Agravain says, wiping the blood flowing from his cut ear onto his shoulder, the rest of him unfortunately still whole.

"That was a warning," I tell him. "You do *not* touch my friends."

"You know what's funny?" Agravain asks, smirking. "Seeing how much you care about all those Fey when all they want is to see you dead."

My stomach lurches. "If you're talking about that prophecy, I already know of it. And you know what I think?" The air around me crackles. "That you can shove it."

I barely register the smoke pooling out of my fingers as I point at the knight. The grey smoke shoots across the landing, turning into tentacles of black tar midair.

Agravain ducks, but he's not fast enough, and my power wraps around his left arm, a black coil that pulls him back to me. With a cry of rage, Agravain turns to hack at the tentacle, but this isn't something human metal can touch. I twist my fingers together, sending another burst of power, and more black ropes whip around Agravain's legs, and sword arm, threatening to pulverize them. At last, he stops struggling.

"P-P-Please," Agravain stutters, pupils dilated with fear.

He's back to being a boy now, a little boy who played with fire before realizing that flames do burn. But there's no pity inside me for him. He burned that away too.

Agravain makes another feeble attempt to pull himself free, the smell of searing flesh and rotten eggs heavy in the hallway as the dark bindings bite into his flesh and metal legs, eating him alive.

394

"You're done killing my friends," I tell him, "you and the rest of the traitors."

I make myself watch until his fingers stop twitching, and his pleas have turned into an indistinct mewling. Then, with a last shudder, Agravain's mouth drops open, drool dripping down his chin, glassy eyes staring sightlessly at the floor.

Only then do I finally turn away.

Arthur is pacing about a wide clearing, pockmarked by strange piles of stones. Cairns, as far as the eye can see, rising at different heights in a convoluted maze. The cousins are with him, as well as Hadrian, Daniel and Keva, all waiting silently, while Sir Hengist, Lugh, Oberon, and my uncle confer together further away.

Somehow, they've lost the dragon. Or, and this scares me more than I dare admit, Carman's sent her beast far away, out of reach.

Arthur finally stops his pacing, and turns to stare at a lone figure standing incongruously to the side. I start at the sight of Mordred, his tattooed body leaning lightly against one of the cairns, golden eyes lost in the distance.

After everything that's happened, I still can't believe it's him, that he's there with the others, working with them. Neither, apparently, can the older knights.

"We have decided to wait here until we get a message for affirmative action from Morgan," my uncle says, arms crossed tightly over his chest. "Going in too soon would be too risky considering the stakes."

"Don't be daft," Mordred says, with barely veiled contempt. "You think Carman's going to wait for us before she attacks my sister?"

"I thought your people were helping her?" Sir Cade says.

Mordred bristles, and I wonder if either Urim or Thummim has managed to report to him what's happened here. "They can't face Carman on their own either," he concedes at last.

Sir Hengist's lips curl in disdain. "The plan was clear. We wait for a sign from the school. Until then, our runners will keep track of the dragon and keep it busy. That's final."

The Errant Companions' leader returns his attention to a map laid out on the ground between him and Lugh. The other knights exchange uncomfortable glances, then fall away as well, leaving Mordred alone but for Arthur.

"You know how I first found out about her?" Arthur asks after a long minute, before going to lean against the stone pillar next to Mordred's.

"Spare me," Mordred says, rolling his eyes.

"It was three years ago," Arthur continues. "I'd been snooping around in my parents' office, when I found a whole pile of unread letters in the trash can."

I gasp in surprise. My letters. The ones I'd written back when I still believed Irene was my mother, telling her about my life at school, hoping that one day I would finally get an answer back.

I'd forgotten about them, but hearing Arthur mention them brings back that sting of hurt and disappointment I'd felt every day when the mail was distributed, watching the other students open their care packages with glee, while my desk remained empty.

"Ah, yes, Morgan's sniveling letters," Mordred says, sounding bored.

Of course, he knows all about them. He was with me during the writing of many of them.

"They weren't sniveling," Arthur retorts, and I can hear the smile in his voice. "They were actually...fun. Full of intriguing details, terrible sketches, and a longing for a home that—"

"If you thought our alliance was an overture for you to pour all your meaningless feelings to me, you were dead wrong," Mordred cuts him off.

"I thought you'd welcome the talk," Arthur says after a long pause.

Mordred snorts. "With you? Are you mad?"

My view bobs up and down as Arthur shrugs. "Who else have you got?" he asks. "I don't suppose those who raised you were much for it, and I know for a fact Jennifer can't stand conversations unless she's the one doing all the talking."

To my surprise, Mordred chuckles. "You're right on both counts, mortal," he says, "but with our probable end near, I don't think I'll change the way I do things now."

"Artie, Rip's coming over," Gauvain shouts from further down the clearing.

Arthur quickly straightens as the strikingly pale man shuffles over, carrying something furry in his cupped hands.

"What is it?" Arthur asks.

Rip lifts both hands up to show Papillon sitting there, long ears drooping in exhaustion.

"What is that...thing?" Sir Hengist asks, having hurried over.

"*Excuse* me," Papillon says, puffing out his heaving chest. "I am the ambassador of none other than her Mightiest—"

"News?" Arthur cuts him off.

Papillon hiccups at the interruption. "Right, right. I'm here to tell you it's time to land the eagle." The flying mouse looks around expectantly, but upon the lack of reaction from the people around, adds, "It's time to lead the dragon back to its nest. The wards are ready, and Morgan's going after Carman."

Keva gasps, but the others are already moving, calling for the troops to march for battle one final time.

# Chapter 37

Light flares in my vision, then something hard connects with my shin. I snarl in response, squinting down at the blinding light.

"How dare—"

"Clearer-headed, hmm?"

I blink in confusion as I try to adjust myself to the fact that I'm no longer with Arthur and Mordred in the vision, but stuck instead in the hallway between the library and armory, Nibs standing before Agravain's remains.

"Yer work?" the clurichaun asks without touching the body.

I nod. Maybe it's from having spent too much time in the company of demons, or perhaps because Agravain's hate turned him into one of them, but I find myself unable to feel guilt at having killed him.

"Banshee?" I call out in alarm, looking for her.

"In the staircase," Nibs says.

I rush over, needing to make sure with my own eyes that the banshee's all right, and find her sitting on the lowest step, holding onto her side.

"Are you all right?" I ask, dropping to my knees beside her.

The banshee flinches away from my touch. "Ffffiinnne," she says, before going stock still, cowl cocked to the side.

398

"What is it?" I ask, ears perked.

Then someone outside shouts, "Incoming!"

It's the same warning cry whenever something large falls through the sky-lake barrier, but this time it holds a note of panic to it.

Dread spikes through me as the cry is taken up by more demons, turning into shrieks of fear.

"Nibs!" I shout.

I barely have the chance to raise a shield around us three when something massive crashes into the courtyard. Windows shatter inward, the whole building heaving and rattling like it's going to collapse on itself. Then the library walls explode as a giant cone of white metal punches through, tearing everything down in its passage in a deafening *crash*.

"To me!" I shout as the eastern wing of the school caves in.

Wrapping my arms around Nibs and the banshee, I close my eyes, concentrating only on keeping my barrier up. I grit my teeth, sweat pouring down my face and back. Pieces of the staircase crack and fall around us, bouncing off my shield. Then at last, the quakes subside.

"Ssssafe now," the banshee says through the ringing in my ears, though she doesn't move away.

It takes another five breaths before I finally let go, and drop to my knees, drenched through and trembling like a leaf.

"A bloody plane!" Nibs hiccups.

I cough out a laugh, nerves frayed from the tension.

"W-would it be t-too much to h-hope it's s-squashed Carman?" I ask.

Nibs rolls his eyes at me. "Ya should know better than that by now," he says. "The two dumbos are keepin' her busy upstairs, but they won't be able to hold her back much longer."

"Urim and Thummim are what?" I breathe out.

But the clurichaun is already speeding up the staircase, moving faster than he ever has, and the banshee and I follow him to the first floor.

"Shhhh," Nibs says before we can barrel into the hallway.

"What are we waiting for?" I ask impatiently.

"Our diversion," Nibs says, staring wide eyed at the scarred metal side of the plane where the library used to be.

The KORT room is just a few dozen feet away, and I can feel the Siege Perilous's presence within, beckoning. But demons are now pouring out the door in a dark ravenous wave to investigate the plane's wreckage, too many for me to face alone, even with the banshee's help.

Yet I can't let them put their filthy paws on anyone that might be in the plane, dead or alive.

"Wait," Nibs tells me, holding me back by my pant leg before I can move. "Keep yer energy, it's my turn now."

Puffing himself up, the clurichaun gives me a mock salute, then launches himself into the corridor, pointing ahead. "DYBBUK!" he shouts at the top of his lungs.

Every demon freezes in its tracks, and I frown at the strange word, trying to place where I've heard it before. I retreat into the staircase as two of the beasts try to push their way to the front, when a large furry creature turns on them with a snarl, jaws snapping. The beast catches one of the two demons on the shoulder, and bites down on it with a loud *crunch*.

Then chaos hits, as demon turns against demon. Only then do I remember what dybbuk means.

"There really is a skin stealer here?" I ask the banshee, repressing a shiver.

"Yesssss," the banshee states.

I lean a little out of the doorway's cover. Could it truly be one of them is a skin stealer? I see Nibs slip behind the corpse of a tall, willowy woman, nearly getting crushed under another falling demon. Then a silent figure turns, kicking a demon in the chest, before spearing two others with her twin blades.

I suddenly feel faint, and find myself clutching the ogham in my pocket, taking comfort in the gem's warmth.

"Kaede?" I whisper.

"Yesssss," the banshee repeats.

"Kaede was a dybbuk all this time, and you never told me?"

The banshee shrugs, and I squeeze the ogham harder, feeling its rapid throb against my fingers, like the beating of a hummingbird's heart. I can't believe we've had a demon at our sides all this time who could have killed us any time it wanted.

Except it never did, did it? And now it's fighting for us still, drawing the other demons' attention away from us.

"Not bad, eh?" Nibs says, slinking back to us. But despite his wicked grin, he's paler than usual.

"A dybbuk," I say through numb lips, still unable to believe it.

"Turned out better 'n expected," Nibs continues, wiping dark blood from his cheek. "Better to kill yer allies than risk havin' one of them turn against ya, eh?"

I stare at the clurichaun as he shifts uneasily from one foot to the next. He glances back out into the hallway.

"Alrighty, almost clear," he says, sounding more nasally than usual.

And in my pocket, the ogham only grows warmer.

"Nibs?"

The clurichaun almost jumps out of his skin, and turns a wide eye in my direction. "Guess it's time to face our demon, huh?" he says, trying to sound as defiant as he always has, and failing miserably.

Iridescent light floods the staircase in rapid pulses as I pull the ogham out of my pocket. Nibs's eyes open even wider, mouth dropping open in shock.

"Yours, isn't it?" I ask.

Nibs can only stare, his Adam's apple bobbing up and down his scrawny neck. It's all the confirmation I need.

"Your arm," I say, holding my free hand out.

"No time," Nibs whispers, but I can hear the longing in his voice.

Finally, seeing I won't budge until he does what I tell him, he slowly extends his small arm for me—the very same Arthur cut open the night we first went to investigate Dub's murders in the surface world.

At a sign from me, the banshee pushes Nibs's red sleeve up, revealing the puckered edges of a long scar. I tighten my hold on him as the banshee slowly draws her knife down his arm. Then, deftly, I push the ogham inside the wound, and Nibs lets out a shuddering groan.

"As promised," I say.

But Nibs's half-melted face breaks into a sweat, pain pulling at his deformed features. His breath hitches. I look in panic at the banshee.

"Hissss body'sssss rejjjjjecting ittttt," she hisses, moving away from us, as if scared. "Notttt ssssstronnng enoughhhh."

Help I once promised him. But now that the time has come, I'm scared I might mess it up and end up poisoning him instead, or outright kill him.

Nibs lets out a miserable yelp.

"I'm sorry," I say. "I can't...I can't do this..."

Nibs's slaps his other hand above mine. "Please," he says through gritted teeth.

I bite down hard on my lip as a spasm tightens his hand around mine, crushing my tarsals. And before I know what I'm doing, power seeps out of me, as if drawn out by an unknown force, to pour into Nibs's arm.

Slowly, the clurichaun's breathing eases, and, as his body reforms the bonds around his ogham that were once so cruelly ruptured, the wound finally closes.

Only then does the strange force release me, and I watch, transfixed, as the burns on Nibs's face slowly disappear, his skin pulling back tightly over his skull, as if I'd never put my iron-laced jacket on him.

Mouth opening and closing without a sound, Nibs gently presses his hand over his smooth cheek, then collapses against me, sobbing.

"I'm sorry it took me this long," I say, patting his back awkwardly.

I stare up at the banshee for help, but she just shrugs, and I finally allow myself a smile. Out in the hallway, I can still hear the sounds of demons dying, but for a moment, I'm happy. Happy to have finally managed to keep a promise, happy to have righted a wrong, and helped a friend in need.

Nibs finally pushes himself away from me, with a long, moist sniffle that makes me wonder how much snot he's left on my jacket.

"OK, stop dallyin'," he says, as if this is all my fault. "We ain't got no time fer a buncha sops."

He turns on his heels, and heads back into the hallway, forcing the banshee and I to scramble along. Kaede, or whoever it is who took her place, has done an amazing job of clearing us a path. The floor is littered with bodies, ichor sprayed on every surface, and she's managed to lead the remaining ones to chase after her, leaving the KORT room wide open for us.

I lose my balance on the slick floor as another explosion detonates outside the school, catching myself on the KORT room's doorframe before pulling myself inside. I blink, letting my eyes roam over the pulsing Gate taking up half the space where the round table used to be, then to the sides. But there's no sign of Urim or Thummim. And certainly no Carman.

"What is this?" I ask, looking for Nibs.

I catch movement out of the corner of my eye, then something sharp pokes me in the ribs.

"Not another step," a high-pitched voice says in my ear.

I freeze, frowning at the red-headed boy holding me at knife point, the Celtic cross and shield on the breast pocket of his school uniform denoting he's a squire like me.

"What—" I start.

The boy jabs his knife a little further. "I said, don't move."

I feel the banshee move behind me, but I motion for her to stay put. The squire's brow and upper lip are covered in a sheen of sweat, his pupils dilated. He's just a scared boy who has no idea what's going on. Time may be short, but if we can minimize the number of casualties, that'll be even better.

"Let me through," I tell him calmly. "We're only trying to stop this whole mess."

"I'd counsel you to shut up," Jennifer's beautiful voice says, making the boy jump.

I wince as his dagger pierces my skin, just beneath my rib.

"No longer sleeping, I see," I say tightly.

Jennifer glides past me, and, dangling a foot above her is Nibs, his tiny fists pumping the air furiously.

"Where's Lance?" I ask.

Jennifer shrugs prettily, her long golden hair almost glowing in the room's dimness. "Don't know, don't care."

Again, I feel that all-too familiar anger surge through me. "Lance risked his neck to save you, and all you have to say is that you don't care about him?" I say.

"That's always been the problem with the guy," Jennifer says, stopping beside the Siege Perilous, "he's always been too good. Always abiding by the rules, except for one thing." She smiles, touching her lips absentmindedly, before sighing. "But no matter how entertaining it may have been with him, it wasn't enough. Not for me."

"What she's trying to say is that all she ever cared for is power," another voice says from the other side of the shimmering Gate.

"Mordred!" I exclaim in relief.

If he's here, then that means Arthur and our troops have arrived too. I look past him through the arched windows in search of our army, and Mordred smiles knowingly.

With all the leisure in the world, he walks over to me, then plucks the blade out of the squire's trembling fingers.

"You know better than to play with pointy objects, Urien," Mordred tells the boy. "And you," he adds, turning to his girlfriend, "should know better than try to betray me."

Jennifer takes a small step back, her blue eyes fierce in her pale face. "I'm not the traitor here," she says.

"Try to?" I repeat in confusion.

Then a second shadow darkens the windows, and fear wells up in me as a blood-soaked Carman floats into the room.

"I am so glad you made it back, Mordred," the witch says, her black feathered dress pooling out around her in a widening circle of darkness. "Algol is at its zenith. It is time to finish what we started."

# chapter 38

My eyes flicker between Mordred and Carman, the whole world around me splintering.

"Tell me this isn't true," I whisper. "You said you'd team up with us."

"Did I?" Mordred says, voice dripping with condescension. "I don't recall making any pact of the sort."

"That's not true, I saw you fight with Arthur, I saw..."

I clamp my mouth shut around a curse. I didn't actually see him do anything but talk. Talk, and attempt to convince the Order to move against the school sooner. And now I know why: Because he and Carman are finally ready to open the seventh Gate of Hell and destroy us all.

I'm clenching my hands so hard they're shaking.

"I'll deal with you later," I tell Mordred, gathering power around me in a shimmering shield.

With a flick of my hand, I shove Urien aside, then walk purposefully toward Carman. Her shadow pushes against my defenses, wanting to strike me down. But just like what happened down in the library, I force her power back, step by careful step.

"Shield us, Lord," I pray, diverting some of my power toward my hand until little bolts crackle along my knuckles. "Aim your spear at those who hunt us down…"

Carman's smirk turns into an angry snarl.

"Morgan, stop!" Mordred shouts.

"And in this last hour, do not forsake us," I finish, lunging at her.

Lugh jumps in front of a swarm of pixies, raising both arms before him as the dragon opens its massive maw and bellows out red-hot fire. The flames part before Lugh, as if they've hit an invisible wall, and Oberon's pixies buzz away in thick clouds to fall onto a group of Fomori that have used this moment to attack a squad of young knights.

"There's too many of them!" Blanchefleur shouts, her crystal sword flashing before her as she strikes a Dark Sidhe down.

"Where are the nets?" Arthur calls out, and my heart does a somersault at the sound of his voice.

"With the cousins," Hadrian retorts, spearing a squat demon in the eye as Keva shields his open side.

Light blooms all around us, followed by a resounding boom. The earth heaves, sending everyone flying back. I scan the burned-up field, scattered with the charred remains of men, Fey and demons alike.

"Anything broken?" I hear Keva ask, helping Hadrian back up.

I catch sight of a Fomori as it charges straight for her, webbed claws out.

"Keva!" I shout in a soundless cry.

At the last second, Keva turns and flings her battered shield up, blocking the demon as it swipes for her head. The blow lands on the shield, sending her reeling into Hadrian. The knight slips, and he grunts as a demon stabs him in the side.

"*Aerouant! Ormrf*" Arthur shouts.

Flashes of green and blue light up the sky, then the world shakes as twin bellows rise in the air. Heart stammering, I watch the two summoned dragons unfurl their long, leathery wings to fly high above our heads, bodies glistening in the veiled sunlight.

I let out a choked gasp as my vision disintegrates, and I'm yanked back inside the KORT room. Carman's hand tightens around my neck.

"Is it fun seeing your friends dying one by one?" Carman asks, sending a fiery wave of pain scorching down my body.

I grit my teeth, scrabbling uselessly against her hold as I slowly run out of oxygen.

"But if your friends think those puny beasts are going to make a difference," she continues, "then they are more foolish than I thought."

"Then why are you so scared?" Mordred asks.

Carman smiles, a cruel rictus on her bloodied face. Her fingers squeeze tighter, and I whimper as something in my neck pops. My hands fall to my sides, useless, all sensations in my body gone.

"That ought to keep you compliant for a bit while your brother frees Balor," she says, tossing my limp body to the side.

I fall onto the flagstones like a ragdoll, stars bursting in my sight as my head strikes the floor. I hear the banshee cry out and tears of frustration well up in my eyes.

"Looks like she peed herself," the squire Urien says in disgust.

My breath hitches, coming out in small, labored gasps. Crap. This is so not how I'd envisioned things to go.

"Wouldn't be the first time, I hear," Jennifer says.

"Shut it, Jen."

"Lance!" Jennifer exclaims, unable to hide her shock at his sudden presence.

I try to turn my head around to get a look at the knight, but all I can see is the banshee's grey cowl as she kneels beside me.

"You should have stayed away," Jennifer says, sounding cold.

She's right. He's going to get killed, and I'm not going to be able to do a thing to protect him.

"I was looking for you," Lance says. I hear footsteps, then Lance's bloodied face comes into view above me.

"I'm OK," I say. "Still alive, but…"

My eyes flicker to where I can hear Carman and Mordred.

"How dare you speak to me thus?" the witch asks, ice in her voice.

"We had a deal, you and I," Mordred says. "To share the spoils of this world between us. No third party involved."

"I don't care what you thought, vermin," Carman says. "Sit. On. That. Throne."

"She…can't…leave," I whisper.

Lance nods. "On it."

"The purpose of this whole exercise was not to free some one-eyed old man who wants to see the whole world burn," Mordred insists. "What's the point of becoming a ruler if there's nothing left to rule over?"

I almost smile at the sound of my words coming out of his mouth.

"You stink of fear," Carman says, the shadows in the room shifting, ready to strike. "If you are going to defy me, you should at least try to be convincing. But we both know the truth, do we not? You are already mine."

"Lance, don't!" Jennifer yells.

Darkness blooms, blotting out the daylight. Sparks blaze in the obscurity as Mordred tries to deflect Carman's attack, power lashing out in sizzling bolts.

Carman laughs. "You are thrice the fool for thinking *you*, of all people, can defeat me."

I close my eyes, urging my body to heal itself faster. My toes and legs are tingling, sensation returning to them. I can almost move my hands.

There's a sharp *clap*, and Mordred lets out a surprised grunt.

"Don't hurt him!" I croak out.

"Shut it, dimwit," Nibs says, as he and the banshee grab me by the arms and legs. "Do you want to die now?"

"But Mordred," I say, finally getting a good look at what's happening in the room.

"His power comes from the very place she currently rules," Nibs whispers, struggling under my weight. "He never stood a chance."

I watch in horror as Mordred rises in the air, ink-black tentacles coiled around his body, dark stains quickly spreading across his torso, obscuring his tattoos.

"We need to clear a path, quickly!" Arthur shouts over the sounds of raging battle and the screeching of the three fighting dragons.

Knights mounted on massive horses sweep across the fields, spearing demons in their passage, while Watchers march through the openings they leave behind to slay the survivors, power crackling from their fingers in efficient bursts.

But it's not enough. The school is still so far, like a black pimple on the horizon, the fields in between dark with demons and draugar.

"Can't do anything without first getting rid of that beast," Gauvain says. He's fighting off a dozen draugar, but his footsteps are faltering, his thrusts and spars slower.

"Timberrrrrr!"

Gareth lands in the middle of the fray, swinging his left arm down. The war hammer's head cracks the nearest draugar's head open with the sound of thunder, the blow's impact ripping through the others with the force of a tempest.

"Thanks for that," Keva says, grimacing as Hadrian pulls her to her feet.

Grinning, Gareth hefts his war hammer arm back up onto his shoulder. "You are always pleasured," he says with a wink.

"Where were you?" Gauvain asks his cousin without bothering to correct him.

"Made a stop over," Gareth says, whirling on another pack of Fomori.

But before the first one can reach him, Gale's there, moving lightly among the Dark Sidhe, his golden spear a bright trail of light as he takes them down.

Keva gasps. "You're back!"

Gale bows slightly, barely out of breath. "Bri's ready to close the wards at your signal, and Morgan's keeping Carman otherwise occupied, as planned."

---

"Mordred should be with her," Arthur says, his voice tight. "He left a while back."

"So she should be OK, right?" Keva asks.

Gale takes a side step so Gareth can punch a demon in the face. "I suppose, or Carman would have made a show by now. But you need to take that sword to her, Art."

With a grunt, Keva pushes Hadrian aside as a demon hurtles their way, long wooden horns pointed forward. The world spins, as Arthur swings Excalibur around. There's a sharp whistle, a bright flash, then the demon's head falls rolling to the ground.

Fire erupts overhead, cutting off dozens of tiny screams. The air shimmers from the heat, and I look up as Lugh and Oberon drop from the sky, hands raised to divert the flames.

"Arthur!" Lugh shouts, muscles bulging under the onslaught. "Go find Morgan, we'll handle things here."

"Stay safe!" Hadrian shouts as Arthur sprints away to come join me inside the KORT room, unaware that he's heading straight for disaster.

"I said sit *down*, Mordred."

Mordred's screams bounce off the barren walls, a terrible wail that sets my teeth on edge.

"No need for tears," Nibs says, spitting. "It ain't like your brother did ya any favors."

He and the banshee have managed to drag me as far away from Carman as possible, and propped me up against the wall. Although I still can't move much more than my pinky, I can at least keep an eye on everything: Jennifer, facing down Lance, and

Mordred, writhing against the Siege Perilous, pinned there by Carman's power.

"Please," I whisper, willing my words to carry to whichever part of Avalon Danu's holing herself up in, "save him. As you've done with me… Save your son before it's too late."

But the familiar warmth doesn't come, the air reeking instead of rotten eggs as the Gates to Hell condense, slowly opening again.

"Save him," I beg Nibs.

But the clurichaun is plastered to the wall next to me, eyes wide in fright. There's a blur of movement at the windows, and I barely have a chance to see Urim and Thummim's silent snarls before the two Dark Sidhe hurl themselves inside.

Thummim dives under the widening Gates, springs to his feet on the other side, scythe in hand, and swings down. The long, curved blade easily severs Carman's bindings, and Mordred slumps onto the Siege Perilous, free.

"Time I taught these two monkeys of yours a lesson in obedience," Carman snarls, the temperature in the room turning arctic cold.

"This definitely ain't good," Nibs says beside me.

My breath fogs in the air as ice spreads across the floor, trapping all it touches in its deadly fingers. With a growl, Thummim hacks at the ice that has spread up his legs. But the scythe isn't meant for close-range use, and the ice keeps rising higher.

Urim jumps to Thummim's aid, long-chained flail whistling sharply as he aims for Carman. But at the moment, the witch brings her hand up, and the bladed lash misses her head to embed itself in a wall of ice. Lance uses the opportunity to lunge at her from her other side, sword flashing in a low arc aimed at her legs. Then Jennifer's moving inside his reach, and knocks him aside with the lightest of touches, sending him crashing to the floor.

"I told you to stay away," Jennifer says, not an ounce of guilt or sadness in her luminescent blue eyes. "But you never listen, do you? Just like all the other men in my life who think I'm just a pretty thing to be ordered about."

"I think that's our cue to leave," Nibs says, grabbing my jacket, and motioning for the banshee to help lift me up.

"No, help him instead," I say, pointing at my brother with my chin.

I watch Mordred slide off the Siege Perilous and the Gates become a hazy blur again. He's too weak to walk on his own, but the two Dark Sidhe are too busy fighting Carman to help him. I catch Urim as he jumps high, twisting in the air to let his flail rip through the ice wall, breaking it into a thousand flying shards.

"Ya tried, princess, and ya failed," Nibs says urgently. "Again. How many more of us must die before ya see this ain't workin'?"

"Go if you want," I say. "But I've got to finish this."

I can't let them fight her alone, nor can I let Arthur get here when it would mean his death.

I slap my hands down onto the cold flagstones, sending a burst of energy outward, letting my anger take the lead. Anger at how Carman's twisted my brother's mind. Anger at how she's used me to hurt my friends, over and over again.

The ice covering the floor cracks, raising hot steam as my power courses through it. Jennifer yelps as the wave strikes her first, but she's not my target, and I let my power surge forward, gritting my teeth as it meets Carman's invisible barrier.

"Yer gonna get us all killed," Nibs says grimly.

His tiny fist is still clutching my jacket, but he's no longer trying to run away.

Thummim's managed to free himself, and joins Urim in the fray. But no matter how hard they fight, they can't seem to keep Carman back as she slowly advances upon Mordred.

I concentrate on a single point in the barrier, letting my power hit it over and over again. At last, her defenses give, and my power pours into the invisible wall's tiny puncture. There's a series of sharp *cracks,* as of dry wood snapping, then Carman's dress catches fire, filling the room with the pungent smell of burning feathers.

Carman whirls around, seething. I smile as the veins in her beautiful face turn black, the stain spilling into her eyes until even the whites are the color of the deepest night.

"Good, got your attention," I say. "Now step away from my brother."

"Over here, knight!" Papillon shouts, zooming around the thick press of demons.

The world tilts as Arthur jumps over the bodies of two fallen knights. The flying mouse motions for him to hurry, pointing at the school's battered door a hundred feet away.

Too soon. I haven't secured the area yet.

A draugar swipes clumsily at Arthur. He ducks beneath the large hand, sliding Excalibur smoothly in the dead man's abdomen before cleaving him in half.

"Hurry!" Papillon tells Arthur, fluttering nervously above.

"Go to Bri," Arthur says, breathing hard. "Tell her to close the wards."

"But I'm supposed to stay with—"

"GO!" Arthur yells, waving the tiny Fey creature away.

I see Papillon hesitate for a moment, before the winged mouse zooms away to deliver the message. Arthur runs another demon through, kicking a third in the legs with his steel-toed boots. But more keep coming, stepping over their fallen comrades in their eagerness to kill Arthur.

My heart thunders in my ears. Why did he come all the way here alone? The cousins should have accompanied him, or Hadrian, or even that Daniel. No matter how good he is, he can't fight against so many people on his own.

But I know why. Arthur, ever the selfless knight, has left them all behind to give them a better chance at defeating Carman's dragon.

Black ichor splatters across my vision as Arthur fells another demon. But his movements are choppier. He's getting tired, dropping his guard. Another draugar rushes at him, mouth red with gore. Arthur twists away from it, stumbling on a dead body.

"Arthur!" I mentally shout.

He's dropped Excalibur somewhere in the mud. All I can see now is the darkening sky as demons swarm over it. Panic tightens my chest. Where is he?

"Arthur!" I shout again.

A blinding flash answers my silent cry, followed by surprised howls. Something falls to the ground beside me with a wet *slop*. Followed by another. My vision returns, and I suck in a surprised breath.

Fish by the thousands are falling like manna from the sky-lake. Carman's demons back away, grunting in confusion at this strange new threat, and Arthur uses that distraction to fish Excalibur out of the mud, then slink away to the school, his road no longer blocked.

No.

I grunt as I force my attention back into my own body.

Stay away.

I blink owlishly at the gaping door. Carman catches my look, and turns as a shape darkens the threshold.

"Morgan!" Arthur shouts, worried gaze finding mine unerringly.

Then Carman's black coils whip around his neck and snatch him inside.

# CHAPTER 39

I launch myself blindly across the room with but one thought in mind: To save Arthur. Eyes never leaving my face, Carman tightens her hold on Arthur a little more, and I freeze midway at the sound of his strangled gasp.

"Don't you dare," I growl, power dancing over my skin in angry red sparks.

"Or what?" Carman asks. "You can barely stand yourself."

I swallow hard. Arthur's hanging upside down in the air, legs trapped by one of Carman's thick, putrescent tentacles. With a sickening grin, she cups his face in a mimicry of affection.

"I think we'd both like to hear what you have to say," Carman says. She catches my horrified look as I watch dark stains bloom on Arthur's golden cheek, and laughs. "Oh, Morgan. If I'd known you'd be this compliant with this pet at my side, I would have fetched him earlier."

I bite hard on my lip, tasting blood. Focus, you idiot. You can't fall into her petty ploy. I quickly scan the room, looking for a way out of this mess. Jennifer's standing to the side, keeping the banshee and Nibs in check. Lance is slowly picking himself up, his head bloody from a nasty gash over his left eye. And both Urim and Thummim are hovering close to Mordred, watching helplessly as my brother thrashes in the Siege Perilous.

A soft light flickers by the windows, pulsing in rhythm with my breathing, and hope flutters in my chest.

Excalibur.

"I'm surprised you feel you need anything to leverage against me," I say at last.

For the barest of moments, I lock eyes with the two Dark Sidhe over Carman's shoulder. It is enough for them to get the message.

"Mordred was right, you are acting less...secure," I continue. "Are you sure you don't want to go back into Hell and stay there? Might be a tad safer for you."

Carman's lips curl.

Then Urim springs upon her from behind, bladed flail hissing through the air. With the barest of shifts, Carman counters the attack, but I'm already moving, sprinting for the windows. Excalibur flashes in anticipation. Then, as my cold fingers close around the sword's grip, Urim's hair-raising shriek cuts across the room.

I whirl around, and bile rises to my throat at the sight of Urim on his knees, weapon abandoned at his side. Blood drips down his hair, scarlet on white, Carman's hand lodged deep inside his skull. Then, with a sickening *squelch,* she pulls her hand back out, an onyx gem the size of her fist clutched in her long fingers.

"Give that back!" Thummim shouts.

In that one moment it took me to grab Excalibur, he's managed to free Mordred. But that moment's cost us Urim's life.

Carman's smile grows wider, until her jaw unhinges completely, lips extending beyond what any normal human could do, to gobble up Urim's ogham in one piece. Catching my look of horror, Carman tosses her hair back, then slowly licks off the dark blood dripping down her chin.

"You shouldn't judge, considering you've partaken of a similar feast yourself," she says, her face glowing with stolen power.

I repress a shiver, remembering all too well the feeling of elation I felt once my body absorbed Gadreel's ogham. And the power that came with it. I let out a slow breath.

"It doesn't matter how many oghams you steal," I say, "you're no match for Balor—either as a partner or as an opponent. You're nothing to him. Just like you were nothing to your parents. And the reason your own people tried to burn you at the stake."

I barely have the chance to see Carman's face contort with fury before her power hits me. I wince against the assault, feeling my shields waver. My grip tightens on Excalibur, but there's nothing I can do to resist the pummeling as utter and total darkness unfurls around me.

I scream, flesh tearing away from me in large strips. My body hits the ceiling or a wall—I can't tell which is what anymore—then stays pinned to it as the gale continues to rip me to shreds.

My lungs struggle to expand. I feel my mind slip away, thoughts sluggish. My whole body goes numb, heart stuttering.

Then all at once the pressure is gone, and through my hazy mind I realize that I'm falling.

I land heavily in someone's strong arms. Arthur?

"Breathe," Lance whispers in my ears.

I try to open my eyes, but everything hurts too much. The sound of crackling thunder bounces around the KORT room. I clutch at Lance's mailed shirt, shaking. Wood cracks as it's hit, burnt splinters exploding out. And, above it all, is the blood-curdling scream of a man.

Fear douses my body in cold sweat, and I manage to force my eyes open. I seek my brother out, and find Mordred's back on the Siege Perilous, blood pouring down his body from a myriad new cuts, Thummim lying stunned at his feet.

A hand pokes out of the reopened Gates, followed by a strangely flat head, before the grotesque creature's body clatters to the floor, pushed from behind by another monster. They're worse than any of the demons I've encountered. Worse than I could have imagined.

Another tremor passes through me as I realize what's happening.

"He's opening them all," Lance says.

All the Gates. That means he's going to free Balor, even if the act is killing him.

Veins pop out on Mordred's forehead and arms as he grips the Siege Perilous, unable to pull himself free.

"Put me down," I tell Lance.

Gently, the knight lowers me to my feet. I take an unsteady step, whole body groaning in protest, then another. One of the demons sees me and pounces. Lance's sword sings as he catches the beast in the face.

"What are you doing?" Lance asks.

Another demon slumps to the floor, throat slit, thick blood gushing onto the flagstones.

"Putting an end to this," I hiss.

I've lost Excalibur again, but no matter. Rage and despair drive me forward as I hone in on Carman. Maybe that's why I can't stop when I see her turn towards me, her full lips stretched thin in a rictus of a smile. Why I can't stop when she raises her hand up in defense. My fist connects with her arm, and I grunt as my bones shatter from the blow.

No matter.

I let my momentum carry me further, whipping my hips around to get another punch in, power gathering in my closed fist.

"Misssstressss!" the banshee shouts in warning, her cry sounding strangled.

Carman slips away, just out of reach, her dress rushing at me like a giant crow's wing, cleaving me open from hip to shoulder. My footsteps falter. I slip in my own blood, feel myself tip backwards. I fling my fingers open, and light blooms from my extended palm in a brilliant ray, hitting Carman's face straight on.

Carman reels back with a bellow, clutching at her face. I roll away from her, feeling lightheaded.

"Mordred!" I yell, crawling on the slippery floor to him as another beast drops down from the Gates. "Close them! Close the—"

A hand twists my arm around viciously. "Enough!" Carman snarls.

Pain rips down my spine as she lifts me high up in the air.

"Look at him," she continues, breath hot on my ear. "Witness this historic moment when the world you once knew is rent asunder and a new age is born."

With a warlike chant, Thummim goes to Lance's help, raging through the growing horde of demons, both of them cutting the creatures down one after another. But always more come. Even together they are no match for all of Hell.

"Any minute now," Carman coos.

My eyes catch movement along the edges of the Siege Perilous, and I freeze completely in Carman's hold. The figures carved within the seat's wood are moving, the winged demons tearing themselves from the armrests to climb onto Mordred's hands. I stare at the black shapes as they crawl over his blue woads. Mordred snaps his head back in a silent scream, eyes rolling back in his head as one of them bites into his flesh, ripping a large hole in his forearm before diving into the wound.

The Gate hums louder as it suddenly expands to encompass half the room, cutting our side off from the windows. Through the flickering gap, I see a large swamp of fuming mud, demons wading across it as quickly as they can, growling and fighting each other to get out of Hell first.

"Look at him trying to resist," Carman says gleefully. "But resistance is futile. He was bound to me the day he was born."

Something inside me loosens, just like when I faced the chimaera. Carman hisses in surprise as my power burns through her, and clutches at her face in pain, finally releasing me.

I scramble to my feet, already turning to help Mordred out.

"It's too late," Carman says, her voice strangely altered.

I glance over my shoulder at her, and nearly miss a step. Her fair skin is now covered in ulcers, pus seeping out from those that burst, as if she's cooking from the inside.

I grin. "We'll see," I say, returning my attention to my brother.

Three lumps are now moving beneath the tattoos of his arms and chest where the carved demons are making their way through. Another sob escapes Mordred's lips.

"Excalibur, to me," I growl, without once looking away from the horrid sight.

I feel the sword before it hits the palm of my open hand, blade incandescent in the waning light of day. But before I can cut the nasty little things out of Mordred, a demon launches herself at me. I instinctively drop to a knee, and the throbbing metal slides easily into the creature's narrow chest. It lets out a shocked hiccup before tipping over as I pull Excalibur back out.

I dodge an extended paw, cut a second demon's outstretched leg, feel claws graze my shoulder. A hand grips my ankle, yanking me up before slamming me into the floor. My head cracks upon the flagstone. Blood fills my mouth. I blink slowly, dazed. A snout appears above my head, foam dripping down yellow fangs.

I hear Carman's gleeful laughter over the ringing in my ears. "Finish her," she commands.

I try to summon my strength again, but my body isn't responding as it should. Then the demon pauses mid-strike, nostrils flaring. I blink uncomprehendingly at the long metal tongue sticking out of the demon's mouth before it retracts again.

"Close one, huh?" Lance asks, offering me his gloved hand.

"How bad are you hurt?" Arthur asks hoarsely, hobbling over.

My throat convulses at the sight of him, and I mentally thank whoever managed to free him from Carman's clutches.

"Alive, you?" I choke back, eyes automatically traveling to the deep stains around his neck.

"Not quite dead yet," he replies.

He picks Excalibur up, and the sword pulses with life.

"Mordred...," I start, knowing what must be done to stop him from freeing Balor.

Arthur nods. "Cover me," he says.

"*Algiz!*" Lance shouts.

A wall of purple air shimmers in front of us, and dark-green phlegm hits the elemental shield with a loud hiss. Calling on my own power, I push back another two demons, and Arthur uses the opportunity to slip forward, Lance on his other flank.

"Open the seventh Gate, Mordred," Carman orders with barely veiled glee.

"Mordred don't!" I shout.

Something heavy slams into me from behind, bringing me down to a knee. I slam my elbow back, feeling it connect with something hard as rock. A fist slams into my shoulder, flattening me to the floor. Wincing, I push myself to my knees, when the demon hits me again. Stars burst across my vision. I hear Lance shout my name. I want to tell him to stay with Arthur, but all that comes out of my mouth is a soft mewl.

Then a bell rings a loud, powerful *gong* that reverberates throughout the school, its peel finding an echo all the way down into my bones.

For a long second, a strange stillness overtakes the KORT room, as if someone's magically taken all of the monsters' batteries out at once. Jaws clenched, I manage to twist myself around, and, summoning a torrent of water, send the creature barreling into the far wall before it can shake off its stupor.

"The wards," Carman breathes, and I hear the fear in her voice.

For the first time since she's been freed, she can see her own plans unraveling.

"Hurry," I urge Arthur as I scramble to his side, half-slipping in the gore strewn across the floor.

Mordred bellows out a cry of pain as Arthur cuts one of the lumps open. Inside it, the carved demon unfurls its wings in protection. But it can't resist Excalibur, and the sword spears it through.

"Watch it!" Thummim shouts somewhere behind.

Then Carman's beside the Siege Perilous, sharp-nailed hand yanking Arthur away by his hair. With a grunt, Arthur swings Excalibur around, flinging the black little creature off the sword's tip in the process.

Lance and I move at the same time, sprinting to Arthur's help, when something red cuts us off in our tracks. Without breaking pace, Lance thrusts his sword out. But the blade goes through the shape without encountering any resistance.

"What the...," he starts.

The blood shadow takes a step forward, sliding up Lance's sword.

"Stand back!" I shout.

Before the blood shadow can touch him, Lance throws himself to the side, careening into an oncoming demon. I throw my hands up, and fire shoots straight for the shade, hitting it in the head. The blood shadow waves uncertainly for a second, then its head reforms, and it turns on me.

"Enough!" Carman growls.

I freeze at the strangled gasp. Arthur's lost Excalibur, and is now standing helplessly before the witch, tendrils of black tar lashed around his limbs, slowly pulling them apart.

A guttural cry tears from my lips, and I find myself vaulting over both Lance and the shade.

This time, Carman doesn't hold back. A bolt of lightning hits me straight on, and I crash to the floor, a foot away from her. I moan as my muscles spasm in protest. Carman's feathered dress brushes against me, slicing through my uniform and finding flesh.

"The time for games is over," Carman says, voice cold.

Frantic, I watch as she steps over me back to Mordred's side. Tears of anger and despair blur my vision. I push unsteadily to my hands, try to stand back up.

I can't let this be how it all ends.

I can't let her win…

A white shape hurls itself over the back of the Siege Perilous, tiny hooves beating the air seconds before landing on Carman's face, scratching and hissing. Carman lets out a curse, twisting away with a surprised snarl.

It's all the time that I need. I lunge, whipping my arm around, and punch Carman straight in the throat, feeling her larynx collapse beneath my knuckles. With a startled wheeze, she doubles over, and the white ball of fur jumps off her face to land in my arms.

"Puck!" I gasp.

The hobgoblin scrambles to the floor, motioning to the Siege Perilous frantically. I start when I notice that Mordred's eyes, as black now as Owen's, are staring straight at me.

"Please, sis," he croaks, voice raw from screaming. "Make it...stop..."

Blink my tears back, I stumble towards him. But as I reach the Siege Perilous, my vision shifts, the world tilting for a second, and when everything rights itself again, I find myself staring at Jennifer instead.

I shake my head in confusion, trying to understand why she's pointing her miniature handgun at my brother.

"You've had a good run," Jennifer tells him. "And it's been fun...some."

"Jennifer, don't do this," Lance says.

"What's happening?" I ask, still lightheaded.

Jennifer smiles at me, her flicking to her squire huddled against the wall. My gaze falls to the metallic net at his feet, Excalibur barely visible through the tight iron meshes. My ogham!

"How does it feel to be fully human?" Jennifer asks, pupils dilated. "I guess we're going to find that out right now."

The blast is deafening.

"NO!" Carman screams.

Mordred's body slumps to the side, then stops moving. I stare at the blood gushing from a hole in his throat, where the bullet punched through the jugular. I hiccup. This can't be right.

Mordred's strong.

Stronger than me.

He can't...it can't end like this for him...

He's my guardian angel!

"And now you."

Jennifer's voice seems to come from so very far away. Slowly, I look back at her, gaze locking onto her piercing blue eyes. Her smile is cold and certain as she points her still smoking gun at my own head. Then her finger pulls the trigger.

*BANG!*

# Chapter 4⬦

My world shatters as Arthur crumples before me, head striking the floor with a dull *thud*. A dark red spot the size of a fist blooms large on his chest, spilling onto the flagstones.

"What did you do?" Lance's shocked voice asks.

"I-I didn't mean...," Jennifer starts, her voice trailing off.

But I don't care what she has to say. I don't care what anyone has to say. I let out a terrible moan as I reach for Arthur. My hands convulse over his wound, trying to staunch the flow, but his warm blood keeps seeping through from between my fingers.

"What did you do that for?" I ask, lip shaking uncontrollably. "That was meant for me, you had no right to...to..."

"Shhhh," Arthur says, struggling to breathe. "You're OK...all...matters."

He coughs, grimacing at the pain. I press my hands harder on his wound, willing it to close back up. I reach for my power, but the usual tingling response isn't there. Instead, I feel...nothing.

Fear twists its cold fingers around my spine. My ogham!

"Urien?" I bark in panic. "Urien!"

The red-headed squire whimpers back. My eyes glide over to the side, finding him lying against the wall in a growing puddle of his own blood, gutted by a demon who's long since left the room.

And, next to him, is Excalibur, the sword still encased in the iron net, cutting me off from my power.

My heart thunders in my ears.

"Lance," I whisper, afraid to leave Arthur's side.

"On it."

He's barely made a step, however, when a dark shape flashes past, then Jennifer lets out a terrified scream.

"How dare you touch my things?" Carman shouts.

Her dress explodes in a shower of feathers that slice Jennifer open with a thousand cuts. Jennifer's scream turns into a high-pitched wail. Before I can stop him, Lance darts in front of her, parrying the deadly feathers with his elemental shield. He twists, swinging his sword arm around, and sparks skitter along the blade as it clashes against Carman's body.

"You puny fool," Carman says, opening her hand up.

The feathers turn into black tentacles that leap out and strike at Lance like vicious snakes. He lashes at them, desperation giving him a burst of speed. He's the best knight I've ever seen after Gale, but even so, his injuries are slowing him down.

Jennifer cries out as one of the tentacles punctures his right shoulder. Then Arthur's hand goes slack above my own. Blood thundering in my ears, I look down at his pallid face.

"Stay with me, Arthur," I say, throat painfully tight.

The world is spinning around me, a confusion of movements and sounds. I will my mind to clear up, finally tearing myself away in search for Urien, and find the squire's dead eyes staring at me. I jerk forward, awkward in my rush to get Excalibur out of its iron net. Sluggish. I've lost too much blood, and my human self can barely stand anymore.

But before my fingers can close around the mesh, a hand hooks around my neck and lifts me in the air.

"Let me go!" I gasp, fighting to keep back the black spots that dance in my vision.

I need to heal Arthur, *now*! If I don't...

Carman releases me, and I double over, gasping for air, when my vision suddenly clears.

"Is this what you're after?" Carman asks.

She's removed the net from Excalibur and is now considering me with some amusement. Panic turns into a tight knot in the pit of my stomach. She knows.

"So you had your oghams merged with Excalibur," Carman says with a sickening giggle. "How very clever. Or very stupid."

She trails a long-nailed finger over the sword's length, watching the warning sparks it generates upon contact.

"It seems to be missing something, however," she says.

My heart stutters as I realize what she means. Excalibur has lost its hilt, only the bladed remaining, like an unfinished weapon. I whirl around, gaze settling automatically on the Siege Perilous behind which lies Mordred's body. If his part of the ogham's gone, then he's fully mortal again, and...

I swallow audibly, unable to make myself finish that thought.

Carman sighs. "I guess you really are the only key I have left."

I look back at her, nerves tingling in apprehension. I can feel my wounds mending, power slowly ebbing back into my limbs. Then Carman's hand closes over Excalibur's tang[35]. The sword lights up with a series of angry lightning bolts, shooting thousands of electric volts straight up her arm. Carman clenches her teeth, face rippling with pain, but she doesn't let go.

"Follow me, Morgan," Carman says, her voice slightly strained.

---

[35] The end of a sword's blade around which the grip, guard piece, and pommel are placed.

A strange feeling washes over me, like I've stepped into a giant wad of cotton. I feel my muscles respond, legs moving of their own volition, tracking Carman's feathered dress across the floor, until I'm standing beside her by the Siege Perilous. Only then does the compulsion fade away, and I wince.

"How did you—"

Eyes wide with terror, I break off. Although the sword clearly rejects her, Carman's evidently still capable of controlling me through my ogham, the same way knights have with countless Fey before.

"If only I'd known about this sooner," Carman says, beaming. She points to the Siege Perilous with Excalibur. "Have a seat."

Despite my best attempt to stop myself, I whirl around robotically, boots squelching in the gore. The remaining wooden demons on the carved chair stare at me eagerly as a hand grips one of the armrests, mouths open, fangs ready to carve a path into my own flesh.

"Come on," Carman presses impatiently. "*Sit.*"

The block of cotton in my mind thickens, and I feel myself lowering to the chair. Then blinding flashes in sudden rapid bursts, searing my vision, and I find myself tipping forward, away from the Siege Perilous.

"Give that back!" Carman roars, power crackling in fury.

Breathing heavily, I look around in confusion, and find Puck bounding away from the witch, dragging Excalibur behind him.

"Misstressss," the banshee hisses urgently from inside a large ring of blood.

A portal.

And within its confines, is Arthur, his beautiful hazel eyes closed.

I scramble forward before Carman can figure out what's happening, but at the edge of the circle, I pause. I can't run away now, not after all the sacrifices we've made.

"Hurrrrryyy!" the banshee entreats, shifting uneasily from one foot to the next.

I look back, and catch sight of Puck heading our way while trying to outrun Carman's reach. He's only a few feet away now, but Excalibur's slowing him down.

"Drop the sword!" I shout at him.

The hobgoblin shakes his horned head, only to trip over a dead demon's arm. As Puck goes flying, a long tentacle from Carman's dress strikes out to coil itself around the sharp blade, and tears it out of his tiny hands.

"Puck!"

I barely register the banshee's soft-spoken words before the circle flares up, activated. But before it can transport us away, I dart back outside its perimeter to fetch the hobgoblin. I dive as another of Carman's tentacles whips overhead, my fingers closing around Puck's shaking body. I spin back around for the banshee's portal, straining not to lose my balance.

"You're not going anywhere!" Carman snarls.

A shudder runs down my spine, body locking in place before I can cross back inside the blood ring. Sweat drips down my forehead. I can sense Carman's satisfied smile as she adjusts her grip on my ogham.

A wall of green light erupts from the portal's edges, and through it I can see the banshee reaching for me, but she's already growing dim, as if turning into a ghost. So, with the last of my strength, I toss puck at her.

"Misstressss, noooo!" the banshee cries out.

"Take care of them," I tell her, eyes falling one last time upon Arthur's body.

Then a loud *crack* resounds, and all three of them disappear, leaving me alone with Carman.

There should be no excitement when facing one's death, no irrepressible desire to laugh giddily. Yet my body feels light as a feather as I slowly turn around to face Carman. Maybe it's because I know this whole mess is finally coming to an end—one way or another, after today, I'll be done.

So, with a confidence I don't quite feel, I strut back to the Siege Perilous where Carman wants me, and let my fingers trail along the seat's back, watching the intricate carvings come alive at my touch. The few angels left on the chair scurry to meet my fingers, chasing away the demons that have taken over most of the fateful chair. Here, too, Hell and Heaven are locked in an eternal fight.

"Good," Carman says, and I can feel her excitement through my link to Excalibur. "Now sit on it."

My body reacts to her order, muscles spasming as I try to resist and delay the fateful moment. I cut a long glance at Carman, ignoring the dark tendrils creeping again from her dress, and force myself to smile.

"Funny how you think yourself so superior," I say, "when really you can't do anything on your own. Couldn't free yourself on your own, couldn't give form to your ogham on your own, can't open these Gates on your own...and apparently you know you can't rule shit on your own either, or you wouldn't be so desperate to free Balor, now, would you?"

I pause, tilting my head at her, arms shaking so violently now, the Siege Perilous is threatening to topple over.

"And you thought you could compare yourself to Danu?" I continue, barking out a laugh that sounds crazy, even to my own ears. "Not in a billion years. You're not *Fey* enough to measure up to her. Not even with that dragon of yours."

Carman's nostrils flare, those black tentacles of hers frozen in shock. Her eyes slide over to the windows, and I follow her gaze. It's not hard to guess where her dragon is, the night sky lit up with blazing trails as it chases after my friends, not realizing they're leading it into a trap. And now she knows I know her secret. And if I know it, then everyone else does too.

The sound of a bell rings out, its note carrying clearly over the distant sounds of battle and the torrential rain. A green light flashes in the distance, the color of a sylph's elemental power. The western ward is back up.

"That's four," I say. "One more, and your so-called reign is over."

Carman starts for the windows, her hold on Excalibur momentarily slipping. I sense her reach out to her beast, calling it back. Not noticing that while she does so, I pluck at that strange cord of power that also links me to the beast, countering her signal. I smirk as her restlessness grows.

"Having issues?" I hear myself ask smugly.

Carman turns her dark gaze back to me, rage kindling in her eyes. "What have you done?"

I shrug. "You should've known better than to use my blood and the Sangraal to build your dragon," I say. "I am now forever bonded to it, and the only way it can be undone is to destroy it completely."

With a violent snarl, Carman slams Excalibur down, the blade sliding into the flagstones until it's embedded all the way up to the fuller[36]. I wince as her power bears down on me, forcing me down to my knees.

"You are going to pay for this when I come back," Carman says, seething.

And when she moves away again, her blood shadow stays behind to guard the sword.

I lift both hands to call on fire and force her back inside, but at my movement, the blood shadow grabs Excalibur. Dark tendrils of smoke jump from beneath its red fingers, and I drop to the floor, pain ripping through my chest.

And through the tears, I see Carman make for the arched windows, feather dress already billowing out to catch the winds.

"Stop...," I cry out.

I can't let her escape. If she manages to fly out to her dragon's help, then our troops are doomed.

Gritting my teeth against the mind-shattering pain, I force myself to crawl across the cold flagstones. But the blood shadow twists its hold on Excalibur, and pain slices down my spine, sending me writhing to the floor.

I can't breathe. Can't think. My heart's about to explode. I arch against the floor, eyes rolling back in my head.

I hear a bone-jarring roar, and I don't know if it's coming from my own lips or someone else's. The stench of charred meat and scorching hair burns up my nose. Then something rings out in the distance. Blue light bursts across my vision. And all at once, everything stops. The agony. The screams. The battle...

Letting out a shaky breath, I look around the room. The blood shadow is gone, leaving my ogham half-buried in the floor, surrounded by dead demons. Someone's crying somewhere to

---

[36] The groove on the long sword that starts about halfway up the naked blade.

my left, yet laughter bubbles out of me. They did it! They've restored the school wards, and stopped Carman's army in its tracks, fencing all the demons and draugar inside the school grounds.

I slowly push myself up, and my eyes fall upon a black figure whimpering against one of the window's columns. For a second, I think it's Thummim, but then I notice the sword gripped in the darkened hand. A sword with light gold and silver traceries on its grip—a knight's sword.

Lance's sword, I realize in a flash.

Except that it isn't Lance who's gripping it.

"Jennifer?" I say in shock.

The girl turns her head blindly at the mention of her name, and I repress the need to gag at the sight of the pus seeping out of what had once been crystal-clear blue eyes.

It's her, all right, covered in open blisters and charred cuts.

Only Carman could have done that to her. And the witch wouldn't have bothered if Jennifer hadn't tried to stop her somehow.

And in doing so, Jennifer's saved us all.

"You're going to pay for this," Carman hisses, whirling on us.

I laugh again, louder. "It's too late," I say. "You can't harm us anymore."

Which leaves only one thing left for me to do. I turn back to the Siege Perilous. Who was it that once told me Mordred and I were two sides of the same coin? Was it Carman? Mordred himself? Danu? It doesn't matter.

A tremor courses through me as my feet return to the seat's edge.

Trepidation, eagerness…and fear.

For to destroy the Siege Perilous, I know I must die too.

I close my eyes, trying to coax my breathing into a more regular pattern. I always knew it might come down to this. It was the one part of the plan I never mentioned to Arthur, though he must've known somehow. Thinking of him now brings back all my memories of our times together. Of the laughter in his eyes despite his too-serious face when he tried to teach me elemental manipulation. Of his constant willingness to give his all the help and protect everyone, including me. Especially me. Until his very last breath.

And now it's my turn to do the same.

I fling my eyes open, grip the chair's carved armrests.

"Your road ends here," I tell Carman, and lower myself upon the Siege Perilous.

The carved demons spring to action, scurrying up the dark wood in excitement. Power surges from the chair, a sickening wave that fills me up like an oily tide, burning all in its passage. I hear Carman laugh, then everything around me disappears.

# Chapter 41

The whole world has turned into a kaleidoscope of greys and blacks—everything's barren and covered in ashes, a smoky haze hanging in the stifling air. The stench of sulfur is so thick I want to retch. I try to shift, and stifle a gasp as pain rips through my chest, as if the Siege Perilous is loathe to let me go. But that's not what makes my hairs stand on end.

I can feel them moving inside me, sharp teeth eating away at my flesh as the wooden demons slowly carve their way into my body.

"Stop them," I plead, shuddering.

Though I can no longer see her, I feel Carman's presence beside me, feel her hot breath warm my cold cheek as she whispers, "Not so proud now, are we?" Her fingers brush my hair back. "The only way to stop this is for you to open that last Gate, and let Balor join me."

"You're mad," I say.

"No, sweetie, just telling the truth. You saw what happens when you try to resist what must be done."

I try to twist away from her, but I'm locked into place, trapped by the very thing I wanted to destroy. How did Mordred ever control the Siege Perilous?

Carman's hand gently forces my head around. "Do you see it?" she asks.

I freeze.

A large red door the size of a tall house is now standing on its own in the middle of the vast, empty plain, the smoke rippling away from it, as if repelled by it. A shiver courses down my spine. It wasn't there a moment ago, did I call it to me?

"Open it," Carman whispers urgently.

All the darkness and emptiness that suffuses this sterile land suddenly finds an echo inside of me, filling my heart with hate and the desire to watch everything burn. I force another long breath through my nose, shocked at the intensity of my emotions.

"The door, Morgan."

Carman's voice is insistent. She's worried. I wince as one of the tiny demons shifts somewhere around my kidney, moving steadily towards my spleen. I lick my parched lips, tasting blood. I can't listen to her. I need to figure out how to close the doors instead of opening them, before these wooden atrocities turn me into human Swiss cheese.

"The sooner you open that door, the sooner you can go back to that boy of yours," Carman croons in my ear.

She means Arthur, of course. A terrible longing to see him again washes over me, to see his slightly crooked smile crinkle the corners of his hazel eyes, dirty blond hair mussed the way it was the night we spent together. Would it be so terrible to stop fighting, close my eyes, and finally let go of everything?

"That's right, go on."

Carman's voice sounds more distant. I shake my head firmly, as if to wake up from a tortuous dream, only to find the red door is now but a couple of feet away. I look over my shoulder in confusion, trying to recall when I moved.

"Hurry, Morgan, there's no time left."

No time left.

Carman's words cycle through my head, over and over again, bringing with them visions of Arthur as he lay in a growing pool of blood, pale and so still he looked dead. All because he took a bullet for me, when all I ever did was cause problems. Rage flows through me at the inanity of this endless war that seems to take the best of us first.

My eyes revert to the red door, and my breath rushes out in sudden panic.

"No," I choke out, staring at the long vertical crack along the frame.

I didn't touch anything, so how could the door open on its own? Intense heat gushes from the narrow gap, plastering my uniform to my body as I try to peer into the darkness that lies on the other side. A terrible pressure settles upon me, and I find myself shaking uncontrollably, unable to move an inch. I am like a bird cornered by a cat, the power of flight forgotten. And I know the reason why.

Balor.

I swallow convulsively. The king of demons knows I'm here, and can already taste the freedom he must crave.

As if aware of my panicked thoughts, a red beam of light suddenly cuts through the obscurity, searing my vision, before winking out again. But it was all I needed to see what lies beyond the door, and nothing will ever erase *that* from my mind.

I collapse onto the ground, legs gone useless. That *thing* is worse than I could have imagined. It is misery and hunger, wrath and pain, mindless evil and horrid death—the four horsemen of the apocalypse rolled into one black hole ready to devour the entire world.

The ray returns as the monster opens its single eye again, red light instantly filling the void. Slowly, the giant's hairy face turns, seeking the exit. I roll out of the way before the laser beam can cross the threshold, and watch in terror as it hits the earth, splitting the ashy ground with a deafening *CRACK*. I stare, shaking, at the yawning chasm of molten rock the light leaves behind as it progresses inexorably further away, burning through every layer of Hell.

The world fragments. Screams of horror in the distance. A part of me can see the KORT room teeming with the demons I helped escape, each one scrambling to get out of the red beam's destructive path. My breath hitches. Fear prickles all my senses raw. At this rate, the whole world's gonna burn within seconds.

Jaw clenched, I slowly crawl forward, pushing against Balor's power that wants to grind me into the ground. I have to pause at the bottom rail's edge to catch my breath. My head's spinning from the poisonous gases spewing from the bottomless chasm left by Balor. I stare up blearily at the giant door, then slowly push myself to my feet.

Another tremor sweeps across the barren plain, and I have to brace myself against the door to keep from falling. There's a sharp *hiss* as the red panel scorches my flesh, charring my skin until it splits and cracks open, fat bubbling from between my splayed fingers.

I fight back my instinct to pull away, and instead lean in to try to force the door back shut. Sweat drips down my face and arms, pooling in the small of my back. The earth shakes again, rattling my teeth, and I nearly lose my grip. Balor's moving.

I push harder, grappling for a solid foothold, put my shoulder into it. Tears haze my view, but at last I feel the door shift the other way, ever so tentatively. I take a half-step forward, reducing the gap by a third. Just a couple more steps, and the seventh Gate will be closed once and for all.

Hands and shoulder slide on the burning door as my scorched flesh parts from my bones in long strips. I snarl. Take another step. Balor's killing beam finally stops in its progress. So close!

Then a dark blur appears above me, and I forget to breathe. My heart's hammering in my chest. I watch in terror as the scarred hand grips the edge of the red door to pry it open from the inside. Blinding pain shoots down my spine, tearing a scream from my parched lips. My knees buckle and I drop to the ground, letting my head hang low in defeat.

I can't do this. Balor's too powerful and I'm not strong enough.

"I'm sorry," I say, hating myself for being so weak. "I'm so sorry…"

The door thumps against my side, gaping wider still.

*Stop fighting, Morgana.*

My heart stutters to a stop. Mother.

*Remember who you are. Remember the good inside you; it is the source of your strength, and will lead to salvation if you so choose.*

The whole earth shudders as Balor tries to force his way past the threshold. My eyes snap up to his knotted hand, burning away against the door like mine did. But the beast is so desperate to escape from its prison, it doesn't care. And, somehow, a part of me finally understands.

Balor's no more evil than Carman, or even me. He's lost in his own rage, a cry of distress that's long been ignored. This place is of his own doing, a representation of himself, of the darkness that has gnawed at him for ages. I know it. I recognize it in myself.

But my friends, my brother, and even Danu, have taught me that I was never truly alone, that there is more to live for. That there is a place for me too, no matter how different I may be.

To my surprise, I find myself reaching up, small fingers coming to rest upon Balor's burning hand to let him know he's been seen. That he's being heard.

And for a long second, everything stills. Balor's stopped trying to pry the door open and must have closed his eye, for the beam of red light has winked out of existence. I feel a soft smile spread on my face, all fear gone. Then a violent tremor passes through Balor's body, and he jerks his hand back.

"Wait!" I call out.

But the red door slams shut again, the wood quickly cooling under my hands.

"It's OK," I say quietly, sagging against it. "There's no need to be afraid..."

Tears stream down my cheeks in the answering silence.

The seventh Gate is closed at last, so why does it feel like I've failed?

*Do not cry, child. You did well, and I am proud of you. But it is time for you to return to us.*

I pull away, and have to stifle a gasp. I'm back inside the KORT room, sitting on the Siege Perilous, a foot away from where Balor's laser beam sliced through the building, the cut extending from the center of the floor to the windows. I expect it must have cleaved through the school grounds as well, though I can't tell how far it went before it stopped.

"NO!" Carman screams as her shoulders hunch over, jet-black hair turning grey in lumpy strands around her now disfigured face.

The others must have finally defeated her dragon and gotten hold of her ogham.

Beneath my fingers, the Siege Perilous's carved angels are pushing the few demons left down to the base of the chair. I lift my hands, noting the rosy new flesh that's replaced the parts that were burned off by Balor's door.

"No, no, no...," Carman keeps repeating, wringing her spotted hands in despair.

She, like Balor, has tried to remake the world in her own image—one where everyone else would be as lost and angry and empty as she feels.

"I understand how one can never truly recover from being abandoned by those who should've been the first to show us love," I say, surprised to feel pity for the old woman now huddling by the arched windows in defeat. "But this path of destruction is not the answer."

Carman's withered face contorts in fury. "Do not presume to know anything about me!" she spits.

I lean back in the Siege Perilous, no longer under its evil influence. The carved angels are now climbing back up towards the armrest, carrying some shapeless thing between them.

"I, too, had to live my life being continuously cast away," I continue wistfully, "as you well know. I always thought there was something wrong with me, that there must've been a good reason for everyone to reject me. And when I found out what I am"—I look down as the first angel reaches my hand and pulls free from the chair, holding out a small lump of metal for me—"I figured that, if they were going to reject me, I would do the same with them."

I grab the surprisingly heavy nodule and, with a slight shock, realize that it's a piece of iron. I smile in derision, wondering how it is that these wooden angels would know what I haven't told a soul about.

"But I later realized," I say, tossing the lump of iron into the air so that it floats at eye-level before me, "that I was focusing too much on what set me apart from everyone else, on our differences, when I should have focused instead on what we had in common."

I direct my energy into the floating piece of iron, heating it up until it glows orange.

I look back at Carman. "In a way, I have you to thank for making me see that."

I let my gaze travel past the windows. Although it feels like an eternity has passed, it is still night, and fires have been lit across the school grounds. My thoughts turn to all my friends out there, to Arthur gone with Puck and the banshee, and I send out a prayer that they're all safe, wishing I could've said goodbye properly.

I take a deep breath. Release it slowly.

Then, with a tiny flick of my finger, the iron flies straight for Excalibur, the blade lying discarded in the middle of the room. At the last second, the sword leaps into the bubbling metal's path until every side of it is covered in iron. All but the tip of the sword, pointed in my direction.

Carman lets out a dry laugh. "You wouldn't," she says, understanding my actions.

I smile despite the woozy feeling that's overtaken me, then give Excalibur—my ogham—one last command.

The sword streaks across the room, so fast I barely see it. I feel the blade slide easily between my ribs, as if it's always belonged there, followed by the dull *thud* as it lodges itself inside the back of the Siege Perilous. Then, with the last of my power, I coax the iron layer to close over the sword's tip, cutting me off entirely from my ogham.

My breath bubbles. I cough, bringing up blood, feeling the sword's sharp edges pull at my lung.

Carman hobbles over to my side, ungainly with sudden age. "You fool," she snaps, grasping Excalibur's tang in her feeble hands. "You ran it through while the chair was still active!"

"All...over...," I say, wincing. This hurts. A lot.

But it was the only way for me to destroy the Siege Perilous, and make sure that no one would ever be able to use it to unleash Hell's fury upon the innocent again.

Carman lets out a startled shriek as a carved demon pulls free from the chair's base to jump on her, claws out. Another follows, then a third, all three eager to escape the inevitable. Behind me, I can hear the Siege Perilous splintering, the sound like ice breaking.

"Get these off!" Carman shouts.

I watch through lidded eyes as she stumbles around in a clumsy attempt to pry the wooden creatures off. But the demons only latch onto her more firmly, biting hungrily at her exposed flesh. I close my eyes in exhaustion. Somewhere in the distance, I hear a horn blast. I feel the corners of my lips lift slightly. It almost sounds like Mordred's back, calling everyone to safety.

I grip the sides of the chair as Lake High starts to shake, heaving violently one last time before the Siege Perilous explodes.

# Chapter 42

There are no flames, no smoke, no skeleton guy to ferry me across some river, nor any judgment scales to weigh my sins against my good deeds. Just lots and lots of dull white, like I'm in the middle of a really thick fog.

I let out a silent sigh, both of relief and of disappointment.

"If someone had told me this was what was waiting for me, I wouldn't have bothered to get here so quickly," I mutter, kicking at empty air.

"You'd rather still be facing Carman and her hordes of demons?"

I jump at the jovial voice. "Who's there?" I squeak out, bringing both fists up defensively. "Show yourself, you coward!"

A bark of laughter greets my threat, and I turn towards the sound to find a form condensing itself into a familiar shape.

"I don't know who taught you to fight, but I can tell you're terrible at it."

The boy steps up to stand in front of me, his long hair tied in a low ponytail to display an open face and large violet eyes full of mirth.

"You always were, you know," he adds, eyeing me up and down as if expecting me to sprout a new limb.

I tilt my head, then let out a gasp of recognition. "Mordred?"

"In the flesh, so to speak," my brother says with a toothy grin. "Thanks to you and the time suspension Danu's holding until this whole business is finished."

"Business? What happened?"

"You sat on the Siege Perilous."

"I know," I start. "I didn't mean...you look so...different."

Mordred rubs a hand down his pristine cheek, the thousands of blue woads gone. "Does it look bad?" he asks, embarrassed.

"Not at all." I smile. "You look better. Younger."

Mordred lets his hand drop back down, and looks away. "I feel naked without them," he admits.

It's now my turn to laugh, and the sound of it surprises me. It's been so long I'd almost forgotten I could.

"Morgan?"

A thrill courses down my spine at Arthur's voice. I turn slowly, scared that this is a cruel trick of my imagination, and suck in a breath at finding him staring at me. My eyes travel down Arthur's body, detailing every inch of him, searching for traces of previous injuries through his torn uniform. But there are none.

Arthur smiles at me, hazel eyes crinkling at the corners. "You did it," he says, voice catching hesitantly, as if afraid to scare a bird away.

Breaking into a smile of my own, I throw myself into his arms, hugging him close, wanting to feel the reassuring solidity of him. If this is a dream, I don't ever want to wake up.

Arthur's lips leave a trail of light kisses along the top of my head, his muffled laugh tickling my ear.

"If I'd known you'd greet me like this, I would have tried dying earlier," he says, his hands warm against my back.

I jerk away from him, punching him on the arm. "That's not even close to being funny," I say, turning away so he cannot see the tears burning in my eyes.

His words have brought the terror and emptiness that followed his loss back in full force, reopening a deep wound that was still too raw.

"I'm sorry," Arthur says, drawing me back into his arms. "I won't joke about it anymore, promise."

I tuck my head against his shoulder, breathing the familiar scent of blooming flowers and ripening fields of wheat on him. A smell that reminds me of rolling hills of flowers in the springtime, and of lazy warm summer days.

"Wait a minute," I say against his shirt. He should be smelling of sweat and coffee, of metal and leather grease. Not like...*her*.

With another hug, Arthur steps away from me, and that's when I hear the soft footfalls making their steady way over to us. I look over my shoulder, and have to squint as a star-bright figure parts the mists around us. Danu, in her full splendor, the way she must have looked at the height of her glory, before she was cast away from Heaven.

I feel Mordred move beside me, and glance at him to gauge his reaction. I almost expect him to burst out in rightful anger at this mother of ours who did even less for him than she ever did for me. But instead, Mordred's eyes grow wide in a face gone pale with shock.

"M-Mother?" he whispers hoarsely.

He may be as tall as she is, but he looks for all the world like a lost child, unsure of the welcome he is to receive now that he's found his way back home at last.

"My child," Danu says, beaming proudly at him. "How I have longed for us to be reunited."

To my surprise, Mordred drops to a knee in front of her, a mute request for her benediction. Danu's smile deepens as she sets her long-fingered hand on his brow. I turn away, feeling like I'm intruding, and frown at Arthur instead.

"Are we dead?" I whisper to him.

"Doesn't matter as long as I get to stay with you," Arthur replies, making my stomach flutter.

I clear my throat, embarrassed at how much I enjoy hearing him say such corny things. "I'm serious," I say. "This whole place, that"—I point behind me to Mordred and Danu—"you..."

"You've got a point," Arthur says, wrinkling his nose. "I doubt you'd smell so bad if we were dead."

"Oh, excuse me!" I say, crossing my arms tightly. "But when one's at war, one doesn't have the time to take a bath, and—"

I pause as his meaning finally sinks in, and I can see Arthur's struggling not to laugh out loud.

"OK, so where are we then?"

Arthur's warm hand grabs mine, and he pulls me after him. The ambient light grows brighter as we go up a hill, stabbing at my eyes until I'm forced to close them. My fingers tighten around Arthur's, trusting him entirely. He could be marching me back down to Balor's Gate, I wouldn't let go of him. Not again. Not anymore.

At last, we slow to a stop. "Open your eyes, Morgan."

I crack an eye open, then both as I take in the tall, ancient tree, its gnarled branches heavy with ripe figs that glow like hundreds of sparkling amethysts.

"How...," I start, voice trailing off as I realize we're somehow inside Danu's cave.

"Your mother used her power and ours to bring you and the rest of us here, before Avalon collapses completely," Arthur says.

He frowns slightly. "Though from what I've heard, that's going to happen any minute now."

"So we really aren't dead," I say.

"We are and we aren't, and we have you to thank for it," Mordred says, startling me.

I didn't realize he'd followed us, and I cast him a questioning look.

"It certainly isn't something I'd expected to happen," he continues, looking at his hands, before dropping them to his sides with a shrug. "But what you did back there…"

A sick feeling slithers up from my stomach as those last, horrifying moments come crashing back down on me. The pain. The darkness. The loss…

"It broke the spell," Arthur says, leaning down so we're eye-to-eye, and tucks a loose strand of hair behind my ear.

"A curse, really," Mordred adds. "Yet here we are, thanks to your sacrifice."

I look back and forth between the two of them. "I don't get it," I say. "Are you talking about me destroying the Siege Perilous? But that's only normal, anyone would've done the same if they could've."

Mordred shakes his head. "Not me. The thought didn't even cross my mind."

"But you were helping me," I say. "I saw you—"

"I wanted to thwart Carman," Mordred cuts in, "but I didn't want to let go of the power the Siege Perilous gave me. But you…you let go of all of that. That's why I'm here now, along with all the others."

"Not everyone," I say, with a twinge of guilt, thinking back of all those who have gone, dead in this terrible war. And I think also of Carman and Balor. They may have been terrible people, and nothing can excuse what they've done, but to live like they do or did is a hell in and of itself.

I feel Arthur's hand tense around mine as Danu joins us.

"Look, child," she says.

She waves gracefully outward, and the blinding light slowly dims to reveal the tranquil lake that surrounds her tree island, its surface glittering like it's made of liquid diamonds. I draw in a sharp breath at the sight of the long line of people that darken the opposite shore, recognizing the little ball of white fur hopping excitedly at its front beside a figure cowled in grey.

"Puck? Banshee?" I whisper.

As if she's heard me, the banshee raises a bony hand in silent greeting. Fresh tears spring to my eyes, thrilled to see that, despite everything that's happened, they're both fine.

And she's not the only one. My throat constricts as countless more people and Fey creatures emerge from the cave's mists to join the others by the edge of the water, their faces glowing with an inner fire, their eyes locked on a spot in the lake.

Taking Puck in her arms, the banshee is the first to move. With a final nod at me, she walks straight into the lake then slips beneath its dazzling surface, disappearing without a ripple.

"Banshee!" I yell.

But Danu holds me back before I can climb down the island to dive after my friends. "You gave them this opportunity," she says, "don't take their choice away."

"Opportunity?" I ask, turning on her. "To go drown themselves?"

Danu's smile is wistful. "To return home." She extends her other hand as more knights and Fey follow in the banshee's footsteps. "Your sacrifice has allowed them to open their eyes and heart at long last, and see what was there all along."

"What?" I ask, voice wobbly.

"Too many believed that death would have sent them into a sea of eternal fire to expiate their sins. So burn they did, until you showed them that what they needed was to let go of their hate and self-loathing. Only then did they understand that the fire they had expected was but an illusion of their own making, bred of their own fear and guilt."

My legs give out from underneath me, and Arthur rushes to catch me. I stare numbly as more of them disappear into the lake. All of them dead. And all of them waiting to cross the final Gate.

In the end, I failed.

I wasn't able to save them.

"Do not mourn for them, Morgana," Danu continues. "They are finally at peace, and moving on to a place beyond sorrow."

"All of them?" I find myself asking.

Danu hesitates slightly. On the far shore, two shimmering figures step together into the water—Myrdwinn and Lady Vivian, clasping hands and smiling brightly.

"Some have lived with fear for so long, they are unwilling to relinquish it, dreading its absence even more," she says at last. "For those, Hell is always open."

I spot another familiar face and a sob tears from my lips. I watch Keva pause in her tracks, Daniel mirroring her like a human shadow.

"She can't be dead," I say, voice quivering.

Keva turns her face in our direction, shielding her eyes against the lake's bright glare. For a moment, I imagine her look of disdain at our torn and bloodied uniforms turn into a knowing smirk at finding Arthur and me practically in each other's arms. Then, with a final toss of her braid, Keva motions for Daniel to keep up with her, and they, too, disappear beneath the lake's surface.

Arthur's arms tighten around my shoulders as we watch more of our friends make their way into the starlit lake: Owen, Jack, and Kaede, Father Tristan and Lady Ysolt, followed by a dapper-looking Sir Boris. Blanchefleur, Lugh, and Oberon are next, bracketed by Urim and Thummim, Lance and Gale close on their tails.

I don't know that I can stand this for much longer. Half our Order, it seems, and many more I've never met, make their way through the golden Gate, and just as many Fey.

Arthur tenses beside me at the sight of Luther. He's standing a little off to the side, looking both fearful and awed at the same time. I reach over my shoulder for Arthur's hand and twine my fingers with his, feel him release a long breath as his father decides to follow along with the others.

"I guess it's my turn now," Mordred finally says, when the flow of people has somewhat abated.

I bite hard on my lip to stop it from trembling. "Please, don't," I manage to say.

Mordred's eyes go round in surprise, then his features soften. He wipes my tears away with a calloused knuckle. "I died back there, sis," he says. "Besides, even if that hadn't been the case, this world—*your* world—isn't made for the likes of me."

"I could show you," I insist, pleading. "It's really not so bad. You could go to school, like you always wanted."

Mordred lets out a bark of laughter at my usual promise to him. "It's all right. Jennifer told me what that's like, not to mention what I saw with you, and I really don't think I've missed much after all."

Then, with a final nod at us, Mordred leaves. I keep my eyes on his back as he proceeds down the island, head held high and shoulders back. The light clings to his body as he wades into the water, welcoming.

And then he, too, is gone.

I rub unconsciously at my chest in a vain attempt to dispel the dull throb I feel there, then sense Danu's attention shift to me, and look up into her golden eyes.

"It is time we said our goodbyes as well, daughter," she says, cupping my cheek in her surprisingly warm hand. "But always remember how proud of you I am."

A new and sharper pain rips through my chest, from front to back, and only then do I remember that I impaled myself on Excalibur after turning mortal. I look down at the gaping wound between my ribs, blood dripping profusely down my uniform. I gasp in shock, no longer feeling the rest of my body. Everything around me is disintegrating.

"It's OK, Morgan," I hear Arthur say, as if from very far away. I try to tether myself to his voice. "I'm right here with you."

I mean to tell him something, something important. But I can no longer form a coherent thought. I rasp in a breath, darkness clouding my vision.

In the end, like in the worst of dreams, everyone I've ever loved is taken away from me, even Arthur.

# EPILOGUE

"Reports have come in from China and Australia over the night, Sir," a deep baritone voice says, "both stating the same thing: That all Fey activity has suddenly stopped, and every single previously-known Demesnes entirely abandoned. Whatever happened to Avalon, it seems it was a worldwide phenomenon."

I stir on what feels like a bed, a dull pain throbbing in my chest at the movement.

"As Lugh had told us." I recognize Hadrian's clipped tone. "But..."

"But it still feels odd to know they've all left."

A shiver runs down my body, to twine itself around my heart, making it skip a beat that's echoed by a machine's *beep*.

Arthur's still here with me. Just like he promised!

I frown at that. When did he promise such a thing? Last thing I remember he was dying, and I sent him away with Puck and the banshee while I faced Carman and—

I take in a shuddering gasp as the rest of my memories come flooding back.

"Arthur, she's moving!" Hadrian exclaims.

"Morgan?" Arthur asks gently, sounding closer. "Morgan, can you hear me?"

I scrunch up my face, finding it difficult to breathe properly while also trying to form an intelligible thought. Too many questions are warring in my head, begging to be answered. Where are we? What happened? Are the others truly gone? What about Carman? The school?

"She looks like she's in pain," Hadrian murmurs.

"Wait, I think she's trying to say something," Arthur whispers urgently.

Something brushes against my chin. I try to open my eyes again, but it feels like they've been glued shut. "...balls...," I croak in frustration.

There's a muffled sound of laughter. "Seems like she's doing all right, actually," Hadrian says.

Rough hands grab mine, squeezing until my carpals grind together, and Arthur bursts into tears beside me.

"Ouch," I mumble, finally able to crack one eye open.

I find myself staring at a pale Arthur, his worried eyes brimming with tears. "Morgan," he croaks, half-rising from his seat. "How do you feel? Where does it hurt?" Without letting go of my hand, he turns to a stunned Hadrian. "Get the doctor in here now!"

"I'm fine," I say, letting out a wheezing breath. "Just...confused..."

Arthur raises my hand to his lips. "You're safe now. We all are, thanks to you and your mother."

"All?"

Arthur scrubs his free hand through his messy hair, looking haunted. "Those who survived and didn't cross over," he says. "The others are...gone. Like Avalon. And, it seems, every other Fey place. But before it disappeared completely, Danu used the last of her strength to return us here. She also warned us that once the final portal closed, all our powers would be gone too."

His words revive the deep wound I feel at the loss of our friends. "It was all true, then," I whisper to myself.

They're all gone. Banshee and Puck will never be at my side again. I will never hear Keva's brutally honest opinions, nor be able to share secrets with her again. Gale will never pop out of nowhere with ready-made solutions whenever we're in trouble. My brother Mordred, my guardian angel, is gone as well. There's no more Blanchefleur, nor Oberon. No Lugh. No Danu.

No magic.

We remain silent for a long moment—I lost in thought, Arthur watching my slightest move. Finally, I return my gaze to him. "Why didn't you go with them?" I ask gruffly.

The question startles Arthur. His thumb rubs the back of my hand nervously. "Danu said to me, when the banshee took me back to her, that my fate became tied to yours the moment you healed me the first time, so how could I leave you?" he says slowly. "But the truth of the matter is that I've liked you long before I ever met you—through those letters you used to write Irene. Then, when you appeared in my life, I only fell harder." His hazel eyes fasten upon mine, so intense that I forget to breathe. "And from then on out, I vowed to always have your back, no matter what, even if…if you didn't want me to be by your side."

The door to the room slams open, making me nearly fall off the bed in shock. "We heard you were awake!" a thickly French-accented voice booms out.

The corners of my mouth lift at the sight of the two cousins ambling their way inside the hospital room.

"Gauvain, Gareth, glad you're alive!"

"So are we," Gareth says.

My eyes drop to the stump of his left arm where his war hammer used to be. "How…?" I start.

"It is a shame I couldn't keep it, *hein*[37]?" Gareth says, tracking my gaze. "I guess I should have smashed that *petit morveux*[38] when I had the chance."

"He means the pixie we freed and who owed us three wishes in return," Gauvain explains, leaning back against the white wall, the pink scars that now cover his entire face garish in the electric light. "Dumbo here used our last wish so we could finally get Carman's dragon to fly over the ward's demarcation line."

"That was a brilliant plan," Gareth says, smiling appreciatively at the memory. "Soon as Bri reactivated the last ward"—he cuts his hand across his throat, whistling—"right off!"

"And the freed pixie decided to take its treasured weapon back," Gauvain finishes, "though it conveniently forgot to return his hand."

Gareth shrugs. "A good exchange, I think," he says.

The door opens again to let Hadrian through, followed by a short woman I assume to be my doctor. I try to sit up for her, but it only makes my head spin, and I drop my head back onto the pillows with a grimace.

"Steady there," the doctor says, checking the machines at my bedside.

"What's wrong with me?" I ask, out of breath again.

I let the doctor check my eyes with her pocket light. "You, young lady, have been in a coma for a month," she says, "it's only normal you should—"

"Coma?" I repeat, before shouting, "For a month?" I turn a furious eye at Arthur. "And I only find that out *now*?"

"After the accident you had, you should consider yourself lucky," the doctor says.

----

[37] *Eh?,* in French.

[38] *Little snot,* in French.

The boys hastily turn away as she opens my shirt to check on my wound. I look down as well, shocked to see the long, puckered scar that mars the side of my breast, dark stitches sticking out from it like dozens of insect legs. And just like that, I am reminded that I've lost my Fey abilities along with my friends and family, and there's no way of getting any of them back.

Not when all the magic in this world's gone.

I turn away, gripping my covers so tightly my fingers hurt, and stare instead out the narrow window on the other side of my bed. The skies are clear, blued tinged with strands of fluffy pink and golden clouds chasing each other above budding trees as the morning dawns. And, if I pay close attention, I can almost hear the faint trills of early birdsong.

"Spring?" I ask softly.

The doctor closes my shirt, eyeing me attentively. "Your temperature's down," she says at last. "Means you're finally getting over your infection."

"Does this mean she can leave her room?" Gareth asks with his most charming smile. "Just for a little bit."

The doctor purses her mouth. Anticipating her disapproval, Gauvain claps Arthur's shoulder, and adds, "Might do loads of good for this young man to soak in some Vitamin D, too."

The doctor lets out a defeated sigh. "Very well," she says. "But only for an hour. And at the first sign of fatigue, you bring her back here. You hear me?"

"Loud and clear."

We watch her leave the room, and when the door closes on her, Gareth says, "It's strange to think we're never going to go back to Avalon."

Gauvain spears him with a glance. "It's strange for you to think at all. You should stop. It doesn't suit you."

"What are you going to do now?" I ask.

The cousins shrug in unison. "Go back home, I expect," Gauvain says.

"And the others?" I ask tentatively, afraid of what else they may not be telling me.

"Jen said something about doing penance and joining a cloister somewhere," Hadrian says.

"So out of character for her," Gauvain says with a small shake of his head.

Not really, I want to say, remembering the burned girl huddled in the KORT room. She's lost everyone who's ever cared for her, and whatever Carman did to her must have left scars that will never go away.

"Sir Cade and that Inspector Bossart are currently helping survivors integrate lay society," Hadrian continues.

"Not until they get their PR back on track," Gauvain says, scratching at the part of his scalp that hasn't been burned away by Carman's dragon. "The way they talk of us on the news, I'm surprised no one's been burned at the stake yet."

"That's so nineteenth century," Gareth says dismissively. He grins. "I'd expect the electric chair, at least!"

Silence greets his words, stretching uncomfortably in the small room. One of the boys clears his throat self-consciously, and I hear someone's stomach growl. I watch Arthur through half-lidded eyes, concerned at how quiet he's remained during this exchange.

"What about you?" I force myself to ask.

Arthur pulls at a loose string sticking out from my cover. "I'm not sure" he says at last. "To be quite honest, I never thought I'd survive the war. And now..." His voice trails off. "Irene says she's still got some funds she stashed away somewhere that the bank can't touch, so I guess we'll be fine too."

"And what about me?" I ask.

All four knights look at me questioningly.

"Weren't you raised in a regular school?" Gauvain asks. "I imagine you could finish up your senior year and go to college, or something."

"You mean boarding school?" I say, repressing a shiver.

"Doesn't have to be," Hadrian says. "You're of legal age now, so you can do whatever you want."

"She sure can!" comes a loud voice from the doorway, and we all turn to find Sir Neil standing there, a beaming Bri at his side.

"Hadrian said you were awake," Bri exclaims, pushing past her father.

I smile at her, glad that she's still with us. "Still feels surreal, somehow," I say. "Like I'm dreaming and am about to wake up any minute."

Grinning maniacally, Bri pinches my arm, and I shout out in pain. "See? Not dreaming," she says, ignoring Arthur's malevolent glare.

"We came as soon as we heard," Sir Neil says with a stern look at his daughter. "Unfortunately, due to some tricky matters with Interpol, your uncle couldn't make it. But he's sent me in his stead to inform you that, as you've long passed your eighteenth birthday—"

"You've got some money too now," Bri finishes. "Although you're not rich anymore, thanks to"—she glances at her father—"prior mismanagement of funds. But hey, you've got your uncle too. So no need to worry."

Sir Neil harrumphs in seeming displeasure, but the fond look he throws Bri tells me he's quite the proud father.

"Just a matter of a few papers to sign and you'll gain full independence," he says. "Bri's correct in that most of the assets left by your father are gone, but it doesn't mean you're lacking. Far from it."

I blink owlishly at the two of them, then turn my gaze back to Arthur. "You mean I can do whatever I want with it?"

"That is correct," Sir Neil says.

I break into a grin, and slide my hand inside Arthur's, enjoying the shocked blush that creeps up his neck at the unexpected gesture.

"Guess you're saddled with me till we're at least both through college, cause I'm not going back to some dreary boarding school," I tell him. "I think you're gonna like college, though it's probably best you don't try to boss everyone around like you used to. You'll be able to find out what you like to do, outside of fighting, that is, and we'll get to see each other every day, and…"

I stop, finding myself turning as scarlet as Arthur.

"I mean," I add, feeling terribly stupid all of a sudden, "I don't want you to feel like you have to…but I thought…I mean, if you'd rather do something else or have other plans…you really don't—"

Arthur leans suddenly forward and presses his lips to mine, taking my breath away and ending my painful monologue at the same time.

When he finally pulls away, my heart is beating so fast, the machine next to my bed is beeping furiously. Arthur smiles. "Haven't you been paying attention?" he whispers, smiling up at me. "I'll always be with you. You are, after all, my knight in shining armor."

I laugh, then wince as the movement pulls at my scar.

"Alright, alright," Bri says, sounding strangely like Keva, "now that we've settled the fact that she'll make an honest man out of you, how about we all celebrate outside before the doctor changes her mind?"

"I know a quiet and cozy place nearby," Sir Neil adds. "The owner's a relative of mine, and I know his wife will make sure Morgan's well taken care of."

"Sounds good to you, Morgan?" Arthur asks me softly.

I grin at him. "I am kinda hungry," I say.

The cousins spring to their feet, evidently glad for the excuse to leave the stuffy room. And after Sir Neil and Arthur have helped me into a wheelchair, we follow suit.

The air outside is cool, with hints of the warm summer months to come. I turn my face towards the sun as we make our slow way to the parking lot, wondering where Keva, and all the others are now, and if any of them can see us.

Arthur stops my wheelchair beside a fiery orange sportscar that I know only too well, and my mouth drops open in shock.

"I know," Arthur says. "But this way I still feel like Percy's with us, you know?"

I nod, swallowing back down the sudden tears. "I don't think he'd approve of the bird shit that's all over his hood, though," I say, giggling as I let him help me inside the car.

As Arthur collapses the wheelchair to stuff it in the back seat, my gaze wanders up the tree's branches where fat buds about to flower can be seen among delicate green leaves.

My breath rushes out as I find myself staring into a single golden eye.

"Ready?" Arthur asks, sliding into the driver's seat. "Morgan?"

"Ready," I whisper back.

As we tear away from the parking lot, I turn in my seat to watch the black feline climb down the tree, its one eye never leaving us. Surely not...

Then the car speeds around the corner and I lose the cat from sight.

"What's the matter?" Arthur asks. "Did you forget something?"

I shake my head. "I'm good," I say with a small smile. "In fact, I've never been better."

# The End

# Brief Glossary of Revised Mythology

**Banshee** – a fairy woman in Irish mythology whose wails and keens mean someone's going to die soon. Banshee wasn't always like that. In fact, she used to be a beautiful Fey, until bad choices and disaster struck. But that's another story for another time...

**Brownie** – Usually found in British houses, this small Fey creature loves to take care of all house chores, particularly at night, when the humans are asleep.

**Clurichaun** – trickster fairy in Irish mythology who lives to drink alcohol, preferably alone. Nibs greatly increased his intake of alcohol once Arthur removed his ogham.

**Dark Sidhe** – technically, according to Scottish mythology, should be called members of the Unseelie Court, but that term went out of fashion in Mordred's time. They hate humankind, and knights in particular, and will do anything to get their revenge.

**Draugar** – term for the undead in Norse mythology, or those who walk again. No matter their previous bodily state. Keva thinks they're disgusting.

𝕯𝖞𝖇𝖇𝖚𝖐 – a Fey creature in Jewish mythology who can possess someone else's body (or steal their skin, if you want) without anyone else noticing—hence why even demons hate them.

𝕰𝖑𝖊𝖒𝖊𝖓𝖙𝖆𝖑𝖘 – basic Fey creatures known across the world, though under different names. The Order has been following Paracelsus's classification since the 16th century, namely:

𝕲𝖓𝖔𝖒𝖊𝖘 to represent the element of earth—they often take the shape of miniature people no taller than three apples;

𝖀𝖓𝖉𝖎𝖓𝖊𝖘 or 𝕹𝖞𝖒𝖕𝖍𝖘 to speak of the water element Fey—their shape can shift and vary, though they like to take on the form of flying fish;

𝖘𝖞𝖑𝖕𝖍𝖘 for the element of air—these elementals can easily be confused with pixies, much to the latter's annoyance; and finally

𝖘𝖆𝖑𝖆𝖒𝖆𝖓𝖉𝖊𝖗𝖘, which are the names for the fire elementals—they take on the shape of either chameleons or lizards, and are often used to light up Lake High and other knights' homes. Dragons are their distant cousins.

𝕰𝖝𝖈𝖆𝖑𝖎𝖇𝖚𝖗 – Fey broadsword that was provided by Caim to the de Cornouailles family, and is known never to break, no matter the foe. Its grip and guard form a large cross.

𝕱𝖔𝖒𝖔𝖗𝖎 – followers of Balor, and foes of the Tuatha Dé, Danu's people. They have become demons that can both haunt the land as well as the seas, and bring chaos and death wherever they go.

𝕲𝖆𝖊 𝕬𝖘𝖘𝖆𝖎𝖑 – Lugh's fiery spear that never misses its mark. According to Irish mythology, the weapon always thirsts for blood, and can only be kept temporarily at rest if its head is doused with a poppy seed-based sleeping draught.

**Geas** – a vow, often sealed in blood. The vow will differ depending on its reason, but is usually used to keep something secret, like Lake High's location.

**Hobgoblin** – a little elf often considered to be hairy and ugly, and usually used to do odd bits and things around one's house.

**Kelpie** – often found in Scottish waters, this water Fey often takes on the shape of a terrifying horse, with a mane of seaweed, and glowing red eyes. Although an omnivore, it does have a predilection for human flesh.

**Leanan Sidhe** – beautiful Fey women who like to take on human lovers, often taking the look and appearance of their lover's sweetheart to more easily beguile them.

**Nephilim** – the children of fallen angels and humans. Although diluted, they have enough Fey blood in them to still command significant powers.

**Ogham** – pronounced "owe 'em", it is the crystallization of a Fey's power, through which it can access its magic, as well as receive that of their Fey Lord or Lady for additional sustenance. It usually takes on the form of a gem, but depending on the Fey's power, can take on different forms, including that of living creatures with a semi-independent will. By knowing the Fey's true name to which the ogham belonged, a knight may be able to call on its power.

**Pair Dadeni** – a giant cauldron recorded in ancient Wales, known to be able to revive the dead, and therefore give an unfair advantage to whoever uses it. Thought once to have been destroyed, it turns up in a rather unsettling location instead…

𝕾angraal – also called *Lapsit exillis*, or the stone that fell from Heaven. It is a stone bowl inscribed with runes along its rim. It once belonged to Lucifer, and, when touched with a true heir's blood, will fill up with liquid that can restore any Fey, angels and demons included, to its full power.

𝕾crying – the practice of looking into a reflecting surface, such as a lake or mirror, to be able to see and communicate with others at great distances, and even in other realms.

𝕿eind – the tithe or tribute, chiefly made up of humans, Dark Sidhe have to pay to Hell to retain their powers. It used to happen once every seven years, but this activity has increased lately.

# Acknowledgments

I would like to take this opportunity to thank a number of people who have helped me make this book a reality.

First of all, I would like to thank my parents for always cheering me on, and for helping me get back up whenever I fell. Mom, Dad, without you, I'd still be working on this today.

I am also very grateful to my friend Jason R., who always knows how to make me laugh, even in the darkest of times.

And, finally, a very special thanks goes to Elisabeth Szentkereszty de Zagon for using up all her free time—lunches included—to edit my story and give me her honest opinion on it.

# About the Author

Ogre killer, witch subduer, bookkeeper for the Gnomes Of Terrible Hirsuteness Society, and Fairy documentarist, Alessa Ellefson uses any spare time she has to write her accounts of the Fey kingdom before her memories can be wiped clean.

*Curse of the Fey* is the final installment in Alessa's *Morgana Trilogy*, a young adult fantasy series based on the memoirs of Morgan Pendragon that were relayed through the goodwill and resilience of pigeon messengers (a true feat in dragon- and harpy-infested skies).

Alessa won the second prize at the CINEFANTASY International Short Film Screenwriting Competition in 2016 for her screenplay *The Seeker's Key,* a tale of two brave children in a tension-filled immigration camp.

To keep up to date with Alessa's activities and latest investigative forays in the magical realms, sign up for her newsletter on www.alessaellefson.com.

Made in the USA
Columbia, SC
14 July 2020